"Imperfect Con † ri † ion"

(Sorrow for sins motivated by fear)

Fourth Mickey Devlin Novel

BY

Inspector Michael P. Cooney (Ret.)

MICKEY DEVLIN NOVELS

TROJAN HORSE 4* (2009)
Library of Congress# TXu 1-685-329
SECOND EDITION 2023

When Philadelphia police recruits Devlin and Odysseus took their oath in 1969, they shared a similar view of the world. Over the next ten years, that view changed radically for one of them. By Constitution Day 1991, Chief Odysseus devised strategies to expose a city entrenched in corruption and racial bias and settle a twenty-year grudge. His stratagem included using jihadist chatter, homegrown terrorists, threats of biological weapons, a presidential visit, a racist black law enforcement association, and cop-on-cop assassinations. Not planned for was Sergeant Mickey Devlin's relentless passion for following the evidence and revealing the truth.

CHILDREN OF THE CLAN *(2010)
Library of Congress# TX 7-357-890
SECOND EDITION 2022

With clan connections stretching back to the great Irish Famine, Philly PD's Lieutenant Mickey Devlin will need to call on old family ties to help impede a drug war, solve the suspicious overnight shooting of a decorated detective, and revisit his past to reconcile a changing neighborhood. Along the way he, his ex-partner from PD Homicide, the newly elected DA with a history of going after the leaders of Philly's illegal drug trade, and a third-year law student from a "cop family" will do whatever is necessary to follow the evidence and get to the truth.

DUBLIN ODYSSEY* (2011)
Library of Congress# TX 7-393-735
SECOND EDITION 2022

After Captain Mickey Devlin had the commissioner's favorite Internal Affairs commander arrested, his chances of convincing the PC to approve an "On Official Business" trip to Ireland to capture a cop killer seemed improbable. But persuading "Higher Ups" to make the right call is a skill Mickey has perfected over his career.

As Mickey crisscrosses Dublin and neighboring towns in hot pursuit of Philadelphia's most egregious home-grown terrorist, a resourceful ex-police chief once in line for Philly's top cop, he learns that "The Greek" is intent on revenge on an international scale. In the end, only one man can prevail.

IMPERFECT CONTRITION* (2012)
Library of Congress# TX 7-683-116
SECOND EDIITON 2023

Continuing their vendetta, the commissioner and his deputy reassigned Captain Mickey Devlin from CIB, "the black hole for commanders," to a patrol district in the middle of a highly publicized corruption probe. Within the first few hours of his new command, Mickey responds to a hostage situation involving an enraged parishioner from a "cop family" and a beloved monsignor. When people die, commanders rush to judgment. Mickey suspects a cover-up and as he conducts his own "under the radar" investigation, he exposes a scandalous conspiracy involving the Mob, high ranking members of the PPD, and the Catholic Church.

IMPERFECT CONTRITION (2018)
THE SCREEN PLAY
Writers Guild of America East
Registration #1305509

CURVEBALL* (2014)
Library of Congress# TX 7-988-233
SECOND EDITION 2022

In March of '98, Philly's mayor hired an "outsider" as his top cop. A few days after taking the helm, Commissioner Delany tracked down Inspector Mickey Devlin who was once again languishing in CIB, the "Bad Boy" Bureau for commanders who dare question the West Wing gang and offered him a "Special Assistant Position" in his new administration.

Four months into his new position, Devlin received an early morning call from Cooperstown, New York. On the line was an animated Delany ordering Mickey to "get his Irish arse" to the birthplace of baseball. It's the 1998 Induction weekend. American Pastime induction ceremony activities will never be the same. Game on!

INSURRECTION* (2017)
Library of Congress# TX 8-516-242
SECOND EDITION 2022

In 2000, when the RNC decided to hold its presidential nominating convention in Philadelphia, the city's Police Commissioner assumed he'd be given the Party's top security position. Unexpectedly, the Chairman of the nominating committee offered that esteemed position to his "Special Assistant," Inspector Mickey Devlin. Needless to say that decision did not sit well with Commissioner Delany. As always, the Commish found a way for the RNC's slight to work in his favor, especially when Inspector Devlin's security strategy was working without a glitch. Then came day three of the Convention, when things changed, and the mayhem began.

GIRLS ONLY* (2022)
Library of Congress# TX 9-155-637

After being released from intensive care, Inspector Mickey Devlin, is convalescing at the New Jersey shore. His recovery is interrupted when the Chief of Police, an old buddy from the Philly PD, asked for his input with the malicious homicide of a young female. The initial investigation goes sideways when the killer quickly follows one sadistic murder with another. Then shockingly he reveals the true motives driving his butchery. That's when things became very personal for Devlin.

(*Available from Amazon in Paperback & Kindle)

READERS RAVE ABOUT
INSPECTOR MICHAEL P. COONEY'S NOVELS

"Thank you very much for dropping off a copy of your book 'Girls Only'. I started reading it this past weekend and I am thoroughly enjoying it. The details and information about North Wildwood are excellent and I enjoy the biographical background about the Mayor."

—*Patrick Rosenello, Mayor*
City of North Wildwood

"In *Dublin Odyssey*, Mickey Devlin is back in intense pursuit of the Greek. Mickey exhibits increased wisdom, as he not only pursues the guilty, but also exonerates the innocent. The work is constructed with twists and turns, so watch out for surprises as you read. With each of his works Mike Cooney writes better and better fiction."

—*Captain Thomas Biscardi,*
Ret. PPD

"I finished the book (*Dublin Odyssey*) last night; it was terrific. I had difficulty putting it down. You really brought all the characters to life."

—*Lieutenant James Kimrey,*
Phila. PD

"Just finished reading your book (*Children of the Clan*). It was so good. When I picked up the book, I didn't stop reading… My favorite so far. You're really some writer!"

—*Kathy Koch, Gloucester County, NJ*

"Great book (*Dublin Odyssey*). Keep up the great work…"

—*Captain Ed Stinson,*
Ret. PPD

"The best way I can describe (*Dublin Odyssey*) is, it was GRAND. Your best one yet."

—*Pat McGee, Florida*

"Just finished *Dublin Odyssey*. Kept me reading… Keep them coming. I'm going to start plugging your books on my Facebook."

—*Eileen Barone,*
Deptford, NJ

"I've read all of the Mickey Devlin novels. *Dublin Odyssey* is the best one yet. I finished it in two sittings. I think your Mickey Devlin series would make a great mini-series. I can't wait to read *Imperfect Contrition*."

—*Thomas, Philadelphia/Florida*

"After I finished your first two books (*Trojan Horse 4*, *Children of the Clan*), I felt like I knew the characters. They became part of the family and I started to actually miss them when I finished. Great reads! *Trojan Horse* was like watching a movie. Can't wait to read *Dublin Odyssey*."

—*Doctor Joel Weissman, MD,*
Phila., PA

"Of all your books, *Dublin Odyssey* is my favorite. The way you portrayed the characters, I felt like I knew them. And the way you described places, I felt like I was there. After reading *Dublin Odyssey,* I can't wait to visit Dublin and trace Mickey Devlin's steps through that city. I'm looking forward to your next novel."

—*Michelle Waters, Delran,*
New Jersey

"As you finish each book (*Trojan Horse 4, Children of the Clan, Dublin Odyssey*), you can't wait for the next one. I understand book four is in the works, can't wait."

—*Bill Craig, Secretary, Ret. Police, Fire, Prison Guard Assoc.*

"Mike, I have read all your books. Each one gets better. But the suspense in *Dublin Odyssey* was great. I felt like I was there. Keep them coming. ...this one (*Dublin Odyssey*) should be made into a movie."

—*Jerry O'Donnell, Retired PPD/Florida*

"The Mickey Devlin series is a perfect opportunity to get your crime fix, with a mix of institutional knowledge of the PPD. Again, these are great books! I'm waiting for the Netflix series."

—*Deputy Commissioner, Willian Blackburn (PPD Ret/Navy Veteran)*

Dedicated to

U.S. Navy Chief Petty Officer David A. Anderson
7/28/1956 – 4/25/2012

Philadelphia Police Officer Irene Cooney
1/31/1953 – 6/22/2012

Captain Thomas J. Biscardi
1939-2020

"There are no strangers, only friends
you have not met yet."

William Butler Yeats

IMPERFECT CONTRITION
TABLE OF CONTENTS

I'll have not lived in Vain

If I can help one lonely soul
And bring new hope to him;
If I can reach one lofty goal
And never take the win.

If I can do one single deed
To help a friend of mine;
If I can lead in time of need
Sure, let my light shine.

If I can ease one breaking heart
Or take away one pain,
Or cause one sorrow to depart
I'll not have lived in vain.

Bernard Howe

Basilica Saints Peter and Paul: Philadelphia

PROLOGUE

"Believe a boaster as you would a liar."

Italian Proverb

Philadelphia, Pennsylvania
"City of Brotherly Love"

In the winter of '97, Philadelphia was being raked over the coals by the local and national media outlets for governmental corruption, mismanagement of the city's pension fund and unprecedented union influence within the Mayor's office and the chambers of City Council. This while Philly was seeing a rash of Mob-related homicides, many in broad daylight as the vics walked their dogs or unloaded their cars in front of their homes.

With the incarceration of Mob Boss Francesco Esposito, the South Philly wise guys are warring over who the next "Capo di tutti capi," boss of bosses, will be. A front-page photograph of a murder victim lying in the street in a pool of blood or sitting behind the wheel of his vehicle with half his head blown off has become an everyday occurrence. The epicenter of the Mob carnage is "Little Italy," South Philadelphia's Councilmanic District 1. With all of this going on, it's no surprise that residents, of all races, are fleeing to other states.

Added to these daily executions are what seem to be the unrelated scandals within the Archdiocese of Philadelphia and the Church's apparent laissez-faire attitude and then cover-up of the molestation of the most innocent by parish priests.

Along with the violence, child-abuse revelations, rising tax rates and a crime-ridden public school system, the lack of leadership starting in City Hall had worked its way downward to almost every other city department. Highest on that "lack of leadership" list is the Police Department's top cop.

For over a decade Philadelphia had a run of less-than-stellar Police Commissioners. One Commissioner, with the approval of the Mayor, unknowingly dropped an explosive device from a State helicopter on a row house in the Cobbs Creek section of West Philly with disastrous results. Unbeknownst to the PC, the bomb was altered. A costly blunder for everyone.

Next top cop, "The Outsider" thought he could "change the culture of policing in the PPD" with his "business model" approach to policing. His abbreviated tenure ended as quickly as it began.

The Outsider was replaced by a man from a list of unqualified candidates who met the current political correctness trend. Sadly, this onerous criterion will permeate the selection of Police Commissioners and Deputy Commissioners through the next decade.

In 1997, the PPD finds itself stuck with another non-achiever the local media calls "Clueless." He's the target of nonstop front-page editorials exposing his "lack of strategic focus, top-down management style and indecisive leadership." One investigative news crew uncovered the Commissioner's practice of sending police officers on "errands" for certain "high-profile community leaders."

A print media outlet called the PC's administration "the most petty, vindictive and visionless" in PPD history. The story followed the commissioner's outrageous statements to city council that "The Mob is dead in Philadelphia, guaranteed." That claim was immediately followed with, "I'm here to tell you people that our City has seen a 17% drop in crime, across the board." Both of these assertions were intended to defuse editorials that asserted he was incapable of identifying, much less reducing, crime in Philadelphia. Crime for the most part being driven by the South Philly Mob, which he claimed was dead.

An off-the-cuff remark by the Mayor overheard at a Union League function was leaked to all the media outlets. "If I could get one do over, it would be my pick for Police Commissioner."

In February of 1997, this unsavory environment is where Captain Mickey Devlin finds himself. Thankfully, Mickey and a handful of others have been able to wade through the cesspool of incompetence and corruption of the PPD's upper echelon and have come out unjaded.

CHAPTER I

"Revenge is the abject pleasure of an abject mind."
Juvenal, 2nd Century Roman Poet

Shortly after Captain Devlin returned from Dublin, Ireland, with Philadelphia's most wanted cop killer and international terrorist in handcuffs, Philly's self-absorbed top cop, threatened by Mickey's celebrity, started "messin' with the Mick" again. He was sent back to languish in the PD's "Black Hole" for Commanders, the Command Inspections Bureau. CIB is where shunned captains and above, deemed "Enemies of the West Wing," are sent to serve out their time. For commanders on the "shit list," it's where careers, new and old, are doomed to crash and burn.

In January of '97, Devlin took the Inspectors Promotional Examination and placed number seven on the list. He never planned to move up the ranks of the PD. He once told his Da that all he wanted to be was a "grunt," a street cop, just like him. Along the way his outlook changed, and encouraged by his wife, Pat, he moved up the chain of command. With twenty-eight years on the job it became more and more about his pension.

There's been no announcement concerning any promotions in the near future. Rumors are flying that perhaps they will be in May during "Police Week." It's the same rumor heard throughout the PD every year, and has always been groundless. Until an actual date is announced, Captain Mickey Devlin is content working nights out of a tiny first-floor room in Police Headquarters, L-8, with the rest of the so-called "Bad Boys of CIB."

Not surprising, a content Mickey Devlin isn't high on the Commissioner's "wish list." Their "history" of butting heads goes back to when Mick was a sergeant in the 14th District and the Commissioner was a "fill-in" Captain assigned to the District in the summer of '89. As the future Commissioner rode the crest of the two Federal Court injunctions claiming racial bias in the PD's promotional testing procedures, he never forgot "that damn sergeant from the 14th," who dared to challenge his mandate of no time off for any officer who refused to donate to the United Negro College Fund.

From that day to the present, the PC never missed an opportunity to take a poke at "that fuckin' Mick." So in February of '97, he took another shot at him. This time he plucked Devlin from CIB, not for a better assignment but to reassign him, "temporarily," to the 3rd District in South Philly. Devlin's transfer doubles his commute to and from work. Something the PC and his inner circle of ass-kissers all have a good laugh over, while sipping coffee from their oversized black Disneyland mugs sitting around the long oak table in the commissioner's conference room. Moving cops as far from home as possible is only one maneuver the PC uses to castigate subordinates. Others include putting cops on his "No Transfer List" and "Transfer for Cause List." All challenged by the FOP.

But increasing Devlin's travel time isn't the PC's major objective. It's more of a bonus. The so-called temporary assignment will put Devlin in the crux of an ongoing, very public corruption probe in South Police Division. Devlin's abrupt transfer is on the heels of a yearlong investigation with a Captain Marvin Blackstone, close friend of the Commissioner, as well as several of his inner circle named as targets.

Allegedly, Blackstone was heard on tape discussing what he "wanted for his special kinda help" when it comes to permitting certain street-level drug activity in the lower end of the 3rd District. Blackstone can be heard laughing and joking with a well- known Vietnamese meth supplier that he wants to "up the ante," from his initial demand of $5,000 to $10,000 a week. "Shiiit! For ten Clevelands, I'll perform magic. Ya get free access in my district. I'll throw in a heads-up call fifteen minutes before the man comes knockin'. Otherwise, shiiit, your gook ass is out of business. Believe me, I got the juice to do it. I got friends in high places. And I ain't talkin' 'bout the top floor of the projects either, my man."

Unbeknownst to Blackstone, Nguyen was already paying "street tax" to the Mob, giving him permission to sell his wares unmolested as long as he continued paying the bill for that privilege. So when a Mob underboss was informed that Captain Blackstone was trying to hustle one of his money sources, he got permission to send Blackstone "a message...time and place TBD."

Captain Blackstone is a stocky man in his early fifties with a closely sculptured haircut professionally dyed too dark for it to be his real color. He's recording secretary for the Brotherhood, a Black police officers' association. Through that association's legal arm, he filed a civil rights brief in Superior Court for harassment. In his brief he claims he's only being targeted because he's a "man of color." At an impromptu media onslaught outside the Brotherhood Headquarters, Blackstone shouted, "This whole thing is bullshit. How come they aren't goin' after the white Deputy? The one whose name ends in a vowel. You know who I'm talkin' 'bout. He's the real corrupt commander. He's the one you should be lookin' at. If I go down, I ain't goin' by my lonesome."

The next day Blackstone's 5 Platoon sergeant and alleged co-conspirator Freddy Carbone was found in the 3rd District behind a "gentleman's club" on Columbus Boulevard. His hands and feet bound with duct tape and his face blown out. It was determined that Carbone's mouth had been stuffed with "Made in Vietnam" red, white and blue firecrackers. The message from the Mob had been sent, big time. Blackstone withdrew his civil rights lawsuit, and stopped bad mouthing the "deputy whose name ends in a vowel." He replaced Carbone with a female sergeant. Not realizing she was a spy for the very deputy he badmouthed. Eventually, for her own safety, she had to be moved out of the 3RD District. But the deputy "took care of her." He transferred her to Homicide in Police Headquarters, closer to him.

The new president of the FOP denied Blackstone legal counsel and pressured the Police Commissioner to suspend and then dismiss Captain Blackstone. "The Captain has disgraced the badge. He and his little band of crooks are a cancer that needs to be cut out." The FOP's demands were rejected outright by the Commissioner. Instead, he reassigned Blackstone to his office. "The man ain't been found guilty of anything. Let's not rush to judgment." When asked about Blackstone's rant outing one of his Deputies, he gave an angry stare and chose not to respond.

It was Captain Blackstone's unforeseen reassignment to the PC's office that left the 3rd District in want of a replacement CO. Who better to fill the bill than the PC's least favorite captain, Mickey Devlin? With the 3rd District crawling with state Attorney General and Internal Affairs surveillance teams, the Commissioner is hoping Devlin will in some way "screw up" and he can, finally, "Make an example of that fuckin' Mick."

As always, Mickey will make the best of his new command. He intends to take one day at a time and continue to do the J O B. As fate may have it, within the first few hours in the District, Mickey will once again find himself in the middle of a "situation." A situation that will expose a bizarre "association" between the PPD, the Italian Mob and the Archdiocese of Philadelphia. All three of these powerful entities are prepared to do whatever is necessary to thwart revealing their "unholy trinity." Endangering their "agreement" is the "temporary" commanding officer of the 3rd District, Mickey Devlin. It's never been in Mickey's DNA to look the other way, regardless of outcomes.

CHAPTER II

February 3, 1997
Staging Area 12TH & Reed

"By learning to obey, you will know how to command."

Italian Proverb

By 5 AM, Captain Mickey Devlin is already in the uniform of the day and on his way to his new assignment in South Philadelphia. "South Philly," unlike Mickey's northeast neighborhood, is a sea of hundred-plus-year-old, two-story, red- brick row houses with flat, black tar roofs that line the narrow asphalt streets like soldiers on a parade ground. Recently, there has been an attempt to "update and flip" some of the century-old homes and advertise them as Center City town houses. Marketing ploys that haven't worked out and have "pissed off" the hard-core South Philly "love it or shove it" types.

The area, on many levels, is worlds apart from Mickey's twenty- five-year-old tree-lined street with single homes at the other end of the city. Truth be known, Mickey grew up in the Kensington and Fairmount sections of the city that share much more in common with the folks "Downtown" than those of his adopted neighborhood in the "Great Northeast."

"South Philly" is approximately ten square miles and covers the lower end of the city. It's bound by South Street to the north, the Delaware River to the east and south, and the Schuylkill River to the west. Being from "South Philly" is more a state of mind than a geographical location. It includes folks who were born or spent some undetermined number of years there, but now live in other parts of the city or even another state. Many of them still insist on telling people they meet, they're from "South Philly."

Politically, the area is represented by two progressive Democrats "from the neighborhood." Council District 1 is represented by a woman who comes from a long line of Democrat politicians, including her father and his father before him. Councilwoman Victoria Russo is known for her hands-on management style and her "list of enemies." It's a list that grows as she gains more power. In an interview with Fox News, the councilwoman made it clear that she likes having enemies. "Having enemies means I've done something right. That I stood up for something in my past. Hell! Even Jesus had enemies." The rumor around City Hall is she'll be Council President in a couple of years. The walls of her City Hall office are jammed with community achievement awards and bronze plaques espousing gratitude from her South Philly devoted constituents.

Council District 2 is represented by ex-committeeman and one- term Register of Wills, Pete "knuckles" DeDanotto. He claims he got his nickname when as a kid hanging at the Capitolo Playground, he used to constantly crack his knuckles. How he really got it was as an "enforcer" for Michael Olivetti, lieutenant in the Vince Cibotti syndicate. He's a big supporter of "Street Cops" and second cousin of the PPD's First Deputy Commissioner.

Although many of the South Philly neighborhoods like Hawthorne, Bella Vista and Queen Village have been home for decades to largely Italian-American families and just a pinch of Shanty Irish, in recent years there's been a stream of immigrants from Vietnam, Cambodia, Russia and Mexico. Many of the "new immigrants" show no signs of "blending in" or even learning to speak English unlike their predecessors. In fact, they have gone out of their way to do just the opposite by pressuring area politicians, looking to remain in power, to change street signs to reflect obvious ethnic names and titles reminiscent of their "native lands."

The 3rd Police District with its Headquarters at 11th and Wharton streets is one of the smallest districts geographically. But with the infamous South Street on the north end, the "Italian Market" in the middle, the Avenue of the Arts and Theater District on the west side, and the ever-expanding River Front Club area on the east end, what it lacks in size it makes up for in around-the-clock "happenings." However, there are rumors that in the future the 3rd District will become part of the 4th District, it's immediate neighbor to the south. Presently, the 3rd has its fair share of political movers and shakers and prominent donors to the city's powerful Democrat Party who are the most vocal when it comes to demanding "special treatment" from city departments, especially from the PPD.

Leaving at five o'clock, Mickey will cut his travel time substantially by avoiding rush-hour traffic getting to the District before the "last out" platoon reports off. He finds it incredible that he's starting this new command twenty-eight years to the day that he and fifty other young men started their law enforcement careers at the Police Academy at 8500 State Road.

Mickey takes I-95 south, one of two interstates through and around Philadelphia. His command car is a hand-me-down 1989, four-door, dark-burgundy Chrysler with 157,000 questionable original miles on the odometer. The paint is peeling off the hood and the AC spouts warm air. A real creampuff in comparison to what some commanders inherited. For Mickey, his '89 Chrysler is a well-appreciated bonus. He makes good time and just eludes the usual early morning backup at the Ben Franklin Bridge egress. He takes the Washington Avenue exit ramp, drives west passes the Mummers Museum at 2nd Street and the Italian Market at 9th Street.

East Coast weather in February can be unkind to both man and beast. But on this day, it appears the weather Gods have decided to play nice for a change. The early-morning host of Mickey's preset Oldies FM radio station owned by his good friend of forty years, Bernie Rabbit, just forecasted that the day would be "mostly sunny and unseasonably warm."

When Mickey exited I-95, he switched his police radio from J-John Band, a citywide band, to South Band that covers the four South Philly Police Districts, 1st, 3rd, 4th and 17th. At five-thirty-five in the morning, South Band is usually quiet, comparatively speaking. So when Mickey heard Lieutenant Rossi, the overnight commander, requesting 3rd District personnel for inner and outer perimeters, a CIB Commander and a hostage negotiator team a stone's throw from his headquarters, Mickey instinctively "rolls in" on the job.

"CO Three to Radio."

Surprised to hear a District Commander coming over the air so early in the day, the dispatcher confirms the source.

"Unit coming in?"

"CO-Three. What do you having going on in the Third?"

"Good morning, Sir. The admin desk got a call from someone who claims to have a hostage inside the Catholic Elementary School at eleven-fifty Wharton. We've got Three Command, Three-B, Three-eleven, Three-sixteen and Three-hundred wagon out at the location. South Detectives were requested to send their negotiation team to the scene. Traffic and pedestrians are being diverted around the area. SEPTA has rerouted their bus lines around the area."

"CO-3...is Stakeout on the scene?"

"Negative. The nearest team, Sam One-oh-five, is on assignment in West Division. They've been notified. ETA thirty minutes."

"CO-Three, receive. Radio, I also want a Stakeout supervisor to respond."

"Okay, CO-Three."

A couple of minutes later Devlin hears the inspector from CIB coming over the air.

"I Isaac Fourteen to South Band."

"I-Fourteen."

"I'm back in service from the Zoo fire, and heading down to the Third District job. ETA twenty-five minutes."

Devlin not one to shirk his responsibility immediately has Radio resume the CIB commander. He'll handle the 3rd District job himself.

"CO-Three to Radio. You can resume CIB. I'm closer and en route."

Hearing Mickey, the thankful inspector doesn't wait for Police Radio to relay Mickey's transmission.

"I-Isaac Fourteen receive. Thanks, Cap. Good luck down at South."

No need for Mickey to respond. Instead he just smiles at Inspector Campanile's communiqué. On one of his many senseless trips to Internal Affairs over his career, Mickey was fortunate that Jimmy Campanile was the assigned investigator. Unlike the present cluster of IAB "everyone is guilty" investigative crowd, Jimmy only was interested in determining the truth, not haphazardly collecting badges to please the head gink who fondly displays the names and badge numbers of fired cops on a huge chart behind his desk for everyone to see. In spite of his exhibit, a good percentage of those identified eventually got their jobs back due to IAB's poor investigative oversight and diligent FOP attorneys. So it's been a real pleasure to work for Jimmy in CIB. He's hoping with a little luck he'll be back working with him again, real soon.

Lieutenant Rossi, hearing Devlin on the air and because of the potential seriousness of the incident violates radio protocol outlined in Directive 6. "No car to car or unit to unit transmissions. All transmissions must go through Police Radio." Rossi raises his new captain directly.

"Three Command to CO-Three."

Devlin identifies the lieutenant's actions as exigent circumstances. He's had to breach a few "protocols" over the years himself. A good commander realizes that many Departmental protocols are just guidelines, and aren't chiseled in stone. Devlin responds to the lieutenant getting the Police Radio Dispatcher off the hook for permitting the lapse in policy. The dispatcher, an experienced veteran, understands completely what's happening and remains silent and relieved!

"Go ahead, Three Command."

"Good morning, Captain. Welcome aboard. I got a staging area in Columbus Square, the ball field at Twelve and Reed, across from Engine Company Ten. The sergeant will meet you there and bring you around to my location across from the school."

"Okay, Command. My ETA is five minutes."

"Roger that, Boss."

Lieutenant Rossi is a barrel-chested, six-foot, thirty-something, olive-skinned man of Italian ancestry. He's been working steady "graveyard shift" in the 3rd for two years. Tony Rossi is someone Mickey knows well from his time working nights in CIB. According to one of Mickey's "highly placed sources in the AG's office," he is not a target in the South Division corruption probe. Lieutenant Tony Rossi is one of the good guys. Mickey will often tap into his expertise of the area and assigned personnel while he's CO of the "Fightin' 3rd."

CHAPTER III

1100 Wharton Street
Command Post

"Better no law than law not enforced."

Italian Proverb

As Mickey pulls up to 12th and Reed, the Sergeant, 3B, greets him with a salute and a handshake. Sergeant Gino Conti, a five-foot-seven-inch, high-strung alpha male who's spent his entire nineteen-year career in South Division. He's a smorgasbord of intel on the Mob, druggies and who the real political power brokers are.

Conti's been a sergeant in the 3rd District for eight years and has seen four captains come and go in that time. He knows every nook and cranny of the district. He can tell you where every "made- man" or wannabe mobster lives, eats and hangs out. Gino and Lieutenant Rossi make a great team. They both grew up in South Philly, and have incredible street smarts and excellent common sense. The latter is often missing in today's new breed of "textbook commanders," all hat no cattle managers.

"Good morning, Boss. Couldn't sleep thinkin' about your new gig?"

The sergeant waves for Devlin to follow him.

"The officer in thee-eleven car will watch your vehicle. He's also keeping the chronology log."

The sergeant yells to the cop standing beside his marked patrol car. "Put Captain Devlin on your log. He'll be our overall scene commander. Look sharp, he's our new boss."

The officer waves and shouts back, "Okay, Saarg. Morning, Captain."

Devlin waves to the young officer standing beside his car, holding a red-plastic clipboard in one hand and a Police Credit Union black pen in the other. As the sergeant walks Devlin through the park and on to where Lieutenant Rossi is waiting, he strikes up a conversation.

"It's just like old times, Boss. Five-thirty in the AM, and you're ridin' in on another pissed-off white guy with a gun call. It's good to see ya, Cap."

"You too, Gino. Figured if I get in here early enough, I—"

"I know. You'd catch me sleeping, right?"

Mickey and Gino laugh aloud. They both know that would never happen.

"You know me, Boss. I'm too scared to sleep. I'd be afraid one of ex-wives might sneak up on me and double-tap a nine-mil upside my noggin."

"How many ex-wives you got these days, Gino?"

"Three." Gino reels off names using his fingers and adds, "In this country anyway."

Mickey laughs again. "In this country. They broke the mold after you, Gino. They broke the mold."

"Probably a good thing, Cap. Oh! By the way…" The sergeant points to a small group of denim-clad men and women wearing a multiplicity of jackets with colorful station logos across their backs standing by the 13th Street entrance of the ball field. "…that's the media shitheads. Rossi wants me to keep them under wraps."

"Good move, Gino. There's only one media type I speak to anyway."

"Michelle, from the Philadelphia Daily. Me too."

"Smart. Gino, I also need them to stay off the air with this thing until it's over. Don't want our moves televised for the bad guy to see. Tell them, if they cooperate, the scene commander will give them an exclusive. A soup-to-nuts interview when we end this thing."

"Thought you don't do on-scene interviews with—"

"I don't."

Gino smiles. "Hello!"

Mickey returns the smile. "Let's move it, Gino. It's too early to be hassled by that crew."

Devlin follows the sergeant to the north side of Wharton Street then east using the parked vehicles as cover to his Lieutenant's position. Rossi is crouched down behind a white-paneled van directly across from the double doors of Our Lady of Sorrows Catholic Elementary School at 1150 Wharton. After a friendly adieu, Gino heads back to the staging area.

††††

The lieutenant salutes his new commander from one knee as he approaches. Devlin returns his salute.

"It was good to hear you on the air, Cap. I heard you were replacing Captain 'where's the money.'"

Mickey smiles. "If half of what I've heard about that guy is true, he should have been locked up a long time ago."

"True story. That's what happens when you got a friend in the front office and you're a big shot in the 'Brotherhood.' It got really ugly down here, Boss. The cops are on edge. They're afraid if they sneeze, IAB, the Feds, or whoever will hand them a tissue. It's like the ginks are behind every pole. One of the guys found a recording device under his dash. It popped out when he was t- boned by a stolen SUV. The guy's too new to be a target of any investigation."

"Ouch! Guess you've checked out the rest of the fleet."

"At the start of every tour. If I were a betting man, I'd guess that IAB placed the little ditty under the dash while the car was getting serviced at the garage."

"They have a history of doing just that."

"I was hoping once Inspector Ziggy was gone things would change at IAB. But I guess I was wrong."

"Seems so. The guys call the new IA boss, Ziggy light."

"Cops, if nothing else, are creative."

Inspector Zigman's reign of terror at IAB lasted just over three years. Then just as he was about to be elevated to Deputy, he fell from grace, for some, proof of the existence of a supreme being.

"Morale must be in the hopper, Ton."

"Morale? What morale? Hopefully, things will change now that you're here."

"That's something we can work on together, Ton."

"Amen! I'm sure you didn't ask for the Third but I'm glad to have ya down here."

Devlin avoids giving the details of his sudden transfer. Maybe later.

"So, what we got here, Ton?"

"One white male with at least one handgun. Looked like a small automatic. He came to the half-opened window." The lieutenant points to the school. "He was holding Monsignor Mario O'Hagorty around the neck. He yelled that he wasn't going to release the Monsignor until he made a public confession. The Monsignor looked terrified. Then the guy closed the window."

"That's a switch. A member of the flock calling for the shepherd to confess his sins. Sounds like you know O'Hagorty. Enlighten me."

"Nothing I can swear to. Just a bunch of shithouse rumors. Gino probably knows more about him than I do. But I can tell you he's considered a big shot in the Church and a neighborhood darling. With a name like O'Hagorty you'd think he'd be one of those 'Quiet Man' kinda priests. But not him. He eats, drinks and sleeps Italian. That's his mom's influence."

"Interesting. Now tell me about the rumors."

"For one he's supposedly 'connected.'" The Lieutenant does air quotes.

"Ya know if he's ever taken a pinch?"

"Negative. But he has lots of friends who have. He's appeared countless times as a character witness over the years for members of the Venti and Olivetti crime families."

"That don't make him a bad person."

"You're right. But ya know what they say about laying in the gutter."

Mickey just smiles at the lieutenant's observation.

Rossi adds, "Gino told me he's real friendly with some pretty bad actors down here, a real goomba. He definitely knows shit. Gino also said the Monsignor lives by the Sicilian code of 'omerta,' the code of silence regarding all his Mob affairs."

"Gino would know. Could you tell if the Monsignor looked injured?"

"Only saw him for a minute. He didn't look injured. But Police Radio said the guy put him on the phone for a few seconds when he called demanding the media be sent to the school. According to the dispatcher I talked to, he wants the Monsignor to 'tell the world' what he's done."

"Any idea what O'Hagorty said to Radio?"

"Not much. According to the call taker, he said he didn't want to die and that he was ready to make things right. 'Make things right in God's eyes' was the phrase he supposedly used. He also supposedly said something about hoping for forgiveness. Radio told me off the record that the Monsignor's appeal for forgiveness sounded more like a scared old man than a heartfelt declaration of guilt. The hostage taker didn't give the Monsignor much airtime. He abruptly hung up."

"Sounds like an imperfect contrition to me, Ton. Remember what we were taught in religion class. 'An imperfect contrition is when we confess our sins not because we are truly sorry but out of fear. As opposed to making a perfect contrition.'"

"Guess that's what ya get when there's a gun pointed at your head, Boss. If a threat of getting your head blown off don't make ya atone nothing will, right?"

Mickey smiles. "Good point, Ton."

"Just a thought, Boss."

"Did you tell Police Radio to mark then pull all phone and radio transmissions on this job?"

"I did. They actually gave me a job number for the detectives to pull the tapes later."

"Great! I take it this block is closed down?"

"Both ends." The lieutenant points behind him. "The folks on this side of Wharton have been evacuated out the back alley to the community center on Passyunk."

"Did you put a cop on the alley so nobody tries to sneak back in? Had a woman shot up in Fairmount sneaking back to a hot scene for her cat."

"People do some dumb things, Boss. I didn't have an available car at the time. But—"

Mickey grimaces. "Check availability again. Get a fourth District cop to cover it if necessary. I don't want another cat-lady incident."

"I'm on it, Boss."

Rossi goes over the air and has Radio assign the closest 4th District sector cop to the alley. Then gets back to his captain.

"Got four-seven car en route to the north-side alley, Boss. West side is a dead end. I'll get him relief when the next Third District car comes available."

"Good!"

With no overt activity from the school, Mickey continues to get more intel. "What else you got going, Ton?"

"The guys at Engine Ten on Twelfth Street, next door, have been notified. Their captain will make the call on an evac. The sergeant also had the last out crew at the Police Maintenance garage next door moved out. I asked Radio to get hold of the janitor for the school who usually shows up around six to open up."

"Did they get him?"

"On his cell. He in turn called the principal who used her 'snow closure phone list' to tell teachers what's up and advise parents to make arrangements for their kids. She closed the school. So we're covered evac and notification wise if things go sideways."

"Good! Our inside guys? Don't want them in the line of fire either."

Tony laughs. "Well there are a few…only kidding. Had them all moved over into the roll room. They ran a couple of phone lines so we're in good shape. All the marked units were moved to the Eleventh Street side of Headquarters."

"Great! With all your time in the Third I guess you're pretty familiar with the inside of the school."

"Been in there tons of times. But I called Rocko from L and I anyway for official blueprints. He came in and one of the inside crew ran them over to me."

Rossi unfolds the blueprints of the interior and exterior footprint of Our Lady of Sorrows. The prints are dated November 1981.

Lieutenant Rossi gives Devlin a quick summary and a few changes he knows aren't on the plans.

"Basically, it has four levels, the top two aren't used. They actually closed off both stairwells with three-quarter plywood walls and doors, installed hasps and put on key locks. So access to the top levels and the roof are blocked. I've never seen those doors unlocked. As far as I know, only the janitor and the principal have keys. So we should only have the ground level and the first floor to worry about if we have to go in."

"How about escape routes?"

"All the windows on the ground floor have grates with access to bolt locks from inside the property. Gino had one of his guys check them out. All secured. So that leaves the two double doors in front and a double door in the back. There's a small schoolyard with a ten-foot fence."

"So far, so good."

"Yes, Sir. There are no side doors or basement doors. There's access to the roof through a trapdoor on the top floor. But even if somebody got up there, the closest adjoining rooftop is the District. That's at least a thirty-yard leap. Unless you're Bob Beamon, that ain't happening."

"Good! Sounds like the place is pretty isolated then."

"Pretty much."

"Do me a favor, Tony. Have Radio contact PECO. If this ends up being a long drawn-out affair and I need to turn off the juice to the school in a hurry, I don't want to have to wait around for them to show up."

"Okay, Boss. You still want to keep the phone lines open, right?"

"Absolutely!"

After Lieutenant Rossi makes his call, Devlin asks, "How about a media timeline?"

"Say again."

"Did the guy in the window give a deadline for getting the media out here? Sometimes they do. They want to feel in control."

"Not that I know of. Radio didn't mention a deadline. Only that the guy wants them here."

"Good. He's probably a rookie at this hostage-taking thing. That's to our advantage. I see you corralled the overnight media guys over on Thirteenth Street. I know they've been crawling over Division with the probe going on. Having them where we can see them is always a bonus. Nice move."

"Thanks, Boss. What do you think time wise?"

"Every hostage situation has its own clock, Ton. Got a number for the school?"

"Right here, Cap. In fact, I got two numbers for you." The lieutenant rips a page from his small spiral notebook and hands it to Devlin. "The first number is for the Administration Office. But according to Radio, our boy called nine-one-one from a cell phone. That's the second number."

"I'll go with the admin number first."

"Point of information, Boss. The window I saw the guys at is definitely one of the usable classrooms. Room four, I think. Gave the kids a class on bullying a couple of months ago."

"Really! How'd that go?"

Rossi smiles. "You kidding, Boss? This is Catholic school. Ain't no bullying in Catholic schools."

Mickey just smiles. "Okay! Guess it's time to get this show on the road and 'reach out and touch someone,' Saarg."

Mickey is well aware of all the universal textbook tactics like "time delay," establishing "who's the boss" and "personalizing a hostage situation." He's also fully aware of the PPD's Procedural Directive covering Barricaded Persons. Supposed, time-tested strategies used to bring a serious confrontation to a successful conclusion. Mickey is also aware that sometimes "textbooks" and "canned procedures" are out the window and replaced with a tactical well-organized "show of force." Today, he'll will try one from column A and one from column B.

CHAPTER IV

South Philly
Detective Gallo's Home

"A man's own opinion is never wrong."

Italian Proverb

Up at daybreak every morning, Detective Carmine "Worms" Gallo, First Deputy Commissioner Antonio Fannille's Man Friday, monitors Police Radio calls over South Band. He likes to keep the Deputy up to date on any "hot jobs" in his boss's neighborhood. "Worms," a nickname he's had since he was nine and was operated on to remove a twenty-foot tapeworm from his large intestine, is a forty-year PPD veteran. He actually admits to being the district cop who "broke in" a twenty-year-old rookie by the name of Fannille. An acknowledgement not every cop would be comfortable sharing with the rank and file.

As the Deputy climbed up the promotional ladder, mostly with a little help from his "politically connected neighborhood associates," he would reach back and bring Worms with him. It had more to do with keeping his first partner's "lips buttoned" about Fannille's "friends" than being a nice guy and helping a buddy. Not that Fannille has any real friends of course. You either hate him or you fear him. Liking Fannille has never been an option, especially if you're an honest cop.

This morning, Worms has been glued to the radio listening to 3rd District cops responding to a barricaded situation on Wharton Street just a few blocks from his boss's private residence. After calling Police Radio for any additional information, including the name of the hostage, he thought it prudent to wake up the Deputy and give him the dire news about his close friend Monsignor O'Hagorty. Gallo punches in Fannille's home number on his department-issued cell phone. After three rings, Gallo hears the groggy voice of his boss.

"Yes! Who is it?"

"Boss! It's Gallo. Sorry to wake ya. But I think I got something you need to be on top of."

"Okay! Spit it out."

Worms gives his Deputy what he knows so far about the Wharton Street job. He ends with, "Oh! You'll love this, Boss. Captain Mickey Devlin is the on-scene-commander."

"Son of a bitch. I can't shake that fuckin' guy. What the hell is he doing in the district at six o'clock in the fuckin' morning? This is his first day down here. Shit! The PC is gonna shit a bird when he hears this bullshit."

While Gallo was telling him about the incident, Fannille was turning on his own portable police radio switching to South Band.

"I got them on the air now. Any idea who the hostage taker is, Carmine?"

"I'm workin' on it, Boss. All Radio could tell me was that when he called nine-one-one he sounded white and young."

"That's a big help."

"So what do ya think? Ya want me to stop by and pick you up? I can be there in ten minutes. Or ya want to go to the location yourself and take it over from Devlin?"

Fannille thinks about what Gallo is saying. On one hand he'd love to ride in and save the day, which would be breaking with tradition. On the other hand he'd like to see Devlin screw up the job so he could fry him in the press. After a few seconds Fannille snaps back.

"Fuck it! No, don't bother coming by. See ya at my normal pick- up time. Just keep monitoring the job and I'll do the same from here. Maybe I'll have you drop by the scene a little later to check things out. I'll let you know."

Gallo was surprised at Fannille's decision to stay away, especially, since he's so close to the Monsignor. Just as he is. But he doesn't push the issue.

"Okay, Boss. If I don't hear from ya, I'll pick ya up at nine o'clock."

"Okay! See ya then."

Gallo hits the end key and lays the cell phone on his kitchen table.

He must really hate Devlin.

It will take a few more tries, but in due course Worms gets the name of the young, white male who's holding the Monsignor at gunpoint from the administration desk in the Radio Room. Once he hears the guy's name, he's sorry he's not pushing his boss harder to respond to the Wharton Street job.

CHAPTER V

1100 Block Wharton Street
Command Post

"Any plan is bad that cannot be changed."

Italian Proverb

Mickey looks at the phone numbers Rossi handed him, takes out his PD cell phone and punches in the ten digits for the Administration Office. Whether the subject answers or not there'll be a time and date indicated. That'll give Mickey cover for at least trying to make contact with the hostage taker. Mickey hears the phone ring five times, then clicks followed by a female giving a canned message.

"You have reached the Administrative Offices of Our Lady of Sorrows Elementary. Your call is important to us. Please leave a short message and your number at the beep and someone will get back to you. Thank you and God bless."

Mickey cups his cell and says to Rossi, "Recording." Tony snickers. "The dude's probably screening the calls."

Mickey nods concurrence. He hears the *beep* and leaves a message for the hostage taker.

"Good morning, Sir. This is Captain Devlin, Philadelphia Police Department." Devlin leaves his cell number. "I'm here to hear the Monsignor's confession. I'll try back later." Mickey hits the end key.

Tony listens to his captain's message, waits for him to finish, then laughs aloud.

"You're here to hear the Monsignor's confession? I never saw that one coming, Boss."

"Isn't that why we're all here this fine February morning? The man said he was 'holding the Monsignor hostage until he confesses.' So I figured what the heck, I can do that. No charge."

"Ya do baptisms and weddings too, Boss?"

"Only in emergencies, lad."

Mickey waits a few minutes, then tries the other number on Rossi's sheet. After two rings a male voice answers the phone in an irritated tone of voice. "This Devlin?"

"This—"

The man cuts Mickey off. "I heard your message. What do—"

This time it's Mickey's turn to interrupt and establish who's really in charge. "This is Captain Devlin. Who am I talking to?"

"Who the hell do you think this is? I said I heard your message. Let's stop the bullshit. So what do you mean you're here to hear the Monsignor's confession? You a priest on the side or something?"

Mickey decides to slow things down and stall for time. "That's a stack of questions, brudder. What do ya say you answer my one question first, then I'll answer all of yours? Deal?"

"Deal. I'm Richie Rugnetta."

"Okay, Mister Rugnetta. How old are you anyway? You sound like a very young man."

"I'm old enough to know the difference between right and wrong. You can cut the mister crap. Mister Rugnetta is my old man. I'm Richie. The Monsignor here is a bad man." Mickey resists any follow-up and lets Richie vent. "I'm from down here. I went to this school over here. My uncle is Deputy Commissioner Antonio Fannille. I'm sure you know him. He's gonna be your next Commissioner. So you mess with me, he'll have you walkin' a beat in some shit hole. Now where's my media? You ain't no freakin' priest."

Mickey presses the phone against his chest, and whispers to Tony, "Says he's Fannille's nephew."

He raises the phone to his right ear again and says, "I hear what you're saying, Richie. Sure I know the Deputy. Do you want me to get him out here—"

"Hell no! That's the last thing I want. The Monsignor is his goomba. They've been in cahoots for years."

Mickey makes a mental note of Richie's uneasiness of bringing Fannille to the scene and pushes the issue. "Ya sure? I can get Fannille out here. I know he's got more drag with the media than me."

"I said no. I only mentioned him—"

"I know why you mentioned him, Richie. I get it!"

Tony and Mickey are well aware of Deputy Fannille and his antics. Since he's been Deputy, "Antonio" has had a string of widely publicized screw-ups. According to one article Fannille is predisposed to "doing favors for his wise-guy friends, like Guiseppe Abbruza and Sheet Metal Workers Union president Dominick Pinto."

Rumor is that when he was promoted to Chief a few years ago, he used his relationship with his Godfather, State Senator Nicodemo DeCarlo, now sitting in Federal Prison, to have the Police Commissioner assign him to South Patrol Bureau. Fannille denied the rumors and told a reporter from the *South Philly View*, "My assignment is just the luck of the draw." He used his new command to strengthen his connection with his "friends from the neighborhood."

Fannille was raised in South Philly and still lives in a very unique three-story, fieldstone row home a few blocks from 3rd District Headquarters. Five years earlier as an Inspector in the Detective Bureau, Fannille was investigated by the FBI for his "Mob Connections." The assigned agents started to refer to Fannille as "Il sporco poliziotto," the dirty cop. Fannille was never charged criminally nor found in violation of departmental misconduct.

The newest buzz is that Fannille is "the target" in an investigation by the New Jersey State Police and New Jersey Attorney General for his recent purchase of a two-million-dollar home in Avalon, New Jersey, and part ownership of a factory newly renovated into a private club, "D.O.A." The club is legendary for the four large front "funeral windows" that open from the floor up to well over six feet, similar to windows used during the Victorian era designed to easily move coffins in and out of homes. The club has a history as a hangout for the "Jersey Mob" and their "Goumada" mistresses.

Fannille is also being "looked at" because of his one-third ownership of a new forty-eight-foot, dual engine, Detroit Diesel, 625 HP, Ocean

Yacht. The *FANABALA*, loosely translated means "Go to Hell," is tied down at a Marina in Avalon, New Jersey.

Devlin tries to keep Richie talking. "So, you're from down here, ya say?"

"Yeah, Nineth Street. Why you asking me this stuff anyway? I told you to get the media down here. The Monsignor has something to say."

"Where is he? I'd like to hear what he's got to say."

Pressing his cell to his chest again Mickey whispers to Tony, "Call Radio and have them run a check on Richard Rugnetta from Nineth Street. Include a firearms' history."

Tony whispers, "Got it." The lieutenant keys his radio and requests the checks as the captain ordered.

Deputy Fannille, who's still monitoring the Wharton Street job from his kitchen, nearly chokes on his espresso when he hears the lieutenant request a PCIC and NCIC records' check of Richard Rugnetta, his nephew. *Holy shit! What's that little dickhead got himself into now? He's gonna piss off a lot people snatching O'Hagorty. I may not be able to save his ass on this one.*

Devlin keeps the conversation going. "Well, Rich. Can I call you Rich?"

"Sure. Sure. Okay. Whatever. Rich, Richie, makes no never mind to me. Now what about answers to my questions? What about the Monsignor's confession? The world's gotta know."

"Well, Rich. First, I realize you got issues with the Monsignor. You made that clear. I'm here to help you work through them. Second, Captains don't walk beats. So cut the threats. My beat days are long gone. Third, I've been a cop for a lot of years. I've taken hundreds of confessions. Some come easy. Others take time. So—"

"You're a funny guy, Devlin. Can I call you Devlin?"

Keeping with the who's-really-the-boss theme, Mickey replies, "You can call me Captain or Captain Devlin."

"Oh! I see how it is."

"Good! I'm glad we at least settled that. Now—"

Rugnetta again cuts off Mickey. "Whatever! The Monsignor's confession ain't the kind you're talking 'bout. That'll come later. The Monsignor needs to cleanse his soul before he dies."

It's obvious that, at the very least, Monsignor O'Hagorty is still alive. It's Devlin's intention to insure that doesn't change. But Richie's future is a little shaky at the present time. Especially, when he seems to be implying the Monsignor's death is close at hand, his hand.

"Look, Rich, being from a police family you know how this works. You give me something and I give you something. I want to talk to the Monsignor first, then you get your media."

"Bullshit! There's news vans running all over down here looking for corrupt cops. You telling me not one of them ain't close enough to come over here? Don't screw with me, Cap…tin."

"It doesn't matter how close they are. It's all about whether I'm going to let any inside my perimeter, Rich…ie. So how about putting the Monsignor on the phone so we can start to settle this thing?"

Silence. "Rich? Richie, ya still with me?"

Click! The phone line goes dead.

Mickey shrugs and says, "He cut me off."

"No way."

CHAPTER VI

Columbus Park

"Bad grass does not make good grass."

Italian Proverb

It didn't take very long for Richie's and Monsignor O'Hagorty's names to leak out. Their conflict became big news throughout the neighborhood. Richie's desperate actions are compounded by the buzz of whom he's taken hostage—Monsignor Mario O'Hagorty, a man thought by some in the dwindling Catholic parish to be almost saintly. Even those who tend to buy into what's been whispered about his "past indiscretions" have been able to overlook those lapses in character because of all the "good he's done" for the image of the Italian Americans in Philly. Not to mention his ability to "get things done" through his many community contacts and his strong relationship with one of the "princes of the Catholic Church" and the city's first Italian Cardinal, Dominic Vuotto. Cardinals are called the princes because only they can select a pope.

For the most part, the neighbors who have gathered on the west side of Columbus Square Park, a short distance from the PPD's staging area, have already picked sides and given predictions on outcomes.

"Richie is a good boy. He wouldn't do anything to hurt the Monsignor."

"This goes any longer, the cops are gonna go in there. If that happens, somebody's gonna get hurt."

"Cool heads will prevail. Nobody needs to get killed because of rumors."

"It's in God's hands now."

Nonetheless, it became evident that most of the earlier-rising parishioners would prefer the Monsignor be the one who walks out of the school building. If young Richie Rugnetta has to pay the ultimate price, then "It must be God's will."

While listening to the neighbors' assessments near his opened first-floor window, Deputy Commissioner Fannille is also monitoring all police operations over his handheld radio. The Deputy is more interested in finding fault with Captain Devlin's handling of the incident than he is with predicting outcomes.

Even more pressing than his dislike for Mickey is how others view Richie Rugnetta's unforeseen actions. All his life Fannille has lived in two different worlds: one as a rising star in the PPD sworn to enforce the laws of the commonwealth and the ordinances of the city. A position that brings with it the understanding that whoever wears the badge must not tarnish it.

Fannille's other world revolves around a hundred-year-old tradition brought to this country by his "Bisnonno," great grandfather, from Sicily, Italy. A tradition, "Our Thing," that continues to operate to this day by fear, a set of archaic rules with linked ceremonies, and a "code of silence" that if violated is lethal. For Deputy Fannille, the old ways have unfortunately influenced how he performs his duties as a cop. It is in this world where impressions are most important to him and his "associates."

Fannille's instincts are telling him young Richie Rugnetta may have opened up a can of worms when he decided to take Monsignor O'Hagorty hostage. Fannille is fully aware of the Monsignor's past and has worked hard to help bury it. He knows if exposed it could hamper the arrangement the Monsignor has had with certain elements of the South Philly Mob over the years and his status within the Catholic Church, specifically with Cardinal Dominic Vuotto, who just so happens to also hail from the same small town in Sicily as Fannille's ancestors. Both men have openly claimed the same "bloodlines."

So far, Fannille has been able to avoid any career-ending conflicts between his two worlds. But he senses that his luck is about to run out. This time he'll need to contend with the proverbial thorn in his side, Captain Mickey Devlin.

CHAPTER VII

Barricaded Man Scene

"There is a cure for everything except death."

Italian Proverb

With a straight face Devlin says to the lieutenant, "He must be thinking about my offer. Give him a few minutes. Like I said he's obviously new at this whole negotiation thing. I'll get him back on the horn in a couple of minutes."

Lieutenant Rossi and Devlin crouch back down behind the van. A few minutes later the lieutenant sneaks a quick look. "Looks like Richie is done thinking, Boss."

The school's Wharton Street door swings wide open and two male figures step out onto the large granite top step. The older man is dressed in a priest's traditional street clothes, a low-end, two- button, black jacket with matching vest and pants pressed so many times they shine, black shoes, matching socks and a small stiff white collar around his neck. His hands are bound in front of him with a clear plastic electrical zip cord.

The Monsignor couldn't be more than five feet four and is slight of build. He looks hunched over a bit, probably suffering from some form of degenerative bone disease in his back. His thick white hair looked disheveled and one lens of his wire-rimmed glasses was cracked. Richie had wrapped gray duct tape tightly around his head covering his mouth and part of his chin.

Richie Rugnetta, standing behind his captive, looks to be only a few inches taller than the Monsignor. He also has a thick head of hair but it is slicked back exposing a pale complexion and looks reddish in the early-morning sunlight. He's wearing a burgundy designer sweatsuit with a small gray collar. The suit has wide gray stripes stretching down both legs to a pair of short zippers along the outside seam. He has on a pair of high-top white jogging shoes. His jacket is unzipped to the middle of his chest exposing a large crucifix. Richie is gripping a compact black automatic handgun and pressing it to the Monsignor's right side. He's holding a black flip- top cell phone in his left hand.

Rossi whispers to Devlin. "Why doesn't the Monsignor run?"

Devlin shrugs. "Too scared? Richie probably told him if he runs, he'll shoot him. Or on some level he doesn't want to escape. We'll have to ask him later when we interview him."

Devlin commits to memory the image of the men, then checks his watch.

"Six-ten. Looks like it's show time."

"Looks like it. I got your back, Boss."

"Appreciate it, Sarg. But do it from the other end of the van. That'll keep me out of your line of fire. Just in case."

The lieutenant smiles and points to his bronze "Expert" firearms qualification pin centered above his round lieutenant's badge. Devlin smiles back and points to his "100" pin, signifying a perfect score. Meaning no misses, and every round tightly grouped within a three-inch circle from various distances.

"Ya got it, Boss. I'm moving." The lieutenant moves to the front of the white van and takes a one-knee, strong-hand shooting position. His Glock 17 unholstered and at his side.

Rugnetta now standing in the open door of the school yells out. "Okay, Captain Devlin, where are ya? Let's talk 'bout gettin' my media people here so the Monsignor can get back in a state of grace."

Devlin gives Rossi the thumbs-up sign and yells back from behind the rear of the van.

"Be right with you, Rich. Just checking the availability of the nearest mobile news crew."

Just then Police Radio tries to contact Devlin. He quickly lowers the volume.

"CO-Three. I got a Stakeout Team on J-John Band. They're at your staging area. They want to know where you want them."

Tony comments, "That was fast. Thought they were thirty minutes away, in West Philly. Maybe a closer team picked up the assignment."

Mickey shrugs. "Let's find out."

"CO-Three, did you say Sam one-oh-five is at the staging area?"

"Negative, CO Thee. Sam one-oh-four picked up the job."

"CO-Three receive."

"You were right, Ton. No matter. Glad to have them on board."

"Guess so."

Devlin thought Rossi's response was a bit odd. But lets it go for now.

Getting impatient, Rugnetta yells again. "That's it, Devlin. No more delay games. I'm—"

Not wanting to tick off Rugnetta any more than he already has, Mickey, a right-hand shooter, stands up holding his portable radio in the air with his left hand and tries to calm Rugnetta.

"I'm here, Rich." Mickey unsnaps his holster with his right thumb and grips his nine millimeter black polymer, Austrian- manufactured Glock 26. The weapon's optional extended magazine clip protruding out the butt of the grip gives the Glock an ominous profile.

"Rich! I told you I'm trying to get the closest news crew for ya. Isn't that what you want? It's early. You're not the only show in town, ya know."

Rugnetta removes the gun from the Monsignor's side and waves it in the air. "Stop shucking and jivin' me, Devlin. I ain't got time…" Mickey instinctively starts to draw his Glock. Lieutenant Rossi also sensing a possible problem aligns the white dots on the front post and rear notch of his Glock 17 for the proper sight- picture on his target, Richie Rugnetta. Mickey backs off when he realizes that Richie's gestures are non-confrontational. He retreats from his shooting posture and motions for the lieutenant to do the same.

Rich does a couple additional loose wrist waves with his gun hand and yells, "Okay then, go on, Captain. Do your thing. Get the news people out here. But I'm telling you I can't wait forever."

Relieved he didn't have to "take the shot," he yells back to a nervous Rugnetta.

"Okay! Just give me a couple of minutes. No need for anyone to get hurt over this. Stop waving that automatic around. You're making my people nervous."

Richie taken aback at Mickey's assertion then realizes how his actions could be perceived and responds, "Oh! Okay." Mickey backs behind the van again. Rossi joins him.

"That was close. How'd you know he wasn't gonna start squeezing off rounds?"

Mickey smiles. "That was an easy one. You should have figured that one out, Mister one hundred percent-Italian Rossi."

Rossi shrugs.

"Rich comes from an Italian background. You know Italians can't talk without using their hands. So…"

Rossi catches himself laughing aloud. "Shit! Ya got me again, Boss. But some of my Irish cohorts can get pretty darn animated themselves."

Mickey smiles. "We're even, Ton."

Mickey has no intention of getting a news crew to the scene anytime soon. He's going to use the time to get Stakeout in place and have the negotiators respond. He keys his handheld radio.

"CO-Three to Radio."

"Go head, Three."

"Have Stakeout move to Twelve and Wharton. The officer on three-eleven car can watch their truck. There's a Third District car parked in the intersection blocking traffic. Tell them to set up there for now. That'll give them a clear line-of-sight on two sides of the school. I also want all Third District units assigned to this job switched to J band. Have Stakeout raise me once in position."

"Okay, CO-Three."

"One more thing, Radio. What's the ETA on my negotiators?"

"We're still trying to raise the last out negotiation team from South Division. The day-work team isn't due in till eight. My supervisor is checking their headquarters."

"CO-Three, no time for all that. Try raising a team from another division."

Police Radio goes silent. Going outside the division is a slap in the face to the South Division negotiation team and could jam them up. Everyone listening knows what Devlin is doing. He's publically embarrassing the detectives and forcing them to stop shirking their responsibility and do their job.

Devlin repeats his request. "Radio, did you receive my last transmission? Try another division for a working negotiation team." Devlin emphasized the word *working*. "Give me their ETA over J Band."

"CO-Three, receive."

Devlin switches to J Band, then turns to the lieutenant. "Let's see if that will light a fire under their butts. As soon as the Sam Team is in position, I'll try to get Rich to play ball."

Impatient, Rich Rugnetta yells, "Hey Captain. What's the holdup?"

Before Mickey steps out from behind the van to engage Richie again he tells Rossi to call the communication desk to get the status of Richie's background check.

Rossi punches in the administration desk at Police Radio on his cell and talks to the shift commander. The captain informs Rossi that Richie Rugnetta has no criminal record, "Not even a traffic ticket as far as we can tell." The captain added, "There is no record of a Richard Rugnetta purchasing or registering a firearm. But based on the address we have for him, there is one S&W thirty-eight registered to Celeste Rugnetta, sixty-two-year-old white female."

"Probably his mom."

"That would be my guess too, Lieutenant. Your hostage taker has an automatic, right?"

"Correct."

Rossi thanks the captain, hits the end key on his cell. He gets Mickey's attention who's been trying to have Richie reconsider his actions, and lets him know the results of the records' check. Mickey goes back to Richie.

"I'm waiting for an ETA on your news crew, Rich. I got one coming from a fatal shooting of a baby girl at Broad and Girard."

Mickey was trying to play the emotional game with Richie's Catholic "holy innocence" emotions using the senseless shooting of a baby. A classic Cop 101 technique, stretching the truth when dealing with bad guys. Mickey calls them "white lies" that don't reach the level of needing to be shared with his confessor.

"Soon as they wrap up their live feed for the early news, they'll head down here. Is there something else I can do for you while we're waiting? Coffee? Something to eat? Did you have breakfast yet? I'd be glad to personally deliver it to you and Monsignor O'Hagorty."

Mickey tries to get some reaction from the Monsignor. "You okay, Monsignor? Just shake your head if you're okay."

Rich whispers something in the Monsignor's ear and presses the gun harder against his right side.

"Stop your shit, Captain. He's all right already. For now anyway."

"Work with me here, Rich. You believe in redemption, right?"

The lieutenant listens with interest. He's been on enough jobs with Mickey to trust whatever he's doing is the right move.

Before Richie can answer, Mickey's radio starts to squeal. He adjusts the volume to prevent Rugnetta from hearing the message. He holds it up to show Rich. "This is probably an update on your news crew, Rich."

Mickey holds the radio close to his mouth.

"CO-Three. Stakeout's in position"

"CO-Three. Receive."

Mickey yells to Rich. "They're on the way. With rush-hour traffic starting to build, fifteen to twenty minutes max."

Rich doesn't respond.

"Ready, Tony?"

"Ready, Boss."

Mickey starts walking toward Richie and the Monsignor.

"Okay, Rich. Since we have a little time, let's talk."

"There's nothing to talk about. Redemption comes at a price."

"So does what you're doing here come with a price, Rich. What would your mother, Celeste, think about what you're doing?"

Richie seems surprised that Devlin knows his mom's name, and responds angrily. "Why you bring mia Madre into this? That's a whole different thing. She thought she was doing right. I wanta just stick with what this man has done to the Church. The man's a thief and a liar. I need to tell my story and this shame of a priest must confess."

"I'm trying to understand exactly what the Monsignor needs to confess. But like I told you before, I don't appreciate you waving that gun around. So please do not point that gun of yours this way. You've been warned."

Rich takes in what Mickey is saying and then glances toward 12th Street. Two black clad, heavily armed Stakeout officers have joined the uniform cop standing behind the white and blue police car in the intersection. They're pointing their Germany-made Heckler and Koch MP5, 9-mm submachine guns in his direction.

"All right! All right! I understand. No more gun waving."

"Good! That'll help things."

Mickey tells Rich he's going to check again on his news crew. He looks back at the lieutenant. Then raises Sam 104 over J Band and whispers into his handset.

"CO-Three to Sam One-oh-four."

"Oh-four."

"You got a clear line of fire on the guy in the burgundy sweat suit?"

"Roger that, Boss."

Mickey takes a stab at where Richie got the automatic. "Okay, Rich. I'm coming to you. But I'd really feel a lot better if you'd put your mom's gun away."

"Nice try! But it's not my mom's. She has a revolver. But you no doubt already know that, Cap…tin Dev…lin."

"Oh no? Then whose is it? Your dad's?"

Richie gets a big smirk on his face and jams the gun back into the Monsignor's side. "It's the Monsignor's. Thank you very much. I got it from him this morning. Maybe you should be checking where he got it." Richie raises the cell phone above his head. "This is his too."

Devlin turns to Rossi, kneeling at the front end of the white van whose been intently monitoring his captain's discussion, and gives him a nod. The lieutenant immediately flips open his cell phone, calls the Radio Admin desk, and gets a weapons' history check on the Monsignor.

Mickey responds to Richie. "Already in the pipeline, Rich. Regardless, how 'bout you put it down?"

"I can't do that, Captain."

"That's too bad, Rich. Then I guess we've got one of those Mexican standoffs."

"What's that mean?"

Mickey decides it's time for a little display of force. He unholsters his Glock 26 and holds it against his right leg with his finger on the trigger ready to take up the slack. As soon as Rich sees him holding his weapon, he immediately starts to back into the school using the Monsignor for cover.

"Hey! What the hell?"

"Hey what? I'd be kinda stupid coming to a gunfight without a gun. Wouldn't I, Rich?"

"This ain't no freakin' gunfight unless you make it one. All I want is for the Monsignor to finally tell the truth about everything."

"Why don't you just have him write it down and I'll make sure it gets to the right people. How about it? Sound like something you can live with, Rich?"

"Maybe as a first step. But..."

Mickey walks to within fifteen feet of the two men careful not to walk into the line of sight of either Lieutenant Rossi or the Sam team. Rich backs up further.

"Shit! What are you doing? I'm the good guy here."

"I'm sure that's not how it looks to all the good people who live on Wharton Street, Rich. If I decide to let the media into my scene, that's not how it'll look to all those folks out there in TV land either."

"This is bullshit. This man is a sinner and liar. He's screwed up the lives of a lot of good people. He took advantage. His time for redemption has come. It's judgment day. This is the end of the line for this Peccatore."

"Peccatore?"

"Sinner. Now where's that news crew? You said they'd be here in fifteen minutes."

"Relax! I said they're on the way."

"You're messin' with me, Devlin. You don't give two shits about me and what this man did. You a Catholic, Devlin?"

"What's that got to do with anything?"

"A lot! Maybe you're in bed with the Archdiocese too, and been lying to me. I don't think there is a news crew coming."

Still trying to stall until the negotiators show up, Devlin tells Rugnetta that a news team is en route. "I told you fifteen minutes, twenty max, and I meant it."

"Stop stalling. Like you said, I came from a cop family. I know the deal with you guys. You stall and stall and next thing ya know the guy with the gun gets shot in the head."

Starting to look more and more edgy, Richie glances up and down Wharton Street as if he's looking for someone to arrive.

"You expecting company, Rich?"

"Say what? No, man. I ain't expecting nobody. It's just—"

Just then Richie's cell phone rings with the sound of string band music. Mickey comments, "That's unique."

Richie looks at the small screen, then puts the phone to his left ear. "Who is this? What? You—"

Richie brings the phone down to his side and again scans Wharton Street. When he's done he glances toward the rooftops on the opposite side of the street and quickly retreats back inside the school. Mickey continues to talk to him.

"Where're you going, Rich? Who was on the phone? Talk to me. What's the matter? What do you want me to tell the media?"

CHAPTER VIII

Budding Crime Scene

"Anger can be an expensive luxury."

Italian Proverb

As the two men back into the school Richie yells to Devlin, "Call me when the news crew gets here. I know you got my number. If you don't—"

"Who was on the phone, Richie? Your Madre? Your Padre?"

Rich doesn't answer. He tries to pull the door shut behind him but the latch doesn't catch leaving it slightly ajar. Mickey backs up to where the lieutenant is kneeling behind the van.

Jokingly Mickey says to Rossi, "I think that went well. Don't you, Ton?"

Rossi smiles. "Like a charm. At least no one got shot. That's always a good thing, Boss. Oh! There's no record of Monsignor Mario O'Hagorty ever registering a firearm."

Mickey shrugs. "Then if Richie is telling the truth about..." Mickey points toward the school. "...that automatic he was waving around, then where did the Monsignor get it?"

"Guess we won't know for sure until this thing is over, Boss."

"Looks that way. You know, my gut is starting to tell me Richie is telling the truth about a lot of things. I'd love to know exactly what the Monsignor did to upset him so much. There's a lot more to the Richie versus O'Hagorty saga than meets the eye, Ton."

"Richie could just be nuts too, Boss. Oops! What do the head doctors want us to call the crazies now...severely mentally disabled persons? Try saying that ten times."

"Academics and their politically correct world! They have fancy names for everything these days. They always try to hook things up with some off-the-wall parent-child thingamajig. But Richie doesn't seem crazy to me. Does he to you, Ton?"

"Not really. But I'm sure his defense team will say he is, at least temporarily."

"Thinking like a lawyer again, are ya, Ton?"

"It's always good to know your enemies, Boss."

"True story. Right up to the time you need a good defense yourself."

"Absolutely! The best the FOP can supply."

Mickey gets back on the air.

"CO-Three. Status of my negotiators?"

"Still trying to raise a team for you, Sir."

"CO-Three. Keep me abreast."

"Yes, Sir."

Mickey turns to the lieutenant. "Let me guess. Detective Deshaun Johnson and his new honey from South Division are the last-out negotiation team, right?"

"You guessed it. They don't like to work past six in the AM."

"It must be great being in the Mayor's gene pool. You get to wear five-hundred-dollar suits, Bostonian wingtip shoes, monogrammed shirts and partner with your girlfriend."

"Don't forget make your own hours, Boss."

"That too."

"Ya know the latest shithouse rumor on Deshaun is he nailed down the team security job for the Eagles."

"Good! That's one more worthless piece of humanity that the PPD has to contend with."

"That only leaves a couple hundred to go, Boss."

Mickey grins and nods in agreement. "We've definitely got some less than desirables on this job, don't we? I had a sergeant one time who would say, 'I didn't sire them. I didn't hire them. Can't fire them.'"

Before the lieutenant can comment, he sees Richie opening one of the classroom windows. "Check it out, Boss."

Richie leans out, looks around the whole time talking on his cell phone. A few seconds later he disappears out of sight.

"Wonder what that was all about?"

"Beats me. Must have got a call from somebody, Cap."

"Or he made the call."

"Maybe it's Uncle Fannille who—"

Suddenly the quiet February morning is shattered by the sound of a muffled—**CRACK**—**THUMP**—followed quickly by a louder **POP**.

Mickey's first instinct is to look up and behind him, toward the roof line on the north side of Wharton Street, but then he looks back and focuses on the open classroom window. He looks over at Rossi, holds up two fingers and mouths, "Two shots?"

Rossi nodded in the affirmative and points toward the school. "From the school?"

Devlin shrugs and gives an uncommitted response. "At least the second one did."

Rossi doesn't respond. But starts to second-guess his first impressions concerning the direction of the shots.

Mick looks at his watch. "Six-twenty-six."

He unsuccessfully tries to contact Police radio. Somebody has an "open mike." When the push-to-talk button of a radio is stuck it prevents everyone else on that Radio Band from transmitting. It's really a dangerous thing to happen. Devlin and the lieutenant can hear someone talking. Rossi says, "Hung carrier." Mick agrees and tries again. This time there's no interference and he gets through.

"CO-three. Gunshots! Eleven-fifty Wharton. Have all Third District personnel hold positions. Have Sam One-o-Four move to my location."

The Stakeout Unit circumvents radio procedures and responds directly to the captain. "Sam One-o-Four receive. En route."

Devlin raises Sergeant Conti. "Three-B. Location?"

Conti responds immediately. "Engine-Ten Headquarters heading up to the roof. I think that hung carrier was me. I got caught up trying to get up through the trapdoor to the roof. Sorry, Boss."

"You okay, Sarg?"

"Yep! Heard shots! What's up, Boss?"

"We heard two shots. At least one sounded like it came from inside the school. Stand by, Saarg."

"Three-B. Okay."

The seriously equipped Stakeout team members cautiously make their way east on Wharton to where Devlin and the lieutenant are crouched behind the van. One of the men is carrying a four-foot- long steel entry device.

"We goin' in, Boss?"

"Looks that way. Unless you two guys have a problem."

The older Stakeout officer, Officer Lee, makes eye contact with his younger partner, then responds.

"Shots fired is a game changer. A tactical entry is warranted. Got to assume we now have injuries, Boss."

Devlin turns to the lieutenant. "Tony? Your thoughts?"

"I agree. Shots fired always changes things. I say we gotta get in there. Sooner rather than later."

"My thoughts exactly. But keep in mind that all we may have is an accidental discharge. Rich seemed pretty nervous. Especially when I told him about you guys." Mickey points to the Stakeout team. "Or maybe the Monsignor decided he wanted out and made a move. I'm gonna give Richie one last shout to see if he responds."

"Okay, Boss. We got ya covered."

Devlin stands up, walks toward the open window, calling to Richie and the Monsignor.

"Richie! Monsignor! You guys okay in there? You still want to talk? I'm here if you want to talk. I'm told the news van is around the corner."

No response. He tries again.

"Richie! I got the media on the phone. Where do you want them? Monsignor, can you come to the window?"

Still no response. He tries calling Richie's cell, no answer. When Mickey gets back behind the van, he notices the younger stakeout officer kneeling a couple yards away and talking on his cell phone.

Suspicious by nature, Mickey asks, "Who you talking to, Officer?"

In a nervous response the officer says, "Just givin' my sergeant a heads up. It's SOP."

A little perturbed Mickey responds, "It's also SOP that your supervisor be on the scene to supervise your search. So—"

"He's en route, Boss. Got stuck on another job. We'll be okay, Captain."

Mickey contemplates asking for a name but decides to deal with Richie and the Monsignor first. He makes a mental note and checks his watch.

"Okay, Lieutenant, show the guys the school's blueprint."

They visually scan it together. Officer Lee asks a couple of follow-up questions to Rossi concerning the upper floors of the school. Once satisfied, he asks his partner which floor he wants.

The younger team member points to the plans. "I went to this school. I know this building like the back of my hand. I'll take here, here and here. You can take this, this and this. Okay?"

"Sounds good to me!"

Mickey reassesses the absence of a Stakeout supervisor but decides to move forward. He gives his blessing to the team's search strategy. "Sounds like a plan to me. Whenever you're ready, guys."

Both men answer in unison, "Ready, Boss."

Mickey gives last-minute instructions. "No friendly fire issues. Deadly force only in a life-threatening situation. Is that clear?"

Mickey gets nods all around. He gives last-minute instructions.

"The initial entry is on you. I think we can pass on using flash bangs. Otherwise we've got to get the Fire Board out here in case the place gets lit up."

Officer Lee answers for both men. "We're ready to do this thing, Boss."

"Good. Let's do it. The lieutenant and I will be with you up to entry. Then it's your show. Once you call the building secure, we'll join you. Keep radio contact."

The men look at each other, adjust their small black earpieces, then look back to Devlin.

"Yes, Sir. Let's do this, Cap." Devlin gets back on J Band.

"CO-Three to Radio."

"CO-Three."

"Have Three-B hold his present position. The same for the crew from Three-hundred wagon. Same one-o-four is about to make entry. I also want fire rescue to respond to the staging area ASAP."

"CO-Three, we already have Medic Twenty-Seven responding. They're coming from Thirteen-fifty-seven south Thirteenth."

"Thanks, Radio."

"Okay, guys. Everybody knows the deal?" Mickey gets three "Yes, Sirs."

"Okay then. Let's roll."

The two Stakeout officers leave their cover and concealment position and makes their way to the set of double doors of Our Lady of Sorrows School. They stop and talk to each other a few seconds, then turn to Devlin and both give him the thumbs-up. Devlin returns the gesture.

The front doors are still ajar so the entry device isn't necessary. They leave it behind and use it as a door jam, just in case a tactical retreat is called for. The team enters and systematically begins the search to clear the building. Officer Lee goes down the worn black-slate steps to the ground level and his partner goes up and starts clearing his assigned area, first checking to confirm the top two upper floors are closed off.

"CO-Three to J-Band. Stakeout clearing building. Have all assigned personnel continue to stand by for further orders. Nobody leave the perimeter."

Before Police Radio can respond, Third District cops fill the airwaves. "Three-B, okay. Three Hundred receive. Three-Eleven okay. Three-Sixteen okay. Four-Seven okay."

Devlin squints and looks at Lieutenant Rossi. "Four-Seven?"

Rossi points north. "Back alley detail."

Devlin smiles and gives a thumbs-up. He and Rossi stand by for Stakeout to call the building clear.

CHAPTER IX

Our Lady of Sorrows
Classroom 4

"Everything may be repaired except the neck bone."
Italian Proverb

Mickey and the lieutenant are just outside the school's front doors waiting for Stakeout to call the building secure. They can hear the team yelling "Clear" to each other as they go through the building. "Classroom two, first floor, clear."

"Ground level, boys' restroom, clear." It only takes minutes for the team to clear all accessible areas of the building.

A few minutes later, Officer Lee, the senior member of the team, returns to the front entry area and shouts to the captain. "Building is clear, Boss!"

Devlin calls police radio. "CO-Three...building secure. Have all Third District units continue to stand by for further orders. Continue to maintain the inner and outer perimeters. Stand-by for conditions. All units can now switch back to South Band. Notify Rescue. I'll let you know if we need them ASAP."

"CO-Three. Will do."

Police Radio relays Devlin's message as instructed. "From CO-Three. All personnel assigned to the Wharton job hold your positions and switch to South Band."

Devlin and the lieutenant holster their weapons and enter the school. Officer Lee points, his MP5 hanging from its black two- inch shoulder strap, down the first-floor hallway.

"I think you'll want to check out what my partner found in classroom four, Boss. The open door. I'm gonna stand by here."

Devlin and the lieutenant walk down the dark hallway to classroom four. When they enter the classroom, they take a quick assessment of the room. The Stakeout officer dressed in his "ninja- like" uniform is staring out one of the classroom's three large wood-framed windows, holding a cell phone up to his left ear and cradling his weapon in his right. He hastily puts his phone away, and starts to address the captain.

"Got a—"

Mickey interrupts the officer. "Updating your sergeant again, Officer?"

"No, Sir. I was just checking that my cell is functioning. I turned it off for the search. Didn't want to—"

"Have it go off and telegraph your position?"

"SOP, Boss."

"Okay! What do you got and what have you done?"

"I've got one obvious five…two…nine…two lying face up over here, Cap. Looks like he caught one in the neck."

"You check vitals?"

"I did. No pulse. Not breathing. Judging from all that blood…" The officer points to the young man lying on the wood floor in a pool of dark-red gooey liquid. "…I'd say he's a couple of quarts light."

"At least! Nothing we can do for him then." Devlin points to the Monsignor propped up against the wall on the other side of the room, the corridor side. "How about the Monsignor over here? What's his status?"

The Stakeout officer walks toward Monsignor O'Hagorty.

"When I first came in to clear the room, he was semi-conscious. He was trying to mumble something. I took the duct tape off his mouth. Couldn't understand a word he was saying. Sounded like gibberish to me." The officer draws Devlin's attention to the right side of Monsignor's head. The thick brownish-red liquid stands out on the Monsignor's white hair.

"Ouch! That had to hurt. When you removed the tape, did you try to question him?"

"To be honest, since he was breathing on his own and talking, I told him to hang in there. I went to check the status of the other guy. Once I realized he expired, I came back over here. I started to help him get up but he went limp, so I set him back down against the wall. He went out on me, but he was still breathing on his own. I'm no doctor, Boss. I—"

"So he said nothing about what happened to him? Nothing at all?"

"Like I said, a bunch of gibberish. That's about it, Boss."

"He wasn't leaning against the wall when you walked in?"

"Correct! He was lying on his side. I figured with a head injury bleeding and all it would be better to prop him up. Ya know. Like they teach us in first-aid class. Keep the wound above the heart to help control the flow of blood."

"Okay! So you never got a chance to ask him how Richie got shot either?"

"No, Sir. I was about to request the medics when you walked in."

"Do you know the Monsignor, Officer?"

"Heard of him but never met the man."

"Really? I heard you tell your partner that you attended this school. My understanding is the Monsignor's been here forever."

"I only went here for two years, sixth and seventh grade. Like I said, I know about him, but I never had any contact with the guy."

"I see." Devlin gets on the air and has the EMT Unit come to the school.

"CO-Three to Radio."

"Go ahead, Sir."

"Building secured. No injuries to police. Have Medic twenty-seven respond to this location. I have one to go. The Stakeout officer securing the front of the building will let them know where we are."

"Receive, CO-Three."

"CO-Three."

"Sir!"

"Have the Sergeant rejoin Three-eleven car at the staging area and stand by. Have Three-sixteen car relocate from his traffic post on Twelfths Street to the front of the school to secure the property. You can resume Thee-hundred wagon. Also notify the ME. We have one to go."

Police Radio does as requested.

Devlin walks over to the Monsignor and checks his carotid artery for a pulse while trying to get him to respond to his name. "Monsignor! Monsignor O'Hagorty, can you hear me?"

There's no response. Devlin address the officer. "Put your gloves back on and cut the zip tie from his hands and put it and the duct tape in his jacket pocket."

"Ya got it, Boss."

Devlin asks the officer, "Any thoughts on how the Monsignor got that head injury?"

"I'm guessing either Richie thumped him at some point, maybe with the butt of his gun, or he could have whacked his head when he hit the floor."

"If he got thumped with Richie's gun…actually at this point we're not sure whose gun that is…there'll be trace in the wound and on the gun. So—"

"They can do that?"

Lieutenant Rossi answers, "Absolutely!"

Devlin looks at the Monsignor's head. "I can't see any other obvious injuries, can you?"

"Negative, Cap. I didn't want to try and move the guy again. Just in case. Figured the EMTs will stabilize and transport. Don't want to be caught up in a lawsuit."

"I hear ya. The Good Samaritan Act only goes so far these days. Last thing we need is the Archdiocese suing the PPD."

After the officer cuts the zip tie from the Monsignor's wrists and flips them palms up, Devlin notices a white dust substance on his right hand, sleeve of his black coat at the cuff.

Devlin points to the Monsignors sleeve. "Tony, what would you say this is?"

Lieutenant Rossi leans over to see what Devlin is referring to. "I'd say it's chalk. White chalk."

"I agree. So the good Monsignor was either writing with chalk or—"

"He was trying to erase something from the chalkboard."

"That's what I would say too."

The two men instinctively look toward the front of the room to where the chalkboard takes up the entire front wall. Interestingly, the Stakeout officer who was listening to the discussion does not. Mickey looks at Rossi, then at the officer and tilts his head and purses his lips as if to say, *What's with him?* Both seasoned commanders make note of the officer's body language.

"Maybe Richie took me up on my suggestion to have the Monsignor write down his confession so I'd make sure it got to the right people."

"The chalkboard in a Catholic school would be the perfect place to do it too, Boss."

Mickey glances at the Stakeout officer for his reaction. There is no noticeable reaction either way.

"It's gonna be hard to prove if the Monsignor actually did use the board the way it looks now. There's chalk marks and chalk dust everywhere, nothing decipherable. Guess we have to place that theory in the 'can't prove yet' folder, Ton."

"Seems that way."

Mickey turns his attention to Richie's body lying in that dark puddle of blood. "I'd say a left to right trajectory. I haven't seen a wound like that for a while. The shot most likely severed his spinal cord."

The officer and Lieutenant Rossi take a closer look. The Stakeout cop offers, "The poor guy must have dropped like a sack of shit. Hey, Boss?"

"Not necessarily. I've been in gun battles when guys shot like that, who you'd think would drop, just keep firing away. Our Doc Steinberg had the reason. He explained that the lowest-most part of the brain, right around the top of the neck and toward the back of the skull—"

"Just like Richie, Boss."

"I'd say so, Ton. The Doc called the area the basal gaglia. It's where the brain controls body movement. Doc said it's possible for someone to continue to use his arms and hands, up to ten seconds, even though his heart has stopped."

"Amazing!"

"I only bring it up because Richie may have had—"

Lieutenant Rossi offers a theory. "Enough left in his basal gaglia to get off a second shot. One to his neck and one—"

"Someplace else. A theory that may need to be expanded, Ton."

Mickey stoops down and checks out Richie's head and neck again. "Still don't see an exit wound though." The lieutenant and the officer join him.

"So, men, in your professional opinion, would you agree that the flight path of the round was left to right?"

The officer puzzles over it. "I don't know, Boss. With all the blood, it's tough to say. I think I'll let the ME make that call."

Devlin leans over the body again. "I definitely see an entrance site but no exit wound... I don't know. Ya would think—"

"That's why I'm not jumping to make the call."

Without looking back at the officer, Devlin agrees. "You're right! It's definitely gonna be the ME's call."

The lieutenant checks out Richie's wound and agrees with his captain and the Stakeout officer.

The young Stakeout officer abruptly walks away while pointing toward the wall-mounted cast-iron radiator under the bank of windows. "I got an Italian-made, blued-finish .22 Beretta Bobcat on the floor over there, Boss. Looks like a two-inch barrel. The standard magazine for that Beretta holds seven rounds. I didn't mess with making the weapon secure. When the threat is gone, we leave that to the detectives and

Crime Scene guys. Oh! I spotted one .22 brass casing lying over there by the leg of that desk.

"How about the lead to go with it?"

"Say again."

"Did you find a lead slug that goes with the casing?"

"Didn't really look, Boss. Guess I just figured it's still in the vic."

"Really! So then you do agree with me that there is no exit site? Because if there was, the round would be somewhere in this room, am I right?"

"Well…Well, maybe I should look around some more, Cap."

Not real happy with the Stakeout's "first officer on the crime scene" performance. Devlin says, "At this point, let's leave well enough alone. The Crime Scene guys will handle it."

The officer nods his compliance.

"You only found one casing? I heard two shots." Mickey turns to the lieutenant. "How many shots did you hear, Ton?"

"Two."

Mickey turns back to the officer. "How about you, Officer?" Mickey reads the black nametag on the chest of the Stakeout cop aloud. "Officer DeMarco? How many shots did you hear?"

"One for sure. But from my set-up position on Twelfth Street, it's hard to say for sure. Could have been two. The sound of gunshots from a block away can bounce off buildings and vehicles and can give the impression of multiple shots. Sorry, Boss. Can't say for certain."

This guy's not sure about anything: bullet trajectories, exit wounds, number of shots he heard.

"I understand. I'm just trying to get an opinion. You're not under oath here."

"I guess, at this point, I'd say one shot."

"Okay. That's all I can ask for, DeMarco."

"Yes, Sir."

Devlin takes another glance at Officer DeMarco's nametag.

"DeMarco! DeMarco! You have family on the job? Your name sounds familiar."

"My dad was a detective. He worked Central for years. He retired in ninety-two. Had twenty-nine years on the job. Figured that's enough."

Mickey keeps running the name DeMarco through his mind.

"That's it. I worked Central when your dad was there. Was your dad's first name Frank?"

"Yes! Same as mine."

"Ya know, without the goggles and headgear, I now can see a lot of your dad in you. It's the eyes."

"People say that all the time."

Mickey doesn't have many fond memories of Detective Frank DeMarco. His so-called retirement was a gift from a Deputy Commissioner who allowed DeMarco to leave the job ahead of an internal investigation to save his pension. The Senior DeMarco got jammed up after being caught in a FBI sting. Story goes he got behind in his "loan shark" payments to a South Philly Mob lieutenant.

But his "marker" got so high, reportedly in excess of twenty thousand, he started trading "the vig," the interest on his loan, for "favors." Favors like alerting the local South Philly "Social Club" when the PPD's organized Crime Unit was about to kick down their door and serve a warrant. Frank was also exposed for his "creative report-writing skills" when investigating certain union activities and mob-run "gentlemen's clubs" in Central Division.

Once off the job, DeMarco was no longer "on the pad" and became a liability to his "wise guy" friends. When the "heat" was turned up on DeMarco, it was believed he tried to "flip," hoping to avoid hard jail time. The ex-detective suspiciously went missing six months after he retired. Depending on the rumor, people suspected that he went into the WPP, Witness Protection Program, was whacked by "Zips" from New York, or relocated to the land of his ancestors, Italy.

One snitch told the FBI "his body was in a double-decker coffin." A popular "Mafia" method of disposing of a body, with the help of a willing funeral home, by putting remains in a secret lower compartment of a coffin and burying them with no one the wiser. A PPD rumor is that a funeral home on South Broad Street, owned by a councilwomen's family, fits that bill. No gravesite was offered.

Mickey's thoughts turn to an old Irish proverb. *Fruit doesn't fall far from the tree.* He hopes young Stakeout Officer Frank DeMarco doesn't follow in his father's footsteps. Mickey drops the family history chat.

"Well, anyway, I'll be interested to see what CSU comes up with. I'd be surprised if they don't find another casing around here somewhere."

Mickey's cell phone in its leather belt case starts to vibrate. He takes it out, flips it open and holds it to his right ear. "Devlin."

"Hello, Captain. Jonas from South Band."

"What you got, Jonas?"

"Aha! Your negotiation team is on the other line. They're asking if you still want them on Wharton Street. I—"

"Hold on, Jonas."

Mickey holds his phone against his leg and whispers to Lieutenant Rossi. "Can you believe those two snakes? Johnson and his girlfriend are now magically available. They want to know if we still want them to respond. They stalled just long enough to bag the day-work crew with this job."

Tony shakes his head in disbelief. "Those little asswipes."

"Ya think?"

Mickey gets back on his cell and tells the dispatcher to have them stand by and he'll get back to her. As soon as he ends his cell phone conversation with the dispatcher, he goes over Police Radio.

"CO-Three to Radio."

"Three."

"We have a scene that needs processing. I need the negotiators to take off their negotiator hats and put on their investigator hats. Get me their ETA. We've got one obvious five-two...nine...two, and one civilian with injuries.

Notify Crime Scene and Homicide Units. They can work out who's the primary and make any additional notification needed upon their arrival."

"CO-Three, okay."

"Three…give me a time check."

"KGF five-eighty-seven. The time is zero six fifty-seven hours."

Tony looks at Mickey and smiles. "Guess those slugs won't try pulling your chain again, Cap."

"It just irks me that they're gonna get overtime for playing the system. But, so be it."

"I can't wait until the Eagles get hold of Johnson's act."

"Act is right." Mickey shakes his head in disbelief. "Man! I can't believe it. I'm in the District an hour and I'm already on the Mayor's radar for messing with a relative. Before this job goes away I'll no doubt make it to a few more hit lists, including Deputy Fannille's. Again!"

"Could be worse, Cap. You could be transferred to CIB."

Mickey laughs.

"Look at the bright side. At least we're all gonna go home safe and sound, except Richie of course. We're not gonna have to be interviewed by IAB's Shooting Team. Which is always a trip."

"That's a win in my playbook, Ton. I can only imagine how the morning papers will spin this one. It's a good thing you had this place locked down so quick this morning. I got a friend in the business. I'll give her a call when I go into the District. At least we'll get a fair shake from her."

"You talking 'bout Michelle Cunay? The retired Chief's kid?"

"Yeah! Know her?"

"I do. You're right. She's not out to make a name for herself by putting cops on trial in the newspaper. The retired cop, Tommy G, in the press room at Headquarters is a good guy too."

"The PC hates both of them."

"Ya know what they say. The truth hurts sometimes."

Mickey restrains from giving a flip response but thinks, *Then the Commissioner must be hurting 24/7.* Instead he takes out a small notebook and makes a quick sketch of the scene, paying particular attention to where Richie and the Monsignor were supposedly found by Officer DeMarco. He has his doubts. Mick also makes note of where the lone brass casing was pointed out. Almost as an afterthought he notes the chalk on the Monsignor's hand.

"Well, guess I'll head into the District. The scene is yours for now. You'll get the neighbors back soon?"

"Already working on that too, Boss."

"Good man. I'll get day work out here to relieve you and your guys, including the Fourth District cop on the alley."

"Already resumed him, Cap. Put one of ours over there. A few minutes ago had him put himself back in service. I also called the community center and had the director let the neighbors know they can return to their homes."

"Good! I want the scene...just the classroom...secured for twenty-four hours. Can you arrange that, Ton?"

"Okay, Boss. I'll take care of it."

"I always like coming back after the smoke clears for a second look."

"No problem, Cap."

"Thanks, Tony."

"Yes, Sir. Always a pleasure."

Mickey thanks the Stakeout team on his way out of Our Lady of Sorrows, and walks back to Columbus Square to get his command car. Sergeant Conti had already gotten rid of the media. So Mickey didn't have to duck them. On the way back, he contacts Police Radio.

"CO-Three. Turn me around from Wharton Street to the District. Three Command has the scene."

"CO-Three. Receive. Oh, and welcome aboard."

"Thank you, Radio."

On the short drive back to the 3rd District Mickey sees the Fire Department's Medic Unit 27 pull up in front of the school. They take out the gurney from the rear of the truck and wheel it into Our Lady of Sorrows. He says a little prayer for the Monsignor. Mickey hopes his first day as CO improves. But he doubts it. He knows all about unintended consequences. His gut is telling him the Richie Rugnetta job will have a bushel full of them.

CHAPTER X

11ᵀᴴ and Wharton Streets
3ᴿᴰ Police District

"The flowers of tomorrow are the seeds of yesterday."
Italian Proverb

Mickey finally pulls into his reserved parking space on the back lot of the 3rd District Headquarters side of the building, two and a half hours since he left home at 7:30 AM. The space is identified by blue and yellow signage hung on a cyclone fence marked Commanding Officer. On the opposite side of the fence stands the District's neighbor, Our Lady of Sorrows. The two properties are separated by a rusty eight-foot fence and a small blacktop schoolyard.

Headquarters is a two-story, concrete-block, multi-function facility. The first floor is shared by the 3rd and 4th Police Districts. There are similar arrangements around the city. Having hundreds of cops share the same facility was said to have been done to "rein in the city's runaway capital budget."

The officers assigned to the 4th District need to traverse the 3rd District to get to their Headquarters. Not only does it cut down on the time officers spend patrolling the lower end of South Philly but it also doubles the number of prisoners housed in the 3rd. Two facts not lost on community activists or their weekly newspapers.

The second floor is home to a satellite office for the Licenses and Inspection Bureau that services the South Philadelphia area. The basement has two large rooms of mostly broken high-school-size lockers, a unisex shower room with occasional access to hot water, a space designated as a gym with hand-me-down equipment, and a small room with oily floors for the high-maintenance utilities equipment. Like most every other police facility in the City of Brotherly Love, the building is listed as "Hazardous."

The asbestos-wrapped ductwork blows cold air in the winter and hot in the summer. If it weren't for the FOP supplying space heaters in the winter and portable sliding screens and the occasional air conditioner in the summer, L and I would have condemned the building and ordered it razed years ago. But as the Mayor told city council, "It's only cops down there. They're 'posed to be on the street protecting the public anyway." An opinion shared by the Deputy Commissioner of Administration who is the PPD's budget watchdog. A man who perceives the PPD budget as his very own personal bank account. An account he holds like a hammer over the heads of subordinate commanders. "Lower your overtime budget and I'll think about getting you heat next winter, Captain."

There's no doubt that Mickey's early-morning arrival was monitored via police radio by every cop and supervisor in South Division. A captain riding his district at five o'clock in the morning is rare at best. So when the 3rd District's new Commanding Officer walked in the back door of the building everyone was on their best behavior. They're all hoping to make a good first impression.

The Captain's clerk, Nora Brown, is the first to greet Mickey. Nora is a very capable and pleasant Black woman in a brown pantsuit and red low-cut designer sneakers. She has over twenty years with the City and ten years as a civilian union representative. Nora's all union. She's heard Mickey is too.

"Good morning, Captain. I'm Nora Brown, your clerk."

Mickey's never had a clerk. Actually, he's never even had an office or any staff of his own. Mickey extends his right hand.

"Nice to meet you, Ms. Brown. I'm Captain Devlin."

"Oh! Yes, Sir. I know who you are. I can tell you we're all happy to see you. We've been havin' a tough time down here because of the actions of a few bad apples. We know that kind of stuff wouldn't have happened if you were at the helm."

"Well thank you, Ms. Brown. I'll do my best to get us off the front page and back to doing police work."

"That's what we all want too, Captain. So whatever I can do to help, I'm here."

"Okay, Ms. Brown. Thanks. You can start by getting either the Five Platoon Lieutenant or the Day Work Lieutenant for me. I need to relieve Lieutenant Rossi and his guys at the scene next door."

"There is no Five Platoon Lieutenant. The Day Work Lieutenant today is Linda MacGraft. I saw her in the operations room. I'll get her, Captain. Please, call me Nora."

"Okay, Nora. Thanks! When you get a chance, I'll need a copy of the District personnel roster and last year's Self Inspection Report."

"I got the roster right here for ya, Sir."

Nora Brown gives her new Captain the "hand-revised" roster.

"I can print out a copy of the ninety-six Self Inspection. I never had a hard copy. But I have it on a disk. I think Captain Blackstone took all the copies with him. He walked in last Friday, packed a bunch of stuff into boxes and left. Never even said good-bye. That was the last we saw of him. I only read about what the Commissioner did with him and his people in the Sunday paper. It's the talk of the district."

"I'm sure it is. I heard some outside agency got into the Captain's office late Thursday night, unannounced, and took several boxes away with them. Supposedly, they never even told the Commissioner they were coming or what they were doing. Bet he's ticked."

"No doubt. Guess they knew Blackstone and the PC are buds."

"Good point, Nora. If you can print me a copy of that report after you find Lieutenant MacGraft, I'd appreciate it."

"Will do."

Nora Brown disappears down the tattered tan-tiled hall toward the operations room to find Lieutenant MacGraft, 1 Platoon's commander.

Lieutenant Linda MacGraft is a rising star in the PPD. The prediction is that she'll be a big boss one day. Temple ROTC graduate, three years active duty in South Korea, a Political Science major and, like Mickey, she graduated number one in her Police Academy recruit class. Also like Mickey, her first assignment was in Northwest Division where she had a reputation as a hard worker and "active street cop," who changed the minds of a lot of the "girls shouldn't be cops" crowd in that Division. She's doing the same thing in South Division.

A couple years out of the Police Academy she started to pile up the commendations including one for Valor. She made detective and was sent back to Northwest Division. Three years later she was number five on the sergeant's promotional list and fought to be sent back to a patrol district. After making Lieutenant she's had two assignments, one in the Organized Crime Unit and now in the 3rd District. The latter again was a request. The lieutenant is a South Philly gal and is a standout patrol supervisor.

Mickey walks through the outer office past Nora Brown's desk and an empty Captain's Aide cubical. He heads for the CO's private office space, his new base camp. First thing he notices is several sealed boxes sitting on the floor under the west-side, double-steel framed windows. The boxes are all marked with thick black magic marker, **"Do Not Remove–CO Internal Affairs."** Mickey takes off his jacket and hangs it in the room's only closet. On the floor of the closet are three lidless boxes filled with files in tan folders with thick red rubber bands around them. There is also a smaller box with a dozen or so VHS videotapes. All the tapes are labeled, "Greek Weekend–South Street." He doesn't bother to peruse them. *Maybe later.*

He walks behind his desk, slides his holstered Glock 26 off his black uniform belt and stores it in the top right-hand drawer of the small executive wooden desk. The drawer is empty except for the two lifeless brown roaches lying on their backs. *Hope this isn't a sign of things to come. Could be worse. They could have attacked me. Disgusting!* Mickey scoops up the pair with a coffee-stained three-by-five index card and deposits them in the trash can under his desk.

A vintage desk is centered in front of the only open wall space in the room. The pale-green wall is dotted with nail holes and dusty outlines of what must have been photos and plaques. Obviously, taken down in haste by the previous occupant.

Opposite the desk is a small three-piece private bathroom right out of the 1950s. Everything is painted brown, even the sink and toilet seat. The tan plastic-tile stall shower is missing the handle for the hot water and showerhead. The room is giving off a strange stench that reminds Mickey of the North Wildwood back bay at low tide. Hanging at eye level on the brown steel door is a small oval sign, **Captain's Quarters**.

Mickey promptly closes the door and removes the homemade nautical signage.

He sits in the black imitation leather executive swivel chair and slowly slides open each of the remaining five drawers, not looking for anything in particular. Except maybe more dead roaches. *Not even a paperclip.*

His thoughts quickly turn to Richie Rugnetta lying on the floor in Classroom 4 of the old school building next door. Running the morning's scene through his mind, what sticks out is the discrepancy on the number of shots heard, a missing brass casing and Richie's neck wound. *I heard two shots...period. DeMarco only found one casing, was a little wishy-washy on the number of shots he heard and didn't follow protocol as the first officer on the scene. Something just doesn't feel right. I'll hold judgment until...*

Mickey's thoughts are interrupted by a knock on his half-closed office door.

"Come in."

"Good morning, Boss. Linda MacGraft. Ya wanted to see me?"

Mickey stands up and shakes the lieutenant's hand. "Captain Devlin."

The lieutenant is a five-foot-ten-inch athletic type. She has straight jet-black hair, cut to regulation, no noticeable makeup, no fingernail polish and no visible jewelry. Mickey's first impression is that the lieutenant is all business. Her uniform is impeccable, and unlike some female commanders, Mickey's sense is MacGraft doesn't use her femininity as a tool to schmooze her superiors to get her way. For her, like in baseball, there's no crying in police work.

"Good morning, Lieutenant. Yeah. I need you to relieve Tony Rossi's people at Our Lady of Sorrows. Guess you heard about the job next door. If you're short, feel free to use Five Platoon personnel."

"I'm on it already, Cap. Had my early side sergeant walk one of his guys over there after the earlier roll call. I got the chronology from Sergeant Conti. After the late side roll call, I'll take a look, see myself and make sure everything is by the numbers."

Mickey smiles and nods. "Outstanding!"

"Saw two Medics take one out on a stretcher earlier."

"That would have been Monsignor O'Hagorty."

"Heard that. I'd ask if you want to address the late side roll call but I see you're still settling in. Maybe some other time."

"Thanks. I'll catch up to you later. I'll eventually get to all the roll calls."

"Okay. Anything else I can help you with, Cap?" "Not right now."

The lieutenant comes to attention and gives a perfect hand salute. Impressed, Mickey returns the salute. The lieutenant then exits the office, leaving the door just as she found it, half open.

She's got things under control. Have to remember Linda MacGraft.

Mickey starts to peruse the District's personnel roster. It's neatly typed separated by platoons and ranked alphabetically. It also gives each officer's appointment date and assignment date. He zeros in on 5 Platoon first. These are the cops and supervisors who work mostly day work, and report directly to the Captain. Five Platoon is where the "specialists" are assigned. Normally, there's a sergeant, a Community Relations Officer, CRO, Victims Assistance Officer, VAO, Sanitation Officer, SO and a handful of other uniform cops who walk "crime beats" or work "plainclothes" burglary details. A real alphabet soup of acronyms.

Platoons 1 and 2 are line platoons working staggered 8 AM to 4 PM and 4 PM to midnight tours. Platoon 3 works the overnight shifts. Unique to the 3rd District, there is also a 7 Platoon. A small contingent of officers, a couple of sergeants and a lieutenant all working out of a neighborhood-financed mini-station on the nine hundred block of South Street, the official northern boundary of the District. Unofficially, the 3rd District covers one block into the 6th District. An "arrangement" created by a chubby, little deputy commissioner to insure his daughter's residence receives "a little extra policing." A setup that will be short lived under the new "temporary" commander of the 3rd District.

Working the overnight tour in CIB, Mickey has had numerous contacts with the South Street Mini-station detail. The lieutenant overseeing the station runs a tight ship. He has great relationships with the neighbors and the business community. Some prominent business leaders joke about the lieutenant running for city council. Neither the West Wing nor City Hall gets too involved with the South Street community's "incivility concerns" for fear of being accused of "taking sides." That too will change under Captain Devlin.

In the last few years, South Street and the surrounding neighborhood has turned more upscale and has attracted thousands from around the city and the suburbs. If it were up to the businesses along the South Street Corridor, they'd be open 24/7 and have festivals and book signings day and night. On the other side are the residents that are kept up at night with the endless yelling, profanity and fights from unruly, intoxicated visitors to the neighborhood. Then to add insult to injury the community is forced to pick up the trash and other unspeakables discarded by the same transient riffraff from the night before.

The South Street lieutenant has been pretty much left on his own to handle the endless events and conflicts on the "Hippest Street in Town." If it weren't for him and his under-manned crew, the area would be an utter war zone.

Mickey isn't a big fan of 5 Platoons in general. Many end up bloated with cops who captains "take a likin' to." Over the years, countless district commanders have gotten "jammed up," professionally and personally, for "getting involved" with subordinates, male and female. A little known scandal usually kept under the radar by a short trip to Night Command for the Captain, and a choice of plush assignments for the subordinate, who the EEO lieutenant refers to as the "victim."

Mickey notices that three names on the roster have been crossed out with a red pen: Sergeant Freddy Carbone, Tactical Supervisor; Officer Neal Cobb, Captain's Aide; and Officer Nicolas Brace, Community Relations Officer. There's a fourth name, a female sergeant circled in black Sharpy. *She must be the spy. Looks like I've inherited a Five Platoon personnel crisis. Stay sharp, Devlin. The vultures are circling.*

CHAPTER XI

8^Th and Race
Commissioner's Conference Room

"A mischievous dog must be tied short."

Italian Proverb

After a short stop "Worms" Gallo picks up his boss at the prescribed time, then drops off Deputy Fannille at 8th and Race streets, Police Headquarters. Deputy Commissioner Antonio Fannille has planned an unscheduled meeting with the PC allegedly to give him a heads up on the Rugnetta "suicide." In reality, he wants to be the first to get to the boss and steer him in the "right" direction, which isn't very hard to do. Fannille is famous for getting ahead of the media and putting his own spin on things. In this instance, the deputy is trying to walk the line between his two conflicting worlds.

The last thing Fannille wants is for anyone to start connecting the sordid dots between Richie Rugnetta's "suicide" and any relationship he may have had with Monsignor O'Hagorty. He plans to do whatever he can to stop that from happening. Which is why Fannille ordered "Last Out" Detective Headquarters to omit any mention of the incident on Wharton Street from the "Commissioner's Overnight Activity Report."

He also doesn't want to upset his arrangements with his South Philly "associates" and the powerful Archdiocese of Philadelphia, that of keeping the Monsignor's persona unsoiled. These so-called "arrangements" are nothing new. Similar understandings between the "associates," i.e., The Mob, and the Church in Philadelphia, extended back to when Fannille's great-grandfather landed at Ellis Island from Sicily.

Fannille finds the commissioner sitting alone at the long oak table in the conference room next door to his executive suite. He's sipping coffee from a large 7-Eleven brown paper cup and has the city's only daily spread out in front of him.

"Good morning, Commissioner. Anything interesting in that rag?"

The commissioner looks up from the sports page. "What are you doing here so early, Fannille?"

"I'm always here early, Boss."

"Whatever! What can I do ya for? Make it fast."

"I just wanted to give you a heads up on an incident that occurred early this morning. Down on Wharton, around the corner from my house."

The commissioner puts the paper down and reaches for the Overnight Activity Report.

"Don't see any mention of no Wharton Street job on my sheet."

"Happened around the shift change. It'll probably show up on the day work report, Boss. But I was monitoring the job from—"

"From as far away as you could, no doubt. Okay, spit it out. What's this mystery Wharton Street job?"

The Deputy disregards the commissioner's wisecrack, and gives him a guarded summary of the incident. When the Deputy revealed that Captain Devlin was the overall commander at the scene, the PC nearly choked on his over-sweetened black coffee.

"What! I can't believe it. I sent that fuckin' Mick to the 3rd District hoping the son-of-a-bitch would tread on his own dick and instead he…" The commissioner can't seem to find the right words. "…he… he…fuck it. Question now is what you gonna do? It was your nephew who got whacked."

Fannille cringes at the commissioner's choice of words. "Richie wasn't whacked. He shot himself. Gotta watch that terminology, Boss. Words are important. Last thing I…we need is for the media to label Richie's untimely death a homicide."

"Whatever! You're telling me there's nothing funny going on with any part of this job. It is what it is, right?"

"It is what it is, Commissioner."

"I hope you're not bullshittin' me, Antonio. Keeping the media on a short leash is your job. I can't believe you didn't ride in on the job and take over. If things blow up for any reason, it's you who will be holding the press conference, my man. Not me."

"Don't worry, Commissioner. Everything is under control. I'm on top of it. Don't worry about that Mick Devlin. I'm gonna push him so far into the weeds on this one his interview won't even make it to the final investigative package. I got Homicide doing it for me. It's a long way from their Headquarters to South Division. Things can easily get lost. I'm keeping everyone away from Rugnetta's parents. I already went to see them. Johnson from South is the assigned by the way."

The only part of Fannille's speech that the PC focuses on is who the assigned investigator is.

"Deshaun Johnson has the job? The Mayor's kin is the assigned?"

Fannille giggles. "The same! It just worked out that way. I sent Worms to the scene to hold DeShaun's hand. He'll do what he's told."

"He better. Or he'll have his skinny black ass writing one-pagers in the basement as far from his home as possible. I'll tear up that letter of recommendation I wrote for him to the Eagles' GM. Now I got your word there's nothing to your nephew's job that could cause the shit to flow my way?"

"Nothing! Nada! Zero! I'm tellin' ya. Trust me. I got this thing under complete control."

"Okay under control."

"Relax, Boss. I even talked to my guys in the Press Room downstairs. They're gonna write up the incident the way I tell them to."

"Really? I don't trust any of those guys as far as I can throw them. They're a bunch of bitches. They'd sell their souls for a front-page story. They keep letting the truth get in the way of a good story. You don't feel you're getting too involved, too close, to this thing?"

"No way. I'm good. By the book all the way. It'll be fine, Commissioner. Trust me."

"Riiight! I hope you're right, Antonio. The writing is on the wall. I'm a short timer around here. If you play your cards right..."

The Commissioner raises both arms and looks around his office. "… all this could be yours."

"Don't want to sound cocky, Commissioner. But I'm told the fix is in."

"Is that so? Don't count your chickens, amico."

"I'm not. Like you always say, 'There never seems to be a shortage of Italians in the PPD looking to be top cop.'"

"Is that what I always say? Guess it has been a while since you people held the reins. Just remember the brothers who helped you along the way."

Fungu! First thing on my agenda is to bury all your freakin' ass kissers. You Back prick.

"Of course! You know me, Commissioner."

With that the Commissioner makes one last stipulation concerning his deputy's obsession with the Rugnetta job.

"This conversation never happened. Keep me out of the loop. I want deniability on this one. I don't want anything to fuck up my pension. Capisce?"

"Ti capisco. I understand, Boss."

Fannille, sensing the Commissioner more or less has bought into his handling of Rugnetta's job, decides it's a good time to take his leave.

"Remember, Antonia, out of the loop."

You want out of the loop? You got it, stupido.

Fannille flashes a wide smile and a thumbs-up to the commissioner.

"Absolutely, Boss. Absolutely!"

Fannille leaves the PC's office, closing the door behind him.

God I'm good.

CHAPTER XII

Captain's Office
3RD District

"Better to ask than go astray."

Italian Proverb

One of the two black push-button phones on Mickey's desk rings. Nora Brown yells through the half-open door, "I got it, Captain." Mickey then hears Nora say, "Hold on, please."

Ms. Brown knocks and pushes the Captain's office door open. "It's the DA's Office. Special investigator, Seamus McCarthy?"

"I'll pick up. Seamus and I worked together in Homicide. Good man."

"Okay, Captain. Line one."

Nora leaves and shuts the door behind her. Mickey picks up and waits for Nora to hang up the extension.

"Seamus. How'd ya find me so fast?"

"I'm a trained investigator, CO-Three."

"Don't tell me. You still spend your mornings monitoring Police Radio calls?"

"Once a cop always a cop. It's hard to break old habits, Mr. Scene Commander."

Through a big smile Mickey responds, "I think this call may qualify as DA harassment. Do me a favor, special investigator McCarthy. Call me on my cell. You got the number, right?"

"Ya kidding? You're my hero. I got your number tattooed on my butt-tocks. I'll get right back to ya."

"Okay butt-tocks. Don't hurt yourself trying to read it, Seam."

Mickey laughs and put the handset back in its cradle. After a few seconds, Mickey's cell starts to vibrate and he answers it.

"Hey, Seam."

"Hey! Things must be pretty bad for ya down there when ya can't talk on your own office phone, Mick."

"Better safe than sorry, partner. Wouldn't be surprised if some outside agency or IAB still has access to Blackstone's office phone lines. Maybe that's something you can help me out with, brudder? You hang with all those fancy outside suits now, don't ya?"

"Wow! That may be outside my wheelhouse, Mick. I'll have to get back to you on that one, Mick. Anyway, where was I? Oh yeah! You think I'm harassing you? Wait till Katherine gets hold of your Irish arse. She's the real pro."

Katherine Desire McBride is Philadelphia's second-term, high- profile District Attorney, Seamus' boss and Mickey's close friend. Katherine was lead prosecutor on the well-publicized "We the People" trial and gained "street cred" when she established her own investigative task force, tagged operation DIVA (DA's Initiative Against Violent Aggressors) to identify and prosecute illegal drug distributors in North Philly. Her initiative led to countless indictments and several high-profile court appearances at the "Bog Trials." The acronym DIVA was Mickey's handy-work and he was also given much of the credit for the operation's success.

She's the first to admit that much of her achievements as the City's top law enforcement official would not have come to fruition without the help of her good friends Mickey Devlin and his ex-Homicide partner Seamus McCarthy with honorable mention going to Alice Elizabeth Gibson, "AE," Kath's relentless ADA. A few years ago Katherine was able to woo away Seamus from the ranks of the PPD. So far she hasn't been triumphant when it comes to Mickey Devlin. But she's still holding out hope. Only time will tell.

Mickey picks up on Seamus' jab. "Katherine's not a problem. I can handle her. How is our bare-knuckles District Attorney doing anyway? She got her eye on the Governor's Office yet?"

"Not this week. Think she'll go for something a little closer to home first."

"Mayor Katherine McBride. Now there's a glass ceiling that needs breaking. Sounds good. You gonna stick around for that, Seam?"

"I doubt it. I'm getting too old for those kinds of hours. 'Sides I'm gonna be a Grandpop again. My son and his wife are expecting a boy. Seamus Patrick."

"That's great, pop-pop."

"Okay, pop-pop. You'll be a Granda someday."

"Sooner than you think, brudder."

"You son-of-a-gun. When were you gonna tell your best friend?"

"You got a lot of nerve. You only beat me with the baby news by one minute."

"That's true. So—"

""My daughter Shellie and her husband are having twins. A boy and a girl."

"All right! Okay, Granda got names picked out yet?"

"Shannon Elizabeth named after a river in Ireland and my mom. David Thomas after my son-in-law and his dad."

"Congratulations, Mick."

"You too, Seam."

"Thanks, partner."

"So now tell me why you really called me so early in the morning. You either want something or—"

"Be nice now. I only called to give you a heads up."

"I like those kinds of calls. So educate me, brudder."

"Katherine wanted me to let you know the FBI is putting together another task force down there in your new neck of the woods and they're asking Katherine to join in."

"Another task force?"

"Yep! Mob related of course. I hear there may even be some very high-ranking 'Philly's Finest' involved, higher than Blackstone. Soo—"

"So, in addition to IAB and a bunch of outside agencies with endless acronyms, I can never remember already imbedded in South Division, Katherine has now been asked to the party? Any idea when this new endeavor will kick off?"

"Probably not for a month or so. I think they're tying up a few loose ends first. Then go after whomever with both guns. The boss lady may be asking you for a little help down the line. But you didn't hear it from me, Mick."

"Hear what?"

"Exactly!"

"Seam, while I got you on the line—"

"Sounds serious, Mick."

"Could be. I'm sitting here with the district personnel roster and trying to separate the good, the bad and the ugly. Trusting anyone down here these days is gonna be a challenge. Blackstone left this place in a shambles, Seam."

"So I heard. I know you already added Tony Rossi to the can-be-trusted list."

"I did! Good man. Sergeant Conti too."

"Right. Well you can add Linda MacGraft to your list! You can trust her."

"I met her this morning. She's definitely one of the sharpest knives in the drawer down here."

"No doubt about it. The lieutenant on South Street is also one of the good guys. I've had a couple of jobs with him over the years. You can trust him too."

"Looks like I got a good cadre of white shirts and at least one blue shirt, Sergeant Conti anyway."

Seamus laughs aloud. "That's a start. Gotta go, Mick. Katherine just walked by with three suits and gave me the high sign. Could be FBI. I'll tell her you were asking 'bout her."

"Do that. Let's do lunch, Seam. On me."

"Call me."

"I will. Soon!"

Mickey punches the end key on his cell. Then he goes back to perusing the District personnel roster. Some of the names in 3 Platoon, the last out cops, are familiar from jobs Mickey handled in South Division during his time in CIB. He puts a check beside their names. *Okay!* There's a couple of supervisors, sergeants and corporals, he remembers as cops working patrol in Central Division. *Good cops.* He puts a check beside their names too. *That leaves a whole lot of question marks. Can't get paranoid. Hopefully, the cancer isn't stage four.*

Mickey opens his door and asks Nora to "round up" all the day work 5 Platoon cops for a "get to know ya" meeting.

"They figured you might want a sit-down. All but the 5 PM to 1 AM plainclothes team have been waiting downstairs in the gym. Guess you saw they lost their sergeant to the corruption investigation."

"You're talking about the red line outs on the roster."

"Yes, Sir. I still have to retype a clean copy. I'll get to it today."

"How long you been in the Third, Nora?"

"Eleven years. I started in the operations room when the whole civilianization of the PD started. Later, I took the clerk-typist tests. After Anna retired, she was the captain's clerk before me, Captain Stephens brought me back here. That was seven years and three Captains ago. Make that four Captains now."

"So you know all the cops in Five Platoon?"

"I do. I work with them every day. What's left of them anyway. Most are good people. Some are still a little wet behind the ears and some are more industrious than others."

Nora looks about the immediate area and then whispers, "But there are rumblings that Blackstone left a few spies embedded in five squad. So—

"Enough said. Thanks. I'll be careful."

"Other than that, they do work pretty good together. Ya know. As a team."

"That parts good to hear. Let me ask you this then. Do you think they can continue to get the job done for me without a supervisor for a little while longer? Or do ya think—"

"Ya mean without their own sergeant?"

"Exactly."

"Honestly? They've been doing just fine without real supervision for a long time. The captain and his little posse were hardly ever here. They were always out hustling. I'm trying to be respectful, Captain Devlin. The district is better off without all of them. I'm sorry. But it's the truth."

"No need to apologize. I appreciate your candor. Makes my job easier. I noticed that one of the sergeants on the roaster was circled. Is she—"

"She's detailed out, Captain. No one knows where. She's supposed to be chummy…real chummy to the Deputy."

"So we're better off without her."

"No lie."

"Understood. Did Blackstone ever request a lieutenant for Five Platoon?"

"Never. Guess he didn't want to share the booty any more than he had to."

"I'm gonna request replacements this week. 'Cause you know Headquarters. If I let it go too long, the desk jockeys at Eight and Race will think they're not needed. Don't want to start setting bad precedents. That's for sure."

"Don't forget, Captain, you got great lieutenants running the other Platoons. The Five Platoon guys have been going to all of them for guidance when they're working."

"What's the South Street Lieutenant working today?"

"Three to eleven. There's a Howard Stern book signing at Tower Records tonight. So he dropped back to cover it."

"Dropped back?"

"Yeah! He does it all the time. Blackstone refused to pay him OT. A real company man, right? Not!"

"That's gonna stop. I'll talk to the lieutenant about giving him an overtime budget based on projected needs."

Being a union rep, Nora Brown, through a big smile, says, "**finally**."

"If things don't get too out of hand, I'll try to catch up to him later tonight. Okay then. Will you get the Five Platoon guys for me?"

"Sure!"

Nora Brown gets up from her desk and starts down the hall. But then Mickey gets a better idea and calls her back.

"Wait! Better yet. I think I'll check out the gym."

Nora Brown smiles. "Okay, Captain."

Mickey is familiar with the layout of the building. He's been there many times over the years. A friend of his, Joe Barone, used to be the CO in the 4th. When Mick was a detective in Central Division he used to stop down regularly and go to lunch with Joe. Mick takes the back steps to the basement, through the locker room to the gym. As soon as their new captain walks in the subduedly lit gym, the remnants of the 3rd District 5 Platoon, all five of them, stop talking and stand up.

They're noticeably nervous about meeting their new CO and worried about their positions. Mickey has a reputation inside the PD as a no-nonsense, by-the-book guy. His FOP activities are much publicized and justified riffs with the West Wing have won him a lot of respect with the rank and file. Not to mention standing ovations at the FOP monthly meetings.

It's not unusual for a new district captain to make a clean sweep of 5 Platoon and move some people out and others in. It's to put his or her own stamp on things. The district's 5 Platoon is also curious about Mickey's intentions concerning supervision. One of the more senior officers breaks the ice. "Whatever they said, Boss. I didn't do it."

Everyone had a good laugh, including Mickey.

Mickey's first impression of his 5 Squad is that except for two cops they're young, mostly men and nervous. Based on his scan of the district's personnel roaster, excluding the two veterans, the average "time on job" is two years. That could be an issue for the new commanding officer. Time will tell.

Mickey takes a closer look at the cop's department-issued nametag. "Officer Brady, is it?"

"Yes, Sir. Gil Brady."

"Well, Officer Gil Brady…" Mickey takes a long pause and looks directly at the officer who now seems to have second thoughts about breaking the ice. "…I'm not the one you got to convince of your innocence." Mickey pauses again. "But for what it's worth, I believe you…for now anyway."

The room lets out one of those relief laughs in unison.

"Sit down, folks. Let's talk."

Toward the end of Mickey's impromptu meeting with his 5 Platoon, he feels a little better about the hand he's been dealt, at least with regard to the five cops sitting in front of him. He tells them at least for the time being, they'll be without direct supervision. He adds that he still expects all of them to continue to do the job and that he'll be sending a request up the chain to fill all vacancies. He adds candidly, "Until that's disapproved, which it will no doubt be, I'll use OT to fill the holes. That should get their attention."

The five officers respond to the welcomed news. "Thanks, Captain." Brady adds, "We'll be fine, Boss."

"That's encouraging, Gil. I understand the South Street Lieutenant and Lieutenant MacGraft have been helping out now and then."

Officer Brady responds again for the group. "They have, Captain. Lieutenant Rossi for the night work BD team. They've all made themselves available when we needed them. Even when they're off the clock, they've been great."

"Well that setup's gonna stop. I'll talk to both of them about being compensated. I'm not against paying OT when warranted. Holes in personnel, at all levels, fall into that category."

Before Mickey heads back to his office, he singles out Officer Brady.

"Brady, I saw your appointment date was seventy-eight. That makes you my senior Five Platoon copper, right?"

"Yes, Sir. Officer Betz would be next. Seniority wise."

Mickey addresses the group. "Okay, if any of you need to get to me, go through Brady here."

Everyone exhibits a big smile. A couple shout out, "Good pick, Captain."

Mickey takes out one of his CIB business cards and writes his cell phone number on the back and hands it to Brady.

Brady takes the card and looks at the number on the back.

"Emergencies only, Brady. Understand?"

"Yes, Sir."

"Okay then. Let's get to work. I'll catch up to the five-to-one BD team later on and fill them in."

As Mickey makes his way back through the locker room, he can hear the cops harassing Brady about being "Captain's pet" and the Captain's "acting sergeant." The normal good humor cop talk. He also hears them talking about Mickey riding the district at five o'clock in the morning.

"This guy looks and sounds like the real deal."

"True story. When I was in the Thirty-fifth, I used to hear him handling jobs in the Fourteenth all the time. He was a sergeant back then. He definitely knows his shit. His guys loved him. They all said he's a cop's cop, no doubt about it. Street cop to the bone."

"He's also the guy who put that cop killer back in Federal prison. He definitely does not play around."

Mickey's first day in the 3rd District will be longer and more hectic than even he could have predicted. But he'll prove to be up to the task.

CHAPTER XIII

3ᴿᴰ Police District
CO's Office

"A bad man is worse when he pretends to be a saint."

Francis Bacon

Back in his office in less than thirty minutes, there's another knock on the door. It's Tony Rossi, the last-out lieutenant, dressed in civvies.

"Come on in, Ton. Thought you'd be long gone by now. I heard Linda relieved you and your guys."

"Oh yeah. Linda jumped right on it. I just wanted to stop by before I head home and run a couple of things by you."

"Sure! What's on your mind, Ton?"

"I...I just want to be certain we're on the same page about this morning. You still agree with hearing two shots, correct?"

"Absolutely! Two shots."

"Good!"

"What else?"

Rossi continues. "It's just, if we're right, where the heck is the other casing?"

"Did CSU came up empty?"

"They did. So as of right now, it looks like old 'Richie from Nineth Street' only fired one shot. The one to his neck."

"At first blush it may look that way, Ton."

Mickey deep in thought starts biting the inside of his right cheek. A bad habit he's had since he was a kid. Then he serves up an alternative.

"Here's how I see it, Ton. Either we were wrong. There was only one shot fired. Or...we were right and the second casing is still out there waiting to be found. Or maybe it was taken from the scene for some unknown reason. I have a third possibility but it's a long shot, literally. It's based on Richie's entry-wound site."

"Good! Because I'm not buying into South Detectives' BS on what happened out there."

"Let me guess. They've already classified the incident a suicide and put themselves in for a commendation."

"Yes to part one. I wouldn't be surprised about part two. The only hope is Homicide will see it differently. They're monitoring the job. Maybe if they can get an autopsy going and change South's classification…"

"Depends on who the assigned Homicide detective is and then getting the right person to do the autopsy. I'll call a couple of people to suggest my picks."

Mickey's "pick" at Homicide would be Detective Ryan. His preference at the ME is Doctor David Steinberg. The Doc and Mickey have worked together on countless high-profile jobs over the years. In 1993, they united along with the DA to investigate the murder of a veteran narcotics detective and the senseless homicide of a senior citizen beloved by the residents of her West Kensington neighborhood, known as "The Bog Murders."

"Bonus! But I still think we're right about the two shots. It's only a matter of time until that second casing shows up."

"And the round that goes with it. If they exist, we'll find them, Ton. The scene is still secure, right?"

"Until Wednesday, Boss."

"Good! That gives me time to revisit it. Now here's another bone to chew on. You remember when Richie was standing behind the Monsignor on the school's front steps?" Mickey doesn't give the lieutenant a chance to answer. "He was holding the gun with his right hand and his cell with his left."

"Sure! I remember. Why?"

"You're right handed, right?"

"Yep!"

"I'm a righty too. I'm saying Richie was holding the gun in his dominate hand, his right hand. That's what I'd do."

"Me too. So—"

"So if we're right, my question is why would he, a right handed man, shoot himself in the left side of his neck? That's why I spent so much time eyeballing his entry wound this morning. So if South wants to spin that suicide thing, then they'll also have to explain—"

"Richie switching hands to shoot himself, which is highly unlikely."

"I agree. Or Richie was a 'switch hitter.' That is easy enough to check."

"Riiight!"

Rossi points his right index finger, thumb in the air, to the right side of his neck. Then he does the same to his left side.

"Awkward!"

"Food for thought, right?"

"Right! But is it enough for the turkeys from South to run on?"

"Probably not." Mickey changes gears. "How about Sergeant Conti, and the rest of the guys out there today? Did you ask them what they heard? Shot wise."

"I did. Remember Sergeant Conti came over the Police Radio and said he heard shots?"

"That's right. He did say shots. Plural! And…"

"And he's sticking to it."

"Good! He was next door at Engine Ten. What about the other guys?"

"The wagon crew was in the maintenance garage around the corner on Eleventh. One of them said he heard one shot and his partner said he thinks he heard two pops. Keegan from sixteen car, who was standing at twelfth Street with Stakeout, said he heard three shots."

"Interesting! Well, until we're proven wrong, my money is still on two shots fired. What else is bothering you, Ton?"

"I just got off the phone with a friend of mine on the day work crew in South Detectives. That's why I'm still here. I called over unofficially, of course, to get a handle on which direction Detective Johnson plans to steer the Rugnetta job. In his report, that is."

"Steer is the optimal word. Good! Were you able to find anything out?"

"Some. First, I find out that Fannille called Johnson soon after he returned from the scene. Johnson's end of the conversation was full of 'yes, sir,' 'no problem, deputy commissioner' and 'I agree one hundred percent' comments."

"Figured the Deputy would be getting involved. Richie was his nephew after all. Remember what he said about the Monsignor, being Fannille's 'goomba.' Go on, Ton."

"I found out right after the Fannille chat, Johnson wrote up his report, cut out the middleman, his lieutenant, and put it in the captain's inbox."

"That was fast. Guess Fannille inspired him."

"It was quick. That's for sure. Record time for Johnson. He's normally delinquent on all his reports. Anyway, it so happened, Johnson's captain was unexpectedly summoned to the PC's office so he hasn't seen the seventy-five forty-nine yet."

Mickey smiles. "But I suspect someone else has. I'd love to see that bad boy."

"Would ya settle for a synopsis, Boss?"

"You're good, Ton. Shoot!"

"Basically, Richie Rugnetta's death was due to a self-inflicted gunshot wound."

"So they really are settling on suicide? Investigation closed."

"Yep! According to the Johnson, Richie snatched the Monsignor while he was on his regular morning walk. Then he made him unlock the doors to the school. Somewhere in the mix, Richie found the Monsignor was carrying a twenty-two Beretta."

"What? I can't wait to see how they handle there's no record of the Monsignor registering a firearm. Can they actually be that stupid, not to run a gun history on him? What was Richie's motive for doing all this? According to super-sleuth Deshaun Johnson, that is."

"Motive? A crazed young man went off his meds, and shot himself in the neck. End of story. Case cleared by investigation."

"He's using the time-tested theory of blame the dead guy? Johnson has a knack for trying to make a murder look like a suicide or vice versa. Talk about fiction. Although, Johnson's little work of fiction could explain how Richie got into the school at five in the morning. No mention in the report about the whole request for media thing, or the Monsignor's sinful ways? Or how about Richie's family connection to the Deputy? I'm surprised Fannille's not demanding FBI, CIA and DOJ investigations into his nephew's death."

"Nope! Not a word about any of that stuff. You're right about the Deputy. It's not like him."

"My sense is he's satisfied to let the incident die a natural death. It is a bit of a mystery. That's for sure."

"Nothing that man does surprises me anymore, Boss."

"Ya know, when I was talking to Richie this morning, I got the uneasy feeling he was a victim of child molestation and that the Monsignor was the doer."

"Funny! I was thinking the same thing. I figured Rich finally decided to confront his assailant and he was gonna make him confess in front of the whole world."

"Just what the Catholic Church needs right now. More abused folks coming forward and more cover-ups discovered. Guess I'd tick off the Archdiocese if I tried to go down that road as a possible motive for Richie."

"I'll say. Does the term excommunication ring a bell, Boss?"

"That would be just like them to blame the messenger, Ton."

"Man! With the juice the Cardinal has in this town, you'd be shipped back to CIB so fast it would take a month to clear your head. You'd be toast, Cap. Burnt toast at that."

Mickey laughs. "It is what it is. Besides, I like burnt toast. My Ma used to say, 'It's good for you. It coats your stomach.' Of course to get me to stop complaining, she'd have to add the part about people starving in Africa, just for good measure."

"Sounds like you're about to make some waves, Boss."

"Could be. Off the grid, of course."

"Well, if you need a wingman—"

"Thanks, Ton. We'll see. I at least want to check out a few things before I jump."

Mickey squints both eyes and puckers his lips. "Johnson and Fannille have taken 'going south with a job' to a whole new level claiming young Rich Rugnetta shot himself."

"Can't forget it was because he was off his meds, Boss."

"Maybe that old adage, 'Blame the dead guy,' really works."

"Every time, Cap. It's kinda like when a plane goes down and there are no survivors, it's always pilot error."

"Exactly! This one's gonna stick in my craw for a while, Ton. Did ya ever hear of Occam's razor?"

"I'm a Norelco razor man myself, Cap."

Mickey smiles. "Me, too. But that's not the razor I'm talking about. Occam's razor is a fourteenth-century theory that the simplest explanation of something, or in this case the dumbest, is the correct one. I'm not a proponent. For cops, Occam's razor makes for a shortsighted investigation."

Mickey senses he's getting a little deep in the weeds with the whole Occam's razor theory thing. "What I'm saying is Johnson either has an extreme case of tunnel vision concerning the Rugnetta job, or he's perfectly happy to be led around by the nose and have some higher authority make all the calls for him."

"How about all of the above, Cap?"

"I like the way you think, Ton. My gut is telling me something much deeper is going on here, maybe even sinister. But then again I come from a long line of doubting Thomases. From my point of view everyone is guilty until proven innocent. I think it's an Irish thing."

"I'm Italian, Boss. That's me too. 'Cept for me it's more a long line of doubting Antnys."

"That's a good thing, right?"

"Absolutely! Oh, by the way, Linda MacGraft said one of her guys told her Deputy Fannille's driver showed up at the school and took Detective Johnson and his partner aside for a little powwow."

"Carmine? That's scary. The guy doesn't blow his nose without checking in with Fannille first. You look up 'butt kisser' in the dictionary and there is a picture of Detective 'Worms' Gallo."

"Ya know Fannille lives around the corner, right?"

"I do!"

"He was probably monitoring the whole job from the comfort of his living room. I wouldn't be a bit surprised to find out Fannille sent Gallo to check things out, after the fact of course."

Mickey laughs. "God forbid he should show up. He may have to make a command decision."

"Maybe 'cause he heard you on the air he decided to avoid the area. You have a history, right?"

"We do. But the guy's a Deputy Commissioner. If I had to guess, the real reason Fannille was a no-show was he hoped I'd fumble the ball."

"The Deputy isn't known as a take-charge kind of guy. He's more of a stab-you-in-the-back kinda guy. I worked with him in Southwest. His rep back then was of a buffoon. A chubby buffoon at that. The guy used to weigh at least two-fifty. He always saw himself as a practical joker. But his jokes always seemed to be at the cost of someone else. He was a lieutenant back then and he used his rank to screw with the troops. He couldn't bear to have his calls being second-guessed. Correction! Second-guessed by his male detectives. His female detectives were... let's say...treated differently. In fact, it was during that time his first wife left him."

Mickey listens, and then comments. "But the nice guy that I am, I'll just say I'm glad he lost his chubbiness."

Rossi chuckles. "You are a nice guy, Boss. Maybe too nice for this job."

"Could be. I'm sure I'll get my reward in heaven." Rossi laughs. "Not me. I'd miss all my friends, Boss."

Mickey smiles. "I think you're selling yourself short, Ton. It's never too late. Or so I'm told."

"If you say so. Oh! Just before I stopped by I heard that Fire Rescue transported Monsignor O'Hagorty to Saint Joe's Hospital."

"Saint Joe's? That's got to be ten miles away. Why not Methodist on South Broad?"

"MacGraft told me she heard one of the EMTs on the cell with somebody he kept calling, 'Your Excellency.' Guess the Church figured the Monsignor's injuries weren't life threatening so transporting him to a Catholic hospital would be no big thing. Could be an insurance thing. Who knows."

Mickey shrugs. "I'll have to look into who made that call. Did you give an interview to the detectives yet?"

"Yes, Sir. So did Stakeout. But as far as I can tell nothing we said made it to Johnson's report."

"They're just covering their butts by going through the motions. Guess they'll eventually catch up with me. I got one thing maybe you could check out for me with the last out Radio dispatcher."

"Sure. What ya got?"

"Remember Sergeant Conti's transmission about his carrier might have been hung up?"

"Right! Yeah, I remember, Boss."

"See if you can at least listen to that part of the Radio tapes they're pulling for us. I'm thinking, if we're lucky, Conti's hung carrier captures the sounds of gunfire."

"Holy shit. If you're right—"

"We got our proof of two shots fired. Two distinctly different sounding shots. A crack followed by a pop."

"Sure I can do that. That's an easy one."

"Anything else on your mind, Ton?"

"That 'bout covers it."

"That's enough for one day. Now go home and get some sleep. If I hear anything interesting, I'll try to keep you in the loop. And Tony... you and your guys did a great job out there this morning."

"Thanks, Boss. Glad to have you on board. Even if you are a short timer."

The lieutenant leaves the office closing the door behind him. Mickey looks at his Da's Timex again. It's vintage 1950. It had been damaged in an explosion while Mickey was in Ireland looking for a cop killer. His wife Pat found a retired jeweler to repair it when he returned.

Nine-thirty? This whole district-commander thing ain't as easy as it looks. As my astute commissioner likes to say, "Things could get even worser." I haven't even had my first cup of tea. Way to go, Devlin.

CHAPTER XIV

Captain Devlin's Office

"A little man often casts a long shadow."
Italian Proverb

For the next two hours Mickey spends his time perusing the assortment of cardboard storage boxes in his office closet. In one box marked REPORTS, there are thirty overdue reports. Another untagged box has Commissioner's Memos from '95 and '96; Procedural Directive #69 "Civil Suits," dated 7-12-96, marked up with red pen; Assist Officer #230, "Off-Duty Firearms" and #231, "Disorderly Conduct" with the word BULLSHIT scribbled across the top in all capital letters. A third box had six CAPS, Complaints Against Police/District Level, investigations assigned to Captain Blackstone, all stamped PAST DUE.

The same box also has five completed Internal Affairs investigations assigned to Captain Blackstone marked "Action and Report." Meaning the IAB's top gink is calling for the Captain to take action, like additional training or discipline for the target(s) of the investigations. These too are stamped PAST DUE.

The next box Mickey comes across is marked Capt. E. Conley, Blackstone's predecessor. Captain Eric Conley was a commander who was promoted to inspector and then rewarded for his years of service to the folks in the 3rd District with a transfer to CIB. Mickey takes a quick look at some of that back and forth memos between the captain and Fannille. *This guy had huge balls. I would have enjoyed working with him. Too bad he took an early retirement.*

Then Mickey starts going through some of the videotapes marked "Greek Weekend/South Street." He slips the most recent, July 1996, into the Toshiba VCR sitting beside the twenty-five-inch Sony TV on the retro cherry-wood laminate credenza against the party wall of the outer office. The screen is cracked in two places and all the little black knobs to adjust sound and color are missing. *Thank goodness the remote still works.*

First to appear on the tape is Captain Blackstone with wall-to-wall young people behind him, mostly African American. Blackstone is trying to outshout the crowd noise. Noise that rivals the notorious 700 level of the Vet Stadium at the Eagles' home opener. At the bottom of the screen there is a military time clock running. Mickey adjusts the volume using the remote. He strains to hear and understand what Blackstone is saying. Mickey can only make out one statement because the captain keeps repeating it over and over.

"This is my last Greek Fest. This is my last Greek Fest."

No matter how Mickey tries to adjust the volume, Blackstone's other remarks become more and more unintelligible. The camera zooms out bringing into view hordes of young people running by shouting "Gun!" Then Mickey can make out a few more of Blackstone's words. "Fannille's in charge. Lord…" The tape goes to black screen. Just as Mickey starts to turn off the tape, he sees more images of young people running all along South Street.

According to the clock in the bottom of the frame, there has been a forty-seven-minute gap. The remainder of the two-hour VHS tape consisted of the camera zooming in and out from some rooftop capturing hundreds of men and women walking up and down the neon-lit South Street. The last ten minutes captured stampeding crowds running west again yelling, "Gun! Gun! Gun!" The tape ends abruptly.

Nora Brown comes in the office. "Watchin' Blackstone's South Street tapes, I hear."

"Tryin'"

"Those kids have no respect." Nora walks back to her deck.

Mickey is very familiar with the Greek Fest. In 1974, he was assigned to Blue Bell Park in Germantown for the very first "Greek Picnic Weekend," then again in '75, when it moved to Belmont Plateau in Fairmount Park during the day and onto South Street at night. As a detective, he handled fifteen cases of reported "Whirling." A term used to describe what happens when an innocent young woman is forced down a long double-line of shouting and groping "fraternity brothers" each snatching a piece of the unsuspecting young woman's clothing as she "whirls" down the line until she exits at the other end near naked. Even with no witnesses coming forward, Mickey and his fellow Central Detectives were able to make several arrests matching images from surveillance tape to photos from "historically black" College and University yearbooks supposedly "hosting" the Picnic.

At the time the organizers told investigators, "You'll see they aren't our people. Those thugs are 'outsiders.' They're not part of the Hellenic Society." To no one's surprise, those thugs were indeed "Greek frat brothers."

Mickey was about to view another video marked "Cheese Steak Beats" and "Bakery Caper–1996," when Nora knocked on the door and announced she had his copy of the District's "Self-Inspection Report."

"Come on in, Nora. Based on some of the images on these tapes it looks like things got a little out of hand up on South Street."

"Always does."

"Seems that way, don't it? Unless promotions come down before July, I guess I'll be here for the next one."

Nora shakes her head. "I wouldn't wish that on anybody. But I bet things will be different with you out there."

Nora hands Mickey the report he asked for. "I made you two copies, Captain. I know Captains sometimes like to mark up and make notes on this kinda stuff. Then you'll have a fresh copy on file."

"Thanks, Nora. You're right about us captains. We're always marking up stuff like this. Questions mostly."

Nora smiles. "Or profanities. Blackstone used to leave his stuff lying all around the district. Embarrassing! Need anything else right now, Captain?"

"Not right now. Thanks!"

Mickey takes the report and sits back down at his desk. *This should be interesting. How the guy put together a report like this when he's supposedly off campus "strong-arming John Q. Public?"*

CHAPTER XV

3RD District
Captain's Office

"An ounce of discretion is better than a pound of knowledge."
Italian Proverb

Mickey starts perusing Blackstone's 1996 annual report. He only gets through a few pages when his pager starts to vibrate. He takes a look at the pager still attached to the left side of his belt. It's a number he knows well, 3334. *That's the Captain of Homicide number. Wonder if he got the call to interview me.*

Don't think Detective Johnson wants to be in the same room with me. Mickey uses his cell to call the Captain.

After only one ring, someone answers. "Homicide. Lieutenant Bloom."

Mickey is surprised to hear his good friend Lieutenant Denny Bloom on the other end. Bloom is known as the number-one "ball breaker in Homicide." So Mickey decides to pull his chain a little bit. A little payback is long overdue.

"Is this the Murder Cop Unit?"

Mickey can easily imagine Bloom's blood starting to simmer. Cops constantly get calls from citizens who just heard the call taker announce the unit's name. But insist on starting with, "Is this...?"

Mickey doesn't give Bloom a chance to answer. "Hello! Is this the Murder Cops? Hello?"

Bloom starts over. This time slower. "Thiiis is thhee Hom-o-cide U-nit. Hoow can I helllp you, Siiir?"

Not wanting to carry things too far Mickey responds, "I want tooo rep-port that da-dea-th of Mic-keeey Dev-a-lin has beeen high-a-ly ex-age-er-ated."

Bloom gives one of his robust laughs. "Son-of-a-bee. You got me. How the hell ya doing, oh wise one?"

"Hey, Den. Sorry! I couldn't resist. I'm hanging in there. I got beeped from this number. Was it you? Or the Captain?"

"Me! The Captain asked me to call ya. He and Joe Lynch had to run up to a shooting scene in East. Three dead ones and one in serious condition at Temple Hospital. They even shot the dog. We think it's drug related."

"Figured! Guess those folks up in East didn't get the latest memo from the Commissioner. The one where he announced that Philly doesn't have a drug gang problem."

Bloom laughs. "My boss uses one of your lines all the time. 'The man has deceptive intelligence. He's dumber than he looks.' Can you believe that guy?"

"No but hang in there. I hear change is a comin'. Starting at the top."

"We're hearing that too, Cap. Rumor is the Chief of Patrol, the Chief of Detectives and the Deputy from Staff Services went to a meeting at the Mayor's office. There were a couple high-ranking commanders from NYPD in town to 'evaluate' our so-called crime-fighting tactics. Such as they are, or are not.

"Inspector McShane got the feeling the Mayor might be looking for a new top cop. He doubts any of the PPD's dinosaurs, including those in attendance, would be offered the job. I know that wouldn't break your heart. Would it? Always on-the-shit-list- again, Captain Devlin."

Mickey steps out of character for a minute and comes close to outwardly badmouthing the PC. "Not a little bit. But I will miss old what's-his-name when he's gone. Now if only the new guy, whoever that is, would show Fannille the door then I'd really be happy."

Both men laugh in unison.

"But enough good news, Bloomy. What's on your captain's mind?"

"Two things. First, for some reason we were given the task of getting an interview from you about your actions at the Dick Rugnetta scene. I guess South is much too busy."

"Or they were told to bag you guys by a certain Deputy. Who knows?"

Mickey questions Bloom about Rugnetta's first name. "You said Dick? The vic goes by Richard."

Bloom chuckles. "If you're dumb enough to shoot yourself in the neck, then you're a Dick not a Richard."

Mickey laughs aloud. "You're bad, Bloom. You gotta tell that in confession, ya know."

"No need! It's not like a lie or anything. 'Sides can't I just tell you, Boss. I heard you volunteered to take that priest guy's confession."

Mickey continues the back and forth with Bloom.

"That guy's title is Monsignor not that priest guy. You're definitely headed for the down elevator after your final roll call."

"Probably! Should I save you a spot?"

"No thanks, Bloomy. I'm on the express to the top floor. I got reservations."

"Okay reservations."

"True story. Now what was the second thing your fearless leader wanted you to relay? You sinner you."

"Fannille is on the warpath. Did you know that Rugnetta was related to the Deputy?"

"Yeah! Richie was quick to announce that bit of information up front. I guess he thought it would mean something. He added that Fannille was gonna be the next commissioner. God forbid! So what's Fannille's problem this time? He's always on the warpath about something. It's not worth worrying about."

"I hear ya, Boss. But what I heard is he thinks you rushed the job this morning. He's telling people you should have waited for the negotiation team."

"How would he even think that unless he was monitoring the job himself? Which I believe he was. If I was doing such a poor job, maybe he should have responded himself and taken over as scene commander. Besides, shots fired forced us into plan B."

"Absolutely! I'm told Fannille's driver talked to Detective Johnson from South at the scene. Johnson supposedly said he was just around the corner when he heard gunshots."

"Really! He said gunshots? Don't suppose he mentioned how many shots he heard from 'just around the corner,' did he?"

"Didn't ask him. Why?"

"There's a little discrepancy among those in attendance this morning. Things range from one shot to three shot to unsure."

"Where do you come down, Cap?"

"Two! I heard two shots."

"That's good enough for me. I heard two shots too. I'll swear to it. I was just around the corner myself."

Mickey chuckles. "You're nuts, Den."

"Great, ain't it?"

"It is."

"So what ya gonna do about the whole Fannille on the warpath crap, Boss?"

"What I always do. Ignore it. That guy's the least of my worries. But I intend to deal with Detective Johnson's BS the first chance I get. That'll border on fun."

"Oh my! Wouldn't want to be on the other end of a Mickey Devlin 'I'll deal with him' whip-ass declaration. No, Sir. Not me."

Back on point Mickey asks, "So how do ya want to handle my interview? Up there? Down here?"

"I know you're just settling in down there. How 'bout I send my top guy, Mike Ryan, down to you? I'm sure he'd like to see ya again."

"Likewise! How'd Ryan end up with interviewing the rogue captain?"

"He volunteered."

"Good man. So does that mean the job was turned over to Homicide? That may rain on Deshaun Johnson's parade. I heard he already wrote up his side of the job, with a little help from his friends."

"Nix! The brass wants us to follow PD-fifty-two."

Out of habit, Lieutenant Bloom starts to paraphrase Procedural Directive number 52: Deaths: Natural and Sudden. "The assigned detective from the Detective Division of occurrence will investigate—"

"Okay, Professor Bloom. I know who's responsible for what according to the PD. I also know you guys are responsible for 'suspicious' deaths. From where I sit, until the ME establishes the cause and manner of death, this job could easily be classified suspicious. So keep your powder dry. It may eventually be reclassified later with a supplemental report."

"Sorry, Boss. But from the 'West Wing' the job stays in South. We're just monitoring it and picking up certain interviews, i.e. Captain Mickey Devlin. But I'm sure we'll be required to do a follow-up at some point though. So—"

"So, Fannille is trying to steer your side of the job too. He's got South jumping through hoops."

"You guessed it. He's already called the Unit twice this morning asking for the captain. I wouldn't be surprised if Fannille hasn't already written up the whole investigation and wants our captain to sign off on our measly part so he can hold a news conference and declare how brilliant he is."

Mickey laughs again. He doesn't want to give up that he's had a sneak preview of Johnson's report. "From what I saw at the scene the suicide scenario is dubious at best."

"Not for Detective Johnson. All his reports are fiction anyway, then he test-a-lies about them in court."

"Testilies, I love it. I don't know, Bloom. Something stinks about this whole job. Too many loose ends for me. People are moving too fast to bury this one. Just haven't figured out why yet. But I will."

"I know you will, Boss."

"First, I need to—"

"Revisit the scene. Do one of those famous Devlin-analysis things."

Mickey chuckles. "Whatever works, right?"

"It definitely works for you, Boss."

"Okay! So you're sending Ryan to my location. Couldn't have picked a better guy."

"He should be there in about thirty minutes. He's with Irene Stasurak at CSU. Say around noonish."

"Sounds good. Thank your captain for the heads up on the Fannille warpath thing. I appreciate it."

"Will do, Cap. Nice to talk to you."

"You too, Bloom. If I don't see ya through the week, I'll see you through the window."

"Hey! That's my line."

"Then you should be flattered."

"Oh! I am."

"Talk to ya, Den."

Bloom waits for Mickey to disconnect, then hangs up. Bloom turns to Detective Golden.

"Sounds like Fannille's already starting a pissing contest with Devlin. Think I'll start a work pool on who wins this time. Like I don't already know."

"I'm in."

Mickey looks at his watch. *Eleven-thirty-two.* While he waits for Detective Ryan to arrive, he goes back to reading Blackstone's Self Inspection Report. *This guy was a master at cookin' the books. Wasn't anyone questioning his crime figures? Or are they in cahoots? Lose the conspiracy theory, Devlin. It'll only get you in trouble, again.*

CHAPTER XVI

Captain's Office
3Rd District

"A candle loses nothing by lighting another candle."
Italian Proverb

At twelve noon sharp Mickey sees Detective Mike Ryan pull into the 3rd District lot and park next to his unmarked. Mickey just finished Blackstone's Self Inspection Report and puts the marked-up, pristine copies in his top middle drawer.

Nora Brown knocks on Mickey's half-opened door and announces Ryan's presence.

"There's a Detective Mike Ryan here to see you, Captain. Said he has an appointment."

"That he does, Nora. Thanks!"

Ryan can light up a room with his smile. He quickly walks to Mickey and offers his catcher's mitt hand to his golfing buddy. Mickey greets his old Central Detectives' deskman with a big smile and hefty handshake.

"Well, if it isn't Mike 'Rolaids' Ryan. Congrats! You finally got your dream job, Homicide cop. 'Bout time the Detective Bureau woke up and put a real gumshoe in that unit instead of some Deputy's girlfriend or the relative of some politician."

"Thanks, Boss. You're right. I found a home. Course nothing will ever be as much fun as Central in the '80s though."

Mickey beams. "We definitely had some good times, Mike. We solved a lot of big jobs along the way too."

"Yes, Sir. We did ourselves proud."

Ryan has been in Homicide for just over a year and has already cleared more jobs than some detectives do in five years. Prior to that he worked out of Central Detective Division, on 21st Street north of the Ben Franklin Parkway, where he spent fifteen years. Central is where Mickey and Ryan first worked together. Ryan is right off the cover of a 1950s *True Detective Magazine*.

What the forty-something, pleasantly plump Mike Ryan lacks in outward appearance, he makes up tenfold in cunning and first-rate cop instincts. Like Mickey, Detective Ryan goes where the evidence leads him, verifies everything twice and always has one eye on the courtroom where most cases are lost because of sloppy police work. Unlike Mickey he'll never take another promotional exam. All he ever wanted to be is a Detective in the Philly PD. He's a lifer. The only way he'll leave the J O B is in the back of a rescue wagon headed for the emergency room.

"Guess my lieutenant told you 'bout Fannille?"

"Yeah, he did."

"Excuse my French. The guy's an asshole. I know you don't like to bad mouth big bosses but—"

Mickey holds up his hand to stop Ryan. "I hear ya, Mike. But you know what they say, 'Dogs bark, but the caravan goes on.' We'll both see Fannille pushed off this job. I'd bet on it."

"I'd go to that party. Hell! I'd even bring a date, Boss."

"I'd pay to see that myself, brudder."

Both veteran investigators and good friends laugh aloud. Nora Brown working at her computer in the outer office smiles at hearing her new captain and his buddy cut up. It's been awhile since she's heard folks joking around in the CO's office of the 3rd District. It feels good.

"So, I hear you volunteered to interview me, Mike."

"Absolutely! 'Sides looking forward to seeing ya. I wanted to hear what really happened down here this morning. Not the crap that's flowing down the pipes from Fannille's office. He's another one of those guys who, if his lips are movin', he's lying."

"Okay then, what do ya say we end your curiosity and get this interview on the fast track so can get back to finding the real bad guys? I got a feeling this is gonna be a long day, for both of us."

"Let's do it."

It took Ryan about twenty minutes to cover the who, what, where, why, when and how surrounding Mickey's part in the Richie Rugnetta job. Ryan uses the computer at the empty captain's aide workstation to type and print out his interview. Mickey proofs it and signs off, hands it back and queries Ryan on South Detective's suicide angle.

"So is your captain buying into the theory that Rugnetta shot himself out of stupidity, Mike? Judging by the way you just conducted my interview, you don't seem happy walking that bride down the aisle. I'd be interested, off the record of course, in what Mike Ryan's gut is telling him at this point."

Mickey already knows his old Central Detective buddy's answer. Mickey's tact isn't lost on Ryan.

"Bullshit! What was that you used to say all the time when some higher-up tried to steer an investigation in the wrong way? Something stinks in Denmark. Well Denmark must be stinkin' to high heaven about now. We both know the cause, Fannille. For the life of me I can't figure out why he's trying to steer this job in a certain direction. But my gut, as you say, is telling me whatever the reason, it ain't kosher."

Mickey grins ear to ear. "Great minds think alike, Mike. So you won't mind me dabbling a little into your sliver of the investigation. Off anyone's radar, of course."

"What the West Wing don't know, yadda, yadda, yadda. I'd be surprised if you didn't do a little dabbling, Boss. It's in your genes. You seem to have an excess of those little babies too. I won't be much help to you though. We're running way behind on trying to clear a hunk of last year's four hundred twenty homicides. Especially, with the batch of do-nothings the PC and his asshole buddy Deputy has parachuted into the unit. Rumor is every one of their past and present honeys have found a home in Homicide. The Patrol guys call us the Love Boat. Morale is in the toilet. But putting all that aside what I can do is keep you in the loop. Even if I gotta do it off the clock."

"I appreciate it, Mike. How 'bout starting by sharing what you heard about the interviews of Rugnetta's family. I'm curious if Richie left a note or ever talked to them about his relationship with the Monsignor. Richie told me he attended Our Lady of Sorrows as a kid. I heard Monsignor O'Hagorty has been vicar there forever. They must have crossed paths on a regular basis."

"To answer your first question, 'bout the Rugnetta family interviews, that's gonna be a little hard to do, Boss. 'Cause there ain't any."

Ryan's response gets a Mickey Devlin lopsided squint. "Ain't any family or ain't any interviews?"

Through clenched jaws, Ryan replies, "Deputy Fannille told us and South Detectives to stay away from the family. Said they're too distraught. He told my captain that since he's 'family'…" Ryan does air quotes. "…he'd grab their interviews himself and forward them to Johnson in South. I called the Admin Sergeant at South. No interviews have shown up yet."

"Fannille never stops to amaze me. He's interfered with so many investigations over the years that—"

"That he should have been jackpotted a long time ago. I know it, Boss. Shit! Everyone knows it. I don't know how he gets away with the stuff he pulls."

"He must have a pretty detailed book on where all the bodies are buried. My guess is he probably helped put some of them there too."

"Now that's an investigation I'd love to be in on."

"Maybe you'll get your chance sooner than you think, Mike. Wouldn't be the first time a big boss got jammed up prying where he shouldn't and thinking he was untouchable. Wouldn't even be the first Deputy at that."

Ryan chuckles. "You're right. But it ticks me off that every time Fannille gets his slimy hands in the cookie jar it's always for either his South Philly Mob buddies, or some thug union president. Now he's added family to that list. I don't know how he keeps his job."

"True story. From what I've been reading about him in some old district memos, he's taken his special treatment act to new heights."

"Right! You mean like a certain Italian-owned and operated steak shop on Passyunk Avenue?"

"I see you read the papers, Detective Ryan."

"I remember when cops were told to stay away from that place because of its Mob connection. That's all changed now they have a goomba in the West Wing, and gets his picture taken with the PC holding a giant check for every PPD cause. What'd the locked-up congressman say, 'Money talks. Bullshit walks'?"

"Welcome to the Philly PD, nineteen-ninety-seven. But anyway, I'm not convinced Fannille is caught up in this job because of Richie."

"Are we talkin' another one of those Mickey Devlin gut feelings again? 'Cause if—"

Mickey smiles at Ryan. "More like I'm whispering down the lane at this point, Mike."

Ryan reaches in his white-collar, canary-yellow shirt pocket and brings out a half-used pack of Rolaids. "I'm listening, Boss."

Mickey chuckles and points to Ryan's Rolaids. "Whoa, Mike. Don't get all frenzied on me. It's just a thought."

Now Ryan laughs and holds up the half-empty white-and-blue Rolaids pack. "Oh! You mean this. No! I was due. I'm good, Boss. I eat these things like candy. What's your thought?"

"I'm thinking maybe this time Fannille isn't mollycoddling some wise guy or union boss. Maybe this time he's trying to protect a higher authority, the Archdiocese. You know, he gets a lot of his juice from his pal Cardinal Vuotto."

Mike gives a one-word response. "Motive?"

"To spare Vuotto and the Church the embarrassment of another ugly abuse lawsuit and expensive court case. They're so deep in that stuff that it'll occupy the Archdiocese's legal department for the next ten years or beyond."

"Man! I really hadn't looked at that angle. Now ya got me going, Cap. I'm starting to wonder if Richie and the Monsignor have more of a history than we're being led to believe."

Mickey smiles. "Now that's the Mike Ryan we all know and love."

"Little bit."

"Good! Now how about the ME's office? Anybody been on the horn with them about doing an autopsy on Richie?"

"Not that I know of." Through a big grin, Ryan adds, "But even if that happens, Fannille will probably do the autopsy himself."

Mickey laughs aloud. "Or bring in his own man to do it."

"Wouldn't be the first time. Remember when he asked for, what the papers called, an 'independent examination' on the homicide of the Mob boss from Ten and Snyder?"

"I do. I also remember how Doc Steinberg refused."

"Absolutely! He put Fannille in short pants over every news channel in town. It was great. The Mayor backed the Doc too."

"You're right. But it didn't stop the Mayor from promoting Fannille to Inspector and telling the Commissioner to transfer him to another 'tit' job."

"The rumor on the street at the time was the Mayor was paying off a debt. Fannille supposedly had used his 'connections' to track down some nasty stuff on our city's chief executive and little boys from his college days in New York."

"I remember. That would have been a game changer for the election."

"So is this just another case of Fannille trying to save the reputation of a dickie shaker? First, the Mayor, allegedly. Now Monsignor O'Hagorty, allegedly. Food for thought, right?"

"Big-time food for thought."

Ryan gets back to the topic at hand. "Cap, I'm gonna play this Rugnetta job sixty, forty. Sixty percent of the time, I'll need to run on it the Fannille way, following orders. The other forty, I'm doing it the Mike Ryan way, follow the evidence and let the chips fall where they may."

"Can't ask for more than that, Mike. It'll be totally off the record, of course."

"I appreciate it. That's the least I can do for the guy who saved my ass on more than one occasion."

"You did nothing to be saved from, Mike. Some of the big bosses in this police department just can't tolerate good police work done by folks who can't be bought."

"Amen to that, Boss. 'Sides if I can be part of the team who nudges Fannille out the door—"

"Let's not count our chickens too fast. We're a long way from any post-Fannille era celebrations."

"Under the radar I know. I'll get back to ya with anything I come up with that seems off the wall."

"Thanks, Mike."

Devlin and Ryan shake to seal the deal. The new Captain of the 3rd District watches his old friend Mike Ryan drive off the lot and on to east-bound Wharton Street. *If the PD had a dozen Mike Ryans there wouldn't be a clearance backlog in Homicide.*

Still looking out his office window, Mickey notices a young, white male in blue jeans and a gray sweatshirt with the word NEWMAN across the front in orange and black letters standing beside a late-model Ford 150 pickup truck that's blocking the crosswalk at 11th and Wharton. The hood of the truck is propped open and the man appears to be fidgeting with something inside as he holds a cell phone to his right ear. He's talking to someone or at least wants people to think he is. *That's not too obvious now, is it?*

Normally, the man's activity wouldn't interest Devlin. What is bugging him this time is that the man has been under that hood since Wharton Street was opened back up again to traffic and the neighbors hours ago. *Either he has the world's worst auto club or he's doing a poor imitation of a "gink."*

With all the outside agencies swarming around South Division like cockroaches in heat, Devlin is leaning toward the latter. *Gink!* He writes down the truck's tag number and asks Nora to have one of the operations room crew run it through the DMV for an owner. Nora leaves and Devlin continues to watch the man while she's away. Within minutes Nora returns with a computer printout and hands it to Devlin.

"Here ya go, Captain."

Mickey reads the results aloud. "No record of an owner."

"Yes, Sir. Want someone to check him out? Ped stop him?"

"Not right now. If he's who I think he is, I don't want to spook him. Whoever he works for will just send another fresh face. Do you know if Lieutenant MacGraft is still in the building?"

"No, Sir. She's on the street."

"Okay. Thanks."

Mickey walks back to the window and while transmitting over his handheld radio, he watches the man's reactions.

"CO-Thee to Radio."

The man presses his left palm against his ear as if he's listening to something through an earpiece. Police Radio responds to the captain's transmission.

"CO-Three."

The young man goes to his left ear again. Mickey whispers, "Busted!" Then he turns up the volume and keys his handset causing a loud squeal to go out over the air. The man jerks his head back and lets go of his earpiece. Mickey grins and goes back over the air.

"Time check, please."

The young man presses his hand against his ear.

"KGF-five-eighty-seven, the time is now..."

Mickey watches the man let go of his earpiece again and go back to his obvious charade. Mick makes a mental note of the man's description and his actions. Then makes a few calls concerning who did what at the Rugnetta scene. First, to the admin lieutenant in South Detectives who tells Mickey the only items the detectives bagged from the scene were an automatic, one .22 brass casing and Richie's hands. "The CS guys processed the rest of the scene. As far as I know Homicide never showed up."

Next he calls Lieutenant Bloom at Homicide again to confirm that none of his guys went to Our Lady of Sorrows.

"That's correct, Cap. We're the redheaded stepsister on this one. Like I said, we got strict marching orders from your favorite deputy. 'Monitor and get an interview from Devlin. Then stand by for further orders.' Ya gotta know I ain't happy sitting on my hands with this one."

"I know you're not, Den."

"How'd Mike Ryan do by the way?"

"The normal Ryan interview. The facts and nothing but the facts. He's the best."

Mickey's not ready to share the sixty-forty deal he has with Ryan just yet. After he hangs up with Homicide, he talks to Lieutenant Scott at the Crime Scene Unit to pump him on what his guys processed. Jesse Scott worked for Mickey in the 35th District. In fact, it was Mickey who used what influence he had to get Jesse an interview with the captain of CSU where Jesse's transfer request was in limbo. Soon after, Jesse's request was moved to the front burner. The captain was so impressed with Jesse's credentials, His transfer was approved a week later. He remained in the unit after being promoted to sergeant and more recently to lieutenant. Needless to say he's been a good "off the record source" for Mick over the years.

Scott responds, "Hi, Boss. That's correct. We processed the whole scene. We lifted several latent prints and collected blood specimens and also personal belongings from the vic's pockets. South took ownership of a twenty-two automatic and the one brass casing found on the floor by one of the Stakeout cops. South Detectives bagged them before we got there. But I believe Firearms Ident has them now."

"Can I ask you what team you sent?"

"Don't think you know them, Nancy Griffin and George Rice. They're my civilian crew."

"You're right. Don't believe I've ever had any jobs with them."

"They're okay. Not the best, not the worst. I didn't realize it was your job or I'd have shot down there myself. Sorry, Boss."

"That's okay, Jes. I'm sure they did fine."

"Hope so. Let me know if they missed something and I'll make it right. Anything else, Boss?"

"One other thing. Did either of your people mention anything about the chalkboard or chalk dust?"

"Not to me. I know there's nothing in their report. Why? What's up?"

"Just a theory I can't prove."

"I doubt that."

"Any way you can fax me a copy of CSU's property receipt from the Rugnetta scene? I'd also like a copy of the sketch your guys did for comparison. I'm doing a little off the reservation investigation of my own. It would be strictly hush-hush."

"I have no problem doing that, Cap. But I'd rather have it hand carried to you. A certain deputy—"

"Say no more, Jess. I know the walls in your building have ears. If you're comfortable with it, I'll send someone down to pick it up in the next hour."

"You know me, Cap. I'm fine with anything you want to do. I'll be here for the next couple of hours. Have your guy ask for me."

"Great! Thanks, Jess. Talk to ya."

"Oh and, Boss, if I hear anything else, I'll give you a call."

"I'd appreciate it."

"Not a problem."

Mickey has Nora send Officer Brady, the bike cop, to Headquarters and the Crime Scene Unit. "Tell him to ask for Lieutenant Scott. He can use my car. Here's the keys."

"Yes, Sir."

Next, using his cell, Mickey punches in Doc Steinberg's number at the ME's office. He gets his voice mail.

"You've reached the office of Doctor David Steinberg. I'm not at my desk right now…"

Mick leaves a short message. "Doc. Mickey Devlin. I was hoping we could talk about a job I got involved with this morning. When you get a chance, call me on my cell. Thanks!" Mickey puts his cell phone in the charger, and walks to the 4th District's side of the building to visit Captain Bobby "Rumors" Bell. *If anyone knows the real skinny in South Philly, it's Bob Bell.*

CHAPTER XVII

Captain's Office
4TH District

"Conscience is as good as a thousand witnesses."
Italian Proverb

Mickey and Captain Bell, surly veteran Commanding Officer of the 4th District, worked together on numerous occasions over the years. So sharing a building should prove to be interesting. The 4th shares the ground floor and a portion of the basement with the 3rd District. They are mirror images of each other. Because the building physically sits in the 3rd District's area of responsibility that gives that captain the added task of landlord. Meaning maintenance goes through Mickey's office. Bell has been a captain for fifteen years. For the past six, he's been assigned to the 4th. Being a huge Philly sports-team fan, having all the sports complexes in his district, even with the headaches, suits him just fine.

Prior to the 4th, Bell worked in Police Radio. That assignment lasted until during a tour of his unit by members of the press, he pointed out several deficiencies with the very expensive "Enhanced 911 System." Deficiencies that could contribute to officers being on the wrong end of serious injury or worse. For his honesty, he was rewarded with a trip to that commander's black hole, Command Inspections Bureau, CIB. Another thing he and Mickey now share. Telling the truth and getting banished for it.

After two years of penance, he was transferred to the 4th District and has been quiet as a church mouse ever since. He stays as far as he can from any media types. He's even stopped reading newspapers. He says it's something to do with "Bad Mojo." He keeps up on current events via Fox News.

Bell joins a long list of high-quality Commanders muzzled by Commissioners who used their power to further their personal agendas.

Some of these men reached their Peter Principle the day after they graduated from the Academy. For many, the present Top Cop proves that very point with his infamous impromptu statement to the media after being "given" the commissioner's job.

"Yesterday I couldn't spell commissioner. Now I is one." Needless to say, that little slip into "Ghetto Grammar" filled the morning papers the very next day. That gaffe was just the first in a long line of "misspeaks" the PC has become famous for.

Mickey walks down the hallway through the front reception area to the 4th District's side of the building. When he turns into the Captain's outer sanctum, he's greeted by a civilian clerk and a white-haired uniform cop sitting at a desk with a plaque above that reads, "You have the right to remain silent if you survive the beating."

"Is your Captain in?"

Officer Terrell Newbury jumps up and answers. "Yes, Sir. I'll tell him you're here, Boss." Newbury heads for Captain Bell's inner sanctum, but stops short when he hears the gruff voice of his boss.

"Is that Mickey Devlin out there?"

His aide answers in the affirmative.

"He don't need no fuckin' announcement. Come on in, Mickey."

Mickey walks in and across the room to Captain Bell who's sitting behind a massive mahogany antique desk. The room is decorated with memorabilia from every professional Philly team. He's got signed baseballs, hockey sticks, footballs and a NBA basketball all prominently displayed. Bell raises his six-three, three-hundred- pound frame to shake Mickey's hand. He laughs and points to the row of sunlit windows along the 11th Street side of his office.

"Guess you're not used to that stuff, are you, Mick?"

Mickey knows his peer is trying to make a little inside cop humor. After commanders are "released" from CIB's steady night work the overused joke is to reintroduce them to daylight. Mickey shrugs and extends the ritual.

"I've been wearing sunglasses all morning, Bob. How long did it take you to readjust?"

Through a big smile, Bell responds. "A good six months. But it's gonna take you a lot longer if you keep coming to work at five o'clock in the morning to play street copper. You're gonna give us nine-to-five guys a bad name."

The two CIB alums chuckle.

"Don't worry. I'm not going to make a habit of it. Not after this morning anyway. I really stepped in it, didn't I?"

"Sounds like it. I heard about the Rugnetta job and his family connection to the Deputy. I also heard about Fannille's 'hands-on' approach to solve it."

"Yeah! Well! I'm not so sure Fannille and South Detectives are being as thorough as they should be on the relationship between Rugnetta and the Monsignor. I'm not buying in. Not yet anyway. I heard Rugnetta's family isn't going to be interviewed by detectives. According to Fannille, they're too distraught to talk to police. Except for him of course. He's supposed to interview mom and pop himself."

"That's merde."

"Merde?"

"Merde...shit!"

"Ouch! I'll have to remember that one, Bob."

Bell shrugs and shakes his head. "I guess that investigation is all but over. Fannille probably already typed up the job and mailed it to the assigned. Who is the assigned anyway?"

"Johnson. But Homicide is monitoring and CSU is helping to process the scene."

"Deshaun Johnson?"

"The one and only."

"Too bad his mom didn't have any kids that lived. Ya know the guy's a nitwit, right?"

"He gives nitwits a bad name. But you better be nice to him, Bob. I heard this morning that he's in line for the Eagles' team security job."

"Ya think your Mayor had anything to do with that? Shit! Wait 'til the boys in the locker room get hold of that jackass. They'll have a field day. Hey, maybe I'll get him to autograph a ball for me. Not!"

"I wonder if he's found a spot for his girlfriend yet."

"Probably! Ya know he used to call Blackstone whenever his uncle the Mayor was heading to Fabulous Deli to keep his cops out of the area. The Mayor hates cops. I think they make him nervous for some reason."

Mickey shrugs and flashes back to what Mike Ryan heard about the Mayor and little boys in New York.

"I give Johnson two months and the Eagles will toss him out on his ear."

"Speakin' of ears, did you know the recently departed Richie Rugnetta has two brothers? They all live with mom and dad in your district?"

"No but what's that got to do with ears?"

"When you said about the Eagles tossing Johnson out on his ear, it reminded me of Richie's older brother, Salvatore 'The Ear.' He has some kind of birth defect. One of his ears never fully developed. It's like a stump on the left side of his head. He's in the system. Did some time as a juvy too. Kid's been trying to find some way to make his bones, a Cugine, for years. One of the Mob lieutenants had him collecting street taxes along the Passyunk Avenue business district. But he's such a 'baggo,' useless wannabe, that the boys at the 'Downtown Social Club' on Moyamesing never took him seriously. He's a hell of a pitcher though. Probably could have gone pro. Threw a perfect game his junior year at Newman."

"Really! Ya know if he was a righty or lefty?"

"Righty! Now the older brother, Rocco 'Guns' Rugnetta, he's a different story. He got his nickname because of the time he spends in the gym working on his arms. The guy's got twenty-two-inch arms. He doesn't work on any other body part, just his arms."

Bell gives out a large laugh. "'The Ear,' 'Guns.' Don't ya just love these people and their nicknames? 'Tommy Sneakers.' 'Vinnie the Chin.'

'No Neck.' 'Tommy Tea Bags.' One of my favorites, 'Johnny Sausage.' Give me a freakin' break over here already."

"Let's not forget 'Tony bag a donuts.' The Organize Crime guys have a hard time keeping up with the wise-guy monikers. So what's Guns' claim to fame? Other than his biceps."

"Cop fighter. But not a very good one. The kid has had more 'Hahnemann Hats' than anyone I know. His noggin has been opened up so many times the scars look like a freakin' map of Jersey. The kid tried bone breaking for an Irish bookie. Bad move! Oil and water. Recently, he's taken pinches for assault and possession of an instrument of crime. He was carrying one of those American Arms mini revolvers."

"Sounds like a real toad."

Bell does his best Schwarzenegger pose. "A toad with twenty-two-inch arms. Forget about it."

"So what did Richie have in common with his brothers other than a last name?"

"Not much. Richie doesn't have an Ident Number. Keeps his nose clean. Works at his pop's store on Nineth Street just north of Washington. 'Rugnettas' Fruit and Produce.' The place has been in the family for years. Heard his Grandpop used to have a pushcart business before he bought the storefront. So I can't really say the three Rugnetta brothers have anything in common. In fact, Richie doesn't even look like his brothers. Richie looks more Irish than Italian."

Mickey pictures Richie standing on the school steps behind the Monsignor and thinking his hair did look reddish, definitely an Irish trait. *Don't know many redheaded Italians.*

"Sounds like—"

"Ya know...sorry, Mick."

"No! Go ahead, Bob."

"I met momma Rugnetta once. She came to the district to get Sal out of lockup. The sector cop scooped him up out of the gutter on Mifflin Street fallen-down drunk. I got talking to his mom and she told me the 'he's always been a good boy routine.' Anyway, to prove her point I guess, she said all three of her boys were altar boys at Our Lady of Sorrows. Hey, Mick did anyone tell ya about the Blessed Mother procession?"

"Blessed Mother procession?"

"Oh man. You got a ton of that kinda shit on your side. Even more of the string band serenades for the goomba brides the night before their wedding."

"Serenades?

"Yeah, you'll get calls from the bride's mom asking to have her street closed down so some string band combo can play Italian music in front of her house. For some reason I don't get many of those calls. But you..." Bell starts humming string-band music. "...you get them weekly. You better not turn mom down. Fannille will be all over you."

"Great! Now what's this Blessed Mother thing?"

"It begins at Saint Mary Magdalen de Pazzi on the seven hundred block of Montrose Street. Great-looking church. The place has been around since eighteen-ninety-one. Heard recently they're thinking about closing it down. That would be too bad and a real bummer for the neighborhood.

"Anyway, once a year, the natives march around carrying a statue of Mary and they all stick money to it. The procession eventually ends up with the blessing of the Nineth Street Market and a big block party with kids trying to climb greased poles for toys. They have amusement rides, lots of Italian food. Cops on the detail love it 'cause it's a free meal. Sometimes things get a little out of hand though. Must have something to do with the amount of dago-red consumed. I hear they get thousands. Yes, Sir. You're gonna love that action. Welcome to South Philly, goombaville."

Mickey refocuses on the Rugnettas being altar boys.

"Sounds like fun. So all three of the Rugnetta brothers were altar boys. Now that's interesting."

Rhetorically, Mickey asks, "I wonder if Sal and Rocco would ever admit to playing 'hide the soap' with Monsignor O'Hagorty?"

"Holy shit! You goin' rogue again, Mick? That always seems to end up not so goodda for youa. Those investigative genes of yours are boiling over, aren't they?"

"More like a low simmer at this point, Bob. But it does give me a new starting point."

"A new starting point? How many times ya gonna buck the system, Mick?"

Mickey grins. "Until I get it right."

"Or piss the big guy off enough he—"

"Transfers me back to CIB?"

"Okay, Mick. You win. How can I help that simmer come to a full boil? I love it when you go against the grain."

"I'm just looking for information right now, Bob. Nothing that can mess up what you got here. Just information."

"Like?"

"Like…if the Rugnetta boys told anybody about playing doctor with the Monsignor, who would they tell?"

"Mom! They're all mommies' boys in South Philly. Momma this and momma that. It's creepy. Believe me if the Rugnetta brothers told pop, the Monsignor would have had his balls cut off and stuffed in his mouth years ago by some wise guy amico."

Through a laugh Mickey asks, "So, the Rugnettas have a store on Nineth Street?"

"Yeah! Nineth and League. The family lives upstairs. But mom and pop are always attending the store. Mostly making sure the workers and the homeless aren't stealing shit. But the rumor is the deputy made them off limits."

"Man! Word travels fast down here." Mickey smiles. "But they're only off limits for official interviews. Not for innocent gossip with paying customers. I figure the Italians are like the Irish. Start them talking and ya can't shut them up. So I think I'll be going shopping for a little produce this afternoon. With any luck 'Guns' and 'The Ear' will be available too."

"I'd love to be there, Mick. But my face and belly are too well known over there. You're the new guy on the block that nobody knows. But ya better hurry up. The neighborhood papers will probably be all over ya for an interview real soon. Especially after this morning. They'll put your mug in the paper listing every assignment you ever had. Man, those people are gonna have a field day with your career." Captain Bell hesitates a few seconds, then adds, "That would be something if all three boys had the same 'I'll show mine if you show me yours' experience with O'Hagorty."

"It would. If that was the case, Detective Johnson and his new buddy Deputy Fannille would have to go back to the drawing board for a new lie, I mean theory."

"So you're going to fall back to that time-honored tradition, 'rounding up the usual suspects.'"

"I see you're a movie buff as well as a memorabilia collector."

"Yep! Ya know, I think you may like it down here, Mick. Did I mention I'm half Italian?"

"No you left that part out! So why don't you school me on the ways of South Philly. My astute half-Italian goomba."

Bell grins. "Mostly good people. Great food. Close-knit neighborhoods. For the most part the races get along. Once in a while you'll have some knuckleheads but when they sober up even they ain't too bad. Of course both of our districts still have their share of cop fighters. Mine more than yours. But don't forget, the Fourth has all the sports venues. I assign the same number of cops to the Seven-hundred Level of Vet Stadium as I do to the New Year's Mummers Parade."

Mickey laughs. "Sounds like my side could be manageable if it weren't for all those wild Mary Mother of God processions."

"Okay! Okay! You'll see of what I speak, Captain Devlin. You'll see."

"You available if I need saving, Bob?"

"Always, brother. As long as it's during the week and it's after nine AM and before five PM. Other than that, you're on your own, oh famous one."

"You got it, Bob. Now tell me the deal with the South Philly Mob. From what I hear they're trying to make a comeback."

"Oh! So ya wanna know about the Cosa Nostra, 'This thing of ours,' do ya?"

"Figured with all the time you got down here you gotta be one of the leading authorities on 'the life.' So yeah. Talk to me, brudder."

"Ya know you got the top..." Bell does air quotes. "...'authority' on everything Mob working for you. Sergeant Gino Conti. The guy's a whiz."

"I know, Bob. But he left on a two-week vacation when he finished work this morning."

"Oh, so I'm your second pick?"

Mickey smiles. "Someday I'll tell you my third."

Bobby Bell asks Mickey to close his office door. Mick gives Bob an inquisitive look and closes the door.

"Have a seat, Mick. I'll tell you what I know."

CHAPTER XVIII

4ᵀᴴ District

"Crooked by nature is never made straight by education."
Italian Proverb

Bobby Bell starts his rendition of the "life as a wise guy" in South Philly. "There's a long history of the Mafia down here. But I'm sure you already know that, Mick."

Mickey is very familiar with the Philly Mob but wants to get Bell's perspective. "A little! But I'm sure you've forgotten more than I'll ever know. Bring me up to speed, Bob."

Bell smiles. "You're such a bullshitter, Mick."

"I'm Irish. I can't help myself."

"Anyway, the wise guys have been in South Philly since the great Italian emigration of the late nineteenth century. There are lots of wise-guy stories I could tell ya. Some of them are even true. The good thing for us is they're always fighting amongst themselves. Even today, one mob family has a hard-on for somebody from another family and if the consiglieres can't iron things out, budda bing, budda bang, someone gets whacked and business returns to normal. The goombas down here kill more of their own kind than Elliot Ness ever did. For the most part, they take care of their own problems. The Mafia is like a police department for wise guys. We just mop up.

"In a nutshell, the Mafia is a handful of loosely connected business types, i.e. gangsters, from a handful of criminal families, some from here, some getting their start in New York City. They supposedly share a common organization structure and live by some bullshit code of conduct." Bobby Bell laughs aloud. "Kinda like the PPD, Mick."

"Man! Sounds like you've given the whole who-are-the-Mafia thing a lot of thought. That was good, Bob."

"Ya liked that, did ya? The Mob is kinda my thing. Maybe I'll write a book like you did, Mick."

"I'd buy it." Captain Bell is urged to continue.

"My grandmom used to talk about the 'Mafioso' in her village back in Sicily as the 'men with swagger' that everyone feared. It's the same way here. Except here it's all about respect. Again just like the PD, each family has its own chain of command. They got the top guy, capo, a second in command, underbosses. We got street cops. They got soldiers. They even have captains. Wonder if we can get a lateral transfer?"

Bell quickly picks up his desk phone and acts as if he's talking to someone. Through a big grin he says, "Only kidding, Commissioner. Devlin made me say it. I'm happy right here." Then he slams the phone back in its cradle.

"You're nuts, Bob. Being next door is gonna be—"

"A trip! Gotta laugh to keep from crying, Mick. Anyway! Stop interrupting me. I'm on a roll."

"Sorry, big guy. Please, go on."

"Wise guys got their own set of rules or codes. Violate them, especially the 'omertá,' code of silence, and you, your wife, your girlfriend and your kids all get whacked. That part's new. The retro wise guys never messed with family members."

"Did you read that FBI bulletin about this guy, Deluca?"

"Alfonso Deluca. I did read it. He's the guy the feds flipped who told them about the so-called 'Ten Commandments for Wise Guys.' The new breed of wise guys could care less about violating any freakin' rules like the one about looking at another made man's wife. Or drinking alcohol in a Center City nightclub. Or having cop associates."

"We know that one's not enforced. Does the name Antonio Fannille ring a bell?"

"Perfect example. Everyone knows about his Sicilian roots and his great grandfather's position in the old Cosa Nostra."

"We can't forget who his 'Godfather' is." Both men say in unison.

"Convicted Senator Nicodemo A. DeCarlo."

Nicodemo "Stubs" DeCarlo was born and raised on south 10th Street of "old world parents." His father, Luigi, started as a day laborer, part-time union organizer and moonlighted as an amateur boxer. The senior DeCarlo quickly rose up the ranks of the carpenters' union with help from a captain in the Vince Cibotti organized-crime family.

After graduating from South Philly High, DeCarlo joined the Army. At five feet six inches and one hundred twenty-five pounds, he was trained as a "tunnel rat," and was sent to "Vietnam Land" to crawl into tight quarters and dismantle Charlie's explosive devices. On his first mission he panicked and ended up losing the three middle fingers on his right hand, thus the "stubs" moniker.

He attended Saint Joe's University on the GI Bill and received a degree in political science. At the urging of his father, he too became a union organizer. Not only did he follow in his father's footsteps into the top ranks of his union, but he also associated with the same influential friend, Vince Cibotti. He used his military injury, his education at a Catholic university, organizing skills and his "connections" to enter the political arena.

Mickey adds DeCarlo's "Federal Prison inmate number 62033- 066."

"Really? You memorized DeCarlo's prison number?"

Mickey laughs. "Didn't you?"

"Man, Mick. I'm glad we're on the same side."

"Me too, Bob. But a number I'd really like to see is one under the name Antonio Fannille."

"That would be something to see, Mick. I have no doubt that over the years Fannille has acted like a private-protection firm for his wise-guy friends."

"The trick is to prove it. You heard of the Teflon Don. Fannille is the Teflon Deputy Commissioner."

"With whatever he's got on the PC, and it must be huge, plus putting his buddy in charge of IAB, Fannille ain't goin' nowhere any time soon."

"You're right. If he's going to get his, it's got to come from outside the PD."

"With any luck that New Jersey probe will get him. 'Til then we're stuck with him."

"You're right. So would you say that the South Philly Mob is dead, dying or on hiatus?"

"Depends on where you're looking. Right now there's a lot of infighting. They're all running into each other and trying to out- Guido the next guy to be boss. From my perspective, it's fun to watch. They're like the gang that couldn't shoot straight."

"In the Third?"

"Not so much. Most of them now live below Tasker Street. The wise guys who lived north of Tasker, on your side, are in jail or in witness protection. With any luck you'll be promoted and out of here by the time the old capos get out of prison. However, a lot of the crews, the soldiers I told you about, from my end, like to dine on your side of the tracks. So, you and yours won't get too involved, unless somebody gets his ass whacked."

"So where do these hotshots like to dine?"

"Rizzo's. It's become a Mob favorite in the last few years. In the past, it was where rival familiar with *Rizzo's Italian Ristorante;* he's eating there a few times with his disk jockey friend, Bernie Rabbit. "In the past, it was where rival families would meet to 'make a marriage.' Ya know…settle any business disputes they may have. Coincidently, it's also where some city bigwigs like to consort. I hear the Mayor and his kitchen cabinet go there a couple times a month. You should ride by the place sometime and check it out. Don't go in though. You'll end up being on the evening news."

"I heard Rizzo's was used as a backdrop in a couple mafia-type movies some years ago."

"Ya could be right, Mick. It is a neat place. Rizzo's is famous for its Ligurian-style ravioli and Railroad Bread. I've been known to go there myself. Gotta try their eggplant appetizer. It's marvelous. Of course with all the IAB ginks and God knows who else staked out down there, the place is too hot. That's your predecessor's fault. He's the reason all the damn outsiders are down here. Putz!"

"No doubt! Bob, I've been going through boxes of stuff Blackstone left in the office."

"You mean what's left after the AG sent the State Police to rifle through his office. I'm sure they took all the juicy stuff already. You're just reading what's left, the crumbs."

"If I'm only reading the crumbs, then Blackstone is history."

"I say Godspeed. He'll make somebody a great bitch in prison. Shit! I think I can even make that happen."

"You're really bad, Bob." Then Mickey decides to give Captain Bell a heads up on the guy with the black F-150.

"No shit. Okay, Mick. I'll pass it along. I agree with ya about not spooking the guy. Thanks, partner."

"Okay, Bob. Talk to ya. Thanks for the history lesson."

"No problem. There's more where that came from. But you're gonna have to buy the book version. Don't be a stranger, Mick." Bell laughs. "But remember nine to five."

"I'll have to remember that, Bobby. Ciao!"

"Arrivederci, Mick."

CHAPTER XIX

The Team Comes Together

"Among men of honor a word is a bond."
Italian Proverb

When Mickey gets back to his office, Nora Brown tells him she heard his cell phone going off in his office.

"Oops! I went next door to talk to Captain Bell."

"Okay! I went looking for you in the operations room and downstairs in the gym. I didn't think about the Fourth. Sorry!"

"My fault. I forgot and left my cell in its charger. Guess I have to get used to telling people where I am. It's different in CIB. I'll let you or somebody know where I'm off to in the future."

"Probably a good idea with Deputy Fannille jogging by here early every morning. He likes to harass whoever's captain at the time with stupid stuff."

"Really? What's his normal flyby time?"

"Sevenish!"

"Too bad. A little earlier and he could have taken over the Rugnetta job. Being his uncle and all."

"I didn't know that, Captain."

"It hasn't been widely publicized. He really jogs by the district every morning?"

"Monday through Friday weather permitting. The sector cop told me he likes to stop for coffee at his buddies' place on Passyunk first."

"The steak takeout?"

"Yep! He's famous for leaving little nasty grams on the office door. Once he left a note that read, 'See three-seven car.' He had fingered WASH ME on the back window of the car in big letters."

Mickey just shakes his head. "Did he follow up?"

"He did, by phone. The Captain took his call and reminded him that three-seven car was a crime scene."

"What?"

"It's true. Somebody had taken a couple of shots at one of our rookies while she was sitting in her car outside Headquarters. The car was being held here until CSU could dust it for prints and stuff."

"I remember that job. It happened on last out. Blew out the passenger-side window. Cop had cuts all over her face from the broken glass, right?"

"Right! She still works for Lieutenant Rossi. Good kid."

"So how embarrassed was the Deputy over his dumbness?"

"Lots! The assigned detective from South lifted a few prints before CSU arrived on the outside chance it was gonna rain. It was a good thing he did. It poured."

"Good move."

"On a hunch the detective ran the prints he lifted through the PPD's employee system. Later he said he did it just in case another cop was the doer."

"Awful to say but it happens a lot. It's hard to count the number of jobs I've handled when some cop pops off a couple rounds over a broken heart."

"Not this time, Captain."

"Good! Let me guess...Fannille's prints were lifted from the glass."

"Exactly! Somebody called the *South Philly Reporter* and the *Center City Weekly*. They plastered the Deputy's face all over the front page. The headline was 'DAAA! HEELLLO!' Fannille tried to take the spotlight off him by blaming Captain Conley for leaking an 'internal police matter' to the press. He actually asked IAB to investigate 'the leak instead of the shooting.' He denied it, of course."

"They probably did it, right?"

"Full blown. Which ended up making Internal Affairs and Fannille look even more foolish. Rumor was the IA buried the investigation after the detective from South dimed out Fannille for trying to squash the latents he lifted. Somehow one of the papers got a copy of the internal investigation. Turns out the IA inspector wrote the conclusion for the assigned lieutenant."

Mickey knows what newspaper outlet got that copy and exactly who the investigative reporter was who got it, Michelle Cunay.

"I remember that article, Nora. Fannille was cleared of any wrongdoing: 'The allegations against Deputy Antonio Fannille are not sustained because he has no reason to lie.' You're right, Nora. IA came out of the whole thing looking even worse than normal, if that's possible."

"A copy of the article was hanging on the bulletin board downstairs until somebody called the deputy's office."

"Cops are something."

"Yep! So like I was saying, it's good for somebody to know how you can be reached."

"Thanks, Nora."

Nora hands Devlin a sheet of paper with names and numbers on it. "That's a list of people who called on your private line while you were out, Cap."

Mickey takes the paper, looks at it and starts to count aloud. "One. two…seven calls already? Not counting calls on my cell. Guess I'm becoming a popular guy. And it's still early."

Mickey walks back to his office and checks his cell for messages. *"One voice message. Doc Steinberg."* Mickey goes through the steps to hear the message. "Yo Mick. Doc Steinberg. We're playing phone tag. You're it. I'm in my office. Call me."

Doctor David Steinberg and Mickey have successfully collaborated on jobs for years. Many of them were considered "high profile" either because of the victims or the doers. In '93 they teamed up to close the investigation surrounding the murder of a veteran narcotics detective in East Division.

Doc and Mickey were the driving force behind establishing the PPD's Cold Case Unit. The Unit's first case was the suspicious death of a Philly Police plainclothes officer in 1952. That officer was Lewis Michael Devlin, Mickey's father. That investigation was later reclassified a homicide, solved and cleared by arrest.

Doc Steinberg and Mickey also co-authored a historical whodunit work of fiction based on the 1832 mysterious deaths of fifty-seven Irish immigrants hired to work on a one-mile section of the Pennsylvania Railroad's Media Line. All fifty-seven men were buried in a mass grave along the tracks they had been working on for two months. *The Slaughter at Duffy's Cut, Solved* became a bestseller. Both men contributed the profits to a college fund for the children of officers who die while in the performance of their duties.

Mickey uses his cell and punches in the Doc's private office number. After one ring Doc Steinberg picks up. "Mickey. Long time no hear. Where are you this time?"

"South Philly. The fightin' Third District."

"Did you ask out of CIB? Or is that shadow of a man you call Commissioner messing with you again?"

"The latter."

"He's such a schmuck. Well, life goes on, right?"

"That it does, Doc. That it does."

"So what's up, Mick?"

"Believe it or not, this morning my first day down here, I was just minding my own business and this citizen decided to snatch a high-profile target from the Archdiocese and hold him hostage. The next thing I knew—"

"Let me guess. The citizen ended up dead. Rumor has it by a self-inflicted gunshot wound. If the ME somehow gets involved with this poor fellow, you want first crack at the prelims. How am I doing?"

"You're doing good, Doc. I guess you also know—"

The Doc cuts off Mickey again. "The vic is Richard Patrick Rugnetta. Youngest son of Celeste and Antony Rugnetta from south Nineth Street."

"Okay! I'm impressed. Now let me do the impressing."

"Be my guest."

"You got a call from a certain Deputy Commissioner. His initials are Antonio Fannille." Mickey can hear Doc laughing. "He told you that Richie Rugnetta, his nephew, shot himself and that he would appreciate it if you would skip your customary perfunctory examination of Richie's remains. He was only asking so the family won't have to wait any longer than necessary to give their boy a proper Catholic burial. Of course the Deputy left out any real details."

"Tried!"

"Say again."

"You said he told me. I'm saying he tried to tell me."

"And?"

"I told him if he called me again I was going to contact my good friend, Katherine McBride, DA extraordinaire, and have her go after him for interfering with my duties as head Medical Examiner."

"You are the man, Doc. What did Fannille say to all of that?"

"I don't know. I hung up on the bastard."

"That's why you're my hero. You got those 'take no prisoners' genes, Doc."

Through his signature chuckle the Steinberg says, "That's why we get along so well, Mick. You've got them genes too."

Mickey laughs. "I can live with that. So back to business. The Rugnetta job?"

"He's still on ice."

"Did your guys pick him up at the scene?"

"Negative. A wagon from the First District dropped the body off. Funny thing. My intake person said the wagon was manned by two guys in suits, detective types."

"That is funny. I'm not talking ha-ha funny either. It's got Fannille written all over it. You wouldn't happen to know if one of the suits was a Detective Gallo."

"Let me check the intake log. Negative! They signed in as Officer Smith and Officer Jones."

"Please! Ya have security cameras out there, right?"

"Outside the loading platform only."

"Can you make me a copy of the security tape? I may need to ID those guys down the line."

"As soon I hang up. I'll give it to you in VHS format, okay?"

"Thanks, Doc. I'll have someone pick it up in a little while."

"I'll leave it with the guard. How's that?"

"Perfect! Any idea if you and your team will—"

Doc Steinberg cuts short Mickey's question once again. "Wow! You're not getting off that easy. I want to hear the real story of Mrs. Rugnetta's little boy. I'm sure there's a Mickey Devlin gut feeling of how and why Richard ended up on a slab. I'm sure it doesn't mirror Fannille's version. Give it up."

Mickey gives Doc Steinberg the unabridged version. It's another one of those Irish things. Any story worth telling merits the full-length edition. Mick covers the early-morning hostage scene and the discrepancies with the number of shots fired, South Detectives' quick leap to a suicide classification, Richie's parents being off limits and Fannille trying to steer the investigation. "Ya know. Kinda like the way he called you, Doc."

When Mickey names Monsignor O'Hagorty as Richie's hostage, Doc Steinberg yells, "Shit!" into the phone. "Wait a minute, Mick. Are you telling me Monsignor Mario O'Hagorty was the high- profile target from the Archdiocese Rugnetta snatched?"

"Yes, but I'm sure once the Monsignor gets interviewed, he'll deny it."

In his most serious tone of voice, Doc Steinberg asks, "You sitting down, Mick?"

Mickey recognizes that tone. It means that Doc is about to throw a hand grenade in the middle of the room, i.e. the Rugnetta investigation.

"Monsignor Mario Francis O'Hagorty is on the slab next to Richie Rugnetta. He was brought here soon after Richie arrived. I was never told there was any connection between the two men, none whatsoever. The EMTs' report is kind of sketchy. It states the Monsignor suffered a massive coronary on the way to the hospital. According to the report, EMT Ligambi unsuccessfully tried to revive him with CPR and a defibrillator.

It goes on to say, Doctor Ignazio Caponigro at Saint Joe's Hospital pronounced the Monsignor at eight-thirty-eight this morning. He supposedly had his heart and BP meds in his pocket so Caponigro was satisfied calling the Monsignor's death 'Natural Causes.' How's all that fit into that gut feeling of yours, Mickey Devlin?"

Mickey doesn't answer right away. Then he asks Doc Steinberg, "Do ya know if Doctor Caponigro called the Monsignor's personal physician for a full medical history prior to making his ruling?"

"I assume—"

It's Mickey's turn to interrupt Doc Steinberg. "If the Monsignor died of natural causes then why is he on ice at the ME's? The remains should have been shipped directly to the funeral home of choice."

"Last question first. Under normal conditions that is correct. But I got a call from the Cardinal who was with Doctor Caponigro at the hospital and he requested the Monsignor's remains be held here overnight. I also got a call from Councilwoman Victoria Russo with the same request. I didn't have a problem with it."

"Russo and the Cardinal? That's a lot of drag, Doc."

"I guess. Seems the Ciro Magano Funeral Home on South Broad Street had no vacancies. Four teenagers from Snyder Ave. were in a compact Chevy when a tractor-trailer hit them head-on on the Schuylkill Expressway."

"Sooo, Magano's is the only funeral home in Philly?"

"It's what you called 'the funeral home of choice,' for what remains of the Monsignor's family, the O'Hagortys now of South Jersey and, in this case, the Archdiocese. The Cardinal told me when a priest or nun dies, the Archdiocese works with the family to insure they get a quick and proper burial along with all that pomp and ceremony stuff they do. He was pretty emphatic that can only happen at two acceptable funeral homes in Philadelphia. Magano's in South Philly and Boyle's in the Northeast. Magano's is in your district."

"Sounds like the Italians and the Irish have the whole Last Rites thing tied up in this town."

"Looks that way, Mick. Another reason the Jews do it right. One, two, three, it's all over. You're in the ground a couple of days later. End of story."

"So you only have the Monsignor until sometime tomorrow."

"Unless something changes and his death is reclassified to a homicide or suspicious. Something other than 'Natural Causes.' Is that something you're working on, Mick?"

"Among other things, Doc. But the list keeps getting longer. Now I'm a bit curious why the Archdiocese's top guy called you and not have some underling do it."

"You're a practicing Catholic, Mick. You can't question the Church. That's a sure way to end up in the fire of hell. See, I'm Jewish so—"

"Doctrine."

"What's that, Mick?"

"I'm not supposed to question the Church on Doctrine. It's the whole 'by faith alone' rule, Doc. Last time I checked Cardinals making phone calls ain't doctrine. You don't have any time limit on keeping Rugnetta on ice, do ya?"

"Just until I can finish my onceover. I told you, your Deputy Fannille wants Richie Rugnetta moved to the head of the line."

"Ya doing it, Doc?"

"I was thinking about it. But after talking to you, I'm reconsidering. It would be nice to have another 'cause and manner of death' though, Captain Devlin. Can you do that for me too?"

"That's the plan. Can I get twenty-four hours regardless?"

"I'm sure I can handle that, Mick. Just for the heck of it, I'm going to give the Monsignor a quick look-over too. Kinda like what you guys in the PD call an 'Inventory Search.' A little wipe-down here. A little blue-light examination there. Nothing too intrusive. Not yet anyway."

"Thanks, Doc."

"Mick. You don't have a problem with what the EMTs reported, do you? You sounded a little wary after I read their report. I've dealt with that crew in the past. Never been a problem—"

"I'm not saying they fudged up, Doc. I just want to keep an open mind. But I do have a question."

Mickey's pager goes off. He looks but ignores it.

"What's your question, Mick?"

"Darn! My pager keeps going off, Doc. I'll get back to you. But can you call me if your 'inventory search' of O'Hagorty comes up with anything? Anything out of the norm or odd?"

"I can do that, Mick."

"Great! I'll call you if any of my 'gut' amounts to anything."

"Deal! Oh, and Mick, don't let that empty shell of a Commissioner get to you."

"Can't happen, Doc. Better men than him have tried."

"Good! Talk to ya."

"Can't wait."

Mickey hits the end key and checks his pager. *Seamus! Wonder what the DA's premier investigator is going to drop on me now. It's gonna be hard to outdo Doc.*

Mickey's about to punch in Seamus' number when Lieutenant MacGraft knocks on his office door.

"Got a minute, Boss?"

"I do. I'm just returning a call. Come on in. Sit!"

CHAPTER XX

The Team Expands

"Desperate times call for desperate measures."
Italian Proverb

Using his cell again, Mickey punches in Seamus McCarthy's office number. While he waits for his old partner to answer, he starts to fill in Lieutenant MacGraft on his intended trip to the Rugnettas' family store on 9th Street. Before he finishes Seamus picks up.

"DA's Office, McCarthy."

"Hey, Seam. Mick...what's up?"

Feeling like the third wheel, Lieutenant MacGraft stands up and mouths, "I'll check back in a little while."

Mickey nods and mouths "Okay."

"Hi, Mick. Look I just got out of a meeting with the Boss Lady and a few suits from the State's AG's Office and a Major Sabella from the State Police. One AG was Pete Wenhoven from the AG's Organized Crime Unit. The other guy, Wily Craig, I never met before. Inspector Nevárez from IA was also with them. You know Nevárez, Mick?"

"Not really. Seen him around. He's PPD's lie detector connoisseur. Nice dresser. Has hopes of being the first Latino PC."

"I don't know much about the guy myself. Must have had a sheltered career. Anyway, the PSPs and IA came sniffing around looking for what they said is 'a little more cooperation' with what's going on with South Division's corruption probe from Katherine. Seems the suits think she's 'holding back.' Their words not mine."

"Really! What did Nevárez have to say?"

"Not much. I think he offered himself up as a liaison with us. I also think he's trying to show he's a team player so that down the road he can grab a position with the state."

"Sounds like something Nevárez would do. But I think they're messing with the wrong lady DA. Katherine isn't the type to stonewall an investigation when it comes to dirty cops or anybody else for that matter."

It's like the AG thinks Katherine is holding out on stuff and just waiting for the right time to showboat. He's probably worried Katherine will take away some of his glory. You know the Gov."

"Do I ever. The guy spends more time in the NBC sports studio doing post-game commentary than he does in Harrisburg. He's a real media whore. Probably thinks Kath may be considering a run for his job. Did the Staties get specific? Or did they try their normal 'show me what you got and if you're a good girl maybe we'll share what we have' routine?"

"Worse! They demand everything but don't want to give up squat. Not that there is anything. They actually threatened Kath with exposing so-called 'embarrassing photos' of her. According to Wenhoven, 'photos that could damage her career.' Kath was hot."

"So what hospital are they in? Don't threaten the street-smart Irish kid from Philly. She'll eat your lunch and take your recess money. Then dare you to rat her out."

Seamus laughs. "No hospital trip this time. But it was a short meeting and she did have building security escort all of them down the elevator and out the door. Of course, she threw in a couple obscenities for good measure."

"That's our Katherine. But I know you weren't trying to get hold of me just to give me the blow-by-blow of Katherine's meeting with the four empty suits. There must be something else going on."

"Always! I'm gonna give you the short version."

"Fat chance."

"Does the name Angelo Lombardo, Esquire, ring a bell with you, Mick?"

"Never heard of him. Should I have?"

"Not really. But chances are you may run into him now though. In fact, you may run into him and Katherine, together."

"Really!"

"Could be. Just saying...anyway Angelo is a product of South Philly. He went to Saint Gabs, then to the Prep. He was supposedly the heir apparent to his daddy's restaurant, Rizzo's, on Christian. Rizzo is Angelo's mom's maiden name. Instead, he was sent off to Harvard prelaw and Yale law school financed by his Godfather, Vince Cibotti. I ain't talkin' about the baptismal stand-in kinda Godfather either."

"Ouch! That could be a messy state of affairs for Katherine if they're seen together all cozy like. But—"

"True story! We're all hoping that that isn't the case. But you know Kath. She's pretty tightlipped about stuff like that."

"What else you got on Angelo?"

"He graduated at the top of his class. Came back to town and got a job at a fancy law firm in Center City...Kline, Leonard and Swartz... working mostly civil law stuff. He lives in Society Hill Towers, the penthouse. Isn't that where your DJ buddy, Bernie Rabbit, lives?"

Mickey laughs. "Man, where did that come from? Yes, Bernie does live there. But he's a whole lot more than just a DJ. The guy's an industry and a friend of mine for over forty years. I worked for him when I was a kid. When Pat and I got married, he got the band for our reception. Anyway, so it sounds like you really did your due diligence on Angelo, Seam. You must be worried."

"Some. But I did my due diligence on the sly. Katherine doesn't know—"

"That's real fatherly of ya. But where are you taking me with this, partner? Does Katherine even know you're making this call?"

"Not exactly."

"Not exactly? You could be in a world of hurt if—"

"There ain't gonna be any ifs, partner."

"Okay! So I'm guessing whatever you want me to do it's because I'm the new sheriff down here in South Philly land, base camp for what's left of the Mob."

Seamus chuckles. "Something like that, Sheriff. So here's where I'm trying to take ya. In addition to bringing in a huge chunk of change for the firm, probably in the millions, Angelo's other job is consigliere to Vince 'Gabagool' Cibotti. The guy who paid the bill for young Angelo's highbrow edjamacation."

"Whoa! This whole thing is getting uglier by the minute. Kath's a smart lady. She must have been aware of Lombardo's affiliations."

"That would be my guess. Ain't love grand, Mick?"

"Not always."

"Amen to that. Anyway the Staties told Kath that they've had a clock on the Cibotti family and their associates for years. Like she didn't know that already."

"So let me guess this time. One of their surveillance teams snapped what they consider 'damaging' pictures for Katherine. Something like the lovely couple walking arm-in-arm joking and laughing all the way."

"Kinda sorta. They got them having dinner at Angelo's parents' place, Rizzo's. After dinner, the boy wonder dropped Kath off at her place. Before you ask, no good-night kiss, nor was he invited in for a nightcap."

"Thank God for little favors. So dinner in a public place and ride home are the so-called damaging images they're trying to peddle? That's what they're threatened Katherine with? Bush league!"

"I told Katherine she shouldn't lose sleep over this stuff."

"You're right, Seam. What did she say?"

"She said she sleeps just fine. But then she said, 'This is bad timing. I really need the Staties to back off.' She seemed more anxious than infuriated. I don't know, Mick. There's something different about this thing. Can't put my finger on it."

"I take it you took her answer to mean a call for a little intervention."

"That's how I'm reading it. Off-the-record kind."

"Ya know this is the second time *Rizzo's Italian Ristorante* has crossed my radar screen today. The Captain of the Fourth District is a big fan of their eggplant appetizers. He also said my predecessor and his dirtball posse were regular 'nonpaying' consumers. So I'm guessing that since Rizzo's is in the 3rd District you want me to do…what exactly? Keep an eye on it? Or—"

"Keep an eye on the place for starters. Ya know, just a casual look-see. Nothing elaborate. Maybe a drive by on your way home looking for anything I can use to turn the tables on those jokers. IDing the Staties surveillance guys could help. Asleep at the wheel would be nice too. I just want something in reserve. It's no secret Rizzo's is the hangout of choice for as you say what's left of the South Philly Mafia."

"Another fact I'm sure Katherine would have been aware of, Seam."

"No doubt she is. But Rizzo's isn't exclusively a Mob shop. It's—"

Before Seamus can finish, Mickey adds, "Yeah! Yeah! I know. It's also a favorite watering hole for some of our city's movers and shakers. Including Mayor what's-his-face."

"Bingo!"

"I got a feeling I know where this is going. Ya know I'll do anything for Katherine. But, as you know, I'm in a rather precarious position right now. Being sent down here by the PC with the hopes I'll screw up. So if I'm gonna get involved in your little endeavor to get those people off Katherine's back, ya got to let me do the Frank Sinatra on this one."

"Meaning?"

"It's got to be done my way. I've got an idea that could make the suits back off."

Seamus laughs aloud. "You're really getting into the whole Italian thing, aren't you, Mister Sinatra? Next thing you'll be telling me is you're gonna give them an offer they can't refuse."

"Just trying to get in touch with my new Italian side, brudder."

"Devlin. You ain't got no Italian side. You're like me, all Mick."

Mickey laughs. "Proud of it, brudder."

"Me too! I know you're a Motown guy but if you really want to go Italian, a friend of mine does a radio gig every Sunday. Four hours of all Sinatra. You should check him out, Johnnydee."

"Sure! I'll check him out. I actually do like Sinatra. My father-in- law got me hooked."

"Great!"

"Seam, I know you don't want to wait around for the Gov and his hatchet men to drop a dime to the media. So, for now, pencil me in for regular drive-bys. I'll get back to you on my other brainchild."

"Thanks, Mick."

"So now that we settled that, it's your turn to do me a favor, partner."

"I'm yours."

"Good! How's thirty minutes at my place sound?"

"Thirty minutes will work."

"When you get down here, I want to take you along on a little field trip around my new stomping ground. Won't take long."

"Field trip?"

"Field trip! Trust me. Wear your best tourist going shopping clothes. That means lose the police scanner and those mirror sunglasses you wear to scare people."

"Oh shit! A Mickey Devlin field trip. Should be interesting. It's been awhile, partner. See ya in a half-hour. Dressed to shop."

"See ya, brudder."

Mickey smiles and hits the end key on his cell with a rigid index finger. *You're right, Seam. It's gonna be interesting.* Mickey walks down the hall to the operations room looking for Lieutenant MacGraft. He finds her in the small computer room off the reception area. She's peering through the old rain-stained curtains that could have been hanging in the room's small window since the building was given its certificate of occupancy. She's watching something on Wharton Street.

"See anything interesting out there, Lieutenant?"

"Hey, Cap." The lieutenant points toward the northeast corner.

"That guy across the street has had his head under the hood of that truck for hours missing with something. Have you—"

"Yes! I have. Not sure from where yet. I know all of IA's surveillance vehicles. A Ford 150 isn't one of them. He's probably a State Trooper.

It doesn't matter, but he's definitely a gink. I caught him monitoring South Band earlier."

"Really? You want to have one of my guys ped-stop Mister Joe Mechanic, Boss?"

"Negative! Don't want to spook the spook. At least we know his mug. I already had the tag run. Came up no record of owner. Give your people and the five Platoon crew a heads up and have them stay away. I already educated Captain Bell on the guy."

"Okay, Boss. Is that what you wanted to see me about earlier?"

"No! What I wanted to let you know was that I'm gonna take a walk over to Nineth Street to talk with the parents of our dead vic. They have a fruit and produce store in the Italian Market."

"Yeah, I know. Rugnettas' Fruit and Produce. So you want me to go with you to do the introductions? Or have the sector cop drop you off?"

"Just the opposite. I'm going incognito. I got civvies in my car. Figure being new down here, nobody will be the wiser. Actually, I won't be alone. The guy I was talking to on the phone when you were in my office, Seamus McCarthy from the DA's office, will be with me. Just have your people go about their normal business. This won't be a meet-and-greet thing."

"I'll take care of it, Boss."

"I know you will. Oh, and Lieutenant, two other things. Monsignor O'Hagorty, our hostage from this morning, allegedly suffered a massive coronary on the way to the hospital."

"Allegedly?"

"Yeah! I find myself using that word a lot concerning the whole Rugnetta job. I feel like a news anchor worried about civil liability."

The lieutenant doesn't push her captain on his obvious skepticism.

"What was the other thing you wanted to tell me, Cap?"

"The DA has a lot of good things to say about you. From what I've seen they're spot on."

Lieutenant MacGraft acknowledges Captain Devlin's comments with a smile and head nod. Mickey does the same and leaves it at that.

"Talk to you when I get back, Linda. Oh! Can you leave something in Tony Rossi's box about the Monsignor's untimely passing? It may or may not be on the news. Regardless, I told Tony I'd keep him in the loop."

"No problem, Boss."

Mickey goes directly to his car and gets his change of clothes for his incognito "field trip" through the Italian Market. Then right back to his office to make a quick call to Michelle Cunay.

Right on time, Seamus arrived and the seasoned ex-homicide partners head out for Rugnettas' Fruit and Produce at 9th and League streets.

"Be back in about an hour, Nora. Gonna take a little walk around the neighborhood. I got my cell this time and Lieutenant MacGraft can find me if needed."

"Okay, Captain."

Thirty seconds into their field trip Seamus asked, "So what's this field trip all about, Mick?"

"Information gathering from the bereaved parents of the young kid who died this morning."

"The Rugnetta job?"

"Yepper! Now stop with the twenty questions, already."

"Okay, Mister Sinatra."

CHAPTER XXI

9ᵀᴴ Street
Italian Market

"Even among the apostles there was a Judas."
Italian Proverb

Mickey and Seamus walk east on Wharton to 9th Street, an area considered the south end of the "Italian Market." Then they head north on 9th toward Fitzwater where the street scene changes. Both sides of the street are cluttered with grocery stores, cafes, restaurants, bakeries, cheese shops, butcher shops and pushcarts overflowing with fresh produce, seafood and curios.

Lined up in front of most of the storefronts along 9th Street are wooden crates or tables neatly stacked with fruit and vegetables from around the world, along with toys, flat-screen televisions and everything in between, all marked SALE or REDUCED. There are delivery trucks with their flashers blinking and private vehicles double-parked, causing traffic backups in every direction. This scene is repeated seven days a week, three hundred sixty-five days a year.

Unlike Mickey, Seamus claims to have only been to the 9th Street Market once to pick up an Italian rum wedding cake for a relative. So the "Market" will be a real visual and sensory excursion for the seasoned Homicide sleuth.

"This is insane. Is it always so damn packed, Mick?"

"Almost always. I'm normally down here after midnight. By then it's mostly the homeless scavenging for damaged produce in dumpsters and draining half-empty soda cans in piles of trash piled up at the end of the cross streets. In the Fall, there are the night crews standing around wood-burning fires in large steel barrels trying to keep warm talking in a whole host of native tongues. Actually, it's pretty cool."

The Market is entirely within the confines of the historic Bella Vista neighborhood in South Philly. Its golden years were during the 1920s and '40s. More recently, the Market has seen an influx of immigrant merchants from Latin America, Vietnam, Korea, Cambodia and others, giving the neighborhood an international flair with its various ethnic specialty cuisines.

The 9th Street Market can trace its roots back to the mid-1880s and the influx of the "new immigrants" from Eastern Europe. The Italian immigrants began to move into the area around 1884, after a prominent Italian businessman opened his first boardinghouse for his Italian brethren. The "open-air market" along 9th Street quickly followed, catering to the new Italian community and has remained to this day.

Many of today's Italian vendors can trace their own roots back a hundred years, to a time when owners lived above their storefront businesses. Today most merchants use their second floors for storage and some as refuges for "undocumented persons." A catchall expression made fashionable by "no boarder" advocates and liberal congressional and Hollywood types. Celeste and Antony Rugnetta, the proud Italian-Catholic parents of the late Richard Rugnetta, still practice the old-school "live-in" tradition.

By the time Mickey and Seamus reach the Rugnettas' store, the afternoon sun is high in the sky baking the tar-coated rooftops and casting huge shadows all along the one-lane narrow 9th Street. Long before they started their stroll through the heart of the market, they were bombarded with a mélange of aromas of spices, cooking oils, newly gutted seafood neatly lined up on elevated rows of ice chips ready for the taking, and live barnyard animals caged in aluminum pens unknowingly waiting to be butchered.

On the way, Mickey explains his intended plan for extracting information from the bereaved parents and siblings of Richard Rugnetta. He is eager to learn if anyone from the PPD informed them exactly how their son died and also ask about his relationship with the late Monsignor Mario O'Hagorty. Detective Johnson's theory that Richie went off his medication is also a topic that he'd like to probe. Lastly, he wants to determine if Richie was a "righty."

Before Seamus got to the 3rd, Mickey called Michelle Cunay, his go-to editor-in-chief for the *Philadelphia Daily*, asking her to put together a thumbnail sketch of Monsignor Mario O'Hagorty's history. According to Michelle, for the most part, the Monsignor had a "normal" South Philly upbringing and stellar religious career. The eighty-seven-year-old Monsignor was the son of an Irish father with roots in County Cork, Ireland, and a mother from a small village along the Gulf of Palermo in Sicily, Italy, by way of New York City. He was born and raised "downtown," a local idiom used for South Philadelphia. Young Mario was a good student, an altar boy and was always helping the Saint Joseph's nuns and parish priests in his tightly knit community.

By all accounts, he had "the calling" to join the priesthood from an early age. Having a devout Italian mama pushing Mario in that direction was also a huge influence. Right after eighth grade he was accepted at Saint Charles Borromeo Seminary on the Main Line. Being the youngest candidate in his seminary class he was taken under the wing by the Rector, Reverend Father Nicholas Bastille and Vice Rector, Reverend Father Dominic Vuotto who would later become Cardinal and head of the Philadelphia Archdiocese.

His first assignment as a parish priest was at one of the oldest Catholic churches in South Philadelphia. He eventually taught at three Catholic high schools around the city. Despite his obvious Irish surname, the Monsignor considered himself an Italian- American. His father, a convert to Catholicism, could care less what heritage his son wanted to claim as long as he didn't turn out to be a "fag." Being homophobic was only one of the senior O'Hagorty's issues. Consuming cheap gin was another.

The Monsignor's father would never live to see how his firstborn would turn out. The hard-core longshoreman got into an altercation with a fifty-year-old intoxicated Puerto Rican handyman in the Oregon Diner. Mister DeJesus ended their squabble by plunging an eight-inch Swiss Army knife into Liam O'Hagorty's chest. He was pronounced dead shortly after arriving at the ER. DeJesus' eventual conviction was overturned and he was released a year later. A week after returning to Philadelphia, the fifty-one-year-old unemployed DeJesus was reported missing by his wife, Nina.

In the 1950s, Father O'Hagorty was sent to Rome by Cardinal Girolamo Santucci to continue his studies. He remained at Vatican City for just under seven years. After his return to Philadelphia, he was elevated to Monsignor, named "Ambassador to the Italian Community," and offered a suite at the Cathedral of Saints Peter and Paul on the Parkway. He thanked the Cardinal for his offer but insisted on keeping his accommodations at Our Lady of Sorrows rectory. "I wish to be close to my flock."

Again, according to Michelle Cunay's research, the Monsignor has spent the last twenty-five years using his "Ambassadorship" to promote the "many contributions of Italian Catholics" to the City's growth. Interestingly, the Monsignor has also been asked to testify as a character witness for some of the less upstanding members of society at highly publicized Federal trials, primarily during the sentencing phase. His appearances have brought into question his relationship with the "Capo dei capi," the boss of bosses, within the South Philly and South Jersey Cosa Nostra. The Monsignor has always shrugged off those questions with his one-liners, like "I've known JoJo since he was a little boy." Or, "Tony is a good boy who comes to Mass with his family every Sunday."

Michelle noted that the Monsignor was never charged with any criminal activity at any time during his long career as a religious. Michelle added one "however" to her research. According to one of her reporters, a South Philly guy, about twenty years ago there were neighborhood rumors that Father O'Hagorty fathered a child with a young woman studying to be a cloistered nun at a facility on Green Street in the Fairmount section of the city.

According to her source, the rumors were never substantiated and died out. Thus, the Catholic Church dodged a scandal. At the time, O'Hagorty told the *Catholic Standard and Times*, "That's nothing but ferocious gossip by people with nothing better to do than spread hateful rumors. My mother would turn over in her grave if she thought I could do such a sinful thing. If it were true, I'd be defrocked by now."

Mickey and Seamus strategically parked themselves on the sidewalk between the Rugnettas' open storefront and the family's three overflowing produce carts lined up along the east curb line. While both of them meticulously start selecting one item at a time and placing them in plastic bags, a Black teenager was watching them. Finally, the kid, wearing a lightweight tan hoodie, jeans and expensive-looking sneakers with red laces, a real "street kid," approached the men and asked, "You guys gonna buy that stuff or marry it?"

Evidently, Mickey and Seamus' effort to look like produce aficionados didn't pass the sniff test for the Rugnettas' observant cart watcher. The duo couldn't help themselves and both laughed aloud. Mickey answers first.

"Buying! But as you can no doubt tell, we're both a little rusty with this whole fruit-picking thing. I was told to smell the fruit."

Seamus adds, "I was told to squeeze it to see if it's ripe."

The kid shrugs. "Whatever! Ya need help, yell." As the kid goes back to straightening the fruit and vegetables on all three carts, Mickey hears him mumble, "Omosessuale!"

Seamus whispers to Mickey, "I think the kid just busted on us."

"I think he called us homosexuals. He thinks we're a couple."

Seamus laughs so hard he drops the fruit he was holding all over the concrete sidewalk. "That little...I'll show him."

Seamus had already started to pick up his items when a white- haired man with a thick Italian accent came running from inside the store waving and screaming at the young boy. "Per favore. What you doin' out here, Terrell? Pick up a that produce."

Relieved the old man wasn't yelling at him, but feeling sorry for the kid, Seamus fesses up that he's the guilty party.

"The young man didn't drop the fruit, Sir. I did."

"That's...an...all right, Mister. The boy...he's a gotta learn. The customer always the right. You looka new around here, Mister. Am I right?"

"Yes! Si! My brother and I just moved to Philadelphia from Pittsburgh. Our wives got jobs at Saint Agnes Hospital. Gordon and I are opening a café up on South Street. I saw the Market in the *Rocky* movie and always wanted to see it for myself."

"Ya don't look-a-like brothers. Si! Rocky. Me not like. Throws the fruit."

The old man holds his open hand in front of him chest high. "Aaa—tappo—tappo!"

The Black kid can tell Mickey and Seamus are not up to snuff on their Italian so he decides to interpret for them. "He's saying little. Ya know, short! He's saying that Rocky is a little short dude."

The man responds. "Si! Si! Shorty! Rocky tappo."

The three men laugh. Terrell goes about his chores.

Mickey asks the old man if he is the owner of the business. A question he already knows the answer to. "Are you Mister Rugnetta?" Mickey points to the signage over the front door.

"Si! Anthony Rugnetta."

Then points toward the inside of the store and says, "Moglie. Wife. Celeste, my wife."

Mickey looking in the direction Anthony Rugnetta is pointing and waves to a woman, wearing a red apron, who is positioning herself closer to the group. Captain Bell's "he's a good boy" discussion flashes through Mickey's mind. "Ciao!"

Seamus plays along and takes out his wallet and shows Anthony recent photos of his grandkids. He points to him and asks if he has any children.

"Children. Si!"

Anthony starts to hold up three fingers. "Children. Si!"

But then he catches himself, makes the sign of the cross and with a tear in his eye holds up two fingers. "Two figli. Two sons, Salvatore and Rocco."

The Black kid pulls Mickey aside and tries to fill in the blanks. "He had three sons until today. His youngest boy, Richie, was killed this morning."

Both Mickey and Seamus' ears perk up at the Black kid's use of the words "was killed" in reference to how Richard Rugnetta lost his life.

Where did that come from? Mickey looks at Seamus, then decides to take a shot at what "the street" may be saying about Richard's death. He goes to work on Terrell.

"Young man. How was Mister Rugnetta's son killed?"

Without hesitation Terrell answers. "Somebody shot him."

"Somebody? Do—"

"Hey! What are you, cops or something?"

Mister Rugnetta shoos him away. "Back to work with ya."

Mickey turns and looks Anthony in the eyes.

"Sorry to hear that about your son, Mister Rugnetta. I can't imagine what it would be like to lose a son. You must be devastated."

The old man looks to Terrell to translate. To which Mister Rugnetta repeats several times. "Si! Grazie. Grazie. Grazie."

Overhearing the focus and tone of the conversation Celeste Rugnetta quickly joins the men on the sidewalk. Without the hint of an accent, she yells at her husband. "You shouldn't be talking about Richie. He ain't even in the ground yet. Boccalone!"

Mickey looks to Terrell to translate. He mouths, "Big mouth."

Celeste makes the sign of the cross twice. "Let it alone. Dirty holy water does not wash clean. Remember what Antonio told us, Antny." Celeste uses her thumb and index finger to twist her lips. "Silence! You, Terrell. Didn't Antny tell you to get back to work?"

"Yes, Ma'am."

Mickey and Seamus sensing the information door is about to close fast decide to double-team the Rugnettas.

Seamus asks, "You Catholic?"

Anthony answers, "Si."

Celeste asks, "Why?"

"We're both Roman Catholic." Seamus points to Mickey. "My mom used to bless herself when she talked about her brother, Jimmy. My uncle Jim was killed. Shot standing in line at the movies."

Mickey and Seamus look for a reaction to the word killed; there was none.

Seamus continues. "My mom said that if she blesses herself every time she uses my uncle's name, he'll get into heaven faster. Kinda like moving to the head of the line at the Pearly Gates."

Celeste responds. "Never heard that. But that's not why I bless myself. It's just a sign of respect for those who have crossed over. My boy, Richie, is gone but I'm sure he's already in heaven with God and watching over us." She makes the sign of the cross two more times, kisses the crucifix hanging from a gold chain around her neck and looks toward the sky.

Mickey quickly says, "I'm sure your son is with God, Mrs. Rugnetta."

Mickey and Seamus continue to show sincere sympathy for the loss of their son. Mickey pays Terrell for all of the produce he and Seamus have bagged. Terrell gives Mickey his change. Seamus starts to walk away, then Mickey stops him, turns back toward the Rugnettas.

"Oh! Speaking of the Deity. Maybe you can help us. My pastor, Monsignor Howard, told me his Seminary classmate, Father O'Hagorty, runs a small parish in South Philadelphia." Mickey points back and forth between Seamus and himself. "We were hoping to become parishioners of his church."

The Rugnettas and Terrell all look at one another but remain silent. It was as if someone slapped them across the face. Then Celeste pushed young Terrell toward the street carts. "I said back to work." With a glare in his eyes he does as he's told. Next she turns to answer Mickey. "Can't help ya, mister." Then she grabs her husband's arm and pulls him back inside their store.

As they walk away Anthony shouts, "Grazie. Thank you! Misters."

Mickey yells back, "Prego! You're welcome, Mister Rugnetta. Nice to meet you, Mrs. Rugnetta. Sorry for your loss."

Seamus shouts, "Ciao! Your son will be in my prayers." Then, the two "incognito shoppers" walk south to Washington Avenue, then West to 11th and back down to the District talking as they go.

"Ouch! So, what do you think, Seam?"

"Other than being called a homosexual by a dollar-an-hour Black teen, I think somebody got to them. I saw your eyes get wide when Celeste mentioned 'Antonio.' I take it Antonio is Deputy Commissioner Antonio Fannille."

"No doubt! I'd love to know what Fannille told them or didn't tell them. They seem upset or in mourning over Richie's death to you, Seam?"

"Not really."

"Me neither."

"Celeste got a bit jumpy when the conversation turned to their son, Richie. I think that she believes if she and Anthony do what they're told, things will work out. That their son's memory will be protected."

"Ya know I got the feeling Celeste and Anthony are concerned about more than just their son's memory. I can't put my finger on it yet. But it'll come."

"I'm sure it will, partner. What about denying knowing the Monsignor? They're obviously lying, right?"

"Big time! All three of Celeste's sons were altar boys at his church. The mention of O'Hagorty's name was like somebody stuck an ice pick in their ears."

Seamus nods in agreement.

"Ya know, I kept getting the feeling the Rugnettas were never told the true circumstances surrounding their son's death. The so-called suicide part anyway. Sounds like somebody told them Richie's death was some tragic accident."

"Ya mean like an accidental discharge of a firearm? Like the 'gun went off when Richie was cleaning it' kinda accident?"

"Exactly! Except it's a little tough explaining away those scenarios happening in a schoolroom at six in the morning. But then again anything is possible for a serial liar like Fannille."

"It would be a walk in the park for him, Mick."

"Ya know the other fly in the ointment is young Terrell, the Rugnetta's hired hand. He's definitely a streetwise young man. He must have heard something. He said Richie was killed. If that were the case, then who killed him? The Monsignor? The—"

"Can't say…yet. But I'm with ya on the kid, Mick. Too bad the brothers weren't around. I definitely can't see getting anything else out of the Rugnettas."

"Probably not. I was also hoping to get into the whole 'off his meds' theory that South Detectives are spinning about Richie. But I'll bet with Terrell working the store with Richie and his brothers, the kid knows stuff. Somebody's got to get to Terrell. He could give us actionable info."

"I hear ya. I'd be willing to bet he knows more about Richie than Richie's parents do. The kid's your nexus."

"I have just the person who can shake his chain too."

"Ya think it might be better coming from the DA's office?"

"Not this time, partner. Katherine's got enough to deal with right now."

"Speaking of my boss. Ya want to clue me in on what you have in mind concerning her little Kodak moment with Angelo Lombardo?"

Mickey deflects Seamus' question with a grin. "So did Richie's mom and pop look upset to you?"

"Not hardly. I'd say more worried than anything. My guess is—"

In unison, Mickey and Seamus bark, "Fannille!"

CHAPTER XXII

Lobby 3RD Police District

"Silent waters run deep."

Italian Proverb

Mickey and Seamus, each holding an overflowing plastic bag of assorted fruit are met at the front double aluminum doors of the 3rd District by Lieutenant Linda MacGraft.

"Hey, Boss. Looks like you were serious about shopping. Great spot! How'd ya do with the Rugnettas? They give up anything to run on?"

"We did okay. Not as much as we would have liked. There's still some digging to do. There's a young teenager that works for the family who could shed some light. I told Seamus I was thinking about—"

The lieutenant interrupts Mickey in mid-sentence. "I can do it."

Mickey and Seamus laugh. Mickey asks, "You volunteering, Linda?"

"Unless you had somebody else in mind, I'm your gal."

Seamus asks the lieutenant, "You know the kid the Captain is talking about?"

"Sure! That would be Terrell 'Stitches' Soetoro. Good kid. Honor student, president of his eighth-grade class. His mom lives in Point Breeze in the Seventeen but he uses his grandmom's address to go to school in the Third. It's safer on this side of Broad Street. Especially for a kid who takes his education seriously."

Mickey smiles. "Why aren't I surprised you have a dossier on Terrell Soetoro."

"I know a lot of people down here, Boss. On and off the job. I'm a Two-Streeter born and raised."

A "Two-Streeter" is a person who proudly resides or resided along a strip of south 2nd Street straddling an area covered by the 3rd and 4th

Police Districts. It also refers to the hundreds of folks who are members of the assortment of "private clubs" that sponsor and house some of Philadelphia's famous string bands and fancy brigades. Second Street becomes, according to some, a big out-of- control party street after the bands march down Broad Street in the New Year's Day Parade.

In '95, by three AM, one commander detailed to the area had enough. He called in every available South Division sector cop and closed the party down, over the objection of a crazed State Senator who lived in the neighborhood. The headlines the next morning read, **"Nazis Invade Party Goers on 2nd Street. Popular Senator Arrested for Disorderly Conduct and Public Intoxication."** The commander was transferred to CIB the next business day.

Mickey responds to Linda admitting to her South Philly roots, "So you're that Irish girl from South Philly? I heard there was one down here somewhere."

MacGraft laughs. She hears that rap all the time. "There're lots of Irish down here. We outnumbered the Italians at one point. We even had our own church, Saint Paul's, Nine-hundred Christian Street. Been around since eighteen-forty-two. The old-timers still call it the 'Irish Church.' I live down in Packer Park now. I outgrew my tiny row house at Second and Mountain."

"Packer Park. Nice neighborhood. Walking distance to Veterans Stadium. Still row house though, right?"

"Yeah, just bigger with wider streets. I like it."

"Back to Terrell. If he's such a good kid, why is he working at Rugnettas' this afternoon and not in school? How'd he get a nickname like 'Stitches'?"

Now it's the lieutenant's turn to smile. "He has the day off, Sir. His school is a crime scene."

Mickey and Seamus look at each other and laugh aloud. "Of course, it is." In unison both men say, "Our Lady of Sorrows," then they bless themselves twice mimicking Celeste Rugnetta.

"Riiight!"

"'Stitches'?"

"When he was going to school in Point Breeze, he would have to regularly fight his way home after school. He won some. He lost some. Either way, more often than not, Terrell needed stitches to close up his battle wounds."

Mickey shrugs and smiles. "Finally, a South Philly nickname that's fitting!"

Mickey points to the slip of yellow paper the lieutenant is holding in her left hand. "Is that for me?"

"It is. Nora Brown had to leave. Her daughter was assaulted by two of her students. She teaches special-ed kids at a school in West Philly. She wanted me to let you know you got a few phone calls. One from Doctor Steinberg, marked IMPORTANT." The lieutenant hands Mickey a slip of paper with three phone numbers written down on it. The Doc's followed by two he recognizes as coming from the West Wing. Mickey resists making derogatory comments on "The Wing" calls in front of the lieutenant.

"The Doc is the top guy at the ME's. He's a personal friend."

Mickey turns to Seamus. "Seamus McCarthy, this is Lieutenant Linda MacGraft, One Platoon." Seamus shakes hands with Linda.

"Seamus is the DA's right-hand man. We were partners in Homicide. He's a good man to know."

"Nice to meet you. Seamus is my dad's name. He was a detective sergeant in Southwest. He retired after thirty years in eighty-six. He got his PI license and later took a security job in AC. Now he manages the 'Cameras in the Sky Unit' at the Tropicana. He loves it."

"Don't think I ever ran into him."

Seamus laughs. "Me either. But there's a good man to know, Mick. Working at the Trop and all."

"You're right." Mickey checks the time and turns to Linda. "Seam and I need to discuss a couple things right now. So I'll catch up with you tomorrow. I want to get your opinion on a couple of things."

"Okay, Boss. Whatever you need. I'll be in at seven o'clock. But can I make a suggestion concerning Terrell Soetoro?"

"Please!"

"He's given the PD some good intel in the past. He's too young to be classified as a CI. He's more like a good citizen who has his ears to the ground. Working on Nineth Street is the perfect place to 'hear stuff.'" The lieutenant makes the air-quote gesture.

"That's good to know, Lin."

The lieutenant continues. "But the kid has, how can I say this, a phobia of cops in suits. I could never pinpoint the reason. But it's an issue with him. But he and I have a history of sharing information."

"Uniforms don't spook him but suits do? Interesting!"

"I'm up for it if I'd know what the end game is. Like what you think Terrell has to offer your investigation."

"That's fair. Seamus, you got a problem with the lieutenant here talking to Terrell? I know at one point on the way back you thought it might be better if Terrell was contacted by your office."

"Negative. It was just a thought. Like you said, we're kinda maxed out right now. And...we're suit coppers. So, let the lieutenant do her thing."

"All right then, 'Stitches' is all yours, Linda."

"Thank you, Sir. Can I make another suggestion real quick?"

"Absolutely!"

"I assume whatever Terrell can supply, you need ASAP."

"Correct!"

"So then I suggest I get to him today. I don't mind sticking around."

Mickey looks at Seamus and smiles. "Then, stop by my office..." Mickey looks at his watch again "...at the end of your tour and I'll fill you in on what I'm looking for."

"I'm done at three-thirty but there's a PDAC meeting in the roll room at four-fifteen. I'm scheduled to give an update to members of the Queen Village Neighbors Association on the recent spike of car break-ins. They'll be happy to know we made a pinch over the weekend. I got a little prep work to do. If it's okay, I'll stop by your office after that."

"That'll be fine, Lin. I'll be working late tonight anyway. Be sure to put yourself in for OT. So I'll see ya, when I see ya."

"Yes, Sir. But in the past we didn't get OT for stuff like community meetings. So—"

"So I heard. All that stops right now."

"Okay, Boss. See you around five-ish."

With that Linda heads to the roll room to prep. After the lieutenant is out of earshot, Seamus says to Mickey, "I think you won the lottery with her, Mick. She's a winner."

"Big time! What do you say we call the Doc back. Then maybe I'll talk about getting the monkeys off Katherine's back."

"Sounds like a plan I can live with."

CHAPTER XXIII

Devlin's Office

"He that seeks finds, and sometimes what he would rather not."
Italian Proverb

With Nora Brown out of the office, 5 Platoon's Officer Brady is manning the phones at her desk.

"Hi, Captain. Guess you heard about Ms. Brown's daughter."

"Yeah! Lieutenant MacGraft told me." Mickey introduces Seamus to Officer Brady. "Seamus, this is Gil Brady. He's my senior Five Platoon Officer. Seamus is lead supervisor at the DA's office."

Seamus extends his right hand. "Seamus McCarthy. Nice to meet you, Gil."

"You too, Sir. Didn't you used to work in Homicide? Ya look familiar."

"I did."

"I thought so. When that Mob boss got whacked sitting in his car down on Snyder, I was detailed to the Fourth District at the time. As luck would have it, I was the first officer on the scene. You interviewed me that night."

"That was some job, wasn't it, Gil?"

"Yes, Sir. It started another Mob war."

"You're right. The war isn't over yet."

Mickey addresses Gil's initiative. "Thanks for stepping in for Nora, Gil. What time you working 'til today?"

"Five o'clock, Boss."

Mickey checks his watch. "Wow! What happened to the day? I'll get one of the night work BD Team guys to relieve you. They're workin' five-P 'til one-A, right?"

"Yes, Sir. That'll be Wong and Kenney."

"Good! I'll have one of them cover the phones until six o'clock. The operations room can pick up the calls after that."

"Okay, Boss. I'll let them know. Oh, and the envelope I picked up for you from the CSU lieutenant is in your inbox."

"Great! Thanks, Gil."

Seamus follows Mickey into his office. Mickey closes the door behind them and takes a seat behind his desk. He picks up the phone and punches in Doc Steinberg's private work number. The Doc answers after one ring.

"Medical Examiner's Office. Doctor Steinberg."

"Doc. Mickey. You rang?"

"Yeah! Mick, I think the Rugnetta slash O'Hagorty jobs are starting to grow legs."

"I thought they might. What ya got for me? Oh! By the way Seamus is here. He stopped down to harass me."

"He's good at that. Say hey for me."

"Tell him yourself. I got you on speaker."

"Seamus, my boy. How's Katherine treating you these days?"

"Hey, Doc. Katherine is treating me just fine. She's almost as good a boss as this Devlin guy."

Mickey jumps in the conversation. "You people finished? If ya don't mind, some of us have work to do. The suspense is killing me. Fire away, Doctor."

"As promised, I did my inventory search of the Monsignor's remains."

Mickey stops Doc. "Ya know what? Let me call you back on my cell."

Doc chuckles. "Okay. Not a problem."

Mickey punches in Doc's number again. Doc answers immediately.

"Hey, Mick."

"Hey, Doc. Sorry about that. I just—"

"I understand, Mick. Walls have ears. Been there myself." "Thanks! I put you on speaker again. Now you were saying."

Doc picked up where he left off. "The Monsignor's pockets were empty."

Mickey interrupts. "Empty? Did you find any duct tape or zip ties?"

"Nope! Sounds like somebody did a little pocket dipping, Mick."

"No doubt about it. I'm sorry, Doc. Go ahead."

"I'm sure the Cardinal took possession of all of the Monsignor's personal belongings at the hospital. I was primarily interested to know what meds he might have been taking. Most times, at the very least, the attending ER physician will make note of the prescription numbers, the prescribing physicians, number of doses remaining, how often prescribed and the number of refills left. If my office is involved, they send the meds in the original containers along with the body. But that's okay. Because in reality, in this case, we're not supposed to be involved."

"I would guess, being in his eighties, the Monsignor probably was taking something for BP for sure. Right?"

"Right! Not having any idea what he might be taking, I made a call to Saint Joe's ER to track down what happened to any meds he may have had or if the EMTs scooped them up."

Seamus asks, "Ya think the EMTs held on to them for some reason, Doc? Is that a policy or something?"

"I doubt it. It's important I know for sure so I can make an accurate call on cause of death...if it falls on me to make the call, that is."

"I know what you're getting at, Doc. I'm still working on it. Are the meds en route to your location? I have a feeling—"

"Ya do? Do ya? Weeell, it seems the Monsignor was on at least three different meds but they're all among the missing. I talked to the head nurse in the ER. She told me she saw a cop take three white plastic medicine containers and put them in a paper bag."

"A uniform cop?"

"No! She thinks he was a boss because he was in a suit and all the uniforms were calling him sir. He had a police ID around his neck, hanging from one of those blue lanyards with police printed on it."

"Did she catch a name? Or how about what color border the ID had? Different ranks have different colors."

"Neither. Guess things got pretty hectic around the ER with the cops and the Cardinal running around. I never thought to ask her about color, Mick."

"Three to one, it was Fannille's name on that ID. I know the head of security at Saint Joe's. He's a retired lieutenant from North Central. I'll have him pull the surveillance tapes. That'll ID the bugger."

"Sounds good. I was able to track down the Monsignor's primary physician through the Archdiocese. I called him to get his medical history and a current list of all medications he may have been taking. I got a voice message. It turns out Doctor James DeStefano's office is temporarily closed due to an electrical fire. No reopening date was given. One of my poker buddies is the Fire Marshal. I called him, off the record. He told me his office is investigating the DeStefano fire. For now the fire is classified suspicious."

"Doctor DeStefano! Ya know, Doc, at the risk of sounding biased, this whole job is starting to read like a Francis Ford Coppola movie. I mean, all the players are of the Italian persuasion. Richie, the Monsignor, half anyway, his family doctor, the attending ER doctor, and the Stakeout cop who found the Monsignor. Then there's Deputy Fannille, South Philly's favorite son who just so happened to put himself in charge of his nephew's death investigation. Maybe you were unaware but the Monsignor had ties to the Cosa Nostra. Maybe it's just my imagination but—"

"Mick, it's South Philly. What did you expect? What's that you say about investigators with preconceived notions?"

"Point taken, Doc. Guess I'll hold off on going public with my

Godfather Ten conspiracy hypothesis for now."

"That would be wise, Captain. But if you find a horse's head in somebody's bed, give me a call. Then maybe we can talk about your Italian connection."

"Will do! What else you got, Doc?"

"Still sitting down?"

"Haven't moved. It sounds like you're getting to the good stuff now. Let it rip."

"Okay! I found a small red spot, a puncture wound, between the first and second metatarsal, of the Monsignor's right foot. That's inside the big toe, for you coppers."

Seamus answers through his signature laugh, "I knew that, Doc."

"Okay, Seam. Anyway I first noted a tad of dried blood and the beginnings of discoloration on the area just above the spot, on the dorsal. Mick, when you saw the Monsignor at the scene, was he wearing both shoes?"

"Yes! Both shoes and socks, black."

"Interesting! Because when the EMTs delivered the Monsignor here, he was missing his right shoe. I guess it could have got lost somewhere in transit. Or after he arrived at Saint Joe's Hospital."

"It happens. Things get a little crazy when a guy is stroking out on ya. I'm a little surprised the EMT guys waited around to transport the Monsignor to your place."

"Probably did it as a courtesy for the Cardinal. But I did think the whole shoe thing was a little odd. That's why I took a peek at his foot. I did try to contact the EMT crew about the missing shoe. Got hold of one of them. Left a message for the other."

"Any luck?"

"Negative! The one I reached suggested looking in the back of their truck. Said he was the driver."

"He wants you to check the truck? Why can't he check it?"

"Don't get your Irish up, Mick. The truck was left here. It's out of service and sitting on my rear parking lot right outside the loading dock. They couldn't start it after dropping off the Monsignor. It's waiting to get towed to the garage. The driver said it has been giving him trouble for a couple of days. He left the keys with our security man at the front desk."

"Bet that wasn't planned for."

"You still on that conspiracy hypothesis, Mick?"

"Just thinking out loud, Doc."

"I'm glad the truck was left. I wanted to check it myself anyway."

"Why's that, Doc?"

"I wanted to look for that darn shoe. When I was checking the Monsignor's jacket, I detected the faint odor of Hoppe's gun- cleaning solvent around his right pocket."

"It was probably trace from carrying his automatic. Richie said he got the gun he was brandishing from the Monsignor."

Seamus yells, "How about his hands, Doc? Any—"

"Another country heard from. No, Seam. Actually, his hand smelled more like vinegar."

Seamus reacts. "Ya know the wise guys like to use vinegar to get the blood off themselves and their clothes after a hit. The plot keeps getting thicker, don't it, Doc?"

"I agree. That's why I got the keys and checked that truck myself."

Mickey and Seamus laugh aloud. "What did you find, Inspector Steinberg?"

Doc laughs too. "No shoe, for starters. Before you ask, yes, I wore gloves. I decided to photograph the whole interior of the truck. Just in case, as you always say."

Seamus follows up on his earlier question. "Did ya smell vinegar in the truck?"

"No, just gasoline fumes."

Seamus suggests that if the Medic vehicle was having mechanical problems the crew probably flooded the motor at some point, causing gasoline fumes to seep into the back of the truck. Mickey and Doc agreed.

"Doc, did you notice any white powder on the Monsignor's jacket sleeves?"

"In fact, I did. It was chalk dust. Why?"

"Just curious. Had this whim at the scene that maybe the Monsignor wrote something on the chalkboard."

"Just one of those gut things again, Mick?"

"I guess, Doc! That Medic truck could be part of a crime scene. Somebody has to go through it before it gets relocated to the garage. Once the mechanics get at it—"

"That would be disastrous. What do you want me to do?"

"I'll get Mike Ryan from Homicide to cancel Tow and head down there on the sly to process the whole vehicle. The cancellation will look better coming from Homicide than from a District Captain. I definitely don't want Detective Johnson from South getting involved."

"Deshaun 'the screw-up' Johnson is the assigned on this one?"

"Sounds like you know him. The last thing we need is for him to get his slimy fingers around the Monsignor's death. Or Rugnetta's for that matter."

"Great! Just in the last year, Deshaun has screwed up six jobs that I know of. Everything he touches turns to shit. Absolutely! Keep that bubblehead away from here, Mick. The knucklehead has delusions of adequacy. Kinda like his uncle, the mayor."

Mickey laughs aloud. "You have a way with words, Doc. I will definitely keep him out of the loop. You gonna be around for a while, Doc?"

"Actually, no. I'm teaching a class at the University this evening. I'll give the keys for the truck back to Myron our security guy and let him know Homicide is en route. I'll be back around eight o'clock. If I'm only keeping the Monsignor overnight, I need to follow up on that very interesting puncture wound inside his big toe. Could be nothing but it's bugging me. Richie Rugnetta will have to wait."

"Ya got enough to at least consider a toxicology, right? Suspicion, of an injection site. Poison or drug overdose, as COD is a criterion isn't, Doc?"

"Suspicion is good enough for an autopsy, Mick, but for toxicology testing I'd need more. They're expensive little ditties and require taking very specific amounts of blood and tissue from the brain, liver and kidneys. As you are fully aware, the result could take weeks, more likely months. I read a paper recently from a leading toxicology lab with twenty full-time examiners. They report requests for ten thousand exams a year. So between doing the actual toxicology tests, appearing in court as expert witnesses and a bunch of other duties, the backlog is humongous."

"That's why I said 'consider' a toxicology, Doc. Maybe just run the idea by the Cardinal, and see if he resists too loud. I'm just trying to get a little time. What if the Monsignor was a doper? That could have contributed to his death. Right, Doc? That little prick mark you found seems like a red flag to me."

"Oh it does, does it, Doctor Devlin? I see where you're going, Mick. Could just be the result of a rookie pedicurist too. He obviously took care of himself...in that way, Mick. If I get to the point where an autopsy is warranted and it needs further investigation, I could classify the autopsy inconclusive pending tox results. I'll do the best I can to get you your time. But—"

"That's a start. Doc, before you go, can you give me the names of the EMT guys?"

"Hold on a minute. I'll check the intake book."

Mickey can hear Doc flipping pages.

"Here we go, Mick. Nicolas Ligambi and Joann Verna-Deloria, Medic Unit-Twenty-seven. That's funny, no payroll numbers. We always get badge and payroll numbers from cops and fire personnel. Just in case we need to follow up on something, or we need them in court. I'm no expert but it looks like the same handwriting for both names. Everyone signs themselves in, period. I'll have to yell at somebody over that."

"Whose name's on top?"

"Ligambi, the driver."

"Then that's your culprit, Doc. Yell at him."

"Okay, Mick. I know exactly what you're thinkin'. Two more Italians added to the mix."

Now both Mickey and Seamus burst out laughing.

"Still think I'm nuts, Doc?"

"That's a trick question, Captain Devlin. Okay! Okay, men. I've given you two old sleuths enough to ponder over for now. I got to prep for a class."

"Thanks, Doc. I owe ya."

"Yeah! Yeah! Yeah! Just keep me in that Devlin loop. I'm starting to agree with you about this job having the makings of becoming a real hummer."

"Good! Oh and Doc, when it's Richie's turn to get the full treatment—"

"I know. You're interested in anything and everything about COD as well as MOD."

"Thanks, Doc. Talk to ya."

"One more thing, Mick. That VHF tape I made for you. You know the surveillance-camera tape from the loading dock?"

"Oh, geez I was supposed to send someone for it. Sorry, Doc."

"Figured you got busy. One of my guys lives on Manton Street around the corner from your district. I had him drop it off at the operations room."

"You're the best, Doc. You're right. Things are starting to jump around here. I'll get it when I hang up. Thanks again."

"Okay, Mick. Talk to you, Seam."

Doc Steinberg hangs up and Mickey immediately calls Detective Ryan's cell phone. He fills him in on the results of Doc's "inventory search" of the Monsignor's remains. Ryan heads for the ME's rear lot to process Fire Rescue Medic Unit 27.

Next, Mickey contacts Julius McMichael, Head of Security at Saint Joe's Hospital, and asks him to make a copy of the security tape covering fifteen minutes before the Monsignor arrived up to fifteen minutes after his body left the hospital.

"You know it's gonna be video only, right? No sound."

"I do, Jules. My main goal is to ID all the players."

"The tape will be ready shortly, Mick."

"Great! Thanks, Jules. Mark the tape Devlin Reunion Party, will ya?"

"Sounds like one of those 'deep in the hat' Mickey Devlin capers."

"You know me, Jules. Can't be too careful. I'll have one of my guys pick up the tape."

"That'll be fine. Have your guy ask for me. I'm here till eight."

"Okay! Thanks, Jules."

Mickey hangs up and calls out to Gil Brady sitting in the outer office. "Brady, can you come in here please?"

"Yes, Sir."

Mickey tells him, "Have whichever BD guy that's not covering the phones go to Saint Joe's Hospital and see the Director of Security, Julius McMichael. He has a package for me."

"Okay, Boss."

Brady leaves Mickey's office closing the door behind him.

"What do you think, Seam? Is the Doc right? Do I have a hummer on my hands?"

"I'd say you got a series of hummers on your hands: the Richie Rugnetta shooting, the sudden death of a beloved South Philly Monsignor and that mysterious red dot, and the one closest to my heart, Katherine's photo display."

In unison, Mickey and Seamus say the name aloud, "Angelo Lombardo."

A couple of minutes later, Linda MacGraft knocks on Mickey's door.

"Come on in."

Lieutenant MacGraft still in uniform comes halfway in the room, unsure if Mickey has time for her. "I got a little time before I talk to the Queen Village folks. You ready for me, Captain?"

"Sure. Seamus was heading out. Take a seat and I'll bring you up to speed on what I'm looking to get from Terrell."

Linda takes a seat beside Mickey's desk and Seamus gets up to leave. Mick tells his old partner to take his bag of produce with him.

"Hey, Seam. Take that bag with you."

"You sure?"

"Absolutely!"

"Okay then. Thanks."

Seam gives an "arrivederci" and leaves. Fifteen minutes later the lieutenant is off to her community meeting. At this point she's less interested in giving good news to the Queen Villagers about the arrest of two homeless men who have been breaking into cars, than she is about talking to Terrell "Stitches" Soetoro. Shortly after five o'clock, Officer Wong from the late-end Burglary Team knocks rhythmically on Mickey's door.

"Come on in."

"Hi, Boss. Ted Wong. I got a package for ya from Saint Joe's."

"That was fast."

"Gil called me at home. I picked it up on my way in to work. I live five minutes from Saint Joe's. So like I said, it was on my way."

"Thanks, Ted."

"You're welcome, Boss. Ya still want Kenney and me on the street by six, right?"

"Definitely!"

"Great. We're working on a strong-arm robbery at the movie theater on Columbus Boulevard. We found a witness."

"Sounds promising. Oh, Ted! There's another package for me in the operations—"

"I'll get it, Boss."

"Thanks."

Officer Wong returns with the surveillance tape from Doc Steinberg.

"Thanks again. Talk to you and Kenney later, okay?"

"Yes, Sir."

Ted Wong gives a wave and leaves Devlin's office.

Seems like a good kid. I know his father. Devlin remembers his personnel folder states that he speaks three languages in addition to English. *That's a bonus.* Mickey slips Doc's tape into the deck and presses play. A few minutes later he presses eject. "Worthless!" *Too dark to even see the wagon number. We gave it a shot, Doc.*

CHAPTER XXIV

3RD District Headquarters

"If you scatter thorns, don't go barefoot."
Italian Proverb

Mickey calls his wife, Pat, to let her know he'll be late coming home, real late.

"Don't wait dinner. I'll grab something in the District. My first day turned out to be a little more involved than I anticipated."

"Okay, Mick. Hey! I heard something on the news about a shooting in your district. I don't suppose—"

"I'll tell you all about it when I get home."

"You're all right then?"

"Sure! Not to worry. There's just a lot on my plate right now."

As always, Pat understands. "As long as you get home safe, Mick. That's what counts. Love ya."

"You too!"

Mickey checks the time. *Doc isn't due back until eight. I hate waiting.*

Mickey tries paging Michelle Cunay. He adds his rookie badge number, 6420, to the end of his cell phone number. A code Mickey uses with close friends to denote callback ASAP. *That should spark Michelle's interest.*

Two minutes later, Mickey's cell phone goes off. "Took ya long enough, Michelle."

Michelle laughs. "Yeah, well I was in the middle of robbing a bank, but I had to stop to make this call. So this better be good, Captain."

Now Mickey laughs. "Is Clyde with ya on this trip, Miss Parker?"

Michelle hoots. "Not this time. You can call me Bonnie."

"Oh! Okay, Bonnie."

"So what's going on, Mick? I was wondering when I was gonna get a call back. So why did ya need the skinny on Monsignor O'Hagorty earlier? He in some kind of trouble?"

"Not the earthly kind. But if my gut is right, his legacy may be in trouble. Saint Peter may have a few issues too. Had a massive heart attack this morning on the way to Saint Joe's Hospital."

"Sorry to hear it. So you writing his obituary or something, Mick?"

"Far from it. I'm just trying to piece some things together about his untimely passing."

"I know that tone, Devlin. By untimely do you mean suspicious? I sense a drama in the making. Ya gonna give me first crack at an exclusive, right?"

"Always, Michelle. I'm surprised you weren't all over the Monsignor thing. You're slipping, kiddo. You need to get out from behind that big desk of yours more often, Madame Chief Editor."

"Stop breakin' them, Mick. It just so happens my guys have been trying, as you said, to get 'all over the Monsignor hostage thing.' But now—"

"You may want to keep that angle going for a bit longer, Michelle."

"How much longer? I hear the new hotshot Captain of the Third District ain't talking. He kept all the media away from the Monsignor's hostage incident this morning, then stood them up for an interview. Wouldn't happen to know who that new guy is, do ya?"

"No! But I'm sure he did the right thing."

"I'm sure he did. I tried schmoozing the PD's Public Information Lieutenant, who gave me attitude. Where'd they get her? Bitches Unlimited? Then she suggested that I call Deputy Fannille. When did he become the Public Information Officer?"

"This morning, when he took over the investigation of the 'Rugnetta takes a Monsignor hostage at gunpoint' job. Because I owe you for the

Monsignor's bio, here's a bulletin from that hotshot captain: Richie Rugnetta was Fannille's nephew."

"You shittin' me?"

"Negative! So that lieutenant was probably given her marching orders from the Deputy."

"No wonder she sounded so pissed off. Fannille probably told her not to give out any copy on either job. Whenever he does that he embarrasses himself and the PD."

"I doubt if he'll be breaking tradition on either job this time either, Michelle."

"Then you better duck. 'Cause he'll be looking for a fall guy when everything goes south. We all know who his favorite fall guy is. Don't we?"

"We do. But he'll need a lot of them on this one. With the commissioner already on thin ice, we can add him to the list of people he can blame."

"All true. Mick, my guys are telling me the PD isn't the only one running close to the vest with anything to do with Monsignor O'Hagorty. The Archdiocese is even worse. I may have to change my religion. Being an infamous and a practicing Catholic in this town isn't doing me any good. You gonna break radio silence and help me out, Captain Devlin, old friend?"

"Why do ya think I paged ya, Las?"

"Okay! Now, I'm sensing there's a but coming."

Michelle can visualize Mickey smiling on the other end of the line.

"You're right. Buuut...I'm gonna need some additional assistance on a few things. Some related to the Wharton Street job and some closer to home. The kind of stuff only you can supply. The kind my department wouldn't touch. Let me be up front about this whole thing. Everything I'm doing or may do is without the blessing of the West Wing. Or any other department for that matter."

"So what's new? That's your MO, Mickey Devlin. Who don't know that? So now tell me about this 'assistance' you need."

"Katherine and—"

"Is somebody messing with our Katherine? I'll hang them in a sea of words. Then bury them in hearsay quicksand. They'll never see me coming. Who is it? Give me names, Mick."

"Slow down, young lady. It's not names I'll be givin' ya. It's letters. AG and IAB."

"Shit! This is gonna be like shooting one-legged men in an ass-kicking competition. Me and those guys have mutual disrespect for one another. They're allergic to the truth. When do we start? What's your game plan? I know you and Seamus got one."

"First, what do you know about Kath's new friend, Angelo Lombardo, Esquire?"

"That's what this is all about? I met him once at a fundraiser for the Mario Lanza Foundation."

"First impressions?"

"He's a looker. He's well off. So he's no gold digger or publicity hound."

"When you met him, did any of those famous investigative- reporter genes start to go off?"

"Not that I can remember. He was just some guy Kath introduced me to on the fly. She didn't make the intro any big deal. Like this is the 'guy I'm gonna marry' intro. Nothing like that, Mick. Why?"

"Just curious. That all sounds innocent enough."

Michelle giggles. "Okay, Father Devlin, what's going on? Like I said, no investigative alarms. Figured Kath's a big girl. She knows the deal. Besides, I was at the party as a guest not the City's top Editor-in-Chief with a team of trained investigative reporters at her beck and call. It was a 'black tie' shindig."

Mickey laughs aloud. "Man, Michelle! That was a mouthful. I don't know where to start."

"Sorry, Mick. Couldn't resist pulling your chain a little. But did I figure right? Katherine knows what she's getting into. Doesn't she? Whatever that means."

Mickey doesn't answer Michelle.

"Oh shit! Your silence is starting to make me uneasy, Mick. Come on, give it up."

"Just thinking, kiddo."

"Yeah! Well how 'bout thinking aloud before I start to hemorrhage?"

"Okay. I know your paper has been covering the Third District's corruption probe."

"From the jump. We'll continue regardless of who's at the helm. You know that. Right, Mick?"

"Wouldn't want it any other way, Michelle. I would never—"

"I know you wouldn't."

"Okay, here it goes. Katherine had a surprise visit by a few career State officials and Inspector Nevárez from IAB. I'm thinking the real reason behind the house call was either they ran into the 'blue wall of silence,' or for some unknown reason, they believe Katherine is Bogarting information that could help their part of the South Division corruption probe."

"Wait a minute. Inspector, 'I'm gonna be commissioner one day' Nevárez, has joined forces with the AG's office? That's hilarious. A couple of years ago the Organized Crime Unit from the State Police raided his office. They were looking at him and his 'too close for comfort' link to the North Philly chapter of the Latin King Nation. Not to mention cooking the books on crime stats in his district. I did a whole two-part story on the guy. Somehow Nevárez avoided getting his neck in a wringer both times."

"No surprise there, Michelle. He was then and still is being groomed as, 'the first Latino police commissioner.'"

"Yeah! But there is more than one qualified Latino in the PPD. A lot more."

"Ain't ethnic politics great?"

"Makes for strange bedfellows. That's for sure. Sometimes I hate this city, Mick."

"Relax, Michelle. Or you'll start hemorrhaging again."

"I guess. I don't know how you do it, Mick. With all the shit that goes on in the PD, your head must explode."

"I take it one day at a time, kiddo. Then I go home. Can't take any of this stuff personal."

"I wish I could do that. But then I guess that's why you're good at what you do. I'm good at what I do."

"Good way to look at it, Michelle. Besides, I don't want to fit into the statistic that cops only live five years after they retire."

"Is that true, Mick?"

"That's what the research indicates. Maybe the cops who retire early have it right, Michelle. Get out while you're still have a life."

"Shit! They don't pay you guys enough. I always thought you should get combat pay. Ya know, like in the military."

"You got my vote. See if you can make that happen, Madame Editor."

Michelle ponders a few seconds, then asks, "What were we talking about? My brain is still fried talking about Il Nevárez."

"Katherine's unannounced visitors. What was their real purpose for their unannounced visit."

"Right! My money is on their 'slam-dunk' investigation has stalled and they're hunting for someone else to blame. They have a history of doing stuff like that, especially IAB. So you better cover up, Mick."

"I've become an expert at bobbing and weaving over the past twenty years, Michelle. What I don't understand is why they think Kath would ever shackle a corruption investigation? That's not her. She's always been hard on that stuff. Above all, if law enforcement is involved. It doesn't add up. If this was an election year then I wouldn't count out dirty politics."

"I don't know, Mick. I think that crap is always in play, especially in the City of Brotherly Love."

"You're probably right. But I'm being told that these guys are pushing the notion that Katherine is dragging her feet because of her 'relationship' with Angelo…who, are you ready for this one, is the consigliere for the Vincent 'Gabagool' Cibotti Family."

"What?" Michelle thinks about what to say next. "But that doesn't make him a 'made man.' In fact, ninety-nine point nine percent of the time consiglieres are not 'made.' Shit, most times they're not even Italian so they can't be made. Even the bad guys deserve good representation now and then."

"Ya done, Michelle?"

"Yes!"

"Good! I could care less about Mr. little-darling Angelo. What I do care about is Katherine Desiree McBride's reputation in this town and beyond."

"Damn! Damn! Double damn. I can't believe Katherine is willing to overlook that part of Angelo's résumé for a little companionship."

"Me either. I'm thinking there's more to this movie than you, I or Seamus know. Katherine's too sharp to allow personal stuff to get in the way of her professional image. Way too sharp."

"Evidently, the AG and that little wimp Nevárez don't think so, Mick. They actually think they can use Angelo's business arrangements against Katherine? That their relationship is motive enough for Kath to fudge a corruption investigation?"

"That plus the surveillance photos of the lovely couple coming out of a Mob bistro looking all cozy."

"Don't tell me. Were they coming out of Rizzo's on Christian by any chance?"

"Bingo!"

"Lovely! Actually, that's good for our side. The whole eating at Rizzo's is no biggie. I know for a fact that every fancy-britches big shot in this city goes there. That includes the Mayor, the City Council President, shit he has a booth named after him, and even that shit-for-brains Inspector Nevárez and his Chief dine there."

"That's probably where Nevárez saw Kath and had one of his roving ginks sit on the place and take some shots."

"I can buy that. What a bunch of hypocrites. Bottom line, dinner at Rizzo's is like having your morning bagels and coffee at Fabulous

Deli on Fourth Street. Everybody goes there. Especially, on election day. They're the hot-spots people want to be seen at."

"Interesting!"

"True story. At one time or another I've seen all those guys at Rizzo's."

"You did. Did ya?"

"A girl's gotta eat, right? The menu is primo. Guess who else I saw there on more than one occasion?"

"Enlighten me."

"The FBI's Special Agent-in-Charge, Ralph Pangallo."

Mickey thinks aloud, "Another Italian."

"What was that, Mick?"

"Just…it's nothing. So it's all fine and dandy that all those big shots patronize Rizzo's. But do any of the aforementioned ever have dinner with Angelo Lombardo or any of his 'associates'?"

Michelle laughs. "Can't say for sure. But it could be arranged."

"You serious?"

"Yep! Would ya like video and eight-by-ten glossies with that?"

"You sound like that kid at Mickey D's, Michelle. Ya want fries with that? Anyway, whatever we do, we do in the dark. No prize- winning exposés. No in-your-face stuff. Agreed?"

"Agreed! For Katherine, anything. Now I got a question for you."

"Go!"

"Is the shooting this morning and what's happening with Katherine connected somehow?"

"Wow! Where did that come from?"

"You're not the only one with gut feelings, Mick."

"Michelle, where are you?"

"I'm mobile. South on I-95. Coming up on the airport. Why?"

"You working a lead or—"

"I'm getting off at Bartram Avenue. Where do you want to meet?"

"Coffee Talk. The strip mall on Columbus Boulevard at Washington. There's plenty of parking."

"I know the place. When?"

"I want to touch base with my four-to-twelve lieutenant first. Just a quick hello, how ya doing, we'll talk later thing. Won't take long. Then I'm outta here."

"Okay! On my way. Ciao, Mick."

Mickey laughs. "Ciao, Michelle."

CHAPTER XXV

The Chase Is On

"A cat pent up becomes a lion."

Italian Proverb

Mickey checks the time. *Ten after six.* He walks to the operations room to see if his 2 Platoon lieutenant is in the area.

The night work operations room of the 3rd District, just like every other operations room, is hoppin'. The small staff of two uniform cops, one mandated civilian as a result of the PPD 'civilianization' plan, and a corporal to handle all incoming calls, arrest paperwork, securing prisoners, filing, "walk-in business," etc.

Prior to having corporals in the PD, the responsibilities of the operations room fell on the shoulders of a "house lieutenant." Those responsibilities proved a bit too overwhelming for those chaps. So the rank of corporal, between sergeants and cops, was created to take the burden off the "stressed out" lieutenants. With their burden alleviated, they were free to go back on the street with the "real cops." Some did. Some didn't.

The operations room crew positions have historically been filled with old-timers, injured and more recently pregnant cops, or female officers with "certain skills" deemed by captains, male and female, as vital to accomplish their mission. The corporal reports directly to the platoon lieutenant, a chain-of-command configuration that bugs the hell out of platoon sergeants.

Mickey gets the corporal's attention.

"Hey, Corp. Everything okay?"

"Hey, Boss. Yeah, we're doing fine. Something I can help you with?"

"Nothing in particular. Working late, so I thought I'd just pop in to see how you're doing."

"Thanks, Boss. Everything is everything."

"Good! Is your LT on the street?"

"He is. I just heard him on the air riding in on an open property on the Fifteen-hundred block of south Tenth. Our Lady of Sorrows Church and a rectory are over there, Fifteen-eleven, I think."

"Is that right? Seems Our Lady of Sorrows can't catch a break. Crime scene at the school this morning, and a break-in at the church tonight."

"When it rains it pours. Want me to give the LT a report?"

"No that's okay. I'll catch up with him later."

"Okay, Captain."

Mickey starts to walk out of the operations room, then remembers he promised his clerk, Nora Brown, to tell somebody where he's going, just in case. He turns and calls to the corporal. "I'm going to Coffee Talk over at Columbus and Washington. I'll be on the air if needed."

"Okay, Boss. Thanks!"

Mickey, still in his civvies from his 9th Street Market excursion, walks out the back door to his unmarked. He drives off the lot, steers east on Wharton, and heads for the Delaware River side of the district. He barely goes a block when Police Radio transmitted a foot pursuit by Officer Kenney, half of the second-shift burglary team.

"All Third District units stand by."

"Plainclothes officers in foot pursuit of a burglary suspect last seen exiting the rear of the rectory at fifteen-eleven south Tenth. Suspect is described as a white male in his early twenties with an Eagles' hoodie, baggy jeans and white sneakers."

"BD-Two, what's your location?"

The officer breathing heavily, adrenaline pumping, obviously still in foot pursuit, shouts into his handheld radio.

"East on Dickinson toward Nineth."

Immediately, 3rd District sector cars put themselves in on the pursuit to back the BD officer.

"Three-oh-three wagon. Put us in."

"Okay, oh-three."

"Three-seven in."

"Got ya in, seven."

"Three-A I'm in. Coming from Eight and South."

"Okay, Saarg. Conditions on arrival." Radio tries to raise the BD officer.

"Three BD-Two present location?"

"Nineth approaching Wilder."

"Three Command I got BD's partner with me."

"Okay, Lieutenant."

The BD officer gets back on the air.

"He just went through the parking lot at tenth. Now he's running east on Reed."

With his adrenaline boiling over now, the pursuing officer shouts even louder into his radio.

"North on Percy. Percy dumps into Nineth and turns into Sears. Get somebody over there."

Mickey has been monitoring the BD team's pursuit with interest on two levels. First, he's concerned about the officer's safety. But his interest is also spiked because of the location where the pursuit originated, Our Lady of Sorrows rectory, home to the late Monsignor O'Hagorty. Mickey doesn't believe in coincidences. So his gut is telling him dots need to be connected between the shooting at the school and a possible break-in at the rectory. He pulls over just west of 9th and Wharton. *They're coming right to me.*

 Three Command gets back on the Radio. "Last location of the BD officer?"

"North on Percy."

Mickey looks at his watch. *Michelle will have to wait.* He jumps out of his car and jogs the half block south on 9th to Percy and takes a quick look down the street. Knowing he'll appear as no genuine threat to the young white male running flat out toward him, he pulls his shirt out of his pants to cover his weapon and presses his holstered Glock against his right hip. *Here we go.* Mickey does that tension-relieving head-tilt thing he does, right then left. He then casually strolls out from behind the corner row house.

With a certain athletic grace in one smooth fluid movement, he brings up his left arm and clotheslines the bulky five-foot-ten suspect. It was a classic Monday Night Football takedown that would surely bring cheers from the hometown crowd and a horde of little yellow flags from the zebra-striped officials.

Mickey's takedown was a technique he perfected during his time detailed to the "Granny Squad." The team that's part of the PD's Stakeout Unit, an all-volunteer group of grizzly street cops, willing to dress as seniors or homeless men and women and offer themselves up as easy targets for lowlife street thugs. They are trained how to suddenly transform into takedown artists and make textbook arrests. All good cops highly decorated for their artistry.

Mickey immediately rolls the stunned suspect over on his stomach, twists both arms behind him. "Police! Don't move." By now Officer Kenney has caught up. Followed by the officers from 3-7 car, 3-A, and Three-Command with Officer Wong, Kenney's plainclothes partner.

"Just happened to be in the neighborhood, fellows. Hope ya don't mind."

Outnumbered and exhausted, the suspect has no interest in resisting. Mickey tells Officer Kenney to cuff his prisoner. The unidentified man is searched and loaded in the back of 303 patrol wagon.

Officer Kenny tells Mickey, "The guy's clean, Boss. No weapons. No contraband. Not even a driver's license. He's a mystery man."

Mickey and the group listen. Then Mick responds. "Something will pop up. I'll catch up with you guys inside. I'd be interested to hear why he would be hanging around the rectory. Especially, Our Lady of Sorrows rectory."

"You got it, Boss."

Officer Wong seeing Mickey's move from down the block comments.

"Man, you came out of nowhere, Boss. Ya don't see that move too often out here. Looks like you played a little no helmet rough- touch in your day."

Mickey smiles. "A little. My Special Ops team was all Army back in the day. Just proving that time-honored scientific theory that the body will follow wherever the head goes. You okay?"

"I'm good."

3A starts doing what a good supervisor does. He checks on everyone's well-being, including the suspect's, then has Police Radio resume the pursuit.

"Three-A."

"A."

"You can resume the pursuit. Apprehension made. No injuries to police. Have the complainant meet the BD team inside. Three-oh-three will be transporting one to the District."

"A. Okay."

Mickey looks at his watch. "Shoot! Gotta get on my horse, fellas. I'm meeting someone at Coffee Talk. Nice job, guys."

The sergeant responds. "Okay, Cap. I got this. Thanks for the help."

"No problem! But I didn't do much. Stepped in the street and the guy ran right into me. Right place. Right time, I guess. Kenney here did all the work."

Everyone smiles. "Okay, Boss."

"I should be back in the district in about an hour."

"Okay, Boss. I'll make sure you get the guy's rap sheet."

"Thanks, Saarg."

Mickey walks back up to his car parked on Wharton a short distance from one of the city's infamous walk-up takeout. While he drives to his meeting with Michelle on Columbus Boulevard he starts to reflect on how sometimes it's as if some pretty dangerous police work occurs in an alternative universe.

A couple of minutes ago a handful of cops, fathers, wives and sons put their lives on the line to apprehend a suspect a half block from dozens of hungry folks standing in long lines for steaks on a roll. *If they only knew. Nix! They're better off not knowing.*

Five minutes later, Mickey pulls in the driveway of the brightly lit strip mall and parks right in front of Coffee Talk's triple-glass windows. He sees Michelle sitting at a table against the rear wall of the store front café. He shuts off his car, and secures it, grabs a jacket and his handheld police radio, and walks to the front door. His own adrenaline level almost back to normal. If there is such a thing for a big-city cop.

CHAPTER XXVI

Philadelphia Free Library
South Broad Street

"Bend the tree while young."

Italian Proverb

While her new commanding officer was involved in a foot pursuit originated by one of his Plain Clothes Burglary Detail Teams on the east side of the district, Lieutenant MacGraft was traversing the 3rd District on her own mission. Trying to track down Terrell "Stitches" Soetoro. After checking the Rugnetta storefront in the Italian Market area and coming up empty, she heads to the west side and Terrell's "pretend Catholic school address." A location his single mom and Gramm Mary Rouse has fourteen-year-old Terrell using in order for him to attend Our Lady of Sorrows Catholic Elementary School.

Terrell is in the eighth grade and hopes to get into a good high school when he graduates in the spring. Already in the "Catholic School System" as opposed to the "Public School System," Terrell's chances are higher, provided he can land a partial tuition scholarship. As an honor student, he has an excellent shot at getting that much-needed help.

Terrell's Gramm has an apartment on the eighth floor of "the projects" at 13th and Fitzwater streets. It's one of many Philadelphia Housing Authority's, partially federally funded, high-rises scattered throughout city. The Fitzwater site takes up a one-block square footprint in the Hawthorne section of South Philly.

PHA is the predominant landlord in the state with over a three-hundred-million-dollar budget. It was established in 1937, and has had its own police force since 1971. Many of them retired PPD officers who were hired because of their experience. PHA offers affordable housing for over eighty thousand city residents with "limited incomes."

Recently, two of the highest-ranking security managers, both retired PPD, have come under scrutiny from the FBI for what some cable networks called "sleazy bookkeeping and unnecessary publicly funded junkets." Rumor is this newest scandal is headed to a Grand Jury.

The officers from the 3rd District have been to Gramm Rouse's building on a number of occasions. On one of them, seven-year-old Terrell Soetoro was kidnapped by a crazed "Meth-head" in an adjoining apartment who threatened to drop him from the screenless window. According to the demented twenty-something Black man, God was telling him that he needed to make a human sacrifice in his name to save the world from Armageddon. The incident ended when a Stakeout officer repelled from the roof and through the open window just as district cops took the door and grabbed Terrell.

From that time on, young Terrell has been "cool" with several of the district cops. A relationship that has helped him work through the shooting death of his father during a robbery at the Chinese takeout on Rodman Street. Being a regular at the neighborhood after school PAL program also helped Terrell "respect the man." A mind-set absent, with so many inner-city young Black youth. An attitude sometimes justified, sometimes not.

Lieutenant MacGraft, out of respect for Mary Rouse's privacy, calls her rather than just showing up on her doorstep.

"Mrs. Rouse, Linda MacGraft."

"Hello, Linda. Is everything all right with Terrell? I always get a chill when I get calls from the police when he's not here."

"As far as I know everything is fine. I'm trying to catch up with him. I think he may be able to help me with something."

"Oh! Okay! He's not here right now. He's at the library on Broad Street. He went there right from work. He's got a research paper due this week. He's trying to get a jump on it. You know!"

"I do. I have a report due myself in a week. Look, would you mind if I talk to Terrell? I don't want you to think I'm going behind your back."

"No, Linda. I don't mind. But his mother is here. Let me put her on the phone."

"Great!"

The lieutenant can hear Mrs. Rouse put the phone down and walk away, calling to Terrell's mother to pick up the extension. A few seconds later, Terrell's mom picks up.

"Hello, Linda. My mom tells me you want to talk to Terrell. Something about he may be able to help you with something. Is that right?"

"Yes, Ma'am. That's correct."

"Can I ask you what you think my boy knows that may help you, Linda?"

"Sure! There was a shooting at his school this morning and—"

"But Terrell's school was closed today. So he wasn't there. He went to work at the Market instead."

"Yes, Ma'am. I know. Thing is, the people who own the store where he works—"

"The Rugnettas."

"Correct. It was their son, Richard, who was shot at Our Lady of Sorrows. We…I, think that because Terrell worked so close with Richard at his parents' store that he might have heard something that could help with the investigation."

"Oh! I see. Well, I guess if you think Terrell can help. But he's not here. He's at the library. The big one over on Broad Street."

"Yes, Ma'am, Ms. Rouse told me. So then you don't mind if I go to the library and talk to Terrell. If you want I can bring you or your mom with me. If you—"

"That won't be necessary, Linda. I trust whatever you're doing is fine. But now can I ask you a favor?"

"Absolutely!"

"Can you drop Terrell off back here after you talk to him? There are a bunch of hoodlums roaming the streets so I would appreciate it if you could do that for me. I was gonna walk over there myself but if—"

"Of course I will, Mrs. Soetoro. That's not a problem at all."

"Okay then, Linda. You have my permission to speak with Terrell. Please, call me Samantha."

"Okay, Samantha. Thank you. I'll have Terrell call you from the library to let you know I'm with him."

"Thanks, Linda. It is always nice to know he's in safe hands."

"I agree. Rest assured I'll bring Terrell home safe and sound."

"Thanks again, Linda. God bless."

"You too!"

Linda presses the end key on her personal cell phone and puts it in the breast pocket of her white uniform shirt. She drives the four blocks to the South Philly branch of the Free Library and parks her marked car out front. All the lights are on inside the all glass-front building and she can see Terrell sitting alone in one of the red plastic chairs on the mezzanine level.

The lieutenant grabs her portable radio, turns it on and adjusts the volume down a notch. She enters the library, waves and nods to the middle-aged Asian woman behind the information and checkout counter. Then she takes the wide marble and aluminum stairs to the upper level. Terrell is so involved with what he's doing he doesn't notice Linda walk up behind him.

"Hey, Terrell. Doing a little extra-credit research?"

Terrell jumps two inches off his chair.

"Man! You scared the…"

Terrell stops short of finishing his sentence. He knows Lieutenant Linda don't like him "cussin'." He respects that about her.

"…oh! Hi, Lieutenant MacGraft. Yeah! I have a history paper coming due soon so I figured I'd get it out of the way."

"I heard."

"Say what?"

"I talked to your mom and asked her if she would mind if I talked to you about the incident at your school this morning."

"Ya did? Ya talked to my mom?"

"I did. On the phone. She told me you were here. I told her I'd have you call her when I caught up to you."

Linda punches in Samantha's number and hands Terrell her cell phone.

Using his best library voice Terrell talks to his mother. "Hi, Mom. Lieutenant Linda wanted me to call ya…I'm fine, just working on my paper…yes, Ma'am…I will, Mom…okay. Love you too, Mom."

Terrell finds the end key, pushes it and hands the phone back to the lieutenant. "Sooo, what do ya think I can tell ya about Richie's killing?"

"For starters, what makes you think Richie was killed?"

"Because…" Terrell looks around the library. "…because he was. Richie was killed."

"You know, the detectives doing the investigation are calling Richie's death a suicide."

"What? No way would my boy Richie ever off himself. He had a girlfriend and wanted to marry her. No way, Lieutenant Linda. No way!"

The lieutenant's questioning is interrupted by an announcement by the woman downstairs at the counter, who's now been joined by an older Black woman.

"The library will be closing in fifteen minutes. Please quietly finish whatever you're working on. Thank you."

Linda waves at the two women indicating she got the message loud and clear. Then she struggles to sit down in the hard plastic chair opposite Terrell. Her bulky work-belt, holding her weapon on one side, her radio and a few other tools of the trade on the other, doesn't seem to want to cooperate. She finally adjusts things just enough for her to settle in the front half of the rigid plastic chair and continues her discussion.

"So I understand you were pretty close to Richie?"

"Richie was my homeboy. We looked out for each other. He was like a brother. Ya know. Like a real brother. Not a brother-brother. Like the brother I never had."

"So then you want to make sure justice is served, right?"

"There ain't no real justice with them people. They have their own justice, 'gold chain justice.' They were always comin' around the store shaking down Mr. Rugnetta. Richie would always tell his dad not to give them anything. But Mrs. Rugnetta would always tell Richie's pop, 'We don't want any trouble. Give them what they want.' They were shakin' down Richie's mom and pop."

The lieutenant, growing up in South Philly, has heard the kind of stories Terrell's telling all her life. She's very familiar with the street terminology "gold chain justice." It refers to how the old- time Italian mob bone-breakers used to wear one or more gold chains around their neck. A fashion statement that seems to have been passed on to their new rivals, Black and Latino drug gangs. A craze that cops refer to as a Mister T start up kit."

"I hear what you're saying, Terrell. But what makes you believe the Mob is responsible for Richie's death? Was Richie into them for any money? Or did he cross the line, or break the street rules in some other way?"

"Richie wasn't a gambler. He didn't need any money. Like I said, he was getting married. He was saving all his money for that. The only line he crossed was movin' on the Monsignor. Ya know, the Italians used the Monsignor to make them look legit. The Monsignor used to tell me that there is no such animal as the Mafia. He said it's all a myth."

Linda thinks, *Sounds like something my commissioner would say.*

"Ya know, Richie took the Monsignor hostage at your school, right?"

"Sure! He said he was gonna grab him when he was on his morning walk. He said he wanted to make the Monsignor own up and face the music. He said he was tired of living a lie. But I never really thought he would do it. It wasn't the first time he said something like that about the Monsignor. So—"

"What do you think he meant by face the music and living a lie?"

Terrell starts fidgeting with his paperwork. His jumpiness doesn't go unnoticed by Linda.

Avoiding eye contact Terrell responds. "Don't know. I asked him but he told me I'd know soon enough. Guess I'll never know now."

"Maybe not. But if the answer is out there I'm gonna find it for you, Terrell."

The lieutenant decides to push one of her captain's working theories, that the Monsignor may have molested kids in the past.

"Did you ever hear anything about the Monsignor and little boys? You understand what I'm talking about. Right, Terrell?"

"I understand, Lieutenant. If you're asking me if I heard stuff about Richie and the Monsignor…the answer is…no way."

Linda pushes a little harder.

"Ya think Richie would have confided in you if something did happen between him and the Monsignor?"

"No doubt about it. I told you we were close. We shared stuff. I could talk to him. Ya know?"

"I do. I'm really sorry you lost such a good friend, Terrell. It must be hard. But he didn't share everything. I mean he didn't tell you about why he wanted the Monsignor to 'face the music.' Am I right?"

"That was different. He was trying to protect me. He said what I don't know can't hurt me."

"He was right about that."

Linda noticed Terrell starting to tear up.

"You going to be okay, Terrell?"

"Yeah! If I can get over losing my dad, I can get over anything."

"You're right, Terrell."

"I know. My Gramm says, 'Time cures all.'"

"Your Gramm is right. So you're positive Richie would have told you if—"

"You don't believe that stuff 'bout the Monsignor, do ya, Lieutenant?"

"I don't want to, Terrell. You know we have to look at everything. But it would give Richie a reason to take the Monsignor at gunpoint."

"No! That ain't right, Lieutenant. The Monsignor never messed with little boys. He was a straight-up guy. I heard a bunch of years ago he fired two priests because they were funny. He was all over that kinda stuff. Not like it is today. Ya know. How the Church hides the pervs or just moves them to some other parish to molest more kids. The detectives are lame for saying that junk 'bout Richie and Monsignor Mario. You're a lieutenant, can't you stop them from telling lies?"

"That's the plan. You know the detectives are also saying Richie did what he did because he went off his medication."

"What? More lies, Lieutenant. Richie wasn't taking any drugs, street or legal."

"Okay, Terrell. If Richie was on any meds, and I believe what you're telling me, we'll find out. But are you absolutely positive about Richie's relationship with—"

Terrell puts down his pencil and looks Linda in the eyes. She backs off pressing him. Then through big sad brown eyes he blurts out, "He was Richie's dad."

The lieutenant has a head-jerk reaction to what Terrell said. She wasn't exactly sure who the "he" Terrell was referring to was. Then she bends forward over the table closer to Terrell and whispers, "Who was Richie's dad?"

"Monsignor Mario. I didn't want to tell ya. But that's what Richie wanted him to confess to. That he was his son. Not the Rugnettas."

"Richie told you that?"

"Yeah! But he told me never to say anything. I swore to the baby Jesus I wouldn't tell. But now that Richie is killed and with those detectives saying lies, I figure it's okay now. Right?"

"You did the right thing, Terrell. You're a good friend to Richie in life and in death. He'd be proud of you doing the right thing. I'm sure he's looking down on you and is smiling at his little brother."

"I think so too. But I still miss him."

"I know you do, Terrell."

Terrell puts his head down on the small tan Formica table between him and Linda and begins to sob. Linda puts her hand on his shoulder, hands him her white hankie and looks around the library. She realizes that she and Terrell are alone except for the two women on the first floor. The Asian woman catches Linda's attention and taps her wristwatch a couple of times, then holds up her open left hand and mouths, "Five minutes."

Linda waves and mouths back, "Okay!" She still needs to ask Terrell several more questions. But they'll have to wait for the ride back to his Gramm's building. Terrell wipes the tears from his eyes and hands the hankie back to Linda.

"Keep it, Terrell. I got another one."

"Thanks, Lieutenant."

"You're welcome. Look! The library is closing in five minutes. I promised your mom I'd drive you home. I got a couple more questions for you though. We can continue our talk in my car, okay?"

Excited at the prospect of getting a ride home in a police car he asks Linda, "You driving your patrol car, Lieutenant? You takin' me home in your cop car?"

"The command car is being used by the night work lieutenant. But I borrowed a sergeant's marked car. He's off tonight. It's just like the one I drive."

"Neat!"

"Grab your things and let's get out of here before those nice ladies downstairs call the cops on us. What do ya say?"

The lieutenant's comments brought a welcomed smile to Terrell's oval face.

"You're funny, Lieutenant. You are the cops."

Linda and Terrell walk down the stairs to the ground level. They thank the two librarians and wish them a good evening on their way through the exit turnstiles beside the checkout counter. Terrell returns the two history books he checked out earlier. The Asian woman follows them out and locks the aluminum and glass doors behind them.

On the ride back to his Gramm's high-rise Terrell clears up some loose ends about Richie and the Monsignor. He also tells the lieutenant that a cop in a suit came to the Rugnettas' store that morning.

"You know me, Lieutenant. Something about cops in suits. It's like they're hiding somethin'."

Terrell tells Linda he heard Mrs. Rugnetta call the man Antonio. The only other thing he remembered about the man was the chrome gun worn on his left hip. Information that will no doubt interest her captain. Linda also asked Terrell if he knew if Richie was right handed or left handed.

"Rich was a righty just like me. In fact, Richie gave me his old first baseman's glove. I'm sure he wrote and played ball as a righty. Why is that important, Lieutenant?"

"It could be, Terrell. I'll let you know."

After dropping Terrell off at the front gate of his Gramm's building, she calls her to let her know her grandson is in the elevator on his way up, safe and sound as promised. Lieutenant MacGraft now heads back to the District to catch up with her captain armed with an eighth-grader's analysis of his world.

CHAPTER XXVII

Coffee Talk Café
South Columbus Boulevard

"A friend in need is a friend indeed."
Italian Proverb

Mickey enters the Coffee Talk Café and walks directly to where Michelle Cunay is sitting alone, staring into her oversized red ceramic cup slowly stirring her Bewley's Black Tea, deep in thought. Mickey notices a legal-size envelope sticking out of the top of her oversized black handbag but holds off commenting.

"Hey, kiddo. Sorry I'm late. I ran into a guy who needed directions. Been here long?"

"Hi, Mick. No! Ten minutes. I saved you a seat against the wall. I know how you coppers like to be able to watch everything going on when you're in a place like this."

Mickey smiles. "Your father taught you well, young lady."

Now Michelle grins. "That he did."

The waitress, right out of a hard-core Goth magazine, suddenly appears at Mickey's side. She has jet-black hair with purple streaks strategically placed all around her head. She has six earrings in each ear of various sizes, mostly sterling silver; one with a skeleton head in the middle, stretching from her earlobe northward along the outer rim of each ear. She also had two side- by-side small gold rings hanging from the left nostril. The empty fissure in her lower lip, covered with a deep shade of black gloss, gives away where she attaches yet another "off duty" ring or hood ornament of some kind. Evidently, even Coffee Talk has standards.

Peeking out at the wrist of her compulsory long-sleeve black and red Coffee Talk waitress attire were several vibrant artistic tattoos of flower arrangements. Also partially veiled by her starched- white collar at the back of her neck is a fierce-looking dragonhead surrounded by intricate multicolored Asian characters.

"Good evening, Sir. Coffee?"

"Tea please. Bewley's decafs with lemon if you have it"

"We do."

"Perfect!"

Mickey waits to sit down before he takes off his waist-length, lightweight, blue-and-tan LL Bean jacket and slides into his seat with a view. Unlike some cops he's not one to advertise he's armed.

The Goth waitress returns with Mickey's decaf tea. "Would either of you like anything else right now? A menu?"

Mickey answers first. "Not for me, thanks."

Michelle agrees. "I'm good, thanks."

Mickey squeezes his lemon slice in his tea and asks, "So what did I interrupt, Michelle?"

"Interrupt?"

"Yeah! Where were you heading when I paged you? You said you were close to the airport. I figured—"

"Oh! No! Nothing! I was just checking out the MG. I had some work done on it this morning. After one of the guys dropped me off at my mechanic's, I took a ride down I-95 to check it out. Ya know, open it up a little bit."

"Everything okay?"

"*Primo*! But that's enough about me. So what's the plan with Katherine? What do you and Seamus have in mind for those toads who are trying to mess with our gal?"

Mickey leans closer to Michelle. "I'm looking to take the wind out of their sails. They think they have Katherine over a barrel by waving eight-by-ten glossies of her having dinner with a friend."

"No scandal there, Mick."

"I agree. Although I still think somebody close to Katherine..." Mickey points to Michelle. "...needs to school her on image and the ways of love."

"Okay! Okay! I'm just hoping Kath has her reasons. Makes no never mind. I promise I'll give it a shot. But you know Katherine."

"Do I ever."

"What else, Mick?"

Mickey continues. "So, based on what you told me about Rizzo's restaurant being a watering hole for the SAC of the Philly FBI and the Mayor, I'm thinking it would be nice to have our own set of eight-by-tens. Ya know. There must be occasions when the Feds and the Mob cross paths at Rizzo's."

"There are. I know for a fact there are. I've seen it up close and personal."

"I believe ya. Now like you suggested we just gotta make it happen..." Mickey winks. "...so we can have our own Kodak moment. It is interesting though the FBI and the Mayor get a pass on their dining experience. But Katherine gets threats."

"So let's even the playing field."

"Airborne! Problem for me, being a government official and the Constitution being what it is, it can't be me aiming the camera, this trip. You get my drift. So—"

"I hear ya, Mick. What I'm concerned about is how and why would my paper justify being interested staking out Rizzo's, if you get my drift."

Mickey shakes his head. "I do. How about a follow-up on one of your past exposés? Like Mob eateries."

"I agree! Maybe if we—" Michelle is interrupted in midstream by the Goth girl holding a stainless-steel pot with steaming hot water.

"Can I warm them up for ya?"

The young lady's polite interruption was actually a welcome sight. Mickey and Michelle respond in unison. "Yes, please."

The waitress fills Michelle's cup just short of the brim and does the same for Mickey. She also hands them fresh tea bags and a small plate of creamers and lemon slices.

Michelle picks up where she left off outlining her own strategy for justifying a covert sting and turning the tables on the AG and IAB goons. Mickey listens, makes a few suggestions along the way, and mentions a friend's name that may be helpful.

"Sounds like a plan we all can live with, Michelle. Of course we have to give Kath deniability and I've already taken Seamus out of the loop."

"Not a word. I know how close you two guys are. But—"

Mickey holds up his left hand. "When this thing winds up, Seamus gets back in the loop first. I have my reasons. Agreed?"

Michelle's eyes get wide at Mickey's stern tone. He gets that way when he has to go against what he calls his "better judgment" for a larger principle. "Agreed! Absolutely? One hundred percent."

As the committed conspirators finish their second round of tea, Mickey can't resist asking Michelle about that white envelope sticking out of her bag.

"What's in the envelope, Michelle?"

"Oh! I almost forgot. I grabbed a copy of tomorrow's early edition." Michelle opens the envelope and unfolds two items from the obituary section of her newspaper. She hands one to Mickey. He reads it aloud.

O'Hagorty

Mario J., Monsignor, on February 3, 1997, at the age of 87. The beloved South Philadelphia Monsignor died of natural causes. Friends and parishioners of Our Lady of Sorrows Parish are invited to the Monsignor's Life Celebration—Wednesday 9–11 AM, 1511 South 10. Donations to the "Save our School Fund" in lieu of flowers would be appreciated. Monsignor O'Hagorty will be interned at Our Lady of Fatima Cemetery, beside his mother.

†Ciro Magano's Funeral Home, Broad and Ellsworth Streets†

Mickey shakes his head in disbelief. "Natural Causes?"

"Oh my. I take it you're not on board with the whole natural- causes thing, Mick. To the trained ear that means—"

"Let's just say whoever supplied your paper with that bit of creative writing either jumped to conclusions or is intentionally giving misinformation. Nobody sent in an obit for Richie Rugnetta yet?"

"Not that I know of. You're working on something, aren't you, Mick? Is Doc Steinberg working with ya?"

Mickey grins at Michelle's investigative instincts. "Look, kiddo. I'm so far off the reservation on this one that...well I'll leave it there for now."

"I've been off that reservation with ya before, Mick. Why not this time? You know I can keep a secret. I've made my bones in that department. Lots of times with you."

"I know. I know. What's that other paper you got there?"

"Don't change the subject, Devlin."

Michelle can see that Mickey is mulling over spilling the beans so she backs off, for now.

"Okay! It's a twelve-paragraph testimonial about the Monsignor. We're adding it to the end of the obituaries."

"Who submitted it?"

"A Mrs. Grace Capaccio."

That brought a series of wide-eyed, "I can't believe it." facial gestures from Mickey.

"Do you know who Grace Capaccio is...was married to?"

"Mr. Capaccio?"

Mickey chuckles. "Wisenheimer! Grace was Deputy Fannille's first wife. Capaccio is her maiden name. Fannille was married to Grace when he was cheating with his present wife. That chump has his hands into everything about the whole Rugnetta versus O'Hagorty hostage job."

"So you are holding back on me? Come on, I can take it."

"Michelle, haven't I always given you first crack at stuff like this?"

"Well yeah. But—"

"No ifs, ands or buts about it. You've always been my go-to media type. That's never gonna change. But right now I'm chasing my gut feelings only. I've got no real evidence to hang my hat on. So if I jump too soon..." Mickey pauses to think how he'll describe his dilemma. "...these are pretty powerful people. They don't mess around."

"Damn, Mick. Who the hell you messing with this time? The freakin' Mob?"

Mickey purses his lips but doesn't answer Michelle.

"Shit, Mick! So does this thing have anything to do at all with Katherine's mess or not?"

"I don't think so. Well, maybe a little. But only because of one of the players. But probably not."

"Geez! I'm glad you straightened all of that out for me, Mick. Shit! You've become the riddler."

"Okay! Look, by the time you get back to me on your undercover work, I'll have something more substantial for ya. How's that? Don't be pumping Seamus or Doc Steinberg either. I don't want to see anything in print until—"

"I know. Until you say so. Deal!"

Michelle makes the sign of the cross across her tightly closed lips.

Goth girl returns with the bill. Mickey insists on paying. He leaves a nice tip. Mick walks Michelle to her white 1973 MGB convertible.

"Thanks for meeting with me, kiddo. I like your plan...a lot."

"Our plan. Any time, Mick. Looking forward to our next chitchat."

"Okay! I have a lieutenant working another angle for me. Gotta get back to the district. When this thing is over, I want you to meet her. She's gonna be a big boss in the PD one day. Smart as a whip. Plus she's Irish and her Da was a cop."

"Okay, Mick. It's always good to know a few big bosses in the PD, right? I'll call ya when I've got all the ducks lined up on the Katherine thing."

"Good. By then I'll have at least the beginnings of a Michelle Cunay exposé."

Michelle tightens her lips and shakes her head. "I hate it when you do that, Mick."

Mickey shrugs. "What? I'm just saying…"

"Okay, just saying. I'll call ya."

Michelle snaps on her seatbelt, revs her tuned-up four-cylinder engine and pulls her MGB off the small strip-mall lot leaving two feet of rubber on southbound Columbus Boulevard.

Mickey yells, "Be safe, kiddo."

Michelle, her red scarf around her neck flying in the breeze, just waves.

Mickey thinks, *another one whose mold was broken.*

CHAPTER XXVIII

A Plan Takes Shape

"A gold key opens every door."

Italian Proverb

Mickey arrives back at the district after eight. He left the door to his outer office open and the light on when he left. Sitting in Nora Brown's swivel chair waiting for him is Lieutenant Linda MacGraft in her civvies.

"Lieutenant! Sorry about keeping you in a holding pattern. I got involved in a couple of things and—"

"Not a problem, Boss. I only just got myself together fifteen minutes ago." The lieutenant smiles. "Oh! About the open field tackle you made on the Lady of Sorrows burglar. Heard it's gonna be on ESPN and make it to John Madden's Iron Man list."

"You know how cops like to embellish."

Mickey still grinning unlocks the door to his private office. Linda follows him inside. "Believe me, Lin, my part in that whole thing was minuscule. By the time the fellow got to me, Officer Kenney had already run him into the ground. There was no fight left in the guy. I just happened to be at the finish line. The young man practically fell over from exhaustion."

"You say so, Boss. You're right. I do know cops. So a conservative estimate would be that by the time your takedown makes its way through the rumor mill, you'll be legendary. These guys aren't accustomed to working for a Captain who...well... who doesn't mind getting dirty. I mean that in a good way of course."

Mickey smiles again. "Okay!" Then he changes the subject. "So how'd you make out with Terrell?"

"Not bad. I think I got some actionable intel for you."

"Great! Pull up a chair. You have my attention."

"First, I want you to know that I did ask Samantha, that's Terrell's Mom, for her permission to talk to him."

"In writing?"

"Negative. But she's a stand-up lady. I've done this before. There won't be a problem."

Mickey doesn't offer an opinion on Linda's lack of a signed consent. Questioning a juvenile without a parent or guardian present can become messy.

"Okay! Now what've ya got?"

"You were right. Terrell and Richie were close. Terrell saw him as the brother he never had…his 'homeboy.' He was adamant about Richie not committing suicide. He said Richie had a girlfriend and that he was saving his money for their upcoming wedding."

"So if Terrell is right about Richie being in love eliminating any chance for suicide, did he have an opinion on who wanted his 'homeboy' dead?"

"Most definitely! The Mob."

"The South Philly Mob? Not many of those guys left, right?"

"Yes, to your first question and no, to the second. According to a guy I know with the FBI's Organized Crime Unit, there are around one hundred fifty wise guys still hanging on…if you count the associate members of the Mob. I still see a few of the old wise guys walking around down here in their pajamas. Seems to be the new 'walk along' maneuver the retro capos prefer."

"Ridiculous. I'll bet those guys are all waiting for trial or sentencing. They're gonna use the, 'Look at me walking around in my PJ's, I must be nuts,' routine to get a reduced sentence."

"They're living in the past if they think that'll work these days. All those 'friendly' judges are incarcerated themselves."

"Good point, Lin."

"These new mobsters are a lot flashier than the original breed was. The old guys were more into making money than headlines, more low-profile gangsters. They had rules they lived by. They let their lawyers do all the talking."

Mickey flashes to Katherine's new sidekick, Angelo Lombardo, the supposed consigliere to Vincent "Gabagool" Cibotti. He refrains from bringing it up to Linda at this time.

Linda continues. "But the young Turks are all about flashy and getting their picture taken all around town. I hear one wise-guy big shot peruses all the area papers hoping to find his name. Allegedly, he gets all perturbed when his search comes up empty. They have no respect for those who came before them. They have no problem breaking all the wise-guy rules."

"Let's say I can buy all that, Linda. Why in the world would the Mob, old or new, want to kill the son of a fruit vendor? That's a little harder to swallow."

Linda holds off on Terrell's assertion that Richie may not be a Rugnetta after all.

"Because everything in South Philly revolves around certain rules, 'commandments.'" Linda does halfhearted air quotes. "Like 'Silenzio,' keeping quiet."

"Captain Bell mentioned the wise-guy commandments to me this afternoon. He called them the Alfonso Deluca, 'Ten Commandments for Wise Guys.' Al was supposedly flipped by the feds and when they rifled his home they found the legendary rules to live by."

"Exactly! Nowadays most of the so-called commandments aren't followed, but the violence once used to enforce them still is."

"Oookay! So according to young Terrell, which commandment did Richie Rugnetta violate?"

"He has no idea. But it only takes one to get ya whacked. He did say that Richie was openly against his parents paying tribute to the neighborhood wise guys. Here's why I'm leaning toward believing the kid, Cap."

Now Linda goes into great detail regarding her discussions with Terrell "Stitches" Soetoro. Along the way Mickey adds the twenty-year-old rumors about the Monsignor's extracurricular activities. Some of which Linda was aware of. Then he asks several probing questions all handled plausibly well by his judicious patrol lieutenant. When she's finished, Mickey plays devil's advocate. He glances at the notes he jotted down while Linda was talking.

"Okay! Now let's break Terrell's revelations down to their lowest common denominators."

Linda readies herself for her Captain's cross-examination.

"So! Let's say I'm okay with your Mob history seminar. That Richie had a big mouth and didn't show the proper respect to the Mob thugs. That every good Italian in South Philly saw Monsignor Mario J. O'Hagorty as a de facto saint sent by the Vatican to spread the good works of Italian Americans."

"Okay!"

"According to more than one source, the Monsignor was the Mob's number-one cheerleader. They've used his saintly status at trial to portray the worst among us as 'community leaders, misunderstood, altruistic gentlemen dedicated to the Church, family values and the good old USA.' Mother and apple pie stuff."

"Right! Sometimes it works. Sometimes it doesn't. Like I said, it depends on if the Judge can be had."

"All right! So let's put all that in the fact column."

"Okay!"

Mickey continues. "So according to Terrell, his 'play brother' found out the good Monsignor, on-call character witness for the Mob, was his birth father. He also found out that the rumors his mother, a cloistered nun in training on Green Street, was impregnated by the Monsignor some twenty-odd years ago are true. Because Richie wanted to announce to the world the Monsignor's flaws, he violated one or more of the South Philly Mob codes. Something the Mob couldn't have. Not to mention a sin or two."

"Correct! Omerta, the code of silence. That whole thing about the Monsignor fathering a mystery love child has been bantered around the neighborhood for years. That's an old rumor. Some down here believe it and others choose to ignore it."

"I'll take your word for it, Linda. I wrote down that you called Richie's birth mother a FOB."

"'Fresh off the boat.' She was a nineteen-year-old from northern Italy whose present whereabouts are unknown."

"So it sounds like you pretty much agree with Terrell that the Mob knocked off Richie to keep their guy's rep from being tarnished, albeit for selfish reasons. I also take it you buy that Richie told Terrell all this stuff and trusted him not to let the cat out of the bag?"

"I'm leaning that way. I do believe Terrell was like a little brother to Richie. Terrell's mom confirmed that for me. If nothing else, it's motive! Besides, I darn sure like it better than Detective Johnson's suicide classification."

"I hear that."

"If Richie were still alive, we wouldn't be having this conversation. With his friend gone, Terrell feels he's no longer bound to keep their pact."

"I wonder how the wise guys will feel about all that. He may need another big brother." Mickey glances sideways at Linda. "Or big sister."

Linda gets wide eyed at Mickey's open-ended hint aimed her way.

"That's a discussion for another day, Cap. But to quote Terrell, 'I swore to the baby Jesus I wouldn't tell. But now that Richie is killed I figured it's okay.' Plus he believes South Detectives are 'lame' for spreading what he says are lies about Richie."

"Hopefully, the baby Jesus will be looking over 'Stitches,' at least for the time being, Lin."

"I hope so too."

"You said you also asked Terrell about other bad habits that may have put him on the Mob's hit list. Habits like excessive gambling or using loan sharks to help finance that upcoming wedding of his."

Linda senses some skepticism in her CO's voice. "Correct! Negative on the bad habits."

"How about the whole molestation angle?"

He said he never saw or heard any of his buddies accuse the Monsignor of 'messing with little boys.' In fact, he gave the impression the Monsignor had zero tolerance for that kind of stuff. Went hard after a couple of priests with those tendencies."

"Little different from what we're hearing these days."

"True. That's exactly how Terrell put it, Cap."

"I don't suppose Terrell gave you the name of the would-be assassin, did he? Saying the Mob did it would be a little vague in a court of law. Might fly in the neighborhood but not—"

"No, Sir. Kid didn't give up any names."

"Well! Let's go back to your original contention. That you have 'actionable information.' Something to run on. A game changer. You still believe it?"

Linda thinks a few seconds. "I do. I also said Terrell gave us motive."

"He did. Plus opportunity and means. But giving and proving are miles apart. Not to mention, how did they pull off Richie's death?"

Linda has no answer. Mickey decides to spring another obstacle on her.

"Okay! For the sake of argument, let's say somehow the Mob managed to whack Richie Rugnetta, in a schoolroom in broad daylight with a street full of cops."

Linda is starting to feel the ceiling is about to fall in on her.

"Oookay, Cap."

"So then who whacked Monsignor Mario O'Hagorty?"

Linda never saw that coming. She was unaware the Monsignor was dead. Not to mention her captain's assertion he was whacked. But to her credit she had a comeback for her captain.

"Ouch! I don't know, Boss. But I bet I can find out."

Mickey laughs aloud. "I wouldn't bet against you, Linda. But right now I'm working with a couple people on that one."

Mickey looks at his watch. "In fact, I should probably be calling one of them about now."

Obviously disappointed, Linda snaps her finger and shrugs. "Oh, well."

"If things are moving too slowly, who knows, I may just take you up on your offer. But I would like you to follow up tomorrow on Richie's fiancée. Find her and get an interview. I'm hoping Deputy Fannille doesn't know about her. We got to get to her before he does. Now go ahead home. We'll talk tomorrow."

"Okay, Boss. Oh, two more items of interest I got from Terrell. Richie was right handed and the Rugnettas were visited by a man who told them about Richie. Terrell heard Mrs. Rugnetta call the man Antonio. He believes the man was a detective because he was wearing a suit and had a chrome gun on his left hip."

"Fannille! That young man doesn't miss a trick. He'd make a great investigator."

"He's a good kid, Boss."

"I agree. Well, if that's it, I'll talk to you tomorrow."

Linda gets up and walks to the door. Mickey calls out, "Ya did good, Lieutenant."

Linda smiles. "Thanks, Boss. See ya tomorrow."

"Hey, Lin. You put yourself down for OT, right?"

"I did. Thanks."

"Good! Talk to ya."

The lieutenant drives off the rear lot but decides not to go right home. A block away from the district she pulls over to the curb and punches in the phone number of Terrell Soetoro's grandmom.

"Hello!"

"Hello, Ms. Rouse?"

"Yes. Who is this?"

"Linda MacGraft. Sorry to bother you so late, Ma'am, but it's important I ask Terrell a couple additional questions."

"Can't it wait till tomorrow, Linda?"

"I'm afraid that if I do the person I'm trying to find may be..." Linda thinks about how she should present the urgency for finding Richie's girlfriend. "...inaccessible."

"Oh! Sounds serious, Linda."

"It is, Ma'am, very serious. This person may be able to supply the PD with information that will help solve the death of Richie Rugnetta. Is Terrell available?"

"Hold on, Linda."

Linda can hear Mary Rouse put the phone down and walk across the laminate floors of her apartment. The next voice Linda hears is fourteen-year-old Terrell Soetoro's.

"Hello."

"Hi, Terrell. Lieutenant MacGraft."

"Oh! Hi, Lieutenant. My Gramm said you wanted to ask me some more questions."

"Yes! Terrell, it's very important that I talk to Richie's girlfriend. If—"

Terrell immediately gives up the information to Linda. "Concetta Bruno. Her dad owns the restaurant at Seventh and Sears, 'Men of Honor.'"

"That's a wise-guy hangout."

"Yeah! That's it. She lives around the block on Earp. Don't know the address. But ya can't miss it. Her house has a black awning with a big white B in the middle. Looks like one of those funeral houses. Ya know?"

Linda smiles. "I do. Thanks, Terrell. You've been very helpful."

"Ya gonna prove Richie was whacked by the Italians?"

"That's one of the things we're looking into. Thanks to you."

"You'll see. It's true, Lieutenant. They have people everywhere in life."

"I believe you, Terrell. But now somebody's got to prove it."

"You can do it. I know you can. You're the best cop I know."

"We'll see. Gotta go. Thanks again, Terrell. Tell your Gramm I apologize for the late phone call. Terrell, it's very important that you keep our conversation about Richie just between your family and me, okay?"

"Yes, Lieutenant. I understand. I already had this discussion with Mom and Gramm."

"Great! If you think of anything else or ya just need to talk, I'm here. Okay?"

"Okay, Lieutenant. Good night."

"Good night, Terrell."

Linda hangs up. Armed with additional intel, she heads home to get some sleep. Now that she's done her extra-credit homework, she's looking forward to meeting with her new captain in the morning. Linda, a lieutenant that's going places in the PD, is hoping to gain points with him. Devlin's reputation as a legit highly decorated investigator who just happens to be sitting high up on the Inspector's promotional list has given Linda a window of opportunity to show she's a team player. It never hurts to impress a big boss in the PPD. One that, like her, is all business. She heads for South Broad Street and on to her Packer Park town house. She doubts if she'll get much sleep tonight thinking about the morning meeting with her innovative boss.

Back in the district Mickey checks his watch. *Wonder how Doc is doing?* He tries calling him first on his cell, then on his private office number. He gets Doc's message machine.

"Doc, Mickey. It's eight-forty-five. Sorry I didn't get back to you closer to eight. I had a meeting with one of my lieutenants. She came up with some pretty solid leads. Guess your knee deep in alligators by now. I'll catch up with you tomorrow."

Mickey walks down the hall to the operations room to check on his BD team. *Wonder how Wong and Kenney did with the would- be mystery burglar.*

CHAPTER XXIX

3RD District Cell room

"Asking costs little."

Italian Proverb

The 3rd District Operations Room is buzzing with activity. In the short time Devlin was talking with Lieutenant MacGraft, there were two sight robbery arrests on the west end and a "walk- in" complaint from a young woman who claimed she was sexually assaulted by a homeless man on South 8th Street. They've also been fielding endless phone inquiries from the cable stations asking about the BD Team's "Catholic rectory burglary" pinch.

When Devlin walks in the room, all three crewmembers are busy on the phone taking complaints or giving assistance. The Corporal is standing at the reception window taking a report from two Asian high-school-aged kids and their parents who claim they were threatened this afternoon by a group of Black students from their high school. Devlin overheard one of the parents complaining about the lack of action by the principal and school security. "This has been going on for weeks. We've been to the principal, the vice principal and the school board. We keep getting the runaround. Nobody is doing anything to help us. I think it's because everyone we talk to is one of them. If something isn't done soon..."

Looking past the corporal and through the waist-high sliding window to the District's lobby area, Devlin can see over a half- dozen civilian types talking among themselves and on cell phones. Some are friends and relatives of suspects temporarily confined for crimes against society and others are police groupies hoping to glean gossip for their next community meeting. The corporal notices his captain enter his work area. He waves, then returns to listening and writing down the Asian kids' allegations.

Occasionally, as a district patrol sergeant, Devlin was assigned to fill in for a vacationing or sick corporal in the operations room. He knows firsthand how hectic the district corporal's job can get. It can go from zero to a hundred miles an hour in the blink of an eye. Fights in the lobby between family members of victims and those of suspects are commonplace. Prisoners who decide to resist the mandatory body searches or those who opt to hang themselves in a cell with their shirt in lieu of imprisonment are also everyday occurrences for the operations crew. Not to mention unannounced visits by political big shots demanding "special consideration" be given to family members of influential individuals or "helpful" business constituents.

Politicians wanting to boost their "grass roots" ties at patrol districts in the middle of the night tend to bring out "pissed-off" bosses from CIB. Bosses who are now forced into "schmooze mode." Some CIBers are better at it than others. It all depends on how long the commander has been shanghaied to CIB and the nature of his perceived crime against the "West Wing." If he's looking for an "early release," then he may lean toward helping build the politicians' "street cred," hoping for a little intervention of his own down the line.

Devlin isn't one to decide these issues based on the position someone holds in the community or city hall. He's an equal opportunist when it comes to politicians. He doesn't trust any of them, regardless of political affiliation. He admittedly makes an exception for one elected official, the present District Attorney.

Not wanting to interrupt the natural flow of things in the operations room, Mick decides to back off and take a quick look in the cell room area across the hall. The officer assigned to that area, the "Turnkey," sees Devlin heading his way and unlocks the outer steel-barred door.

"Working late?"

"Yeah! It's been a long day." Mickey looks for the officer's nametag but it's missing. The officer sees him look and immediately says his name.

"Claus. Nick Claus."

Devlin smiles. The officer is used to his captain's reaction. He gets it all the time.

"I know. My pop had a sense of humor."

With a grin still on his face Devlin adds, "Could be worse."

"It is! My middle name is Rudolf."

Most, if not all, "Turnkey" cops don't wear their nametags, or badges primarily for "confidentiality reasons." A practice the virtuous investigators, who don't wear uniforms, from IAB go batty over. Dealing with prisoners all day and night has many understandable pitfalls. Frivolous IAD complaints being high on the list. "He didn't feed me when I woke up." "When he cuffed me, he made them too tight." "He called me…" "I pay his salary and he wouldn't give me my one phone call." The complaints are never ending and, in the eyes of the head gink, worthy of a comprehensive investigation. Not by him but the district captain, of course.

The working conditions in the cell room are the pits and the "customers" are usually the lowlifes of society. The Turnkey must "babysit" them in eight hours shifts day after day. However, from the Turnkey's perspective, the advantage of the job is bosses normally stay away from the putrid-smelling, flea-infested area and they're not tied to endless police radio calls. Out of sight, out of mind is the Turnkey's motto.

All six cells are at full capacity. In cell 3 there's a prisoner lying in his own urine on the concrete floor in his cell. He overheard his custodian's conversation with Devlin and unwisely decides to "break balls."

He yells, "Hey, Santa. Where did ya park your sleigh?"

Officer Claus tells Devlin, "That's one of the reasons I avoid wearing my nametag."

"You'll get no argument from me. Probably a wise decision, officer."

"I think so."

"I was looking for the BD team's prisoner. They made a pinch over on Percy Street earlier. I—"

"Sure. Oh, and I heard Vince McMahon from World Wrestling wants to offer a certain captain a contract. I'd like to have seen that takedown."

"Cops!"

Officer Claus smiles. "Riiight! Anyway, I had the guy from Percy Street with me for a little while. Our o-three wagon transported him to South Detectives to get interviewed about thirty minutes ago."

"Sorry I missed them. You got a copy of the guy's criminal history printout?"

"I do. Not much to see though. The corporal ran the name he gave us. South will print him and run him through the system again I'm sure."

Officer Claus takes two five by eight and a half inch stapled computer printout pages off his brown-plastic clipboard and hands them to Devlin, who scans the first and flips over to the second.

"You're right! Nothing much here. No record found on our Smith. The address is probably a vacant lot, the DOB fictitious and the name, Smith, is a no-brainer."

"Wouldn't be the first time, some toad thought he could beat the system."

"It won't be the last."

"Actually, the guy seemed like a pretty nice guy. Got with the program and didn't complain about anything. Unlike most of the other slugs that come through this place." Officer Claus points over his shoulder to the wise ass in the supine position on the floor of his cell with pee stained jeans.

"Did Mr. Smith say anything while you had him? Anything at all?"

"Other than…yes officer, no officer…not a peep. Not to me anyway."

"Shrewd. I'm sure if South delves in a little deep to Mister Smith's family history they'll find he's no stranger to the judicial system."

Devlin hands the cell room copy of Smith's records' check back to Officer Claus.

"What cell were you holding our Mr. Smith in?"

"Smith was in with Mister pee the bed over here."

"Really! I need a minute with Smith's roomie. Put me on your prisoner visitors' list, Claus."

"Ya got it."

Still in civvies Devlin approaches the cell of the semi-conscious "Mister Pee the Bed." He quickly stands up.

"Excuse me, Sir. I was—"

"I heard all that. If you people are talkin' 'bout that young WOP kid who was in here with me, then I can—"

Mickey holds up his right hand and shushes the animated thirty-something jailbird. He walks closer to the man's cell. Officer Claus wary the guy was up to no good stands between his captain and the prisoner. Just in case.

"I'd like to hear what you have to say. Go on, finish what you started to say."

The man rudely responds, "First, who the fuck are you?"

Over the years Devlin has conversed with hundreds of detainees just like the one standing on the other side of the steel bars. Realizing Officer Claus never addressed him as captain or boss, Devlin gives one of his classic introductions.

"I'm Sam Clemens from the Public Defender's Office. I'm here to represent another young man incarcerated on the other side." Mickey points over his shoulder. "Ya know, the Fourth District side. I make it my business to check on other 'so-called' suspects…" Mickey violates his own rule and does the air-quote thing. "…while I'm here. Are you represented? Even if you are, I may still be able to give you some guidance. So anything you can offer to help yourself…I think you know what I mean."

"Hell yeah! I know what you mean."

Even more surprised than the prisoner by his captain's believable sales pitch was Officer Claus. Evidently, he's not familiar with rule number one from the "Investigator's Unauthorized Handbook," lying is always optional when talking to prisoners.

"Did you say Sam Cummings?"

"No! Clemens. Samuel Longhorn Clemens. My daddy was a founding member of the ACLU."

"Whatever. Anyway, sure, I can give you something. That guy, that WOP who was in here, he told me he could get me a fancy lawyer, 'cept he called him a consiglironi, or something like that. Sounded WOP to me."

"Consigliere?"

"Yeah! Yeah! That's what he called him. What you said."

"Why would he do that for you? He must have wanted something in return."

"No shit, Sherlock. You sure you're an ACCU lawyer?"

Devlin doesn't bother correcting Mister Stinky Drawers.

"He wanted me to go to a location, not far from right here, and pick up a package, something in a paper bag, and then throw that something in the Delaware River from the Camden side. He said if I did that for him, he'd help me get out of going up to State Road. I can't do any more time up there. It's all Blacks and Ricans. They're down on white boys."

"I understand your trepidation, Sir."

The man gives Devlin a blank gaze.

He continues. "So what did you tell him?"

"What do you think I told him? Hello! I told him no problem. Piece a cake. But that was then. I'm still waiting for that constiglaroni-macaroni guy. If you're offering a better deal, I'd be stupid not to jump on it. Right?"

"Okay! Let's see now. I'm guessing, that you're offering to give up the location of said paper bag. That you believe whatever you're picking up and disposing of must be pretty important."

"Incriminatin' is more like it."

"Incriminating! You're hoping I feel the same way. So much so I'm willing get you a deal. How am I doing?"

"You're doin' fine, Sammy boy. So if you can get me out of here, right now, then I'm ready to consumerate the deal."

This guy sounds like he went to the same high school as the PC. Consumerate. You can't make this stuff up. I love this job.

"What are you in here for anyway?"

"Some bullshit retail-theft pinch. I'm no petty thief. I'm a burglar. A damn good one."

"Hey! I believe you. Okay! So here's what I'm willing to do. I have an excellent relationship with the captain of the district. I just saw him in his office before I came in here. So, I'm willing to go talk to him and do my best to convince him to go along with our proposed arrangement. So shall I go work my magic?"

"I'm thinkin' on it, Sambo."

"Riiight! Don't think too much. Time is money. Once I leave this fine establishment my offer to intervene on your behalf expires."

"Okay already. Yes! Intervent me."

"Hey, slow down now. This isn't his first rodeo. The Captain will want to check out the merchandise. So if you give up the location of that so-called 'incriminating' package so he can see if it's worth giving you a 'get out of jail free' card, then I'd say you'd be back on the street in a matter of an hour. What say you? Talk to—"

"Tenth and Reed."

"Ya want to be a little more specific?"

"There's a parkin' lot at Tenth and Reed. The guy said he threw the bag into one of the big wooden planters on the lot. He said it was the one closest to Reed."

"Did he tell you why he threw the package away?"

"I didn't ask him. I could care less. So ya gonna talk to the captain now? Get me out a here?"

"I said I would. Shouldn't take too long to check out your story."

"Good. How 'bout in the meantime getting me something to eat? A super meal from BK would be nice. What do you say, Sammy?"

"If things turn out the way I'm hoping, I'll buy you a four-course meal at Rizzo's. How's that?"

"That's exactly what I'm talkin 'bout. Can I bring my girl?"

"Sure! Why not!"

Devlin turns to the shell-shocked Turnkey and winks. "Thanks, Officer." Using a cops first name is always a no no in this situation. "Guess I got my work cut out for me. I'll try and catch up with the BD's guy over at South Detectives. You know who caught the job?"

"I heard Kenney talking on the phone to Lloyd Idelson." Officer Claus joins in the fun. "He's top shelf, Mr. Clemens. If anybody is gonna 'dig a little deeper' on the Mister Smith, Lloyd will."

"Okay! Thanks again."

Officer Claus unlocks the outer cell room door and lets Devlin out. He whispers, "I think I just witnessed the makings of another legend. For a minute there even I started to believe ya."

Devlin laughs. "Me too!"

Officer Claus locks the cell room door behind is thought-provoking new boss. He walks to the small desk in the back of the room. Mister Pee the Bed is still standing at the front of his cell, nose between the bars. "Hey, Santa. Get that lawyer back here. He never asked me my name. What's up with that?"

"Not to worry. Mister Clemens knows who you are. Go back to sleep. I'll wake you up when your 'get out of jail card' arrives."

"Okay, you better. Or my ACC...U mouthpiece will be all over your shit."

"Right. Say good night, Gracie."

"Whatever!"

CHAPTER XXX

10ᵀᴴ & Reed
Crime Scene Grows

"One may have good eyes but see nothing."
Italian Proverb

As Mick walks past the Operations Room, he sees Officer Stu Guckin talking to the corporal. Guckin was a rookie in the 6th District when Mickey was in Central Detectives. He was older than most new cops, which gives him a maturity that was a refreshing change for Mick.

Guckin sees Mickey. "Hey, Boss. I heard you were coming down. It's really nice to see you."

"Hi, Stu. When did you make the move to the Third?"

"I'll be here four years this May. Best move I made so far. I heard you're high up on the inspectors' list. That's great."

"Thanks. Didn't I see your name on the new detectives' promotion list?"

"Yes, Sir. I'm fourteen. Heard there may be promotions soon."

"Your lips to God's ear. What are you doing right now? You on a job?"

"Not right now. I put myself out at Headquarters dropping off paperwork. Need something, Boss?"

"Actually, I do. I have the perfect mission for a future detective."

"Sounds good to me."

"Put yourself back in service then out on a district assignment. I'll square it away with your sergeant."

Mickey sends the future sleuth Stu Guckin out to 10th and Reed to retrieve "the package" from the parking lot planter, with instructions to call him from that location. Mick hopes whatever is out there will tie mysterious John Smith to the rectory job. For Mickey having Our Lady of Sorrows victimized twice in one day is not a coincidence. His gut is telling him whatever is in that planter will help prove him right.

Mickey walks back down the hall to his office. He sits down behind his roach-hotel desk, takes a deep breath and checks his watch. *Nine-twenty.* He notices a yellow Post-It on the floor beside his chair. He picks it up and reads it aloud.

Captain Devlin,

Sorry I had to leave you short on your first day. My daughter was injured at her job. Be in early tomorrow.

Nora

PS I set up your voice mail on your private line for you. The instructions are in your top left drawer.

Mickey checks his drawer for the instruction sheet. He reads them silently. *Sounds easy enough.* He takes a practice run and is surprised by what he hears.

You have two messages. Press five to hear your first voice message.

Mickey presses 5 on his private touch-tone phone.

First message.

"Hey, Cap. Mike Ryan. I processed Medic Twenty-seven. I found a silver antique pillbox with a white crucifix and the word ROMA in caps on the lid. Found it in between the wall and the aluminum floorplate. It had two white pills in it. Must have gotten jammed in there somehow. Had to pry it out with my knife. I also found three syringes, one with a broken tip, five alcohol wipes, a few two-by-two sterile gauze pads with a dark reddish-brown substance visible and three pairs of blue extra-large rubber gloves among the hazmat trash. I tagged everything for investigation. I also found some duct tape and zip ties under the front passenger seat. Tagged them too.

"Oh! I had the truck towed to Headquarters. It's parked on the ramp outside the Detention Unit bay garage doors. It'll be safe there until I can get the Lab boys down to check some more. The Fire Commissioner is mad as hell I'm keeping one of his Medic vehicles off the street." Ryan laughs into the phone, "Guess he'll have to resurrect one of those units he put down for 'Budgetary Economy.' Or maybe he'll reassign one of the three trucks he's got servicing his West Oak Lane neighborhood. Fat chance, right, Boss? Okay! I'll call ya if I get anything else interesting."

A canned message kicks in. *End of message. To save this message press seven.*

Mickey saves Ryan's message. Just in case.

To hear the next message press five.

Mickey presses 5.

"Me again, Boss. I forgot to tell ya. Before I bagged the pillbox, I showed the two meds to Doc Steinberg. Based on what he calls identifiers he believes the little white pills are oxycodone."

Wow! That's opium derived. A schedule-II drug. The Monsignor may have been a prescription junky.

"Gotta run. Talk to ya, Boss."

End of messages. To save this...

Mickey presses 7 to save Ryan's second message, then puts the handset back in its cradle. Mickey stands up and stretches. *What a day. And it ain't over yet. Guess I should eat something. Maybe later.*

Mickey tries to catch up with his BD team. Using his private line he punches in 3313, South Detectives' general phone number.

"South Detectives, Whatley."

"Hey, Whatley. Captain Devlin over at the Third. I'm trying to catch up with my BD team. They had a prisoner transported—"

"Hey, Cap. I got your guys right in front of me. Hold on a sec."

Officer Kenney gets on the phone. "Hi, Cap. What's up?"

"How you guys coming with John Smith?"

"Better than we thought."

"How so?"

"Idelson found our mystery man ain't what he appears to be." "Figured as much. Pray tell!"

"His real name is Pollina. Johnny 'Little John' Pollina, son of Big Johnny 'The Nose' Pollina, Atlantic City wise-guy underboss. The old man supposedly committed suicide six months ago waiting for his racketeering trial to start."

"Supposedly is right. Go on."

"After the funeral, junior headed back to Italy. Organized Crime believes Little John wants to follow in his pop's footsteps but decided to cool it for a while. Guess he thought he may be next to be suicided."

Mickey laughs. "Probably a good move."

"I'd say."

"So he came back to Philly, has been waiting in the wings for a call to prove himself. Looks like whoever made the call to have Little John burglarize Our Lady of Sorrows should be whacked himself. Kid got caught."

Officer Kenney adds, "Yeah! He almost got decapitated for his trouble, Boss."

Not wanting to revisit the whole John Madden Iron Man thing, Mickey asked. "How is the kid anyway? Looked a bit dazed when you cuffed him."

"He's fine, Cap. He doesn't even remember how he was taken down out there."

"Good! So what did he take?"

"According to Father Natale nothing is missing from the rectory or the Church."

Mickey doesn't immediately respond. He swivels back and forth a few times in his squeaky hand-me-down chair doing that bottom lip-biting thing he does when deep in thought. Another one of those involuntary habits Mick got from his Ma.

"So the wisdom now is that some South Philly wise-guy captain has the son of a Jersey underboss relocate from Italy to our city to show he's worthy. The whole make your bones BS gets bizarre."

"It does. What you said sounds about right. No one ever said these guys are Rhodes Scholars, Boss."

Mickey agrees. "So tonight, this kid gets the call to burglarize a priest's residence. He gets in, but takes nothing, gets eye-balled at the back door of the rectory by you and ends up taking a pinch for burglary."

"That's my story and I am stickin' to it, Boss."

"Okay! Look, I need you to make sure that Little John doesn't go anywhere. I sent Stu Guckin out to Tenth and Reed—"

"Tenth and Reed is where I lost Johnny boy for a few seconds. I figured he ducked behind a car or something. But then I picked him up again heading east on Reed."

"I remember you going over the air with that. You think our boy could have unloaded whatever he took when you lost him?"

"Possible!"

"I'm not buying Father Natale's version of what was or wasn't taken from the rectory."

Kenney laughs. "He's a priest, Boss. He wouldn't lie."

"Riiight! If you believe that—"

Kenney laughs again. "I already bought that bridge, Cap."

"So you're the guy." Mickey gets back on point. "I take it Little John was in system."

"Correct! He took a stolen car pinch when he was here for his pop's funeral. He—"

Mickey interrupts. "Not that it means anything to this case. But do you or your partner remember which funeral home handled Big Johnny 'The Nose' Pollina's viewing?"

"Sure! We were teamed up with the Feds to ID some of the locals who showed up to pay their respect. It was Ciro Magano's at Broad and Ellsworth. Why? What's up, Cap?"

"Nothing. Just playing gotcha with a friend of mine. Thanks."

"Glad I could help, Boss. By the way, when the Highway team that made the stolen car pinch searched the SUV, they found a Sig nine millimeter under the driver's seat."

"Being the son of an underboss, that sounds like some pretty dumb move. The kid keeps making rookie mistakes."

"I've seen dumber things, Boss."

"I bet you have. But I'm leaning toward maybe the young wannabe was trying to put something in the rectory, not take something out. Specifically, the Monsignor's room."

Kenney doesn't respond.

"So with nothing missing, at least according to Father Natale anyway, ya think the DA will be able to actually charge him with burglary?"

"If we can prove intent, she can. Ya know like he planned to take something but—"

"Was anything moved? Did the kid line up any goodies on the floor already to bag and take with him?"

"Nothing was moved. But the kid was seen running from the scene, Boss."

"That's an easy one to explain away. Kid was scared. He had old pinches on the books. On his way from church he saw what looked like the rectory had been burglarized. He made you guys, and took off. Does the rectory or the church have a working alarm system?"

"Nothing in the church. The place was built in the 1800s. It has a fire alarm for insurance purposes and L and I probably made them get one. Same with the rectory. Father Natale told us God protects Our Lady of Sorrows."

Mickey smiles. "Really! God must be taking a little vacation time. Our Lady of Sorrows has had a bad day."

"Looks that way, Cap."

"So as far as you two guys are concerned, Monsignor O'Hagorty's room had not been disturbed?"

"Correct!"

"Then maybe we have one of those jobs where the absence of evidence is evidence."

"Never heard it put that way before. But—"

Mickey interrupts. "Hold on. The Corporal just walked in my office." Mickey cups the mouthpiece of the phone.

"What's up, Corp."

"Got Guckin on line two. Said the package isn't where it's supposed to be. He's holding for you to pick up."

"Okay, thanks."

Mickey gets back to Kenney. "Still with me, Ken?"

"Yes, Sir."

"I got Stu Guckin on the line. Hang on. I'll get back to you in a few seconds."

"Okay, Boss."

"Hear you're coming up empty, Stu."

"Yes, Sir. You did say large flower box closest to Reed Street, right?"

"That's what my guy told me. How many flower boxes are out there?"

"Six."

Mickey has an idea. "Hold on, Stu. I'm gonna try something. With a little luck…"

Mickey takes out his notebook and slides out the small piece of paper Lieutenant Rossi gave him outside the school this morning with two phone numbers on it. He disregards the school's admin number and points to the other number. The one Police Radio said Richie Rugnetta called them from.

"Stu?"

"Yeah, Boss."

"Stand by."

Mickey punches in the number using his cell.

"Hey, Boss. I can hear a cell phone going off. It sounds like a string band. Wait…I got it. I got the package. It's a paper bag with a black Konica inside."

"Outstanding!"

"It just stopped ringing, Boss."

"I know. I ended the call, Stu. Close the bag and bring it to South. See Detective Lloyd Idelson. He's the assigned on the Rectory burglary from South Tenth."

"You got it, Boss."

Mickey hangs up on Stu Guckin. *So how did Little John come into possession of a cell phone used at the scene of a crime. According to Richie Rugnetta, the Monsignor's cell phone.* Mick gets back to line 1.

"Kenney."

"Yeah, Boss."

"Guckin is en route to your location with a cell phone. Little John Pollina's fingerprints will be all over it. I have a witness that will state your prisoner told him he chucked it into a flower box at Tenth and Reed. Do not let Little John walk."

"Hope Guckin gets here quick. Pollina's high-priced attorney is making a lot of noise over here."

"Got a name for the kid's lawyer?"

"I got one of his cards right here, Cap. Angelo Lombardo. Know him?"

Mickey shakes his head in disbelief. "Heard of him. We have a mutual friend."

"All the guys over here at South seem to know him. Idelson said he's some kind of big-shot Mob mouthpiece. I know he's wearing a five-hundred-dollar suit. So—"

"Five-hundred-dollar suit or not. Do not let your guy walk. Tell Idelson if he needs me to personally call the DA, I will."

"Okay, Boss. Hey! I just heard Guckin tell Radio he's en route to South."

"Good! I'll let you go. Keep me abreast."

"Okay, Boss."

CHAPTER XXXI

3RD District

"A little truth makes the whole lie pass."
Italian Proverb

A short time later, officers Wong and Kenney return from South Detectives. They're surprised to see the light still on in the CO's office. Kenney knocks on the captain's door. "Captain. It's officers Kenney and Wong."

"Come on in."

The officers walk into Mickey's office and stand in front of his desk.

"Sooo?"

"As of now, Little John Pollina is gonna hit the books."

"For?"

"At least receiving stolen property. The burglary charge is pending."

"At least he didn't walk. That's good."

"Oh! Detective Idelson sent his partner over to interview your witness, Don O'Drain." Wong smiles. "Heard some public defender sealed the deal with O'Drain."

Mickey laughs aloud. "You mean Sam Clemens."

Wong laughs aloud. Kenny adds, "Like to meet Mr. Clemens someday, Cap."

"Never can tell, Ken. Guy seems to keep a low profile."

"I hear ya, Boss."

"I'm still looking to wrap up some loose ends. What I need you guys to do now is go back over to the rectory. If we're lucky, nothing has changed. Have Father Natale sign the Consent to Search form. Tell him the ME needs to find the Monsignor's heart and blood-pressure meds to close out his report. Legally, that should get you in every nook and cranny of the Monsignor's suite."

"Father Natale locked the Monsignor's door when he left. Said the Monsignor's relatives were coming by Wednesday for the funeral and that they would pick up his remaining personal belongings then. So we should be okay."

"Good! Oh, and get the name and number of the housekeeper. Every rectory has one. They could also have volunteers who keep the place clean, answer phones for the priests. You guys report off at one o'clock, right?"

"Right!" Wong answers. "You gonna be around a little while longer, Boss?"

"I'll be here when you get back."

Officers Wong and Kenney head back over to the Monsignor's suite on south 10th. The four-to-twelve corporal knocks on Mickey's half-open door.

"Hey, Boss. We ordered pizzas. They just arrived. There's plenty. We got Tran Lee, our civilian guy, a birthday cake. Since you're still here, thought you might want to join us."

"Love to! Be right in."

After two slices of Sicilian thin pizza, a can of root beer and a little "cop talk" Mickey feels semi-rejuvenated. It's been "one of those days."

††††

At ten-thirty-five, Officers Wong and Kenney find Mickey sitting at his desk writing in his Daily Planner, a Christmas gift from his wife, Pat. Mickey waves them in.

"How'd you do?"

Kenney speaks first. "Not too good, Cap."

"Define not too good."

"We had a problem getting Father Natale to sign our Consent to Search form. Said he had to run it by the Archdiocese's legal office first. That wasn't gonna happen until tomorrow morning at the earliest. But the real downer was that two guys from the Diocese got there before us and packed up three small boxes with the Monsignor's belongings."

"According to Father Natale, correct?"

Wong and Kenney look at each other, then respond, "Correct!"

Wong continues. "Natale said he had to let them go through the Monsignor's room. He said he got a phone call from the Cardinal's office right after we left and just before the guys showed up. I asked Natale if the Monsignor's family was told about the burglary or the late-night visit from the Archdiocese."

Kenney adds, "He said neither. He was told that information had to come from someone higher up than him."

"Sounds like whoever the two guys were, they came prepared. Oh well. We gave it the old college try."

Wong jumps in. "We did convince Natale to let us do a limited walk-through looking for the Monsignor's meds though. Came up empty."

"Not surprised. I'm sure the two guys from the Diocese were pros."

Wong responds. "I got the feeling Father Natale knew it too."

"How'd you do with a housekeeper?"

"Part-timer. Theresa Casella. Lives in the neighborhood. We got her address." Kenney holds up his small black Police Credit Union notebook.

"That it?"

Wong looks at his partner. "That's it."

"All right! Follow up with the housekeeper tomorrow. Won't hurt. If you find anything good, get back to me."

"Will do."

"Regardless what the DA decides about the burglary, you guys did a good job. Guess the next thing for Little John and his lawyer will be an IAB complaint."

"Funny you should say that. The kid's lawyer told the lieutenant at South that a visit to IA was on his to-do list."

"Also not surprising. I'm sure Lombardo is hip to Internal Affairs ten-thousand-dollar-buyout deal."

Kenney looks at Wong and shrugs.

"Guess you guys never heard that brilliant policy. IAB is authorized to disburse up to ten thousand to a complainant if he or she withdraws their complaint. It's one way the PC and the chief at IA have been trying to reduce the number of complaints filed before they hit the books. It's all about image. They say it's cheaper to write a check than tie up an investigator and go to court."

"That stinks. I'll bet the word is out on the street too."

"True story. I've tried to find out how much has been paid out since the buyout began and who got checks."

"Any luck?'

"Not yet. But stay tuned."

Wong and Kenney smile and nod.

Wong asks Devlin if he needs the team to do anything else.

"Not right now, guys."

Wong responds. "Okay, Boss." Kenney gives a wave.

CHAPTER XXXII

Stakeout Bares Fruit

"Bad news is the first to come."

Italian Proverb

As soon as the team leaves, Mickey pages Michelle Cunay and leaves his cell number. *She'll love this one. The DA's dinner companion is the mouthpiece for Little John Pollina, burglary suspect and son of Big Johnny "The Nose" Atlantic City wise-guy underboss.*

Five minutes later Michelle returns Mickey's page.

"It's eleven o'clock at night. You still in work?"

"Yeah! But leaving soon, You home?"

"I wish. I figured tonight's as good a time as any to do a little fishing."

"You in my neck of the woods?"

"Yep! Hold on a sec."

Mickey can hear Michelle talking to someone.

"Yeah! Cream, no sugar. Here's a ten."

Mick now realizes why Michelle wasn't using his name. She doesn't want to give him up to her surveillance partner.

"Sorry, Mick. I didn't want to take a chance of my guy overhearing something he shouldn't."

"I appreciate it, kiddo."

"Okay! So enlighten me."

Mickey tells Michelle about Katherine's friend's late-night legal endeavor. Michelle nearly chokes on what's left of her cold Dunkin' Donuts French-vanilla latte. "Are you shittin' me?"

"No! I'm starting to believe we're on a slippery slope. Katherine needs to decide if she wants a career or be married to the Mob."

"Not looking too good, is it, Mick?"

"Ya think? But I'm starting to think maybe you should back off having that girl-to-girl talk with Katherine."

"That's okay with me, Mick. I wasn't really looking forward to it."

"That settles that then. I think Katherine is way too smart to chuck it all for a life partner. I can't help but think she's hiding something. Probably to protect folks, is my guess. Whatever it is, I'm certain she has a good reason. So let's give her room on this one."

"You really think Katherine would do something like that, keep us in the dark?"

"She would if whatever she's doing is important to her. If we're being honest, to a certain extent we all, as you say, keep friends in the dark. Eventually we let the cat out of the bag and all is forgiven."

"That's true, Mick."

"Trust me. I know Katherine. This is one of those cases, Michelle."

"Okay, Mick. We'll give her room."

"So tell me how your surveillance is going."

"Slow! I'm out here with my apprentice camera guy, drinking cold coffee out of paper cups and freezing my butt off."

Mickey wonders how much Michelle shared with her apprentice. Hopefully not very much.

"You'll survive. You always do. How long do you intend to be out there?"

"Depends."

"How 'bout you, Mick? When you going home?"

"I'm getting ready to get out of here soon."

"How 'bout I call ya in the AM?"

"Okay! Talk to ya then. Be safe."

"You got it, Mick."

"See ya, kiddo."

Michelle tosses her cell on the dashboard just as her cameraman returns with her third round of sixteen-ouncers.

"Cream not sugar. Here's your change."

"Thanks, Al."

"Did I miss anything?"

"Nothing important."

Al decides not to inquire about whom his boss was talking to. An astute call for the new guy. For the next hour or so Michelle's outing doesn't show much of a result. Then Michelle notices that Alan is adjusting his "old-school" 75-300mm zoom lens on his Canon EOS-1N/RS. Alan Ebner has been with the paper part time for about three months. Prior to that he worked at a couple of neighborhood weeklies in North and West Philly. His dad was also in the newspaper business in the 1980s in New York City.

Michelle has gone through two other "hopefuls" to replace her original "go-to guy," Kim Chow, who went rogue on her and flipped sides in 1991 while working on a "cop killer" exposé. So far Alan seems to have just the right temperament, drive and ability to button his lip when necessary. Michelle is hopeful he'll be "a keeper."

Alan's Canon, a present from his dad, is billed as the world's "fastest AF SLR camera," and can continuously shoot at 10fps. Michelle starts to enjoy her java as she watched Al trying to focus on three streetlight illuminated male figures coming out of Rizzo's Ristorante's back door. He brackets several shots to better his chances of finding the correct F-stop. Then lets his Canon continue to fire away, a few shots at a time, as the three males walk past Rizzo's bank of picture windows to the corner. Alan shoots off the remainder of his twenty-four exposures. He takes the camera away from his face and lays it on his lap. He's smiling cheek to cheek.

"I think we got the money shots you're looking for."

Michelle looks at the men through her WWII, US Army–issued 7X50, M17A1 binoculars. Al reloads his Canon EOS with another roll of 35mm black and white film.

Alan looks at Michelle and smiles. She returns the gesture.

"Out freakin' standing. This stakeout is over. I'm starving, Alan. How 'bout you?"

"A little."

"What do you think? Cheese steaks all around? My treat."

"Ya talked me into it, Boss Lady."

Michelle asks the most important dining question when it comes to Philly cheese steaks, "Wit or witout?"

Wit or witout are terms used when ordering one of Philly's famous cheese steaks. It's street slang for with or without onions. The wall menu at Michelle's favorite steak takeout actually encourages customers to use "wit and witout" when ordering.

Alan, the fine Philly boy he is, answers, "Wit!"

Michelle starts up the company car, a green '95 Ford Explorer and heads to the all-night steak walk-up at 9th and Passyunk. It's said because the place has so many multicolor fluorescent lights outside that NASA astronauts can see it from space. The owner's family is given credit for conceiving the idea of a steak on a roll, and the world famous "Philly cheese steak sandwich was born." Some others have tried to "rip off" his creation but he remains the king of cheese steaks, hands down. A title easily proved by the hundreds of signed photos of politicians and Hollywood types that grace every available wall in front of his establishment.

After finishing their late-night banquet, Alan takes a cab to his rented studio apartment just off Temple University campus.

Michelle decided she would run Alan's roll of 35mm, 800ASA Kodak Gold black and white film through the processor at work herself. It's not that she doesn't trust her new camera guy, well maybe just a little, it's more that she's protecting him from any future blowback around her covert, "stakeout to help a friend" gambit. She also wants to avoid the possibility of any nosy newspaper night editor looking for a "scoop." She makes a contact sheet of the roll and prints eight-by-tens of Alan's "money shots." Michelle puts all of them in a messenger's envelope and takes them home with her.

On the way to the elevator she thinks, *Now, let's see how Mister Attorney General smarty-pants deals with our Kodak moment. How dare he threaten a friend of mine. Bitch!*

Michelle drives her MGB out of the building's underground parking lot on the 15th side of her building, and heads south. She owns a small town house on Delancy Street a short distance away in "Old City."

CHAPTER XXXIII

3RD District
Day Two

"A rainy morn oft brings a pleasant day."
Italian Proverb

Mickey got home by midnight. He tried, but didn't get much sleep. He kept wondering how Michelle made out on her late-night "hush-hush stakeout."

Or if Doc Steinberg or Detective Ryan came up with any new leads. By six-thirty he's awake and a short time later he's in uniform and heading out the door for the district. He leaves a note for his wife, Pat, that he'll be late coming home again.

Tuesday, February 4th, Mickey's second full day as CO of the 3rd District isn't going to be as nice weather-wise as his first day. Chilly rain showers off and on are forecasted until sometime mid- afternoon. The rainfall is making the trip on South I-95 a real mess. He's hopeful his second day in the district will be less hectic than his maiden voyage.

He finally arrives at work just shy of eight AM. Nora Brown is sitting at her desk going through the mail. When Mickey walks in, she greets her new captain.

"Good morning, Captain Devlin. Sorry 'bout yesterday. But—"

"No problem, Nora. Really! Family always outranks everything else. How's your daughter doing?"

"Minor bumps and bruises. She's back at work this morning."

"Sounds like she's a real trooper. How about the kids who attacked her?"

"Suspended for one day."

"That's it? They attack a teacher and the school district gives them a one-day vacation? Aren't the detectives gonna tack on charges?"

"Yeah! Assault, terroristic threats and some other stuff, specific to classroom teachers. West Detectives is handling the job. School Board Police are also assigned to escort my daughter to and from her car."

"At least that's something. Any Fannille sightings or calls, Nora?"

Nora chuckles. "No sightings. But the Deputy did call you twice."

"Any idea what he wanted? Any message?"

"Nope on both accounts."

"He calls here all the time and never leaves any message. He only talks to the captain."

"I have a sneaky feeling he does talk to some other people. But that's—"

"Ya mean, like spies?"

Mickey smiles. "You get that feeling too, Nora?"

"Totally! I'm not the only one. Ya know he lives around the corner, right?"

"I do. I had a job in front of his house while I was working the five-to-one tour in CIB. Some citizen liberated the Deputy's radio from his city vehicle. My guess was he left it unlocked. Didn't push the issue at the time."

"That had to be hard to explain."

"Evidently, not for him. IAB got the job and classified it lost property. I heard two weeks later the manager of the diner on Oregon Ave. called nine-one-one. Said he found it in the men's room."

"Riiight! Somebody tacked a copy of a newspaper article about that on the board in the hall.: Norn points out her door. "Fannille heard about it and sent his aide to dispose of it. Somebody put another copy up the next day."

"Cops. Don't you just love them?"

"Yep!"

"So any other messages?"

"No more calls. But Lieutenant MacGraft was in around seven o'clock and asked me to let you know she's on the street doing 'follow-up.'

She said you'd know what she's talking about. Want me to have the corporal call her in?"

"That's okay, Nora. When she's finished with what she's doing, I'm sure she'll find me. Thanks. That's it?"

"That's it, Captain."

Mickey unlocks the door to his private office and leaves it open behind him. Last thing he wants staff to think is he's too cagey. That's what Mickey's good friend, Officer Jimmy Waters told him might happen. Jimmy will eventually become Devlin's righthand man. For the most part, cops are a paranoid bunch, Mickey included. Bosses who live behind closed doors make cops nervous. You hear it all the time. "I think the boss is hiding something." "What's he scared of?" Worse yet, the message is these bosses don't trust the people who work for them. For bosses who try to lead from behind closed doors, there are always unintended consequences, none of them beneficial.

Mickey sits down at his desk, turns on the TV and slides the surveillance tape he had picked up at Saint Joe's Hospital in the VCR. He pushes play and waits for the tapes to begin. A small military-time clock appears along the bottom right-hand corner.

Initially, there doesn't appear to be anything out of the norm for an emergency room. There are several adults and a few young children sitting in light-blue molded plastic chairs lined up in two rows facing each other. There are also a handful of adults standing around three vending machines a short distance away. Mickey scans the faces and the body language carefully of the people in the waiting room. No one stands out. Not yet anyway.

At 08:29:14, things change substantially. Several nurse types in assorted colored scrubs and doctors in white smocks start running toward the front doors. Then Mickey can see the Fire Department's EMT team rolling a gurney into the ER. One uniformed guy is pushing and one is running alongside pressing on the man's exposed chest. *CPR.* Mickey rewinds the tape a few frames. He's interested if the man on the gurney is wearing shoes. He presses play and the VHS tape moved forward again. *Darn, the sheet is covering the guy's feet.* One of the white coats is running beside the team holding a clear plastic mask over the man's nose and mouth.

The gurney wheels through the ER waiting room, through a set of automatic double doors and down a well-lit hallway. After a few quick bleeps, the tape picks up again. The gurney can be seen being wheeled into a white-curtained exam room. The two EMTs remain in the hall. Six minutes later the curtains open and three nurses and two doctors exit. By that time, several uniform police and religious have joined the two EMTs outside the exam room. He also sees a man carrying a suit coat and wearing a PPD identification badge around his neck. Easily noticeable is the chrome automatic on his left hip. *Fannille!* Standing beside the Deputy is Detective Carmine "Worms" Gallo and Cardinal Dominic Vuotto. The threesome is huddled in conversation.

During "hard times" in the late '50s, Mickey's Uncle George, his wife and their "deaf" daughter Anna moved in with Mick's family. Anna and Mickey were the same age and became best friends. During their stay with the Devlins, Mickey picked up sign language and lip reading from his cousin. Skills that came in very handy in Mickey's chosen profession. *Okay, Devlin, make Anna proud.* He rewinds the tape. He can only pick up parts of a conversation between Fannille and the Cardinal.

"I'll take care of _____ on _____ my, your Excellency."

"All right, Antonio. I'm depending _____ to keep this thing from _____ out of hand."

"I've been _____ from the _____ beginning."

"God bless, _____ son."

Toward the end of the tape Mickey sees the EMT team replace the two white sheets and wheel their empty gurney back down the hall and out the ER doors. Close behind them Mickey can see Detective Gallo holding a cell phone to his left ear. Mick can't pick up any of what he's saying. *Darn!*

Thirty seconds later Gallo walks back through the ER followed by the EMTs wheeling their empty gurney. *Wait a minute. What...*Mickey rewinds the tape to the beginning and stops it. *Okay! Two guys wheel the Monsignor in.* Mickey fast-forwards the tape to when Gallo brings the EMTs back. *Wow!* The tape now shows that one of the male EMTs has been replaced by a female. *Bingo!*

Mickey lets the tape play out. As the EMTs wheel who Mick believes is the Monsignor back out of Saint Joe's he sees Detective Gallo stop and discretely hand a young man standing by the open doors a brown paper bag. Mick hits the pause button and takes a closer look at the man. *Are you kidding me? Little John Pollina at Saint Joe's. That's how he got the Monsignor's cell phone. Worms gave it to him. Two down and who knows how many to go. Keep your eye on the ball, Devlin.*

Mickey takes the videotape out of the cassette player and tries to put it back in the messenger box. It's giving him trouble. He looks inside and sees a typed note from Julius McMichael, Director of Security at Saint Joe's. He removes it and reads it.

Mick,

I included a list of the people on the tape. I got their names off our mandatory sign-in sheet. And hospital employee directory. Hope it helps to ID the actors.

Jules

Mickey smiles. He looks at Julius' list and fingers down to and stops at the first EMT team: *Nicolas Ligambi and Seth Melloni. Ligambi was supposedly the driver of Medic 27.* Then he checks his notes for the names of the EMT team that Doc Steinberg told him transported the Monsignor's remains to the ME's. *Nicolas Ligambi and Joann Verna-Deloria. Gotcha! I owe ya, Julius McMichael.*

My interview wish list just got longer.

CHAPTER XXXIV

Eight and Earp
Concetta Bruno's Home

"A secret imparted is no longer a secret."
Italian Proverb

Early on her shift Lieutenant MacGraft heads for Concetta Bruno's two-story brick row home on the eight hundred block of Earp Street. As she pulls into the street, she's reminded of what Terrell told her: "Looks like one of those funeral houses. It's the home with the black awning covering the entire front of the building with a massive white *B* in the middle of it."

He was right about that: huge awning, turned wide brick front steps, oversized first-floor picture window. All that's missing is a line of black town cars out front with orange and white **FUNERAL** stickers on the front windshield.

The lieutenant walks up the immaculate five brick steps to the matching brick landing and knocks on the swanky, black-framed storm door also with a white *B* strategically placed. The solid-oak front door swings open and a curvy ponytailed, brown-haired, twenty-something woman, gripping a white hanky just stands in the open door and says nothing.

Linda breaks the ice. "Hey, I'm Lieutenant Linda MacGraft, Third District. I was hoping to talk with Concetta Bruno."

"I'm Concetta Bruno. You're Terrell's friend, right?"

Linda smiles. "Yes! I'm friends with Terrell and his mother, Samantha."

"How's Terrell? He and Richie were like brothers. He was gonna be in our wedding."

"Terrell's…Terrell's going to be okay. He's a tough kid. How are you, Concetta?"

"Oh...I'll be okay. I have my family. And..."

Concetta's red eyes start to swell with tears. It's obvious that she's been crying and only stopped to answer the door. This is when the lieutenant would normally suggest coming back at a better time to talk, but not today. She's on a mission. A mission with a time clock attached. In response, Concetta opens the door and asks Linda to come in and join her for a just-brewed cup of coffee. Linda acquiesces. Two feet inside Linda's right leg is attacked by a small snow-white fluff of a dog dragging a five-foot plastic pink leash behind it.

"Precious is my mom's dog. She calls Precious her 'other daughter.' Down, Precious. Sorry, Lieutenant. She loves people."

Linda chuckled. "I can see that."

Precious waddles over to a customized doggy bed complete with a pink pillow carefully placed by the front window.

Linda follows Concetta to the classic six-foot Greco-Roman-styled sofa with mahogany-wood trim traditionally fitted with clear plastic slipcovers. The gentle ᴡʜᴏᴏsʜ sound when she sits down has Linda feeling right at home. It's like sitting in her grandmother's house, Ann Marie Mooney-MacGraft. Concetta pours her a cup of Lavazza Dark Italian coffee.

Concetta takes a sip of her coffee, puts her cup down and then begins to tell Linda about her fiancé. Starting with what she believes is why the lieutenant came to talk with her. Richie's past.

"Richie said when he was ten he heard his parents talking one night about him being a 'gift from God.' He thought that meant he was special. He said it made him happy. Later, he asked his older brother Salvatore what his parents meant. Sal said it meant that his mom wasn't his mom. Richie said he was confused. Sal told him he was adopted. That he came from a Catholic orphanage. He called Richie a 'milkman's baby.' He told him that his real father was from the neighborhood. When Richie asked his mom about what his brother said, she called Sal 'oobatz' crazy. Then she made Sal apologize to Richie and told him to get to confession and tell the priest he was cruel to his brother."

"You said this all happened when Richie was ten?"

"That's what he told me."

"Did he ever tell you anything else about his childhood? I heard he was an altar boy and—"

"No! No way. I know where you're going with this. A couple of years ago, some priest from the Cardinal's office was interviewing all the boys who were altar boys at Our Lady of Sorrows back in the '70s and '80s. No! Richie was never molested as a kid. Not by a priest. Not by anyone."

"He told you that?"

"He did."

"How about Richie's brothers? They were altar boys too. Did Richie ever—"

"Ya know Richie's brother Rocco is recchione, a fanook. Ya know, homosexual?"

Linda is taken back by Concetta's question.

"No, never heard that about Rocco. He seems like a big ladies man."

"Yeah, weeell. He's a closet homo. One hundred percent."

Linda moves on.

"So the subject of childhood molestation came up with you and Richie because of…"

Linda senses Concetta is getting upset so she backs off. Concetta finishes her coffee and stares into her empty cup.

"Concetta, you okay?"

Concetta avoids making eye contact and reaches for the gold crucifix around her neck. "I brought the subject up. Not Richie. I brought it up."

"Oh! I'm sorry, Concetta. I really didn't think—"

"I brought the subject up because I loved Richie and I didn't want any secrets between us."

Linda doesn't respond. She takes Concetta's free hand and lets the moment pass. Concetta puts her cup down on the glass coffee table and looks at Linda.

"I told Richie I was molested when I was eight years old. I told him because I loved him and he loved me no matter what."

"I'm so sorry, Concetta. That must have been a terrible burden to carry around all these years. Did you ever report the incident to the police?"

"I never even told my parents. There would have been hell to pay. Believe me. Until right now, Richie was the only person I told."

Concetta's revelation was another total shock. But Linda feels compelled to say something.

"I'm sure you feel you did the right thing at the time. But ya know it's not too late to talk to authorities. PA law gives special time limits in child molestation cases. Basically, you have until you're thirty to report it. That timeline may be extended in the future. So if you ever want to, I'm here for you, Concetta. Okay?"

"Okay!"

Linda quickly changes the subject before Concetta shuts down on her.

"How did you get along with Richie's brother Salvatore? He sounds like he was pretty malicious to Richie."

"Sal is a spiteful person. It shoulda been him who got killed."

Killed? There's that word again. Linda questions Concetta's use of words.

"Concetta, I was told Richie committed suicide."

"No way! He'd never kill himself. Richie was killed. I know it. Richie and I were gonna get married in two weeks."

"Sorry for having to ask you some of these things but—"

"It's okay, Lieutenant. I want to talk to somebody. I'm glad it's you. I'm sure you're not aware of this. But Terrell used to talk to Richie about you. He told Richie he could trust you."

"That's nice to hear. Terrell is a good kid." Linda gets back on point. "So you mean no one from the PD has come to interview you. No one from South Detectives? No one from Police Headquarters?"

"No! Why should they?"

"Well, because you were Richie's fiancée. Because you might know something about why he did what he did."

"No one knew 'bout us 'cept little Terrell. We didn't even tell Richie's parents because they wouldn't approve. Something to do with my dad's buddies."

"You didn't get along with Richie's parents?"

"We get along all right, I guess. It wasn't that. It's just that Richie wanted it that way. That's all."

"How about your parents? Did you tell them?"

"My mom knows Richie and me are friends, but that's it. She's cool with it. She loves, loved Richie. Me and Richie was gonna tell her about getting married last weekend, but Richie put it off. Guess he wanted to talk to the Monsignor first. I'm just guessing 'bout that part."

"Your dad? What does your dad know?"

"Nothing. No way. He thinks me and Richie just know each other from the neighborhood. If he knew we were gonna get married, he'd kill Richie. Nobody, especially Richie for some reason, is good enough for his little princes. 'Sides, my mom and dad are estranged. He lives in the apartment above his restaurant over on Seventh. Mom doesn't like his friends. She told me they're either crazy Nam vets or Mob wannabes."

Linda knows all about Concetta's father's infamous 7th Street restaurant. It's called "Men of Honor." It's basically a Mob hangout pretending to be an Italian deli. The lieutenant served a couple of search warrants on the place when she was in plain clothes. Years ago somebody blew the place up trying to assassinate a Mob underboss from the Colelori Family. Concetta's dad is an ex-Marine sergeant, who volunteered for two tours in Vietnam. To his credit he earned several medals, including the Purple Heart awarded after he took a burst from a Russian AK-forty-seven in his right leg. It earned him a ticket home in nineteen-seventy, and a lifetime disability. He still walks with a noticeable limp. Thus the nickname "The Gimp."

"Sorry to hear about your mom and dad having trouble."

"That's all right, Lieutenant. It's not the first time they broke up. He likes catering to the neighborhood wise-guys or wannabe wise- guys and his old army buddies. Like I said, they all seem a little weird to me and my mom. But I know she still loves him. Me too."

"I'm familiar with your dad's place, Concetta. I don't know if Terrell said anything to you, but he believes the Mob was somehow involved in Richie's death."

"Yeah! Terrell told me that."

"Do you believe him?"

"I do but I can't prove it."

"Why would the Mob want Richie dead?"

"They don't need a reason. They do stupid stuff all the time. Them and their rules. It's all che cazzata, bullshit. Who knows, maybe one of my dad's crazy Nam friends found out about me and Richie and…but that would be even too dumb for those guys. I do know that Richie argues all the time with his parents 'bout paying tribute to the thugs from Christian Street. Maybe they just wanted to shut Richie up. Teach him a lesson. Who knows?"

"Concetta. Do you have any reason to believe Richie was in debt to the Mob? A bad loan? Anything?"

"No never. He made good money at the store. He worked his hours and his brothers' hours. Neither of those dummies helped out with the business. They're too busy hanging out with all the neighborhood losers. He didn't need to borrow from anybody. I have all of our wedding money in a safe deposit box. No way was Richie involved with those people. No way, Lieutenant."

"I believe you, Concetta. Sorry! But—"

"I understand. You're just doing your job. It's okay."

According to Concetta Bruno, she was aware that Richie was going to confront Monsignor O'Hagorty yesterday about being his biological father. *That confirms what Terrell told me.* But she denied knowing that he was going to kidnap him and cause such a "ruckus." Linda revisits a couple of unresolved issues with Concetta.

"What makes you so certain that Richie didn't commit suicide? You seem so sure."

Concetta pours herself another half cup of coffee. She adds sugar and cream and stirs it to an even blend of light tan. Then she turns and looks at Linda.

"Because he wanted to be a daddy more than anything in the world. He would have been a great daddy."

Linda's eyes widen and she thinks. *Holy shit, here comes another bomb.*

Concetta takes another slower more deliberate sip of her coffee this time and holds the gold-edged China cup on her lap with both hands.

"I'm four months pregnant."

Linda is a little surprised at Concetta's openness about such a private matter. But she refocuses on the task at hand.

"Congratulations! From what I've heard about Richie, I'm certain he would have been a great father."

"Thanks! So now ya see why I say he would never intentionally leave me alone to raise our baby. He loved me and loved that we were gonna have a baby."

"Yes, I can see why you feel that way. Thank you for sharing that with me. I'm so sorry for your loss. Did Terrell know about the baby?"

"Thank you, Lieutenant. No, Terrell didn't know. Richie thought he was too young for all of that stuff."

"I see. If it's okay, I have a couple more questions."

"It's okay. Like I said I needed to talk to somebody."

"Earlier you said that Richie wanted to…" Linda refers to her notes. "…confront the Monsignor. Was it just for the sole purpose of—"

"About his mom. Stuff like, is she still alive, and if she is, how can he contact her? Plus was the Monsignor ready to be a better grandfather than he was a father."

"I see. Sounds natural enough to me. He went about it in an unconventional way but…nothing else?"

"That's it as far as I know. I can't imagine how things got out of hand. Maybe the Monsignor said something. Or Richie was pushed into it. Don't know."

Linda pushes on. "Concetta. Do you know if Richie was on any kind of medication? Or if he was into any other drugs."

"Nothing! He wouldn't even take an aspirin. He was in great shape. He's done the Broad Street Run for the past six years. That's ten miles long ya know. He definitely wasn't on any meds or drugs. Is that what those detectives are trying to say? That Richie was some kind of junk? Or that he went off his meds and went nutty?"

To spare Concetta the details, Linda tells a white lie. "No! But I just wanted to make sure that if the subject came up, I could dismiss it from the jump."

"Good! Richie was not into drugs, never. Is that all you need, Lieutenant? I'm kinda tired. I didn't get much sleep last night."

"Just two more questions, if it's okay, Concetta. How did you find out about Richie?"

"Terrell. Terrell told me. He came here and told me."

The lieutenant wants to try one last time to have Concetta address the subject of her unreported molestation.

"Last question, Concetta. I'm sorry for bringing it up again, but as a cop I'd be remiss if I didn't. I apologize in advance for being so blunt."

"All right!"

"Who molested you?"

Concetta slowly puts her cup down on the table. For a few seconds she doesn't speak. She just stares into her empty China coffee cup and begins to sob. Then she turns to Linda and through glassy eyes gives a two-word answer.

"Monsignor O'Hagorty."

Linda uncharacteristically barks, "The son of a bitch."

"That's what Richie said."

Linda knows it's time to close down the conversation. She suddenly is aware that Concetta inadvertently just gave Richie the ultimate motive for snatching and wanting the Monsignor dead.

"Okay, Concetta. I'll let you get some sleep. You've been very helpful. Again, I am so sorry for your loss."

Linda takes out one of her business cards and writes her cell phone number on the back.

"If you think of anything else, or if you just want to talk, please call me on my cell. It doesn't matter, day or night. I only live ten minutes away. I gave Terrell the same offer. Maybe all three of us can talk. You'll let me know, right?"

Concetta takes the card, looks at it a few seconds and puts it in the back pocket of her designer jeans.

"I will, Lieutenant. Thanks."

Concetta walks Linda to the front door.

Linda hurries to her car hopscotching over dirty rain puddles in Earp Street and drives back to the district. Although heart-sick over the cards Concetta Bruno and Richie Rugnetta were dealt, she feels energized about the results of her interview.

Just prior to knocking on Concetta's front door Linda had put herself "out of service on a district assignment" over Police Radio. She goes back over the air to change her status.

"Three Command to Radio."

"Command?"

"Turn me around from Eight and Earp to the district dropping off paperwork."

"Command okay."

Mickey's been monitoring South Band from his office over his handheld radio. He heard Linda turn herself around to the district. He's curious how she did with Richie's girlfriend.

CHAPTER XXXV

The Usual Suspects?

"Deliberate before you act."

Italian Proverb

At 9:05, Mickey's cell phone starts to vibrate on his left hip. He literally hates cell phones. He's bought into the research that contends they cause brain cancer. "Darn!"

He struggles to get the phone out of its stiff leather pouch, next to the double ten-round, 9-mm magazine case for his Glock 26. He presses the talk key. "Devlin."

"Hi ya, Mick! Michelle. Got a minute?"

"Always! How did you make out with your undercover job?"

"We got the money shots, Mick. If you're not too busy fighting crime, I'd like to stop by and show you what I got."

"How's noon sound? I got a lieutenant heading into the district with the results of an unrelated matter."

"Unrelated matter? Unrelated to what, Mick? Are you hiding stuff from your favorite big-time news editor again?"

"Who me? Never! She's doing a little follow-up investigation for me."

"Sounds like you finally found somebody you can trust down there on the South Forty."

"I did. Seamus gave me a heads up that she's one of the good ones. From what I've seen so far, he was dead on."

"Can't wait to meet your trustworthy lieutenant, Mick. Maybe you'll do the introductions when I come down."

"Absolutely! You two have a lot in common."

"Really! Ya mean she's smart and beautiful?"

"That's something you're gonna have to judge for yourself, kiddo."

"Ya know I will too."

"Okay already. So let's say my office at noon."

"Sounds good. Don't forget your promise. My exclusive—"

"I'm good for it, Michelle. Two or three loose ends and—"

"Okay! I know you're good for it. See ya at noon."

Mickey waits for Michelle to hang up.

Five minutes later Lieutenant MacGraft knocks on Mickey's door. Still wearing her long black raincoat, she stomps the excess rain off her black-leather boots on the rug outside his office door.

"Come in."

Linda cautiously peeks from behind a half-opened door.

"You got time for me, Boss?"

"Absolutely! I was going to call you in but heard you turn yourself around from Earp Street. Figured you were coming from Richie's girlfriend's."

"Yes, Sir."

"Great! Come on in. Sit down."

Linda slips out of her raincoat and lays it over the cardboard boxes next to the window and sits down. Referring to her notes, she tells Mickey about her revealing discussion with the pregnant Concetta Bruno. Mickey listens with interest. After which he comments, "That's one heck of an interview, Lieutenant. Sad! But enlightening."

"Yes, on both counts. I feel so sorry for the direction Concetta's life is going. I'm just hoping now that we've been told about the connection between her, Richie and the Monsignor, it doesn't drive her over the cliff."

"We have to make certain that doesn't happen. If she'll let us, we'll get her whatever help she needs. We have to do that."

"Yes, Sir."

"I was hoping to glean enough information from Concetta to change the direction South Detectives and the First Deputy are heading with Richie's case. But it is, what it is."

Mickey finishes writing down a few notes of his own, while Linda mulls over her captain's comment about the Deputy.

She waits until Mickey puts down his pen then asks him, "So Deputy Fannille is definitely involved in the Richie Rugnetta job?"

"He's running it and it looks like the Monsignor's job too."

"Ya think the commissioner knows what the Deputy is doing?"

"I believe he knows about it and condones it. But I'm also certain he's positioned himself to be able to deny it down the line. He may have been born at night, but not last night. He's not going to do anything to jeopardize whatever he's got lined up when he's finally bounced."

"So much for stepping up to the plate. You really think he's gonna get bounced?"

"You can bet the ranch."

"Wonder if Fannille will get bounced too?"

"Time will tell. But what I know for sure is he's the driving force behind having Richie's job classified as a suicide. He's also the guy who put Richie's parents, or should I say adopted parents, off limits. I would have loved to be a fly on the wall when the Deputy talked to them."

"Probably more like talked **at** them, Boss. Guess all we can go on is what Terrell added to the equation about that."

"That's true. Oh! I viewed a security tape from Saint Joe's Hospital. I saw Terrell's chrome-toting detective."

"Fannille. What's with him? How's he get away with carrying that thing? It's clearly a violation of policy."

"It's great to be the king's alter ego. Ya know when Seamus and I went over to Richie's parents' place, they did seem a little jumpy. Actually, a lot jumpy. I have to wonder why a high-ranking police official wants to limit the scope of an investigation."

"I can tell you for sure Deputy Fannille doesn't do anything in a vacuum, Boss. There's always a reason. Albeit not always a moral one."

Mickey adds, "Or legal. He does seem to have his fingers into everything South Philly. I guess you know he's been looked at by the Feds on more than one occasion."

"I do. I was here when he tried messing with Captain Conley. He was constantly trying to middle him. Good thing the Captain documented everything the Dep and his lackey lieutenant wanted him to do. Believe me, there was a lot of shaky stuff they were trying to get the Captain to do. Really shaky stuff. He was way too smart for those two though."

"I heard all about Conley's troubles with Fannille. It was the talk of the command meetings. Hard to believe the Deputy never got jammed up behind all the favors he did or tried to have Conley do for his wise-guy buddies."

"Bone yard! He knows where all the West Wing's bodies are buried."

Mickey smiles. "I agree with you on that one, Linda. I'm starting to think he holds the same position in South Philly politics. Knowing where the bodies are, that is."

"No doubt! I think he may own that graveyard down here."

"I wouldn't be surprised if he helped dig a few of those graves either, Lin."

Linda smiles. "No disrespect, but do you know what the merchants along Nineth Street say about the Deputy?"

"School me."

"They call him, 'Pezzo di merda,' that 'piece of shit.'"

"Ouch!"

Mickey avoids going into his own history with the Deputy. Maybe some other time. He gets back on point.

"The Deputy is also trying to put Homicide on a short leash behind Richie's job. Thankfully, the guy that's been given the job to monitor doesn't take lightly to being led."

Linda smiles. "That can only be one of two Homicide guys, Nobles or Ryan. My money is on Mike Ryan."

Mickey returns the smile but doesn't give up his friend because of their "under the radar" pact.

"You know, Mike?"

"Most definitely! Had some jobs with him when I was assigned to Organized Crime. Good man. He can be cantankerous but he's an outstanding investigator. He has incorruptible ethics."

"You pegged him to a tee. Guess you do know him."

"Yes, Sir."

Linda doesn't push her captain for a confirmation on Ryan's connection to Richie's case. She understands the need for discretion in police work. Even among people on the same team.

Mickey moves on. "So let's summarize. We have two sources, albeit the two people closest to Richie, convinced that he would never take his own life. Both agree that he was looking forward to his upcoming wedding and that he was never molested as a kid.

"Concetta Bruno is positive Richie was not taking drugs, prescription or otherwise, and he wasn't into anyone for money. In fact, she told you he was a veteran long-distance runner. Did the ten-mile Broad Street Run the last six years."

"I already confirmed that, Boss. I've done that run myself. My source even gave me Richie's times. No doper could put up those numbers."

"That's great, Linda. Speaking of verification, with Richie and the Monsignor sharing a room at the ME's a quick blood test hopefully followed with a DNA test should confirm any linkage."

"To the ninety-nine point ninety-ninth percentile. If they match, it will prove Richie right and give him a double motive to want to whack the Monsignor. He impregnated his mom and walked. Then molested his future bride and covered it up."

"Back in the day the Monsignor could not have gotten away with either of those disgusting things without help, Lin."

"Big time. The kind that can put the fear of God in ya, Boss."

"But let's not take our eyes off the ball. Richie did threaten to kill the Monsignor, in so many words."

"So if we establish motive to kill the Monsignor, does that take suicide off the table and change who investigates?"

"It could. It's all in the presentation. We on the same page so far, Lin?"

"So far!"

"Like you said if that isn't motive for revenge, nothing is. It's definitely enough to drive someone to take a hostage."

"I've seen hostage takers with less of a motive, Cap. But I agree. Richie must have been really ticked off."

"Ya think? So here's the million-dollar question that needs the million-dollar answer."

Linda bites her top lip waiting for her captain's query.

"If Richie was so ticked off, most folks in his position would be, then why the heck would he…" Mickey and his streetwise lieutenant answer in unison. "…kill himself and not the man who caused chaos in his life?"

Linda now starts biting her bottom lip. Then gives her gut answer.

"You know where I fall, Boss. He didn't. Based on what I know about Richie Rugnetta, I'm certain he had no intention of dying yesterday. Not a little bit."

Mickey smiles and nods in agreement. "I'm moving in that direction too. Now we need to prove it. Regardless of who gets ticked off."

Linda shrugs. "So be it."

"Right answer. Sooo…then, who killed Richie? I'm not talking about some far-ranging opinion like 'The Mob did it' answer. We need a suspect. Somebody we can charge and put on the stand. So let's start with who had the opportunity. But I think we should also get ready for some pushback from Fannille and his tragic accident theory."

"So let's make our list, Boss."

Linda flips the page in her small notebook.

"Okay, I'll start. The Monsignor."

Linda smiles and writes down the Monsignor's full name. She finishes and looks back at her captain.

Mickey is smiling. "Pretty short list, isn't it, Lieutenant?"

"That's it? Nobody else makes the list?"

"Everybody else arrived after Richie was dead. So let's make a second list, Lin. It's something I do to prevent me from getting tunnel vision on a case."

"Second list? Who—"

"The TUPS."

"Say again."

"The temporarily unidentified perpetrators, TUPS."

Linda runs her left hand through her close-cropped thick black hair and then writes T U P S in caps to her sparse suspect list. She puts her pen behind her right ear and looks at her captain quizzically.

"Wow! You think someone else was in the school and he was missed by Stakeout?"

"Or her."

"Her? The only hers in play so far are Richie's mom, or moms, and Concetta Bruno and her mom."

"You're right. But let's hold off on adding them to our list just yet. I'm not saying missed. I'm thinking more in the line of came along with Richie and was readily ignored by one or both Stakeout cops."

"Holy…are you thinking one or both of the Stakeout cops are part of a conspiracy? That officers DeMarco and Lee let an assassin escape? That's—"

"I'm not saying anything. I'm just saying add the unknown subject to your list. Most homicides start out with an unknown suspect. You just need to work all the possibilities."

"I'm with ya, Cap."

"Good! It's not an indictment of anybody. We're just brainstorming here, Linda."

"You're right. What's next?"

"Let's start with family and friends of both Richie and the Monsignor. Separate the good from the bad. Establish and verify their whereabouts and compare those with time of death. We already know that Richie told at least two people what his intentions were, a fourteen-year-old kid and a pregnant woman."

"Right! Not the perfect duo when it comes to keeping a secret."

"We need to know who else could have had access to the scene. Who has keys. If the rectory and church are any indication then the school probably doesn't have a security system. It will become obvious who can be purged from that list."

"Okay!"

"Basically, it's a process of elimination."

"I'll start the process ASAP."

Linda puts her notebook back in the pocket of her white shirt. She grabs her raincoat and starts for the door. Mickey has one more idea. He calls to Linda.

"Hey, Linda."

"Sir."

"Before you start your follow-up, I'd like you to take a walk next door with me. Lieutenant Rossi worked it out with the principal to keep the classroom secured until later today."

"I heard. Sure, I'm available, Cap. Street's been pretty quiet. Just want to tell my sergeants where I'll be if they need me."

"Good idea. That's something I got to work harder on myself. Letting people know where I'm going. See you in ten minutes?"

"Ten minutes, Cap."

CHAPTER XXXVI

Our Lady Of Sorrows
Crime Scene Do Over

"Desperate times call for desperate measures."
Italian Proverb

Standing at the front door of Our Lady of Sorrows School is a lone uniform officer. When Devlin and the Lieutenant get within a few feet of him, the officer comes to attention and gives a hand salute.

"Good morning, Captain…Lieutenant."

Devlin returns the salute. "Good morning to you too, Officer. You keeping a crime-scene log?"

"Yes, Sir. I got it from Officer Ortiz, three Platoon. You and Lieutenant MacGraft are my first police visitors. When I got here…" The officer checks his log. "…the maintenance guy was waiting for me so I could open up the school for him to do whatever he does." The officer hands the log to his captain.

"Good!" Devlin peruses it and hands it back.

"Nobody after CSU left. Just how I like it. Ready, Lieutenant?"

"Yes, Sir."

The officer immediately opens one of the double doors for Devlin and his lieutenant. Standing at the top of the short charcoal-slate staircase is an elderly Black man dressed in jeans, a light-blue work shirt and tan work boots laced to their dark-brown leather crest. Devlin climbs the slate stairs. Linda does the introductions.

"Captain Devlin, this is Cliff Davies. He's the caretaker for the school. Been here for what…twenty years, Cliff?"

Cliff offers his right hand to the captain. "Nice to meet ya, Captain. Been here twenty-two years, actually. But who's counting. Heard ya had an exciting first day in the district, Sir."

"Ya could say that. Nice to meet you too, Cliff."

Devlin starts a friendly Q and A with Cliff. He can't help himself. As far as he's concerned, everyone's a potential TUP.

"I was told you were notified by cell phone about yesterday's activities."

"Yes, Sir. Got a call from Police Radio."

"Hope they didn't wake you, Cliff."

"Not hardly. I was on my way in. After I got the call, I called the principal. She used our phone chain-list plan to let teachers and students know school would be closed for two days. But she has the teachers and admin staff reporting to the church basement auditorium this morning for meetings and updates."

Devlin looks at the lieutenant and shrugs. "Good thing the church didn't turn out to be a secondary crime scene."

Linda nods.

"So when you arrived yesterday—"

"I was met by Sergeant Conti. He asked me to hang around the staging area just in case your guys needed something. I was there when you pulled up."

"So you never got into the school yesterday then?"

"That's correct, Captain. In fact, I gave my door keys to the sergeant."

Lieutenant MacGraft confirms Cliff's statement. "The keys have been passed on with the security log."

Cliff adds, "The only other door keys are the ones the principal and vice principal have. As far as I know anyway."

"Excellent! So with that in mind, I'd be interested in hearing your opinion on how someone could get in here. I was told there were no signs of forced entry."

"Can't say, Captain. Maybe somebody had one of them skeleton keys. Or a professional burglar was able to pick that door lock of ours."

"Who secured the school last Friday?"

"Probably the principal. I work six to three, adding in my lunch break. The building stays open for at least two hours after I leave. So the principal or vice principal has that responsibility. But I can tell you that the principal has already asked me to change the locks again."

"Again? Have many burglaries, Cliff?"

"No, Sir. In my twenty-two years we've only had two. One in seventy-six and one in ninety-one. Both times the district cops made an arrest. Both times the cops said the robbers came in those doors..." Cliff points down the steps toward the Wharton Street double doors. "...I did change the door locks after the first robberies. So we're due."

"What was taken in seventy-six and ninety-one?"

"Office supplies. There was some minor vandalism. The principal has an inventory of all the stuff taken. I know 'cause she had to give it to the detectives and insurance company."

"I see. Well I don't think we can classify either of the two men, if that number holds, that were in here yesterday as 'professional burglars,' Cliff. But maybe one of them knows a pro. We'll have to look into that. I appreciate your thoughts on the matter though."

"Glad to be of help, Captain."

Mickey points down the hall. "I take it you've not been in room four today, Cliff?"

"No, Sir. Not today. Not yesterday, no, Sir."

"Outstanding! I'm hoping that when the lieutenant and I are finished, we'll be releasing the scene. Please thank the principal for all her cooperation. The Police Department is sorry for the inconvenience. I'll stop by the first chance I have to thank her personally."

"No problem, Captain. We know this is serious business. It's not every day we have someone killed in our school. I'll surely let Principal Duffinette know what you said."

Devlin can't let Cliff's explicit assessment of Richie's death pass unchallenged.

"You said it's not every day we have someone **killed** in our school. Our detectives have classified the victim's death as a suicide, Cliff. Maybe you can—"

"Oh! I only meant the man died inside our school. I guess in my civilian mind killed and suicide aren't that far apart. Obviously, I'm wrong. Sorry, Sir. I—"

"I understand, Cliff. It's like when you called the previous two burglaries, robberies. It's just a word issue not a classification. Sorry if I jumped—"

"No, Sir. Guess I watch too many TV cop shows. I learned something today."

"Hollywood is the worst with cop talk, Cliff. How about the Monsignor's death? How would those TV cops say he died?"

"On that one, I can only go by what I read in the papers. Natural! The Monsignor died of natural causes."

"There ya go. Okay, thanks again for your help. You know I'm right next door now, so if you need me for anything, don't hesitate. Okay?"

"Yes, Sir. Thank you, Captain."

Devlin shakes hands with Cliff and then has Lieutenant MacGraft accompany him to classroom 4. Cliff walks down the stairs and starts a conversation with the uniform officer at the front door.

"Your captain is all business ain't he."

"That's what I hear, Cliff."

When Devlin gets to the classroom, he gingerly removes the yellow and black crime scene tape in an X-pattern from one side of the doorframe and lets the ends hang. He puts on a pair of rubber gloves he got from his back pocket.

"Now let's see what else this scene can tell us. What's not looked for will never be found, right, Lin?"

"Right, Boss."

Devlin offers his extra pair of gloves to MacGraft. She pulls out an identical pair from her back pocket.

"Got my own, Boss."

Devlin smiles, gently turns the tarnished brass knob and pushes open the classroom door. Inside the room Devlin tells MacGraft to grab a chair and join him in the middle of the room.

"You familiar with the adage, 'Mortui vivos docent,' let the dead teach the living?"

"Think I read it somewhere."

Devlin chuckles. "Okay! I always like to revisit a scene after all the hustle-and-bustle processing is over. It gives me a chance to reflect on everything with a clear mind."

Devlin points out where Richie and the Monsignor were when he entered the room. Where Officer Demarco said he found the weapon and the one spent casing. Fresh from witnessing her captain's "words are important" shootout with Cliff, MacGraft astutely latches on to her captain's verbiage and inflection.

"I'm getting the feeling you're suspicious that the scene you saw and the scene Stakeout found are not one and the same."

"It's always a possibility, right? You know how cops move stuff without thinking about it. I can't even count the times I walked into a scene, as a supervisor, and the cops are walking around, touching stuff, smoking or worse."

"You're right. I walked in on a residential burglary once, and there were three cops sitting at the vacationing victim's dining room table drinking the poor guy's bourbon out of his wedding- reception silver goblets."

"Wow!"

"You got that right, Boss. That was the night a burglary job turned into an IAB investigation with one thieving cop getting fired. Two more lost time and were transferred to the Subway Unit. They're still down there."

"That could be good or bad. I'm not one for transferring problem cops from one command to another."

"I hear ya. But moving bodies and evidence at a scene seems way out there, Boss."

"Wouldn't be the first time. All I'm saying is if I can't testify to exactly where something was then—"

"Never really thought of it that way. But you're right. Guess it all depends on who's asking the questions."

Since MacGraft arrived at the original scene after Devlin yesterday, he wanted to get her impressions of how the room looked to her currently.

"Does everything look the way you remember it, Linda? Notice anything, anything at all, that may have been moved, altered, added to the room. Minus all the different color fingerprint powder around here. Or does anything seem out of place for a grade- school classroom to you?"

MacGraft starts looking for any changes to the area. Starting with the ceiling and ending with the floors, the room appears to be how she remembered it. When she's satisfied with her inspection, she responds to Devlin.

"Everything looks just like it did when I left, Boss. But I'm getting the feeling something isn't sitting right with you."

"I'm not sure, Lin. But something seems different. Let me think about it for a minute. You do the same."

After a couple of minutes MacGraft still can't see anything different between the scene she saw yesterday and the one she's looking at today.

"Looks about the same to me, Boss."

"Okay…well I called the Captain of South Detectives earlier. He was emphatic that his guys only took into evidence one automatic and one twenty-two brass casing. My contact at CSU told me they processed the rest of the scene." Devlin doesn't mention the property receipt and scene sketch waiting for him from Lieutenant Scott at CSU. "Plus, Homicide confirmed that they're just monitoring the job and never responded."

Devlin continues his own re-examination of the room. For some reason, he kept returning to the chalkboard in the front of the room and the three large windows that face Wharton Street.

MacGraft walks to the front of the room. "I got it, Cap." She walks to the small wooden desk and pulls out the matching chair from underneath. "When I was here this chair was out and there were several hand-printed papers on the seat. They looked like something the kids handed in for homework. Now that I think about it, what was written on the kids papers is note-worthy. It was the Act of Contrition. I didn't think too much about it then. But now I'm thinking how appropriate."

"Right! I can hear the Monsignor now, 'Oh my God, I am heartily sorry for having messed up Richie and Concetta's life...' That is appropriate. Richie is demanding the Monsignor publicly confess for his sins and twenty copies of the Act of Contrition are staring him in the face."

"Appropriate! Interesting! Even a little spooky."

"But don't mean a thing in a court of law, Lin."

Through a big grin MacGraft adds, "It is kinda like divine providence though. Right, Boss?"

Devlin smiles. "More like the Devil made me do it, Lin. I'm sure it'll become part of some way-out cop gossip. My question is, what happened to the kids' homework?"

"Maybe somebody didn't appreciate the irony, Boss."

Devlin snaps his fingers. "I know what I'm doing wrong. I'm limiting my scope." Devlin's face lights up and he smiles. "Of course..." He points to the window nearest the front of the classroom. "...that window was wide open. Richie opened it and was talking on his cell just before Rossi and I heard the two shots. When I came inside that window was closed. It didn't register until right now."

"You said Officer DeMarco cleared this floor and found Richie and the Monsignor, right Cap?"

"Correct! Then...why would he close that window?"

"Devil's advocate...maybe to protect the scene from the elements."

"What elements? Unlike today, it was unseasonably warm, no wind, and no rain in the forecast. I remember hearing the forecast on my car radio on the way in."

"So if he wasn't protecting the scene from the elements—"

"He must have been protecting something else, or maybe someone else's actions."

"I'll be damned. If you're right—"

"We have a snag, a huge snag, in the Richie Rugnetta investigation. Now all we have to do is untangle that snag."

"What or who would a Stakeout cop feel he needs to protect...and why, Cap?"

Only half listening, Devlin gets up and walks to the front window and opens the bottom sash all the way up. "That's how it was when I heard the two shots." He points across Wharton Street. "Rossi and I were standing over there behind a white van."

Devlin leans out the window and looks up and down a dreary rain-soaked Wharton Street. He looks across the street at the three-story red-brick row homes. Then he looks up to the rooftop on the north side of Wharton, trying to mirror Richie's actions. He tells Linda to get the officer at the front door.

"Get your detail cop in here and have him stand in front of this open window."

"Yes, Sir."

The lieutenant leaves and heads back down the hall. Devlin yells to her.

"Get the Fire Board out here. I want a ladder put up to those roofs across the street."

Devlin keeps asking himself why Richie would open the window in the first place. *Better cell reception?* The more obvious reason is he was looking for someone. Devlin's thoughts turn to his old sniping days. None of his targets were "under glass." They were all in the open. The glass would have changed the trajectory of his shot. *Too chancy. Somebody told Richie to open this window. Somebody called him. Someone he knew. Someone who knew he'd only get off one shot. One unobstructed shot.*

Devlin is moving the goalpost again. He just moved the classroom from a suicide scene to a homicide scene. Better yet, an assassination scene. If he's on target, he believes that the mysterious second brass casing could be somewhere on one of those tar roofs across the street.

MacGraft contacts Police Radio and relays her Captain's request. On his way out of the classroom Devlin catches a glimpse of what looks like a spitball stuck to the base of the ornate white-wood crucifix strategically hung above the classroom door. He comments to himself, *Kids. Some things never change.* Then he walks down the hall passing Cliff on the way.

"Gonna need the room a little longer, Cliff."

"Yes, Sir, Captain."

Within ten minutes the PFD Ladder 11, from 10th and Reed, arrives and two husky firefighters unload a thirty-five-foot extension ladder.

One of the firemen asks, "Where ya want it, Boss?"

After conferring with the homeowner, Devlin directs them to lean it against the row house that lines up with classroom 4. It doesn't take long for the district operation room crew to gather on the street and watch the goings-on. It's rare to see bosses about to climb a ladder. In fact, it's a little bizarre. Big bosses don't do stuff like that.

"Let's do this, Linda."

Without hesitation, Devlin leads the way up to the rooftop.

"Right behind ya, Boss."

CHAPTER XXXVII

11TH and Federal
Secondary Scene

"A thousand probabilities do not make one truth."
Italian Proverb

When Devlin and the MacGraft reach the top of the FD heavy aluminum ladder and climb up on the roof, the small group of uniform spectators applaud the two white-shirts. Patrol lieutenants and above wear white shirts; everyone else wears blue. Rumor is that may change. Agile climbers acknowledge the group's attempt at humor by waving from their perch. Then with a smile Devlin yells down, "Okay, you can get back to work now, fellows. Show's over." Everyone laughs and the witty gawkers do as ordered.

MacGraft asks, "What are we looking for, Boss?"

"Any sign that someone could have climbed up here and may have been watching the goings-on yesterday morning." Devlin points to the back of the Wharton Street roofline. "We're still unsure who else had prior knowledge of Richie's plan. Check all the backyards and the alley for extension ladders, and see if there are any skylights or trapdoors. Look for cigarette butts, gum wrappers and stuff like that. My hope is we'll find a brass casing up here somewhere."

Before MacGraft sets off on her task and with a quizzical look on her face, she asks Devlin, "Boss, I thought Lieutenant Rossi put a cop at the end of the alley. Don't ya think he would have seen somebody climbing up here?"

"Normally, yes. Problem was Rossi had to get a cop from the Fourth District until one ours became available. Even he wasn't assigned until we were well into the Rugnetta job. So there was a window of opportunity to climb up here, lay low for a while, and then get out of Dodge when we opened up the street and pulled the cop."

"Oh! I didn't know about the delay part."

"Ya know, Lin, I just can't get out of my mind the look on Richie's face when he was talking on his cell. Whoever called, he caught him off guard. The way he looked up here from the classroom window… he looked scared."

MacGraft doesn't verbally respond just nods. She hesitantly turns and begins walking along the north side, rear roofline, looking down into the small yards below for "any sign." Devlin stands frozen at the front edge of the rooftop located directly across from the open window of Our Lady of Sorrows, classroom 4.

He is fixed on the uniform officer who's now standing just inside the room watching the activities. He gets the officer's attention and instructs him to turn and face the front of the room exposing his left side from the waist up. When he turns Devlin kneels and takes a shooting position, a sniper's shooting position. Visualizes what it would take for a shooter to execute the perfect neck shot. A shot Devlin and his sniper buddies call "slicing the apple core."

Sniping is something Devlin knows a lot about having been a decorated combat sniper serving with the Special Forces Group 5 (Airborne), in Vietnam. He got his revered "Hog" classification on his second day in the <u>Mekong Delta</u>, with a perfect kill shot of a Vietcong sniper, who had his scope trained on Specialist E-4 Devlin.

It was the fleeting glare of the scope that gave "Charlie's" position away. As Devlin quickly found out, the most dangerous thing for a sniper out in the field is another sniper. "The shot," as it became known, was just over seven hundred meters downrange that went through the scope into "Charlie's" right eye, blowing out the back of his head. Immediately, there was a bounty on Spec E-4 Mickey Devlin. They called him the "Shamrock" because of the black three-leaf clover painted on the front of his helmet.

True to the "Sniper's Code," Devlin retrieved the chambered 7.62X54R round from the North Vietnamese Army sniper's, Soviet SVD rifle. The "Code" can only be satisfied and the "Hog" tag bestowed on a sniper when the chambered round of the vic is retrieved and made into a necklace. The round that was intended for a twenty year old kid from Philly. He keeps his and several other items from his days in "The Nam" locked in a safe deposit box.

Devlin yells to the officer in the classroom. "Come closer to the window." The officer waves and moves right up against the old cast-iron radiator attached to the wall under the window.

He yells again. "Good! Stop right there." Devlin again visualizes the shot required to execute Richie Rugnetta from that position. *Bad angle. Too close. Violates a prime sniper rule: don't give away your position.* He looks around for higher ground. He finds it further north on a rare four-story property with a one-of-a-kind roof deck. *Bingo!*

Devlin calls to Linda. "Find anything?"

"Nothing. No ladders anywhere back here. Negative on trapdoors."

"Not surprised. Come on. Let's go. I see a better spot."

Linda gingerly walks back across the spongy tar-covered rooftops to her captain and the PFD aluminum ladder.

"You find anything, Boss?"

"The only thing I found was that we're probably on the wrong roof." Devlin points to the wood-roof deck further north on 11th Street. "That's where we need to be. Looks like the perfect FFP."

Linda looks toward the only roof deck in the area. "A what?"

"Final firing position. It's sniper-speak."

"If you're saying Richie was shot from up there…that would be one hell of a shot, wouldn't it, Cap?"

"A walk in the park for a military sniper school grad. The best of them will have shoot one hundred thousand rounds a year to prepare for it."

"I take it you've got your diploma?"

Devlin chuckles. "Actually I got my sniper training long before the military got so formal." He leaves it at that.

"Let's see about getting up on that deck."

"I know that property. It's been up for sale for a while."

"It's vacant?"

"Owners moved to Ireland. Dublin, I think."

"Good for them. I'm jealous."

"Yeah! I know for a fact the realtor on Washington Avenue has the key. I had to get in there about a month ago. A neighbor called nine-one-one. Said she smelled gas coming from the basement when she walked by."

Devlin smiles. "Leave it to you to find a way."

"Didn't want to kick down the door for a lot of reasons. Including taking a cop off patrol to guard an open property. I don't have enough people for those kinda details anymore. Sooo—"

"Good move."

Devlin and the MacGraft climb back down the ladder to street level. Pressed for time, Devlin asked the driver of the FD's ladder truck if his equipment is long enough to reach the roof of a four- story building.

"Got ya covered, Cap."

The FD crew loads the thirty-five-foot ladder back on the truck and moves the truck around the corner and follows Devlin and MacGraft north on 11th Street to the deckhouse. On the walk around the corner to the FFP Devlin asked the lieutenant, "Do you think any of our Stakeout cops have the range time to make the kind of shot I'm talking about?"

"If it's military you're looking for, I know one or two, ex-Marine snipers, who—"

Devlin interrupts MacGraft. "I need to know if they were working on Monday and what was their assignment. If they were off, then they need to be interviewed."

"We're eliminating **tups**, right?"

"You got it. All part of the process."

"Give me a minute and I can check that for you right now."

"Do it."

MacGraft makes a quick call on her cell and gets back to Devlin just as they arrive in front of the 11th Street deckhouse.

"They were both at the range yesterday qualifying. Started at seven and were cut loose at three. So—"

"So that's two less interviews somebody has to contend with. Thanks, Lin."

The FD crew decides it would be safer to use the hydraulic cherry picker to reach the deck. This time Devlin decides to check out this rooftop solo. He doesn't want the neighbors to think there's an invasion. Once he reaches the twelve-by-twelve, redwood-stained, pine-and-plywood deck, he walks to the south side. He separates two of the four large potted evergreens just enough to check his "line of sight."

He finds the perfect "sniper's hide" needed to make the downhill shot through the opened window and into Richie Rugnetta's neck. With the officer still standing in the window, Devlin takes "the position" again and goes through his sniper routine. *Distance. Yesterday's conditions were ideal. Aim. Sight alignment. Breathing. Follow through. Ding! Piece of cake.*

The exercise brings back memories of the endless "Hunting Grounds" he set up in over his thirteen-month tour in Vietnam in the late '60s. Mickey never talks about his "kills." His military records will only confirm "sixty-four high-value targets."

In the process of finding the best position to make the shot, he keeps kicking the unseated cover of a small deck drain. He fits the four-inch PVC cover back in place after taking a quick look inside. *Nothing.* Next, he looks over the edge of the deck and sees the drain is tied into a long white aluminum downspout that empties into the unkempt weed-covered yard a foot or so from the building. *That's gotta be checked out.* Devlin yells down to Lieutenant MacGraft standing in the street next to the cherry picker truck.

"Linda, can you get in the backyard?"

"Absolutely! What do ya need?"

"There's a downspout coming off the deck up here. I need you to check out the end of it for me. Check around the immediate area."

"I'm on it."

Devlin goes back to his "sniper hide," looks toward the school, while he waits for the lieutenant to get in position. Yes! *Definitely doable.*

The lieutenant yells up to Devlin. "I'm here, Boss."

Devlin waves and yells back. "I'm going to drop my lucky silver dollar into the downspout. I got it from my Ma. Watch and see where it ends up."

Linda waves. "You got it, Boss."

MacGraft can hear the coin clattering off the sides of the four-story long downspout. The clatter suddenly stops.

"I think it shot out the end of the elbow, Cap. It's hard to tell with all the crabgrass down here."

The lieutenant kneels down and feels the inside of the white aluminum elbow and shines her black mini "Maglite" inside. Then, yells up to Devlin. "Nothing, Cap. Gotta be here somewhere. Let me...oh shit!"

"What's the matter, Lin?"

"I knelt on something in the grass. It's killing my knee. Give me a minute. It's tangled in this crabgrass down here."

MacGraft combs through the thick grass looking for what she knelt on. After a few seconds she yells to her captain, "You gotta see this, Boss."

"What is it?"

"A spent brass casing. Looks like a...nine mill to me."

Devlin yells down. "Don't touch it, Lin. I'll be right down."

MacGraft backs off and waits for her captain to join her.

Devlin takes the cherry picker back down to ground level and finds the open gate in the alley to the yard.

"Outstanding, Linda. You may have just found the game changer we need."

Devlin decides against calling the assigned Detective Division, a decision that will no doubt bring a lot of heat from the West Wing. He instead calls Detective Mike Ryan at Homicide.

"Homicide, Stasurak."

"Hey, Irene. Captain Devlin. Ryan around?"

"Hi, Cap. Sure, hold on."

"Hi, Boss."

"Mike, Devlin. Ya want to get homicide back on the front burner in the Richie Rugnetta job? If ya do, I think my observant lieutenant may have just found a way to do it."

"I'd love to. Where do ya want me?"

"We're in the backyard, Eleven and Federal, west side. Look for the Fire Department's truck."

"I'm on my way, Cap."

"Okay, Mike."

When Detective Ryan arrives, Devlin escorts him back to where Lieutenant MacGraft is standing over the flattened grass area two feet away from the end of the long downspout.

Ryan greets Linda. "Well if it isn't Lieutenant Linda MacGraft. I should have known you'd be the captain's 'observant lieutenant.' How the heck ya doing?"

"Hey, Mike. I'm doing fine. Better now that we got a real CO down here."

"Ain't that the truth. So what ya got?"

Linda points to the matted-down spot in the grass with the shiny brass casing partially exposed lying in the middle. Ryan immediately places a small yellow ruler beside the casing and takes a couple of photos with his privately owned Canon F-1.

Ryan asks Linda, "So what makes you folks think this baby is gonna get Homicide to the front of the pack on the Rugnetta job?"

"Better let my boss explain that one, Mike."

Ryan turns to his old partner. "Captain?"

"I'm working on young Richie was assassinated. The assassin used that deck up there..." Mickey points to the roof. "...to do the deed."

"Whoa! That's way out there, Boss. If that's true, sounds like a professional hit job."

"Correct! Not your run-of-the-mill hit man either. I'm going for a sniper-qualified hit man. I'm thinking that little baby there…" Mickey points to the brass casing. "…will seal the deal."

"Haven't had a sniper job in a while. Can I ask ya how you think that casing ended up here? Any pro worth his salt would have policed up his brass before he left. Am I right?"

"That you are, Mike. But this guy didn't realize he had set up on the edge of our perimeter yesterday morning. That was his first mistake. Then I believe he had to bail sooner than planned. When he ejected the casing it hit the wood deck and bounced into the small roof drain, then dropped through the aluminum downspout, ending up right where you see it. Probably hoped to come back later and clean up."

Ryan takes a few more pictures of the downspout, the building and what he can see of the roof deck from ground level.

"I'll need to get some shots of that drain up there, Cap."

"Definitely! You okay with a cherry-picker ride, Mike?"

"Not a problem. You probably don't know this about me, but I started as a fireman. Worked out of the Arch Street firehouse. I transferred over to the PD after two years."

"Didn't know, Mike. You're a real renaissance man, aren't you?"

Ryan chuckles. "Sure, why not?"

Linda, Mickey and Ryan all have a good laugh.

"Mike, I'm gonna leave Linda with you, okay? She may need your help with a little follow-up thing. I got to get back to the district. Got someone coming in at noon."

"Sure! We're good. I'm just gonna bag my evidence and take a few more shots from up on the roof. Then, I'm outta here too."

Linda agrees. "I'm good too, Boss. I'll see you back at the district when I'm done. Oh! Here's your lucky silver dollar. Found it a couple of inches from the casing."

"Thanks, Lin. Don't want to lose that."

"Sometime, I'd love to hear what makes it so lucky, Cap."

Ryan laughs aloud. "Oh, you'll love that yarn, Lin. It's a classic."

Devlin smiles. "One day, Lin. Look. Gotta go. I have someone I want you to meet when you you're done here."

"Okay, Cap."

Devlin calls to the cherry picker crew. "Ten minutes max." He thanks them and walks back down 11th Street to the district.

CHAPTER XXXVIII

Devlin's Office
The Money Shots

"Dirty water does not wash clean."

Italian Proverb

When Mickey gets back to the district, he's met by Nora Brown holding her small yellow notepad.

"Hi, Captain."

"Nora. Anything hot?"

"Ya had seven calls while you were out, three from Deputy Fannille. He sounded annoyed."

Mickey shrugs. "C'est la vie. That's life. Guess his network of spies in the district are alive and well. Who were the other four calls from?"

Nora seems a little befuddled with her captain's devil-may-care attitude about the deputy's calls. The previous captain would always call the deputy right back but not her new CO. She doesn't say a word, just continues to read who the other three callers were.

"Doctor Steinberg. Said he'll be in his office till six-thirty."

"Great! Who else?"

"Jim from the Keller-Williams real estate agency. Wanted to talk to ya about a property he's managing on Eleventh Street. Something about the fire department and a roof deck."

"Figured that might happen. Probably got a call from one of the neighbors when they saw the Fire Board run a cherry picker up to the roof of the property he has under contract."

Nora smiles. "You also had a call from the Archdiocese of Philadelphia. A woman by the name of Rice, Amanda Rice. Said she's an attorney. Refused to leave a message."

"Never heard of her. Who else?"

"Last call was from your wife. Said she'll call back later."

"Okay, Nora. Thanks."

"Did you find anything on the roof across the street, Captain?"

"No! But Lieutenant MacGraft found a little something around the corner that I believe will change the focus of yesterday's shooting."

"Lieutenant Linda found something?"

"Yep!"

"I'm not surprised. She's sharp as a tack. Always goes full throttle."

"I'm lucky to have her on board. That's for sure."

"Yes, Sir."

"She and Lieutenant Rossi will make my job a lot easier."

"Amen to that, Captain."

"Amen!"

Nora smiles. Mick goes straight for his private bathroom and cleans up from his rooftop inspections.

Ten minutes later the buzzer on Mickey's private phone goes off. It's Nora Brown from her desk in the outer office.

"Captain?"

"What's up, Nora?"

"Officer Branch is out here. He says there's a Michelle Cunay at the operations room window. She says you're expecting her."

Mickey looks at his watch. "That I am. Have Branch show her back."

"Okay, Captain. Is she the reporter who likes cops?"

"Honest cops. That's her."

"Okay, then. I'll get Branch to bring her back."

A short time later, Nora Brown gives two quick knocks and pushes open Mickey's door. She's followed by Michelle carrying an oversized manila envelope.

Mickey waves to Nora, "Thanks, Nora. Hold my calls until Ms. Cunay leaves, okay?"

"Even the ones from the Deputy?"

"Especially the ones from the Deputy."

"Yes, Sir."

Nora Brown leaves closing the door behind her. Mickey points to one of two black-leather, wood-legged chairs.

"Sit, Kiddo!"

Michelle settles in and her first comment is, "Ms. Cunay? Aren't we formal? That's a new one."

Mickey, sitting in his lopsided executive swivel chair, smiles. "The less said, blah blah blah. So you did good last night?"

Michelle grins. "Yes, real good."

"Sooo!"

Michelle takes the black and white glossies out of the envelope and hands them to Mickey.

"One, or should I say twenty-four pictures are worth a thousand words."

Mickey takes the photos, dated and numbered in sequence at the bottom-right corner with black marker, and starts perusing them. As he goes through them he starts making comments.

"Omigosh, Bat Woman."

"Whoa! Showing your age there, Mick."

Through a wide grin, Mickey responds. "I have no problem with being twenty-nine, Michelle."

"Okaaay!"

"These are unbelievable. What hypocrites. Rizzo's really is the hot spot down here. Who was working the camera again? Each one of these is better than the last."

"Alan Ebner. He's my new go-to cameraman. He's good with stills and video. He's old school. Seems to be working out."

"Ebner. Ebner. Does he have any family on the job? I knew an Ebner that used to work at the Academy. He was an animal. Good guy to have on your side. May still be up there."

"Not that I know of. At least he never mentioned it to me." Mickey gets to photos 18 and 19, then stops. He looks at them side by side. He glances at them back and forth. Then he smiles.

"See something, Mick?"

"Think so! You got one of those loop thingies with ya? Those magnifying glass things the squints in the lab use to eyeball stuff up close on photos."

"Sounds like you're old school too, Mick. It just so happens..." Michelle reaches in her oversized handbag. "...here ya go. Why? What caught your attention in those two shots?"

"I think..." Mickey takes the loop from Michelle and positions it over two people sitting in a window booth inside Rizzo's Italian Ristorante. He looks throw the loop first with his left eye then his right eye, his shooting eye. One photo, then the other. "Gotcha!"

"Who ya got, Mick?"

"My Third District gink. At least one of them anyway. I'm sure there's more though."

Mickey hands photos 18 and 19 to Michelle along with the loop magnifier.

"Thank God for candlelight dinners. Check out the lovely couple in the window seat in those two shots."

Michelle strategically places the small round device over the couple in the window.

"Okay! I see them. A middle-aged, dark-hair guy in a suit with a younger-looking woman. So who are they?"

"The female is one of my sergeants from the South Street Mini Station. I ran into her up there on a couple of CIB jobs I responded to. The male is Deputy Commissioner Fannille. The married Deputy Fannille. Albeit his second attempt at that sacrament. I heard the sergeant was married to a cop who divorced her when he found out about her squad party activities. My last-out lieutenant gave me a heads up about her seamy relationship with Fannille. Looks like he nailed her act."

"So what's the Deputy's possible infidelity got to do with the matter at hand, i.e. Katherine's little problem with the AG and your Internal Affairs?"

"Nothing! Not a darn thing. It's just that you and Ebner's after- hour's excursion doubled down on success. You got the Mayor and his aide dining with the consigliere for the Mob, then slithering out of Rizzo's back door looking all friendly. That should make those toads back off a notch. Wouldn't you say?"

"That was the plan."

"Plus, I got a bonus."

"Glad I could make your day, El Capitan."

"How'd you know the mayor and Mr. Mob mouthpiece would be having a late-night dinner together last night anyway? Potluck?"

"Yo, Mick. I'm good, not lucky." Michelle smiles. "I used the contact you gave me, Ken Coons, the dinner maître d' at Rizzo's. I reached out to him after we talked. I didn't mention it to you last night because—"

"Because of Alan Ebner. Smart!"

Michelle smiles. "That's me! Turns out Mr. Consigliere made a reservation for the Mayor and two guests early yesterday afternoon. That's why I jumped on the job last night. One was a no-show, so Katherine's friend Angelo took his spot at the table. Must know the Mayor pretty good to just invite himself."

"I'm gonna owe Coons big time. We were classmates at Roman Catholic. He was in my homeroom all four years. Heck of a soccer player. Made all Catholic three times."

"Seems like a nice guy."

"Aces! You guys got the 'Kodak moment' we were hoping for. I caught a kiss-up spy having a candlelight dinner with Fannille. Outstanding! The proverbial two birds with one stone."

"If she is his gink or his honey, or both, I won't be able to touch her. He'll no doubt protect her." Mickey shrugs. "Nothing's forever, right?"

"Right! Sooo who's gonna tell Seamus? I think you should."

"Thanks, kiddo. I'd love to. We'll let him tell Katherine, right?"

"Absolutely."

"You and Ebner did great work. I'm sure you'll find some way to make your little Sneaky-Pete mission work for you."

"Hello! I'm thinking a City Hall favor down the line. Okay Mick, I did my part. That means you owe me, right?"

"I do."

"Then is this the scene where you keep your promise and spill the beans on who you're going after that's so—"

"Connected?"

"Yes, connected. How'd you put it last night? 'Pretty powerful people who don't mess around.' I think I got that about right."

"Close enough, las."

Mickey starts that lip-biting thing he does. A habit he picked up watching his mom worrying about Mick's Da, Lewis, when he was late for supper. The original Officer Devlin was a highly decorated and active Philly cop. Worrying about him coming home safe was a regular happening in the Devlin house. Mickey's wife, Pat, has the same worries.

Mickey decides to "spill the beans'" on what he's been running on. Some of it anyway. With the stipulation that it doesn't leave his office. Besides, Mick may need to tap into Michelle's expert research capabilities in the near future, again. He hints that the game is only half over and he still needs to connect some huge dots. Michelle doesn't respond right away. Prize-winning investigative reporter that she is, she's trying to put what Mickey is telling her in perspective.

"So let me get this straight in my mind. You're running on the belief, a gut feeling, that—"

Mickey smiles. "Let me stop you there. It's not just my gut. That was what got the ball rolling. I've got witnesses, young, old and in between, plus pretty solid evidence, to throw into the mix, Michelle. I told you I'm still putting the pieces together. I'm giving you what I got so far. With the understanding—"

"Ya got my word. It's just…Damn! Well, I've seen you solve jobs with a lot less, Mick. But you really jump off the reservation with tying your favorite Deputy, the South Philly Mob and maybe even the Archdiocese all together in some kind of conspiracy."

"I keep telling you—"

"I know. You're still putting pieces together."

"Figure if I say it enough, you'll believe me, Michelle."

"Maybe! But remember I'm Irish. You know that ticket for the express train you tell everyone you have directly to the Pearly Gates, Mick? Well it may get rescinded if you start messing with the…" Michelle does air quotes. "'…Diocese.' The train may leave sooner than you expect if the wise guys get wind of you."

Mickey laughs and shrugs his broad shoulders. "Guess that about says it all then, kiddo. Does sound different when you say it out loud. I told you, if I'm right on this one, those 'connected' people I mentioned are going down."

"Man! If you're even a quarter right, this city is in for a shocker."

Michelle really only knows bits and pieces of Mickey's theory. It's way too early to share the more sinister component. Michelle's a good kid and one hell of an investigative reporter. Mick will eventually give up the whole nine yards to her. She earned it.

"Michelle, you got to promise me that the genie won't be let out of the lamp. Because if I'm wrong—"

"Not to worry, Mick. I'd never do anything to jackpot you. You gotta know that by now."

"I do, Michelle."

"Good!"

"When it's time, I'll need you and your paper to help carry the ball over the goal line. 'Til then—"

"When you need me, I'll be there."

"Okay, kiddo. Now let's wind up the whole Katherine McBride thing. I'm gonna call Seamus shortly to give him the good news."

"Sounds good. We'll talk later, right?"

"Soon! Real soon. Promise. I expect this whole thing will be over in the next twelve hours."

Michelle gives Mickey the envelope with the set of black and white glossies to show Seamus and gets up to leave.

"Don't go yet, Madam Chief Editor. I told you I want you to meet somebody." Mickey buzzes Nora Brown.

"Yes, Captain."

"Nora, is Lieutenant MacGraft back yet?"

"Yes, Captain. She's standing in the hall."

"Have her come into my office."

"I'll send her right in, Captain."

"Thank you."

Seconds later Linda knocks on Mickey's office door.

"Come on in, Linda."

Mickey makes the introductions as promised to both Linda and Michelle.

"Pleasure to meet you, Michelle."

"Right back at ya, Linda. Your captain has told me a lot about you. He thinks we may have a lot in common. I'd very much like to have a sit-down with you some time. How about lunch one day, my treat? Let's see if your captain is correct."

"From what I've seen so far, he's seldom wrong. So sure, a sit- down will work for me too. Sometime when I'm off the clock. As far as lunch goes…we'll go Dutch."

Michelle smiles. *She is sharp.* "Dutch it is then, Lieutenant. Here's my card. Call me with a time that works for you."

Linda glances at the card. "Oh! You're *that* Michelle?"

"In the flesh."

"I'm a big fan. I make it a point to read all your articles. Especially, those on the PPD. All home runs."

"Well, thank you, Lieutenant."

"So you'll give me a call? Sooner rather than later."

"Will do!"

"Great."

"Okay, Mick, I'm outta here. Be safe."

"Always, Michelle."

Lieutenant MacGraft also takes her leave.

Mickey, still holding the black and white photos, separates photos 18 and 19. He'll need them when he's ultimately called to the West Wing to explain his actions. A meeting Mickey is looking forward to.

After Michelle and Linda leave, Nora Brown taps on Mickey's door.

"Captain, this envelope was sitting in my inbox. Must have been left there yesterday after I had to leave to meet my daughter. The sticky reads 'Officer Brady.'"

"Great! Better late than never, right? Thanks, Nora."

Mickey takes the sealed messenger envelope, sits down at his desk and rips off the end with the shipping tape. He pulls out the CSU property receipt and reads it to himself. Then he takes a quick look at the crime-scene sketch Lieutenant Scott's team did. *As suspected, no cell phone.* He smiles. *We already know where that baby is, don't we, 'Little John' Pollina? Thanks to the ring tone of a string band Little John will spend time in the big house?*

CHAPTER XXXIX

3ᴿᴰ District CO's Office

"By asking for the impossible we obtain the possible."
Italian Proverb

Armed with a fresh theory on manner of death, MOD, Mickey contacts Doc Steinberg on his cell.

"Come on, Doc. Pick up."

"Steinberg."

"Hi, Doc. Mickey."

"Mick, I was just going to call you. What's up?"

"With good news I hope. Go ahead. You first, Doc."

"Two things. First, I took a look at Richie's neck wound. It's an obvious left to right trajectory with a downward track. Didn't Richie supposedly shoot himself with a twenty-two?"

"As far as I'm concerned the jury is still out on that one. But Richie was brandishing a small automatic at the scene. The Stakeout cop who found Richie and the Monsignor did find a twenty-two Berretta in the room with them. According to Richie, the Berretta belonged to O'Hagorty. FIU is test-firing the weapon."

"For the sake of argument, let's say he did pop himself."

"Okay. Let's."

"Where's the exit wound? I realize twenty-twos like to bounce around a lot inside the body. But…I guess that little bugger could be anywhere."

"If method of death was indeed via a twenty-two, Doc, I'm not so sure it was. I'd like an independent opinion on that one. Like you said, 'those little buggers like to bounce around'—"

"I'll need to do an x-ray and an autopsy to be positive. I need more time. The Monsignor has been getting most of my attention lately. So—"

"I'm trying to get it for you. Time, that is."

"Fair enough. My pre-autopsy observations on the Monsignor indicate bruising to both shoulders and bicep areas."

"Ya think the EMTs or the doctors in the ER might have done the damage moving him around? Seniors can bruise easily. Or—"

"In my professional opinion, I'd say the Monsignor was conscious and being held down. The old guy put up a fight, judging from the bruises on his hands. That's my opinion. Anyway I decided to do a series of x-rays on his upper torso. Plus—"

"You found fractures, right?"

"To his right clavicle, the anterior portion of his shoulder, and to his scapula, the back part of his shoulder girdle. I'm also of the opinion the man was forcibly restrained by someone with very large hands. Say a size twelve or larger glove. My theory is he regained consciousness either in the rescue truck or at the ER."

"Ya know one Stakeout cop did tell me the Monsignor was conscious when he found him, but then went out. Oh, and Mike Ryan found a few pairs of used extra-large rubber gloves in Medic Twenty-seven."

"I know. He sent me a copy of his property receipt."

"So let's add the classroom to your list of restraint zones, Doc."

"Sure, why not. The damage may have happened while he was trying to get up but somebody wasn't having it. He also had contusions across the back of his legs. Which led me to think all the activity took place while he was lying down. Like on a stiff gurney or table."

"You still insist those EMT friends of yours are righteous folks, Doc? How about this…if I remember right, their report stated they 'unsuccessfully tried to revive the Monsignor.' That sound right?"

"It does."

"To me, that means CPR or a little paddle action. Ya know, a defibrillator."

Doc Steinberg chuckles. "Paddle action. You're nuts. But yes, that sounds the most likely action."

Mickey doesn't skip a beat. "So if they did perform—"

"My turn. If they did CPR, and because of the Monsignor's age, there would be bruising or worse to his chest and possibly his xiphoid appendix. But—"

"But your x-rays in that area were negative for fractures. Correct?"

"Correct! Doctor Devlin. What else ya got?"

"Well! Expanding on your theory of forced restraint, what if the reason was to inject him with something…a toxin, poison or even OD him with prescription meds? Say oxycodone."

Doc Steinberg doesn't respond. He lets Mickey continue.

"What about that small puncture in the web of his right foot? How do you feel about that, Doc? Is that something that can raise the bar away from natural causes to suspicious? Is that a possibility?"

Mickey can hear the Doc flipping through papers.

"Doc, still with me?"

"I'm here, Mick. I'm kinda sold that something suspicious went on. Enough anyway to schedule the Monsignor for an autopsy today."

"Outstanding! How about I get Mike Ryan to observe? He's monitoring the Rugnetta job. As far as I know, I haven't checked the district's incident control log yet, but the O'Hagorty job is probably being classified as a hospital case, no report to follow. Destined to be lost among the other eighty-five thousand plus hospital cases the PPD handles each year."

"Ryan sounds like a good idea, Mick. I'll need to notify the Cardinal and the family I'm keeping the Monsignor on ice. After I'm finished, I'm going to send specimens off to the toxicology lab. This job is turning into a hornets' nest, Mick. Now it's your turn. Why were you calling me?"

"It's about the Richie Rugnetta's part of this hornets' nest. I just came from a little rooftop fishing expedition with one of my day- work lieutenants. Are you ready for this?"

Doc Steinberg is never surprised at the lengths Mickey will go to get to the truth. *Rooftops!* "After the Monsignor prelims, I'm ready for anything. Fire away, Mick."

"I think Richie was whacked."

"What?"

"I'm not talking about some young Turk hired by the Mob. I'm thinking more battle-hardened sniper-type assassin. Probably Marine Scout or Army Special Forces–trained kinda sniper. Have any cases that fit that MO lately, Doc?"

"Last sniper case I had was a woman shot from the South Street overpass. She took one to the chest. Guy shot her through the windshield. The woman died instantly. She flipped her van and caused a two-mile backup on I-Ninety-five for hours. The doer never left the overpass. He claimed to be a Vietnam Vet suffering from PTSD."

"That's right. I remember that job, Doc. Summer of ninety-three."

"That's the one. Then you'll remember that the perp wasn't a vet at all. He was a walk-off from a mental facility in New York State. He never served in the military. He used his father's customized, M-fourteen-AR rifle with a scope, to do the shooting."

"I do, Doc."

"So tell me why, out of the blue, you're going down the sniper road with Richie's shooting. I know you've never bought into suicide. But sniper? That's a big leap. Even for you, Mick. What's your foundation?"

Mickey explains why he rejected the suicide label including Deputy Fannille's interest in the case, his personal recollections of the original incident, interviews from Terrell Soetoro and Richie's fiancée Concetta Bruno, and the surveillance tape from Saint Joe's hospital. He adds the mysterious burglary at Our Lady of Sorrows rectory, the Monsignor's cell phone episode, and the suspect's Mob connections. He wraps up with his recent rooftop adventures leading to the discovery of a lonesome brass casing in the yard of a vacant property a city block away from where Richie was shot. When Mickey finishes, Doc Steinberg asks the obvious questions.

"Who's your prime suspect? What about motive?"

"I'm working on that, Doc. Can you hold on a minute? Ya got my wheels turning." Mickey flips through the notes he jotted down when Lieutenant MacGraft outlined her interview with Concetta Bruno. *Found it.*

"Here it is, Doc. This is what Richie's future wife and mother of his child, Concetta Bruno, told my lieutenant about her dad. Who happens to be the owner and solitary employee of a restaurant, 'Men of Honor,' a known Mob hangout. I quote, 'If he knew we were gonna get married he'd kill Richie. Nobody, especially Richie for some reason, is good enough for his little princess.' Of course that could just be an off-the-cuff remark with no basis in fact. Or—"

"Or Concetta knows her dad. That's why she didn't keep him in the loop about her plans to marry Richie or her pregnancy. But to kill the father of your grandchild—"

"Or have him killed. I have a lieutenant running on family and friends who may fit the bill for means and opportunity material."

"Either way. Offing your grandkid's dad…that's really sick."

"Ya think? Hold on, there's more. Concetta like young Terrell thinks the Mob had something to do with Richie's death. Their reasoning is a little shaky but…oh yeah, here's what I was looking for. Concetta's dad also caters to a crew of his old Marine buddies from his 'Nam' days. Concetta's fallback assassins are those 'crazy friends' of her pop who if they 'found out about her and Richie' would…she believes would off Richie as a favor to her dad. Farfetched, but I added them and her dad to my very short list of possible shooters. Keeping in mind the shot Richie took was right out of the sniper handbook. A classic, one-shot, one-kill scenario."

"As long as we're pulling out all the stops you might as well add Concetta's mom to your list. She lives in the same house as her daughter. Just think of the potential embarrassment for a Catholic Italian mother and—"

"Annnd anything can happen."

"Believe me, Mick, you haven't seen anything until you throw an incensed Italian mom into the mix. Things can really hit the fan, quick. Second only to an angry Jewish mother of course."

"We're already looking at mom. Hold on, there's something else in my notes somewhere. Got it! My lieutenant said when she was in Organized Crime she served a warrant on Concetta's dad's restaurant."

"Men of Honor...Men of Honor...right! I knew that sounded familiar. I did an autopsy on a Mob guy dismembered in an explosion at the place. The guys from Organized Crime used to call it the 'Bomb Bistro.'"

"That's the place. Anyway, my first impression about that name was that it was a Mob phrase. A respect thing for his Mob associates. But now, I'm leaning more toward it's out of respect for Mister Bruno's military buddies. Mr. Francis 'The Gimp' Bruno was a Marine in Vietnam in the Sixties.

According to the lieutenant, he served two tours over there. Got an early ticket back to the world after he took a ding from an AK-forty-seven in the right leg."

"So your prime-prime suspect is now the father of the girl Richie impregnated? You think this Nam vet, what is he, fifty- something, assassinated Richie with a single round through the neck from a roof deck a block away. I guess you can find motive in there somewhere, Mick. Maybe even a movie script."

"Let's stick with the motive part, Doc. You know there is a wise- guy code that states, 'You'll know the person who whacks you.' Bruno definitely knew Richie and supposedly didn't like him."

"Wise-guy codes. Can you believe those shitheads?"

"Just saying, Doc."

"I guess. Sniping was once your specialty, wasn't it, Mick?"

"Among other things. But there's something else, Doc."

"Are you shittin' me?"

"Negative. Now hear me out, Doc. After I returned from where the casing was found...by the way it looked like a nine-mil not a twenty-two. My clerk told me the realtor who's handling the sale of the property we were at called me. So when I returned his call he confirmed that it was a neighbor who called his office about the police being on the roof. On a hunch, I asked him if any neighbors called him about suspicious activity around the same property any time early Monday morning. That's when we closed down Wharton Street because of Richie's escapades at the school."

"How'd your hunch pan out?"

"Same neighbor who called about me being at the property, and a natural gas leak a while back, also left a voice message Monday after seeing a guy in his fifties carrying what she described as 'a black trombone case' checking the side door of the same house around six-thirtyish. According to the neighbor, Mrs. Helena DiCicco, the man walked north on Eleventh then east on Federal."

"Don't tell me. The guy walked with a limp."

"Hello!"

"Holy shit! You can't make this crap up. Mick, I have a question for you."

"Good! I want your feedback."

"You said you and Mike Ryan used a cherry picker to get up on the roof deck, right?"

"Right!"

"How'd the crippled guy get up there at six o'clock in the morning? I doubt the realtor was available to give him a key."

"Good question, Doc."

"How 'bout a good answer?"

"How's this? During my conversation with Jimmy Downs, from Keller-Williams, I discovered he's a retired PPD lieutenant. So I decided to pump him a little more. I asked him if it was his agency's policy to personally escort interested buyers through properties under his control."

"Annnd?"

"It is, unless he knows the person. Then he has no problem giving a key out. I asked him to check to see if the house on Eleventh Street was shown recently. His answer was interesting to say the least. 'Not for a couple of weeks.' With that, I thanked him for his help and apologized for causing a ruckus with the Fire Department. He seemed okay with it."

"Now what?"

"I'm not done. A few minutes later Downs called me back and said he just checked the wall cabinet where he keeps all the keys for properties they're selling or renting and—"

"The keys for your Eleventh Street property are missing."

"Bingo! You'll never guess who has a realtor's license and works for Keller-Williams part time?"

"Francis Gimpy Bruno?"

"No! But close. Neal Olivetto, one of Frank Bruno's Viet Nam buddies and a 'Men of Honor' regular."

"Oh my!"

"Ya got that right, Doc."

"What's next?"

"More interviews for Ryan. But I'm ready to hand this monstrosity off to the DA. It's starting to go viral. First, I need to get hold of Lieutenant MacGraft to find out what she saw in Bruno's place when she served those warrants. I'm guessing he and his service buddies are gun enthusiasts. I want to dig into Olivetto's military record a little deeper. If he or his pal had sniper training, I think I've got enough to at least call Katherine and work with her on a couple of search warrants. But I'm also still waiting to hear what Mike Ryan came up with on that nine-mil casing."

"It does sound like you're going to need some outside help on this, Mick."

"I agree, Doc. I can't think of any better 'outside help' than Katherine McBride. Besides, she's gonna owe me."

"I'm sure she'll pay up too. So are you ready to school me on that 'not fully developed' theory you have on Richie's wound?"

"Oh, right. Like I said, it still needs some polishing. It kinda depends on if your x-ray of Richie's head and neck finds lead. If it comes up negative, then I'll need a little Michelle Cunay research. But just for future reference, let me tell you a short story. Might help down the line. Who knows?"

"Shoot!"

"When I was hot and heavy into the PD's shooting team, I met a guy at a match in South Carolina. Interesting guy. He was an advisor in Nam maybe six years before I made the trip over there. He was one of the first men selected for sniper training. More like an on-the-job sniper course. It was put together by a couple of Marines on the famous 'Hill Fifth-five in South Vietnam. Tough guys, all of them. Crack shots. Invented the whole 'Known Distance Shooting' philosophy."

"Is that where you got your training?"

"It is, after they opened it up to Army and Air Force shooters. Anyway, this guy was a member of the 'Vietnam Hunting Club' a bunch of snipers before the military had a MOS, military occupational specialties, for snipers. Originally, my MOS was Eleven-B-Bravo, rifleman… grunt. Back in the day, ya had to have at least an E-4 pay grade, and be Eleven-Bravo qualified."

"Wow! Sounds like a guy with a sniper's MOS, is someone you'd want on your team when the shit hits the fan."

"Absolutely! Those guys racked up more kills than any battalion of grunts. Anyway, my guy told me he was developing a round that would penetrate a soft matter, like flesh, but would break up when it hit, say, bone. He called it a frangible bullet. Supposedly, the weapons company he was hooked up with was also working on a 'green bullet' since nineteen-seventy-four. A no-lead bullet made from a composite. Anyway he said this frang-round is designed to break apart when it contacts anything harder than itself."

"Wait! So now you're telling me you think Richie was shot from a block away with a 'frangible bullet' that fell apart when it hit a bone in his neck. I don't know. Sounds like science fiction to me. Beam me up, Mick."

"Okay, Scotty. How about you explain the seemingly lack of an exit wound anywhere on Richie. The guy did tell me that with his frangible round, the further away a shooter is from his target, it would lose velocity. Making it more prone to break up on impact."

Doc Steinberg doesn't respond.

"Maybe you ought to invest in the company, Doc. The guy said he's gonna market the round and target it for urban law enforcement, to prevent ricochets and over penetration. No collateral damage. Ya know, with rounds going through the perpetrator and hitting some kid on a bike. Situations like that."

"Does it come in nine-mil, Mick? Isn't that what the casing was you found?"

"Good question. I remember he said the frang and green bullets were being tested with the NATO rounds, 7.62. I think he wants to offer it as an alternative to the troops first. Lead bullets cause a lot of health problems. Some of the guys at our pistol range have heightened lead levels in their blood from working on our weapons and digging brass rounds out of the mound for salvage."

"A green bullet! Sounds like a great idea. So let's say I'm getting close to buying into the frangible-bullet hypothesis. How do I go about—"

"My whole hypothesis, as you call it, gets blown out of the water if you find a twenty-two slug on your x-ray of Richie's neck. But if you find a bunch of little foreign fragments, and when you extract them they're not made of lead, then—"

"If that ends up being the case, we'll need to continue this conversation. Deal?"

"Deal."

"Got this whole movie figured out, don't you?"

Mickey laughs. "Trying! Just need to find the right guy to play you. I'm not certain of the ending just yet. Too many possibilities, Doc."

"What you need is a good director. That's a part I can play, mister. Oh, and I didn't see any signs of GSR anywhere around the entry site."

"Wouldn't be if the shot was fired from a block away, right?"

"True! Without searing, soot, powder burns or an abrasion ring around the entry site, suicide does lose its appeal."

"Come on, Doc. Take the leap. For a whole host of reasons, Richie did not shoot himself."

"Okay, Mick. Richie's job does not fit what we forensic pathologists normally see in ninety-nine percent of suicides."

To help make his own point, Mickey pushes Doc to enumerate what a pathologist would normally see in most suicides. "Like?"

"Well, like if a handgun is used, the typical wound is behind the ear, in the mouth, or in the head. Not the neck. I've never seen a suicide vic who didn't move clothing out of the way first. Even when a rifle or shotgun is used to the chest, the vic more times than not will open his shirt to expose the skin. It's like they just want to be sure. Nutty but ya gotta be a little nutty to off yourself anyway, right?"

"Rodger that."

"Anyway, Richie's designer jogging outfit had a small collar. The top of his collar had a half-moon type hole that lined up with his entry wound. It doesn't appear he even bothered to move his thick gold chain aside either. It was nicked too. We already talked about the absence of searing, or powder burns. Nevertheless, I'm still going to have his wound and hands scanned with an electron microscope x-ray. If trace is there, that analysis will find it."

"I like it, Doc."

"It's a start. But just because we're moving toward disproving suicide, doesn't mean we've proved homicide."

"No. But I've learned that sometimes the absence of evidence is evidence. Sounds like we have some additional homework to do, Doc. You up for it?"

"Is the pope Catholic? Hell yes. I'm up for it. Damn! That's my pager going off. Perfect timing. It's the Cardinal's office. We'll talk later, okay, Mick?"

"Most definitely, Doc."

When Mickey disconnects, he asks Nora Brown to have Lieutenant MacGraft stop by the office.

"She's back on the street. I'll have the corporal give her a Headquarters."

"Thanks, Nora."

Looks like another long day, Devlin. Such is life.

CHAPTER XL

Strategy 101

"It's not enough to aim, you must hit."
Italian Proverb

Mickey's been monitoring South Band with his portable radio. He hears Lieutenant MacGraft tell Police Radio to take her out of service at the Captain's office. *Good! Got another mission for Linda.*

Mick calls Seamus at the DA's office and without going into detail sets up a sit-down with his old Homicide partner.

"I think you're going to like what I'm holding in my hands, brudder. You and your boss."

"I like the sound of that, Mick."

"Think you can tear yourself away from the office around five or so?"

"Sure. Just tell me where."

"I'm feeling like Irish tonight. How about a sit-down at Casey's, Two and South?"

"Perfect! Heard they put together a top-shelf shepherd's pie."

"Doubt it can top Sean O'Leary's shepherd's pie up in the old neighborhood. But I will give it a shot. See ya at five then."

"Okay, Mick."

When Seamus hangs up, he calls his wife and tells her he won't be home for dinner. When he tells her it's because he's meeting Mickey, she's delighted.

"It's about time you two broke bread together again. Good for you. Enjoy, honey."

A few minutes later Linda MacGraft appears at Mickey's door. "You rang, Cap?"

"Hey, Lin. Question. When you served those warrants on Bruno's place, did it include the upstairs apartment and the business?"

"First time only covered the restaurant and the basement. The last time was for the whole property."

"What were the probable cause specifics on the second?"

"We were looking for two handguns. They were part of a load that 'fell'…" Linda does air quotes. "…out of the back of an EPW on I-Ninety-five. The wagon was hauling a hundred and ten weapons turned in under the Mayor's Guns for Sneakers Initiative. They were en route to a foundry to be melted down. Police Radio lit up when the guns started dropping out of the door on the Interstate northbound. Between good citizens and one of the recruit classes from the Academy hustled to the area to do a grid search, all the guns were recovered except a Browning M-nineteen-eleven, forty-five caliber and a two-inch black matte S and W Model-six-thirty-seven, Pro thirty-eight-SP. Radio got an anonymous call that both weapons were stashed in Bruno's property.

"Bruno's place is a well-known 'drop' and 'table' location for wise guys. Street on him is he's a smalltime 'earner' for the Mob. Some of the old heads in Organized Crime told me that years ago, I believe right after he mustered out of the Marines, Bruno offered his services up as a 'Button.' You familiar with that term, Cap?"

"A hired gun for a Capo."

"Exactly. As far as the guys knew at the time, he was never taken up on his offer. The reason I heard was, he was oobatz…crazy even by Mafia standards."

"Interesting! That's the same expression…crazy, that Concetta used talking about her father's Marine buddies."

"Riiight! Anyway we tossed the whole place. We got into every nook and cranny, no guns. At least not the two we were after. My captain always figured Bruno or more likely someone higher up in the organization got a call from some cop on the pad, and told Francis the man was en route. Why ya asking? What's up?"

Mickey skips over Linda's question. "Sounds like you did find other firearms though. How about long guns, rifles?"

"Several. We seized them for investigation and put them on a property receipt. Turned out they were all legal and no record of them used in a shooting. He had some pretty fancy firearms displayed on his living room wall. Nice stuff. Firearms Ident had a field day with them."

"Do you remember what kind of rifles he had?"

"Not offhand. But I kept a copy of the property receipt listing all the stuff we confiscated. It's in my locker. I'll get it if you want."

"That would be great. I'm curious to know if he had any rifles with scopes or that may have been customized for long-distance target shooting, competition stuff."

"Let me go get the receipts. But I know for a fact he had at least half a dozen rifles. I'll be right back."

Five minutes later Linda returns and hands Mick a copy of a three-page PD property receipt, seventy-five dash three, filed after a warrant was served on Mr. Francis "Gimp" Bruno's property.

"My captain got a copy of his Military record before we hit his place. I know he was awarded a Silver Star on one of his tours in Vietnam."

"That's impressive. Did his record indicate any special weapons' training?"

"You mean like sniper training, Boss?"

"Exactly."

"Not that I can remember. Basically, he was an O-Three-Eleven…rifleman."

"A prerequisite for sniper training back in the day. Saves me the trouble of getting his records. It was on my to-do list. How about his Marine buds? They ever take a pinch?"

"No idea. My LT didn't go that deep, Boss. Maybe—"

"How about tapping your sources in Organized Crimes for some names?"

"Absolutely!"

"Good. Like to have a better feel for those guys in case we decide to pay the 'Men of Honor' an unscheduled visit."

Linda nods her compliance. Mick starts to peruse the first page of the property receipt.

"You weren't kidding, Lin? The Gimp has some serious armaments."

"That's what the firearms guys were saying, Cap."

"This is one heck of a list. What is this guy, a dealer?"

"Not a licensed dealer anyway."

Mickey scans the list and reading out loud. Barrett 82-A1 Rifle. Springfield AA9122 Scout semi-auto rifle 308 Winchester. Winchester Mod 70, 30.06 bolt-action rifle with Unertl 8X scope. M40A3 rifle. M-14 and M-1 Garand Rifle, with barley-com aperture sights. This is some list, Lin."

"It is. Wait until you check out the next page."

Mickey flips the page and starts reading from the page labeled "Miscellaneous Items."

M-21 with auto-ranging telescopic sight. M-40, a WWII, M1, Garand Carbine Rifle, M1G1 Manual (M1, M1C, M1D sniper 1947). US Army Ranger Handbook, FM23-10 Sniper School Training Manual, and TC25-8 Training Range Manual.

Mickey turns to the last page. "Two reload presses (Progressive/single stage), one shell holder/powder measuring device (scoops), and a bunch of reload data manuals/scales/dial caliper/case trimmer/reload table."

Mickey puts the three-page property receipt down.

"If Bruno didn't get sniper training, according to some of the stuff on this list, he sure liked reading about it. You said all the weapons were registered all legal like?"

"Yes, Sir. I know that everything listed there was eventually returned to Bruno. He probably even has more by now. That warrant was five years ago, Boss."

Linda hesitates asking Mick why all of a sudden he's so interested in Concetta Bruno's dad. *What the heck.* "Can I ask what's going on, Boss?"

"Oh, sure, Lin. I'm just trying to connect some dots. That casing you found got me thinking."

"About?"

"About adding another name to our tups list. In fact, Doc Steinberg at the ME's suggested adding another one. Mrs. Bruno."

"You think Concetta's father or mother could have been pissed off enough to kill Richie Rugnetta because they found out she was pregnant?"

"Or, like I said to the Doc, had him whacked. You remember what Concetta said about Bruno's crazy Nam buddies. So...anyway, I'd like to find a way to get back in Bruno's entire property. Maybe I'll run what I got by the DA. If she thinks I'm on solid ground, I'm sure I can get a Judge to approve a warrant."

"Ya want to do this legally, right? 'Cause—"

Mickey stops Linda in mid-sentence. "Book legal. Don't want to blow this one because we didn't dot all our Is and cross all our Ts."

"Absolutely!"

"I'm gonna call in some favors. Lin, keep this discussion under your hat. We don't want Bruno getting any more 'the man is coming' phone calls from anyone. The Rugnetta job is supposedly off limits, all right?"

"What Rugnetta job?"

"Exactly!"

Mickey holds back on letting Linda in on the recent discovery of a certain female sergeant...Fannille's spy. He doubts she'd be surprised.

The buzzer on Mickey's private phone buzzes twice.

"What ya got, Nora?"

"A detective Ryan on line two, Captain."

"Thanks! Linda, give me a few minutes."

Linda salutes and leaves, closing Mickey's office door on her way out. Mick pushes the blinking light under line two.

"Hey, Mike. You were next up to call. What's up?"

"I got something for ya, Boss."

"Let's have it."

"I lifted two sets of usable prints from that drain cover on the roof deck." Ryan chuckles. "I got two hits. **You** and a Mister Francis Bruno. Bruno was in the system for a bunch of old numbers stuff and an agg assault job on an off-duty cop by the name of DeMarco."

"Junior or Senior?"

"Repeat!"

"The assault was it...what's the cops DOB?"

"Let's see. Six, six, thirty-nine. Why?"

"Just curious. His kid is the Stakeout cop who found Richie Rugnetta and the Monsignor."

"Ain't that interesting? The assault was dismissed by the way. The complaint was dropped because DeMarco FTAd. He failed to appear every time he was scheduled to testify. He ended up losing time over it, fifteen days."

"Bingo!"

Ryan moves on. "Annnd! I got a thumbprint off the casing from the yard—"

"Please make my day and tell me it's a match for Bruno."

Ryan chuckles. "Double bingo."

"There is a God, Mike. That proves he's on our side. So was it on a nine-mil?"

"A homemade nine-mil. It's obvious somebody is pressing their own reloads, Boss."

"I saw a property receipt for items taken on a warrant served on Bruno's place five years ago. The man was all set up to do just that. He had two reload presses, die sets, shell holders and a reload table."

"Sounds like Mister Bruno is open for business, Boss."

"I think it's getting close to serving our own warrant. You in?"

"I'm in."

"Good!"

"Now why were you gonna call me, Cap? Ya said I was on your call list."

"Doc Steinberg has decided to probe a little deeper into COD and MOD for Richie and the Monsignor. He scheduled an autopsy. I hope you don't mind I suggested that you sit in. It's the next step in having South Detective dropped as the assigned unit."

"Don't mind a little bit, Boss. If that's all ya got, I'm out of here and on my way to see the ME's."

"Keep me in the loop, Mike. Unofficially of course. Oh, and I'm moving toward a nighttime warrant for Bruno's place, top to bottom. If your captain can't handle the overtime, I'll have you detailed in the Third. Your OT will be on me."

"You can do that?"

"I've done it with uniforms into Homicide. No reason I can't go the other way. Don't worry. Your captain and I will work it out."

"I'm not worried a bit. Just don't want to see you get jammed up, is all."

"Appreciate it, Mike. Not a problem."

"Sounds like a doable plan then. Talk to ya later, Boss."

As soon as Mickey hangs up he asks Lieutenant MacGraft back in his office.

"Come in. Close the door, Lin. Something else's is starting to jell. Sit! Listen to this."

Mickey outlines his discussions with Doc Steinberg and Mike Ryan.

"Man! What a turnaround. Yesterday, South Detectives was handling a suicide. Or so they wanted everyone to believe. All we were involved with was writing up the initial incident report, a hospital case on the Monsignor. Now everything is upside down. All based on a couple of hunches."

"Don't forget the initial job, Lin."

"Oops! Sorry, Boss."

"Lin, remember what I told you. 'Mortui vivos docent.'"

"Let the dead teach the living."

"We just need to listen. I want you to check something out for me. On my way out of the classroom earlier, I saw what looked like a white spitball stuck to the crucifix above the door. It was just below Christ's feet. I didn't see any other, what I'm calling spitballs, around. Don't know why it caught my eye but it did. So—"

Half kidding, Linda spouts off, "Maybe it's a sign, Boss. I'll check it out. Be back in a wink."

Fifteen minutes later Linda returns with a small plastic baggy in her hand. "We were both right, Cap. It was a spitball of sorts. But it wasn't stuck to the crucifix. It was stuffed into it. It is a sign, right from the man himself."

Linda holds up her baggy. "Well, here's your unraveled spitball."

She hands the sealed baggy to Mickey. "When I got that out of the small hole, I unraveled it. What do you think? Yes I used gloves."

What he's looking at doesn't look like a spitball at all. Mickey flips the baggy back and forth. Then answers the animated lieutenant.

"It's the top half of an incident report form. What are the chances some kid would have one of those in his pocket. Not to mention launch a spitball with it."

He answers his own question. "Zero."

Mickey now asks the million-dollar question. He's hoping for a bombshell of an answer. "When you removed the wad of paper could you see if anything else was in the hole?"

Through a huge smile Linda answers, "A small lead cartridge."

Mickey closes his eyes and runs both hands through his blondish- gray hair. "The slug from the Richie's...O'Hagorty's weapon."

Before Mickey can follow up with the normal "what did you do next" questions, Linda lets her new boss know she didn't attempt to retrieve the round and that the room is still secured.

"I got a uniform cop sitting on it. I figured you want to keep the wraps on this thing. Personally, I'd call in Mike Ryan again. But—"

"Under normal circumstances you'd be right, Lin. But since Homicide was never called to the scene—"

"CSU was. You don't want to jam up Lieutenant Scott's techs. So you want me to reach out and give him another shot at processing the scene? A mulligan, right?"

"Exactly! But if you're worried about fallout from the West Wing, and you'd rather I do it, it's your call to make."

"No way, Boss."

"Good! Lin."

Linda without hesitation takes out her cell phone and pushes in the number of CSU. Mickey listens attentively to Linda's conversation with Jesse Scott, the CO of the Crime Scene Unit. *This lady is head and shoulders above the competition. I'm listening to a real pro.*

Linda presses the end key on her phone.

"The lieutenant and one of his guys are en route. He wanted me to thank you for a second bite of the apple."

"Jesse is good people."

"I'm gonna walk over and let my guy know the CSU team is on the way. I left orders not to let anybody in the classroom. With Officer James there's only black and white. He'll follow my order to a tee."

"Sounds like a good man. Go! Lin, ya did good. Oh, and I've got a dinner meeting with Seamus at Casey's at five. So, I'll catch up to you about the Bruno warrant. You've been in the Bruno property before, so you already know the lay of the land. I'm going to get Lieutenant Rossi involved too."

"Sounds good. Is there anything else I can do in the meantime to move things along?"

"Just keep your eye on the goal, getting to the truth."

"Always!"

Linda gets up to leave but stops short of the door.

"Oh, Cap."

"Yeah, Lin."

"I know you're a short timer down here but for what it's worth you've already done more to make this place the real deal than the last guy did in years. It's fun being a cop again. Real police work is fun, ain't it?"

"Absolutely!"

Linda heads next door to Our Lady of Sorrows School to meet the CSU lieutenant.

CHAPTER XLI

2ⁿᵈ & South Street
Casey's Irish Pub

"A gift with a kind countenance is a double present."
Italian Proverb

Mickey quickly gets back to the task at hand. At four o'clock Nora Brown knocks on Mick's half-opened door to let him know she's going.

"Captain Devlin, it's quitting time for me. Is everything all right? Ya been kinda quiet in here. Is there anything you want me to do before I go?"

"No, I'm fine. Just putting the finishing touches on a couple of things. I can't think of anything for now. Go check up on your daughter. I'll see you in the morning. Be safe!"

"You too, Captain. See ya then. You be safe too."

"That's the plan, Nora."

Neither Mickey nor Nora Brown know what will have happened by the next time they talk again. Nora will read about it over breakfast with her daughter. In disbelief, she'll drive to work in a semi-stupor, arriving an hour early. No one at the Fightin' 3rd will take the news worse than Nora Brown.

Mickey calls his wife, Pat, to let her know he'll be working late again and that he's having dinner with Seamus. He drives to 2nd and South and arrives at Casey's Pub five minutes after Seamus.

"Waiting long, brudder?"

"Just got here."

The waitress seats them at a small round table for two, with two, high, barstool-style seats, overlooking the dinner crowd volleying for parking spots along South Street.

"Drinks, guys?"

Mickey responds first, "Iced tea for me."

"Make it two. I think we already know what we want."

"Great! What can I get for you?"

"Shepherd's pies all around."

"That was easy. I'll put your order right in and bring your drinks. Thanks, guys."

"So Mick, tell me all about the good news you got for me and Katherine. Anything to do with that envelope you brought with ya?"

Mickey decides to string his old partner along a little before he shares Michelle's "Money shots."

"I'm starving. Things are really starting to pop in the district. In fact, I want to run something by you. But let's eat first. What do ya say?"

"I say stop breakin' them for me. What's in those envelopes? We can eat anytime, brudder."

Mickey smiles. "Okay. Man, you're getting all fluppy duppy in your old age, Grandpop." Mick hands Seamus one of the envelopes holding twenty-two of twenty-four of Michelle's photos. He holds off on giving him numbers 18 and 19, showing his district's spy and Fannille having dinner. "Here, knock yourself out, Seam."

Seamus slides the black and white photographs out of the legal- size manila envelope and starts eyeballing them up and down, side to side. His smile keeps getting wider with every new photo.

The eight-by-ten glossies showed the mayor, his aide and Angelo Lombardo, the consigliere to Vince "Gabagool" Cibotti, having dinner together. They also showed Angelo exiting Rizzo's rear door and walking the mayor and his aide to a waiting black-on- black Lincoln Town Car. In the last photo in that series, Angelo can be seen handing the city's top executive a letter-sized white envelope, contents unknown. Not that it matters. Image and impressions are the name of the game in Philly politics.

"Man! How good are these? You say Michelle took these?"

The waitress arrives with two unsweetened ice teas.

"Your pies will be right out."

Seamus responds, "Sounds good."

Mickey continues. "Actually, Michelle set up the surveillance for last night and brought her new camera guy to take the shots. Before you go off half-cocked. The guy, Al Ebner, was working blind. He thinks he was out in front of Rizzo's working on a future Mob-related story for Michelle. When the job was over, she took the roll of film and ran it through the processor herself. Sent the kid home in fact with a pat on the back and an, 'I'll see you tomorrow' line.' Not my name, not your name, and not Katherine's name was ever mentioned."

"Thanks, partner, I owe ya."

Needless to say, Seamus' boss, Katherine McBride, will be surprised and elated with what her friends did for her. Michelle's late-night stakeout will accomplish what it was intended to do, get the AG and IAB to back off, giving her the time needed to resolve whatever is going on with Angelo.

Seamus hasn't stopped smiling since he put the photos back in the envelope. "Now it's your turn. You said on the phone that you're looking for a little help from me. What's up? Is it the Rugnetta job? My spies back in Homicide said Fannille's on the warpath 'cause you're going off the reservation again and refuse to take his calls. I know how he hates that stuff."

"News travels fast in the PD, don't it. The guy's got ginks everywhere." Mickey hands Seamus a second envelope with two missing pictures, 18 and 19. "I held these back on you, partner."

"Must be eighteen and nineteen. I noticed they were missing. Figured either they were doubles or—"

Mickey laughs. "You may be old, but ya still have your powers of observation, Grandpop."

"Not Grandpop, Mick. I'm all Irish with my grandkids...**Granda**. They call me Granda. You're awful cocky yourself for someone who's looking for a favor from this old man."

"Ya got me there, Granda. So here's what I'm thinking…"

Mickey fills Seamus in on everything that's been happening over the day and a half with the Richie Rugnetta and Monsignor O'Hagorty jobs. Most surprising to Mickey's old Homicide buddy is the covert role of the Archdiocese.

"Look, my intention is to hit Bruno's place with a no-knock, nighttime warrant. I want to do it tomorrow morning."

Seamus doesn't answer initially.

Mickey continues, "Mike Ryan is sitting in on Doc Steinberg's autopsy of Richie Rugnetta as we speak. CSU guys are at Our Lady of Sorrows School to collect that missing lead slug. Like I said, I believe it's the round that Richie popped off, probably a reflex after he took one in his neck. I believe that round will match the casing found at the scene."

"What's that gut of yours tell you about the whole spitball thing, Mick?"

"It's telling me that any prints found on it won't be from a fourth grader. So what do you think? Can you run interference with Ryan on my warrant? Can you do that for me, brudder?"

After a few seconds of thought, Seamus' first reaction is one of concern. "Holy shit, Mick. Do you realize all the different entities you're getting involved with? Ya got the Mob, the Catholic Church, not to mention your chain of command. No wonder Fannille is jumping mad."

"Yeah, well. It is what it is. I'm not the one who started the 'cover-up' ball rolling down conspiracy hill. But I can be the one who stops these dirtballs from getting away with murder. More specifically, *murders*. Richie and even the Monsignor with all his flaws deserved their day in court. Wouldn't you agree?"

Seamus shrugs and shakes his head in agreement. "So when can Mike be at the office?"

Mickey with a big grin says, "I'll set it up."

The waitress arrives and sets huge shepherd's pies in front of Mickey and Seamus.

"Enjoy!"

The two seasoned sleuths end their dinner over a pot of Bewley's Irish tea. Seamus takes the opportunity to inform his closest friend he has decided to, finally, fully retire. After twenty years with the PPD and another "good run" with Katherine McBride at the DA's office, now he hopes to spend more "quality time" with family, especially his wife and grandkids.

Fate will intervene and Seamus will have to postpone his retirement plans. After a couple of years in remission, his prostate cancer returns. He decides to remain on the job for the medical benefits as he faces six months of chemotherapy. Everyone prays to Saint Jude and Saint Anthony for his full and speedy recovery.

CHAPTER XLII

Devlin's Office

"A mad parish a mad priest."

Italian Proverb

Even Mickey's taken aback that what started early Monday morning, as a "routine" barricaded situation, could end the way he believes it will a day and a half later. Namely, the shattering of hopes and dreams, the shocking end of promising careers, a Catholic Church cover-up scandal and the devastating loss of lives.

What some initially wanted to portray as an unfortunate suicide of a young delusional gun-toting hostage taker, intent on forcing a beloved Monsignor to confess his fictitious past transgressions, did not pass the sniff test for Mickey Devlin. Then when Monsignor O'Hagorty, who suffered a minor head injury, suddenly suffered a massive heart attack while being transported by a Fire Department EMT crew, Mickey's famous "gut feelings" started to emerge.

Back in his office Mickey looks at his watch, and wonders what his Da would think about the kind of cop he's become. That question has crossed Mick's mind more and more in the past few years. He chalks it up to being on the tail end of his law enforcement career and the whole "mortality" check cops go through when they've reached the half-century mark. A time that was stolen from his father by an assassin's bullet. An assassin hired by the Mob to prevent Officer Lewis Devlin's testimony in Federal Court. Mick hasn't lost sight of the possibility that the remnants of the same Mob that assassinated his Da may very well be behind the Richie Rugnetta and Monsignor O'Hagorty deaths. *The more things change, the more they remain the same. C'est la vie.*

Mickey gets a call from Doc Steinberg. The Doc explains how with "curious trepidation," Cardinal Dominic Vuotto of Philadelphia's Archdiocese was persuaded to use his considerable influence to have the Monsignor's toxicology exam at the Maryland lab moved to the top of the list, which was no small feat. Knowing how Mickey hates it when politicians and the like try to throw their weight around and try to influence outcomes, he summarizes his discussion with the Cardinal.

"I told Cardinal Vuotto that I appreciated him intervening on my behalf. A certified toxicology report routinely takes up to eight months. It tests for a wide range of poisons, prescribed and illicit drugs, and various toxins." Amazingly, Doc Steinberg had his results hand carried to his office within five hours.

"The Cardinal assured me he only wants to help. Then he asked to be discreet with the results. To quote the Cardinal, 'The Diocese cannot afford, and I mean that on many levels, another scandal. It's my job to make sure that doesn't happen, at all costs.'

"You know me, Mick. I didn't go for his tone. I felt he was trying to intimidate me. So I had to set his Excellency straight. It must be from hanging around with you too much. I got my Jewish up. So I told him straight out, 'Cardinal, I'm all about getting to the truth. I get there by using my professional skills, instincts and by following the evidence. The Monsignor's case is no different.'"

"Good for you, Doc."

"I think he got my drift. He told me that there was 'no need to get irritated.' That he's just 'trying to protect the Church.' Give me a break, please."

"I know you jumped on that."

"Hello! I told the Cardinal, 'I'm just trying to help catch a murderer.' I quoted my translation of Exodus twenty:thirteen, 'You shall not murder.' He started to mumble something like, 'All I'm trying to say—' but I cut him off."

"I'm sorry I missed all that, Doc. Sounds like what legends are made of. Go on. What did you tell the good Cardinal?"

"I said, 'Believe me, **Cardinal**...' I accentuated his title. '...I know what you're trying to say. Now if you don't mind I have to get back to work. I'm on a very tight schedule. I do appreciate your help. Shalom.' Then I hung up on him."

"Guess you won't be converting to my side anytime soon, hey Doc?"

"Guess not, Father Devlin. Look! That's enough fun for one day. I really do got to get back to work. I'll call ya, Mick."

"Okay, Doc. You made my day."

"Glad to hear it, Mick."

Doc Steinberg hangs up and continues perusing the tox results. His autopsy along with the toxicology certified report revealed that Monsignor O'Hagorty did, in fact, suffer a massive heart attack. However, it was not due to "natural causes" related to his age or any other medical condition.

In point of fact, the reports provided irrefutable evidence that the Monsignor, a Type 1 diabetic since adolescence, was injected with a "lethal dose of insulin." Confirmation received shows one hundred times his prescribed amount of insulin was in his system causing a massive heart attack. There was credible evidence that because of the dosage administered, Monsignor O'Hagorty would have lost consciousness and died quickly.

Just as the Doc predicted, the site of the injection was between the 1st and 2nd metatarsal, of the Monsignor's right foot. He noted the "inflamed" area with the remnants of dried blood when he did his initial "inventory search" of the Monsignor's remains. Of even more importance was the tip of a syringe he found in the wound during the autopsy. The tip matched the broken syringe Mike Ryan found in Medic 27. The Doc determined that the syringe broke off during a struggle, which indicated the contents of the syringe were forcefully injected into the Monsignor. The sterile swabs that Detective Ryan found also had traces of the Monsignor's blood and a unique brand of insulin not prescribed to him.

Working feverously, the ME's Office simultaneously worked on the remains of Richie Rugnetta. First on the agenda was Mickey's request for x-rays to be taken of Richie's head, neck and shoulder area. The images and later the autopsy confirmed Mickey's theory that, A, the round that entered Richie's neck on the left side, then severed his spinal cord, was not a .22 caliber; B, it was not comprised of lead; and C, the trajectory was indeed left to right but at an angle inconsistent with Detective Johnson's assertion of a self-inflicted wound. Nor could the wound be initiated by a right- handed shooter even if that right-handed shooter used his left hand. In fact, only his right hand tested positive for GSR.

Doc Steinberg was able to identify and retrieve over thirty fragments of varying sizes and shapes all comprised of an unknown composite. However, when the pieces were reverse- engineered they took on the consistency and volume near to that of a lead-based 9-millimeter round. The autopsy examination also established that Richie Rugnetta was drug free.

At Mickey's urging, Doc Steinberg took blood and requested a DNA comparison. The results were ninety-nine point ninety-nine that Richie and the Monsignor were blood relatives.

The next call Mickey received was from Katherine McBride, who thanked him for "having her back." She didn't elaborate and Mickey didn't expect her to. Then Katherine informed him that her "techies" were able to get into the Monsignor's cell phone memory card. They verified that on the morning of February 3rd, his cell, the one used by Richard Rugnetta and later recovered in the large planter at 10th and Reed, received calls from Mickey and two calls from a cell listed to one Francis Bruno. The times of those calls coinciding with those Richie received while at Our Lady of Sorrows Catholic School. Thus answering the question of who called Richie after he took the Monsignor hostage. Almost certainly addresses why Richie appeared so spooked when he received Bruno's calls. What was discussed is still unknown.

Katherine also told Mickey that she issued a warrant for the phone records of Cardinal Dominic Fazio Vuotto's private suite on City Line Avenue. Those records revealed that he made a call, also on the morning of February 3rd, lasting thirteen minutes to a city- issued cell phone assigned to EMT Nick Ligambi, Medic 27. It's noted that he also made three calls to another city-issued cell phone issued to the Police Department's Deputy Commissioner Antonio Fannille on February 3rd, and two more on February 4th. One additional call was made on the 5th at one AM, to a landline located inside the "Men of Honor" restaurant at 7th and Sears. The duration of that call was ten seconds.

CHAPTER XLIII

Police Headquarters
Homicide Unit

"A hundred years cannot repair a moment's loss of honor."
Italian Proverb

Fire Department EMTs Seth Mellone, Joann Verna-Deloria and Nicolas Ligambi were interrogated within hours of Monsignor O'Hagorty's toxicology results and the DA's cell phone inquiry. Their interrogations were handled by Homicide Detective Ryan and Detective Stasurak, and were videotaped in conjunction with the DA's office.

Mellone, through his union attorney, volunteered to be questioned in contrast to EMTs Deloria and Ligambi. Both, following advice from counsel, refused to cooperate with the joint investigation. An investigation labeled a "witch hunt" by their attorney.

EMT Mellone was questioned by Detective Ryan pertaining to inaccuracies in the "action taken" section of his submitted handwritten report concerning the transportation of Monsignor O'Hagorty to Saint Joseph Hospital on Monday, February 3rd. Mellone was given a facsimile of his report; he read it and then handed it back to Ryan.

"Yes, I wrote the original report. I did so based on information given to me by my partner that day, EMT Ligambi. With only a year on the street, I'm ashamed to admit it, but I was intimidated by Ligambi. The guy's seen it all during his twenty-three years with the Department. I realize that's no excuse for what I did but…but I'm ready to make things right. That's why I volunteered to talk with you."

Mellone told Stasurak and Ryan that he heard Nick Ligambi struggling with the Monsignor in the rear of Medic 27 en route to the hospital. "At first, I thought the Monsignor was delirious and Nick was trying to restrain him so he wouldn't hurt himself."

"So you were the assigned driver not Ligambi?"

"Correct."

"Interesting! Has that happened before? Someone you're transporting starts to struggle, or tries to stand up?"

"During my time on the job, it's happened a handful of times. Somebody will wake up and not remember they're shot or cut and have no idea where they are. So yeah, it happens."

"When it does occur, is it required to mention that in the submitted report?"

"Yes. For obvious reasons. Liability stuff. You know."

"Go on."

"When the struggle continued I thought maybe my partner needed my assistance. I slowed down and started to pull over. Ligambi yelled, 'What the fuck are you doing? We got to get this guy to the hospital. Get going.' So that's what I did."

"What happened next?"

"The Monsignor started yelling, 'God help me. God help me.' Then I heard Nick hitting the Monsignor and say, 'Not today, Father.' But I also heard what sounded like the Monsignor hitting Nick. So… like I said, I figured the Monsignor was…havin' a fit or something."

When asked why he didn't pull over and stop the truck at that point, Mellone thought about the question a few seconds, then responded, "I should have. Maybe if I did, the Monsignor would still be alive."

"By your answer, I take it you believe Nicolas Ligambi had something to do with Monsignor O'Hagorty's death."

"In hindsight, yes. When I pulled up in front of Saint Joe's ER and swung open the back doors, I saw Nick holding one of the Monsignor's black socks. His left sock and shoe were still on. I noticed blood around the Monsignor's right toe. His big toe. Then I saw Nick throw a used broken syringe in the hazmat wall dispenser. That's when I really started to think Nick did something. Something that was intended to hurt not help the Monsignor."

Mellone tells his attorney to give the detective the brown paper bag he's been holding. Detective Ryan looks inside.

"Nick told me to grab the Monsignor's sock and other shoe and bring them. I stuck them in my bag. I figured somebody in the ER, a doctor or a nurse, would see the blood on his toe and red flags would go up. But they didn't. I told Nick that my pregnant wife was taken to Rolling Hill Hospital and I had to leave. I had already called Headquarters to send a replacement. I took that stuff…" Mellone points to the paper bag. "…with me when I left. For the record, my wife isn't pregnant. I heard the ME did question the blood spot. Thank God."

"Whose decision was it to take the Monsignor to Saint Joe's? There are several hospitals a lot closer to Our Lady of Sorrows School, where you picked him up."

Mellone shrugs. "I'm guessing the Cardinal. I only base that on overhearing Nick talking to someone on his cell about needing time while we were getting the Monsignor ready to transport. He kept calling whoever was on the other end, 'Your Excellency.' Shortly after we arrived at the hospital, I saw Cardinal Vuotto in the hall. I heard Nick say to him, 'I took care of it, Your Excellency.' So, my guess is…it was the Cardinal who Nick had been talking to at the school and who made the call where to take the Monsignor.

"Again, in hindsight, I guess…Nick needed more time to do whatever he did. The further away the hospital, the more time he had. But I'm just guessing."

CHAPTER XLIV

7th and Sears Streets
Men Of Honor

"The morning hours are the most precious of the day."
Italian Proverb

Two hectic days after Richie Rugnetta's murder, a search warrant for Mr. Francis "Gimp" Bruno's residence and the attached "Men of Honor" restaurant were approved. Based on prior history, Mickey arranged to have a team "sit on the target property" and watch Bruno's white Ford F-100 with a PA tag of "OOBATZ-1" (Italian slang for crazy). He also requested to have L and I and Philly FD on standby. Mickey had Detective Mike Ryan work with the DA's office for a "nighttime" warrant. Submitted with the affidavit were copies of radio tapes from the 3rd of February that clearly identifies two gunshots, one more audible than the other. Judge Joe Walters, a retired PPD Captain, and Academy classmate of Mickey, enthusiastically approved the requested warrant adding a "no knock" provision.

Since the property is in close proximity to the District, Mickey used his Headquarters' basement gym as the initial staging area and pre-raid instruction briefing location. The briefing also included the updated L and I blueprints for Bruno's double-lot, corner property.

The plan was to serve the warrants at two AM. The team included uniform officers and supervisors from Stakeout, a supervisor from Homicide, Detective Mike Ryan, along with his partner Detective Irene Stasurak. Also present from the 3rd District were lieutenants Tony Rossi and Linda MacGraft, plus the two last-out wagon crews to cover escape routes and transportation of potential prisoners. Because of Fannille's deep-seated spy network covert methods were employed.

Mickey was the overall scene commander and was to monitor the two-stage operation from a strategic street-level location. To quash the possibility Bruno has access to a police scanner, Mickey arranged initially to use his cell phone to liaison with Police Radio. A method he's used in the past with great success. Once Stakeout made entry, he would switch over and continue communication with Radio via his handheld radio. Each team member carried a 150 radio, with extra battery, giving them long term person-to-person communications without transmitting via the Radio room. Supervisors carried 150s and handheld radios.

At one-thirty AM, residences in close proximity to the target property were quietly evacuated and a perimeter established. At two AM, under a moonless sky, Mickey had L and I shut off the electric to the property. Thirty seconds later Stakeout made simultaneous forced entries into the Men of Honor restaurant and the side door leading to the second-floor apartment of Frank Bruno. Lieutenant MacGraft, a heavily armed Stakeout team and a supervisor entered the first-floor eatery. They were able to secure the entire restaurant and kitchen area with no resistance. Within ten minutes the lieutenant reported over her 150 that portion of the property secured.

"Team one to CO-Three. First floor secure. No apprehensions or injuries. Moving to secondary objective."

"CO-Three, receive."

From his command post Mickey turns to Mike Ryan. "One down. Two to go."

The second team's search of the second-floor apartment was also uneventful, starting with the two small rear bedrooms and strategically securing the remaining two bedrooms, galley kitchen and large bathroom, moving toward the front living area. With each subsequent room searched and secured, Lieutenant Rossi informed Mickey.

"Team-Two to CO-Three. Second floor secured. No injuries…no… apprehensions. No access to roof identified."

"CO-Three, receive. Post a detail…return to my location."

"Team-Two okay. En route."

Detective Ryan overhears Lieutenant Rossi's last transmission. "You ready for me and Irene to start processing the apartment, Boss?"

"Not yet, Mike. Let's wait till the whole property is secure. Linda still needs to secure the basement. I'm not comfortable with sending anyone else in harm's way. I have this thing, about basements, especially this one. When she's finished I'll cut you and Irene loose, okay, buddy?"

Mike Ryan is one of the ever-growing numbers of cops who believes that Mickey possesses an extra gene when it comes to gut feelings.

"I'm with ya, Boss. Security first, absolutely!"

Mickey's "thing about basements" goes back to the June '94 fire of a South Philly landmark, Palumbo's Café-Restaurant at 9th and Catharine Street. The one hundred three-year-old banquet hall was a short distance from where Bruno's property is located. As fate may have it that day, Lieutenant Devlin was detailed to South Division and was first to arrive at the lunchtime blaze. While escorting folks out of the building to safety, he noticed a male wearing a white shirt and pants, similar to what a chef or baker might wear, running toward the ever-growing inferno. When the young man failed to heed Mickey's order to vacate the building he immediately became a suspect. Mickey went into pursuit through the back of the restaurant and the massive industrial-equipped kitchen to stairs leading to the basement.

By the time Mickey reached the bottom of the oddly longer than normal basement steps the man was gone and a pair of white pants and matching shirt were lying on the floor in front of an old wooden plank door on the north side of the building. The brass-hinged squat door opened to a maze of dirt-floor tunnels leading in three different directions. Mickey followed one of the tunnels east, then north fifty yards to another even smaller set of wooden doors that emptied into another damp-smelling basement. When Mickey found his way back up to street level he discovered he was outside a private residence at 11th and Warnock. The residence had been evacuated due to the four-alarm fire. The "suspect" was in the wind...gone.

When interviewed by Fire Department investigators, Mickey discovered he had accidently stumbled, lucky for him because Palumbo's had already collapsed, into one of the old "speakeasy escape routes" found throughout the Italian Market area during prohibition. Armed with that knowledge Mickey passed on his Palumbo experience to Lieutenant MacGraft.

He looks at his watch. *It's taking too long.* Concerned, he tries to raise Linda over her 150.

"Team -One, conditions."

No response. He tries again.

"CO-Three to Team-One...what's your status?"

After a nerve-racking couple of minutes, during which Mickey contemplated taking Rossi's team into the first floor, Lieutenant MacGraft finally responds to Mickey.

"We're good, Boss. Must be in a dead spot. Couldn't transmit. He's got a pretty sophisticated armory down here. We've found a sub-basement. I'm taking two Stakeout cops with me to check out what's below us. It's slow going in the dark. I'll get back in a few."

Linda's comment has Mickey rethinking his decision to cut utilities. A decision that will eventually prove to be the right one.

Linda gets back on the air. "There are wooden crates stacked up against the south wall. Hold one..." Linda's 150 goes silent. "...Cap one of the Stakeout cops thinks he smells Butyl and the bottom of some of these crates are oozing some kind of oily...maybe—"

Mickey cuts off Linda's transmission. Calmly but with authority he orders her to stop transmitting and to extract her team from the building.

"Stop all further transmission. Terminate your search. Get your team out of the building. Now!"

Sensing the urgency in her captain's voice, Linda immediately does as ordered. From his street-level command post, Mickey can actually hear Linda yelling at her team members to get out.

"Let's go guys. We're out of here. No! Get the hell out. Now!"

The lieutenant's transmission abruptly breaks off. Then the chilly early-morning stillness is broken with what sounded to Mick like a NVA ambush. An experience Mickey knows all too well from his time in country. The hair on the back of Mickey's neck stood up. He simultaneously called an "Assist Officer," the highest-priority assignment, over the team's 150s and over South Band.

With the unremitting sounds of small arms' and automatic weapons' fire ringing in his ears, Mickey leads Lieutenant Rossi's team, Mike Ryan and his partner through the "Men of Honor" restaurant to the rear of the first floor where the stairs to the basement are located. Mickey makes note of a carved plaque hung over the door. "Head of the Spear." A phrase often used by snipers to describe themselves. A favorite slogan added above Army Special Forces and Marine sniper body art. Mick moves his team down the steps and stops at the top of the sub-basement stairs.

From that position they were shocked at what they heard and saw. The basement was lit up like the finale of a New Year's fireworks display. Tracers, sited every fifth round in automatic ammo belts, were ricocheting off every surface making it dangerously near impossible to get down to help Team-One. Plaster, splintered rafters and decades-old dust fell like rain in the sub-basement.

"That's an M-sixty, Mike. Bruno was ready for us." Mickey risks raising Lieutenant MacGraft over her 150.

"CO-Three, to Team-One. Ready to reinforce. Advise."

"Negative. Still too—"

Mickey turns to Lieutenant Rossi. "Don't sound good. Get out front and use all responding units to the Assist to tighten our perimeter. This whole neighborhood is loaded with old speakeasy tunnels. Get on the horn and tell Radio I want the bomb squad ASAP. Bruno's got C-four down there. I want the PFD to run a hose to the front of this building in case this place goes up. Then stand by. Got it?"

"Got it."

"Okay. Now give me your extra magazines."

Lieutenant Rossi nods, hands over his two extra magazines and then hurries out to 7th Street where he starts directing and controlling the adrenalin-driven arriving cops.

With no indication the basement mêlée was going to end anytime soon, Mickey turns to Mike Ryan and his partner.

"That's a hot zone down there. Give the Stakeout sergeant your extra magazines."

"But—"

"No buts, Mike. Uniforms only down there."

Mickey points down the sub-basement stairs. "Don't need you and Irene being mistaken for the bad guys in your soft clothes. Now get out of here."

"Yes, Sir." Without hesitation Detective Ryan and his new partner head for the front door.

Next Mickey turns to the Stakeout sergeant and his heavily equipped trio.

"You ready to roll, fellows?"

All the men nod in the affirmative.

"Good!"

Mickey raises Lieutenant MacGraft over her 150.

"Make room, Team-One. We're on our way. Lay down cover."

Mickey hears an increase of small arms. "There's our cue, guys. Let's do this."

With that, Mickey leads reinforcements into what the Stakeout sergeant would later call, "the mother of all urban firefights."

CHAPTER XLV

Men Of Honor
Sub-Basement

"A wise man does at first what a fool must do at last."
Italian Proverb

One of the Stakeout officers assigned to Team-One with Lieutenant MacGraft would later describe in his Internal Affairs Shooting Team typed interview what transpired in Bruno's sub-basement. His view confirms the time-tested adage, "No plan survives the first shot."

"All hell broke loose. It was like I was back in Nam. The lieutenant told us to open up. So we did. I emptied my MP5, and my Glock 19. I reloaded and emptied two more extended magazines. We were in a world of hurt.

Tracer rounds were coming at us nonstop. Then I heard the captain coming down the steps with backup. When the captain reached our position he gave me, my partner and the lieutenant a fully charged 9-mil mag. I was ready to go again. Once reinforcements got in the fight, things started to change in our favor.

Then suddenly, everything got serene. We stopped taking fire. At first, I thought we eliminated all the shooters. Then there was a stream of light and what sounded like a squeaky-door hinge coming from the back of the sub-basement. I heard the Captain yell, 'They're in the tunnels.'

"The lieutenant ordered me and my partner to move closer to what looked like a fortress, a bunker inside a bunker. The captain compared it to the basement bunker found in the 'MOVE' house on Osage Avenue back in '85. I started to pull the front of the bunker down, and then the LT found a way around it and waved me and my partner to follow her through a rickety plywood door and into a dirt-floor maze.

I saw at least two dead ones behind the bunker on my way in. The M60 was resting on a row of sandbags with the breach slide wide open and the ammo case beside it was empty. The tip of the weapon was actually glowing red hot. Being over six foot, I had to squat down to get through the door. The winding system of tunnels was illuminated with a string of candles along the floor. We didn't get very far when we started taking fire from two camouflaged figures. We hugged the dirt walls and let loose with a volley of our own.

"One of the shooters fell immediately but the second guy ran at us indiscriminately firing away with two handguns. By then I was out of ammo again. I think my partner was too. I thought...I thought we bought it. The guy was covered in blood. He was bug-eyed. I was about to jump up and go for him when I recoiled at hearing two rapid deafening shots coming from behind me. **POP–POP!**

When I refocused, I saw the guy drop like a sack of shit. He was no more than a yard away. He got domed. Blood was squirting from two tightly grouped holes in his forehead just below his WWII steel helmet. I glanced back and realized Lieutenant MacGraft had put two right between the old guy's eyes. She saved our butts, big time. At the time, my partner and I didn't realize the Lieutenant had been hit."

An examination of all four men "eliminated" that morning revealed they suffered numerous gunshot wounds to various extremities. All four shooters were covered in body armor. Several police officers suffered blunt-force trauma from rounds that hit but did not penetrate their protective vests. Francis "Gimp" Bruno, the last man standing in the tunnel, had seventeen gunshot wounds. Most prominent were the two blood-soaked cavities centered in his forehead. The other three decedents suffered over a dozen wounds each.

Another Stakeout officer told his IA interviewer: "Everything slowed down and sped up all at the same time. I thought I was a dead man."

The only life-threatening injury to police was to Lieutenant Linda MacGraft who suffered one 9-millimeter round to her left temple. She was transported to Jefferson Hospital's trauma center by EPW 301.

The Crime Scene Unit retrieved one thousand, nine-hundred and eighty-seven brass casings from Bruno's sub-basement and the adjoining tunnel. Most were 9 millimeter but there were also 40 caliber and 7.62 NATO brass found. If the firefight had taken place anywhere except in the close quarters of Bruno's sub- basement, there certainly would have been untold "collateral damage" at street level.

CSU also recovered twelve-weapons: three custom rifles, one M60E3 machine gun mounted on a M122 tripod and eight handguns from the property. With the exception of Bruno's two handguns, all the automatic weapons' slides were locked open. Meaning all the weapons had been emptied. Every firearm was legally purchased and registered to Francis Bruno or his three accomplices. Also taken "for investigation" from Bruno's sub- basement were three unopened cases of 9-millimeter ammunition. The PPD are classifying them as "leadless/green, experimental 9-millimeter munitions."

One of the rifles, a customized "sniper" M-1, and the brass casing found by Lieutenant MacGraft in the yard of a vacate property on 11th Street were hand carried to the FBI facility in Virginia. The customized M-1 was eventually positively identified as the weapon used to assassinate Richie Rugnetta.

Based on entries in Bruno's "data book," a day-to-day chronology every serious sniper faithfully maintains, PPD Homicide reopened and eventually cleared five additional "cold cases." For many snipers, luckily including Francis Bruno, keeping a data book doesn't stop once he musters out of the military. Essentially, it's a very private, handwritten in-depth record of every combat mission and/or kill shot. It also includes weather conditions, type of weapon and round used for starters. Mickey destroyed his when he was discharged from the Army.

It was established that Bruno was a serial assassin. It's chilling to read Bruno's words after a 1993 "kill." *"His head exploded. It's such a rush. I love dinging unsuspecting people. A sniper needs to stay sharp. Perfect practice makes perfect."* The pages of his books were dotted with perplexing 444s, Mob talk for an ordered "hit." Homicides most likely never solved…till now.

Lastly, ATF and the PPD Bomb Disposal Unit removed eight cases of Military C-4. Two of the cases had become "unstable" and were leaking an oily substance. Because C-4 has no real odor of its own, manufacturers add butyl or methyl mercaptan to help detect a breakdown or seepage of the material. Mickey's recent ordeal in Dublin, Ireland, with seeping C-4 is why Mickey ordered Lieutenant MacGraft's team out of Bruno's sub-basement.

The homes of Bruno's co-gunmen and ex-Marine "buddies," Timothy Sabella, Mitt Dovi and Phillip Manzella, were searched. Numerous handguns, vintage rifles and stockpiles of 9-millimeter and 40-caliber munitions were confiscated and classified "for investigation." None of the men had any past contact with the legal system. For all intents and purposes they were, until February 5th, model citizens.

Licenses and Inspections was charged with identifying and eliminating any and all of the so-called "speakeasy tunnels" located under the 9th Street Market area. In the first six months of their inspection they discovered sixteen tunnels. The burrows found under Bruno's Men of Honor restaurant snaked in two directions ending in row home sub-basements, one under two homes on the 700 block of Fairhill, the other one to 500 Earp. When interviewed, all of the present residents of those properties claimed to have no knowledge of the tunnels. A shaky claim at best, but unchallenged by the PPD.

The Police Commissioner repeatedly rejected Mickey's very public contention that Frank Bruno was given a *"heads up"* prior to the warrant service on his property. In time, the PC will be proven wrong. The DA indicated she's bringing the matter to a Grand Jury.

CHAPTER XLVI

City Trauma Hospitals

"A friend is not known until lost."
Italian Proverb

After a twenty-four-hour vigil outside the hospital room of Lieutenant Linda MacGraft by her family, Mickey and several of the men and women who worked with and for her, the lieutenant sadly succumbed to her wound at two-thirty-two PM, February 6th. It was her thirty-seventh birthday. A message went out over the PD's computer system ordering all officers to wear the ceremonial black crepe over their badges for thirty days, and flags to be flown at half-mast until after the lieutenant's internment.

At the 3rd District and out of respect for Linda's military service, Mickey had his Headquarters American flag lowered one flag width down the hoist. Tradition has it that by doing so it leaves room for the "invisible flag of death" to fly above, thus signifying death's presence, power and prominence. A fitting tribute to all who serve in the military, as well as in law enforcement.

Lieutenant MacGraft was afforded full military rites, complete with bagpipes, riderless horse plus a one-hundred police car procession. Services were held at her childhood parish, the "Irish Church," Saint Paul's at 900 Christian Street. Captain Mickey Devlin gave a moving eulogy and was honored to present the flag to her father, retired PPD Detective Sergeant Liam MacGraft, and her mother, Bridget Alice (nee O'Flynn) MacGraft. They were grateful but understandably crushed.

After the funeral service, several members of the media asked Mickey for his comments on the Bruno warrant services and who should be held responsible for the flawed operation. Breaking his own rule he addressed the impetuous media: "I take full responsibility for the entire operation. My actions are under scrutiny by a whole host of agencies, including my own. When the dust clears... Well let's just wait and see. But I will say this about who I believe is responsible for Lieutenant MacGraft's murder.

It's Francis Bruno and the lowlife who called him and his fellow assassins and let them know the PD was coming."

Mickey's comment brought a horde of follow-up questions from those present. His only response, "It took me twenty years to find out who murdered my Da. If it takes me another twenty to find the scumbag or scumbags who enabled the murder of Linda MacGraft, so be it."

Needless to say, Mickey's admonition and his history for settling scores reverberated through the PPD rapidly. It especially echoed behind the doors on the third floor of Headquarter…the "West Wing."

EPILOGUE

"At the end of the work you may judge of the workmen."
Italian Proverb

In early March of 1997, the spiritual leader of Philadelphia's Archdiocese, Cardinal Vuotto retired. Although retiring Cardinals have two years to "wind down," Vuotto abruptly vacated his suite and relocated back to his birthplace, Abruzzo, Italy, fifty miles east of Rome. Within days the DA's office sent investigators to Italy to interview Cardinal Vuotto concerning Monsignor O'Hagorty's death, and the Cardinal's cell phone records. They were turned away and told that the Cardinal was suffering from dementia and was on intensive insulin therapy for his Type 1 diabetes and Cozaar for high blood pressure, making him "unavailable" for interviews. The DA's office made the same interview request for the next two months.

In May of '97, Cardinal Dominic Fazio Vuotto was rushed to the hospital with chest pains. Within two hours the Cardinal lost his fight for life. The attending physician read a brief statement to the Italian media.

"Our beloved Cardinal Dominic Fazio Vuotto was taken from us at 9:04 this morning. His death is classified as due to 'natural causes.'" He added, "It's very common, sixty-five percent or higher, for people with Type 1 diabetes to die of some type of heart or blood-vessel disease. The Cardinal will be sorely missed. Funeral arrangements will be forthcoming. Thank you. Please keep the Cardinal in your prayers."

Philadelphia's DA is still looking into the Cardinal's involvement with Monsignor O'Hagorty's demise. The Archdiocese's position on the matter is, "The man is dead. Leave it alone." A spokesperson for the Diocese's legal department was quoted in the Catholic Standard as saying, "Any investigation targeting the Cardinal that might mar his reputation and good works will never see the light of day." She added, "I've been assured by a high-ranking police official that is the case."

Katherine McBride, Philly's "take no prisoners" DA, took great joy publically reminding the Archdiocese that she never has and never will work for the Philadelphia Police Department. She works for the people, all of the people of the City. That they outrank all PPD high-ranking officials.

One day later, Katherine sent her top ADA, Alice Elizabeth Gibson, and Senior Investigator Seamus McCarthy to Abruzzo, Italy. They were accompanied by Doctor David Steinberg, Chief Medical Examiner for the City of Philadelphia. Katherine contends that since Cardinal Vuotto was a naturalized United States citizen and a seventy-year resident of Philadelphia she has the authority to conduct a full investigation, including an autopsy and toxicology examination, into the cause and manner of his death.

The DA's representatives were abruptly turned away and handed an official letter from Vatican City that Cardinal Dominic Fazio Vuotto's remains were cremated at the request of the new Cardinal of the Archdiocese of Philadelphia. His ashes were spread over "the two cities he loved so much," Abruzzo and Philadelphia.

The DA's office also continues investigating how the Monsignor came into possession of a .22 Berretta reported stolen in 1969 from the home of Grace Capaccio. Ms. Capaccio is Deputy Police Commissioner Fannille's first wife and author of Monsignor O'Hagorty's published newspaper testimonial.

†††††

Philadelphia Fire Department EMTs Seth Mellone and Nicolas Ligambi were "Suspended for 30 Days with Intent to Dismiss," by the Fire Commissioner. Due to his willingness to cooperate, the District Attorney's Office has decided not to criminally charge Mellone. That is not the case with Nicolas Ligambi. Based on credible evidence gathered by CSU and the ME's office that included matching several unique palm impressions on Monsignor O'Hagorty's shoulders and upper arms to Nicolas Ligambi, together with Seth Mellone's incriminating eyewitness statement to IAB, plus trace evidence found by Detective Ryan in Medic 27, all eventually led to the felony conviction and loss of all pension benefits for the twenty-year-plus PFD veteran.

EMT JoAnne Verna-Deloria, with less than one year in the ranks of the PFD, was "Rejected During Probation" for refusing to cooperate in a criminal investigation. Being in "Probationary Status," she has no legal recourse forever returning to the Fire Department. She now works construction in New Jersey.

††††

Stakeout Officer Frank DeMarco was questioned by Homicide detectives in the presence of his attorney and Internal Affairs investigators, concerning his actions at Our Lady of Sorrows Elementary School on February 3rd. Specifically, he was questioned about how he and his partner received the assignment, his actions at the crime scene, Monsignor O'Hagorty's head injury, the Monsignor's missing cell phone, and his partial prints on a 75-48 form apparently used to conceal a .22-caliber cartridge found in the wall of classroom 4. Investigators believe DeMarco did not have time to extract the lead from the wall. So he concealed it.

At first, under advice of counsel DeMarco refused to answer questions. However, after a requested short break, DeMarco returned with his lawyer and made one short statement. He told investigators that he was contacted by cell phone and told to pick up the school job by Deputy Fannille. A piece of the puzzle Mickey had contended from the start.

DeMarco was then questioned about his relationship with the Deputy, Francis Bruno and Monsignor O'Hagorty. Again following the advice of his private attorney, he refused to answer any further questions. For his refusal to cooperate fully in an internal investigation, the Police Commissioner immediately suspended him for "Thirty days with intent to Dismiss."

The DA's office approved criminal charges against DeMarco, ranging from interfering in a criminal investigation, tampering with evidence and entering into a conspiracy to cover up the assassination of Richard Rugnetta. At his preliminary arraignment, cash bail was set at five hundred thousand dollars. His family magically put up the ten percent required, and over the objection by the DA that he was a flight risk and should be incarcerated until his trial, DeMarco walked out of the cell room in the basement of the Roundhouse twenty-four hours later.

One week after making bail, DeMarco's wife reported him missing. "He went out to get the paper and he never came back." Mickey's first impression of Officer DeMarco was that he may be just like his father, Detective DeMarco. That of having more loyalty to his underworld roots than to his profession.

When DeMarco went "missing," he immediately went on Mickey's list of who may have facilitated Bruno's "heads up,'" probably using his position as a Stakeout officer to gain information about the intended raid. Mickey was able to convince the PPD not to classify DeMarco as a missing person, but rather as "absconded." An arrest warrant was immediately filed and approved by the DA.

On a hunch, Mickey called in favors from the US Postal Authority and UPS to monitor "overseas" mail going to the DeMarco residence on Ritner Street in South Philadelphia. Sixteen months later Mrs. Mary DeMarco was scheduled to receive a UPS package originating from Venice, Italy. There was no return address.

After being photographed and checked for prints, the package was eventually delivered. A single thumbprint on the brown paper packaging around the small package was identified as that of Ex-Stakeout Office Frank DeMarco. The scrutiny of "out- of-country" mail for the Ritner Street address continues. Detective Mike Ryan has been working with Italian law enforcement to locate and return Frank DeMarco to Philadelphia. Ryan has been keeping Mickey Devlin in the loop, under the radar of course.

††††

The burglary charge brought against Johnny "Little John" Pollina, son of Johnny "The Nose" Pollina, former wise-guy underboss from the Atlantic City Mob, was dropped, "Lack of Sufficient Evidence." The charge of receiving stolen property, conspiracy and interfering in a criminal investigation were also dismissed in front of The Honorable Dante Sambocca, Common Pleas Court. His decision was partially based on Little John's 3rd District cellmate recanting his discussion with Mickey (AKA Samuel Longhorn Clemens) concerning his part in disposing of a "package" later found in a planter on Reed Street.

Judge Sambocca chose to disregard the fact that John's fingerprints were found on the phone in said package.

††††

Monsignor Mario Francis O'Hagorty's funeral arrangements were put on hold until after the Medical Examiner's toxicology and autopsy results were completed, evaluated and signed off on by Doctor Steinberg. The postponement angered the devoted parishioners in the Monsignor's small South Philly parish of Our Lady of Sorrows. Criticism shrugged off by the Doc.

††††

In late May, at her annual Memorial Day barbeque, attended by her closest friends, Katherine McBride finally came clean concerning her "problematic relationship" with Angelo Lombardo, Esquire. Turns out she was collaborating with the SAC of the Philadelphia FBI. Katherine had been asked to act as go-between with the FBI and Lombardo. Angelo approached the FBI about testifying against his Godfather's, Vince Cibotti's, crime activities.

Additionally, he was prepared to give the FBI information that showed an ongoing "association" between two high-ranking Police Department officials and the Atlantic City Mob. A condition of his testimony was placement into the Federal "Witness Protection Program." His one and only other demand was that Katherine act as link.

When Katherine shared her FBI activities with her friends, it took the form of an apology. As expected, no apology was needed. However, Mickey couldn't resist reminding Michelle that as predicted, "Katherine would never allow anything to get in the way of an investigation. Especially, when corrupt cops are involved."

Talk of Katherine McBride running for mayor was shattered when she announced her candidacy for another four-year term as the City's DA. Mickey predicts her next move will be at the state level. But that's just another one of those gut feelings Mick is famous for.

††††

Antonio and Celeste Rugnetta, Richie's adopted parents, suddenly decided to move back to Palermo, Italy. Their two sons, Salvatore and Rocco, took over the family business on 9th Street. Not being business types they were eventually forced to sell the business and the residence upstairs. It went for under market value to a Vietnamese family who after minor renovations reopened under a new name that no one can pronounce. So the neighbors unapologetically started calling it "That VC's Place."

Sal and Rocco pursued different career paths. Both are trying to move up "the organizational" flowchart of the new action South Philly Mob. Glorified errand boys will be it for them.

††††

The PPD's forensic document unit was given the task of all thirty years' worth of Francis Bruno's "Data Books." They found that on January 4, 1997, Bruno made note that his wife suspected his "little princess" Concetta was pregnant and that Richie Rugnetta was the father. He ended his inscription on the day with a telling entry in red ink, "Someday I'll kill him."

On the 5th of January he pens that an "associate" for Vince Cibotti, identified only as CH405, contacted him about taking on a "contract." Mickey's theory, that never gained much traction, was CH405 stood for City Hall Room 405. That's the office of Councilwoman Victoria Russo who represents District 1, the larger of the two Councilmanic Districts covering South Philly.

Mickey could never get anyone to bite on the City Hall connection to either Richie Rugnetta or Monsignor O'Hagorty's demise. Even Katherine McBride told Mick, "Until you have something really solid, something that we can take to a Grand Jury, I'm taking a pass. You get the stuff and I'll hand carry that bad boy over myself." Mickey agreed his theory was thin so he filed it away for another time.

Bruno's data book revealed that his proposed contract was Monsignor O'Hagorty. Other entries indicate the Monsignor was losing his "usefulness." He goes on to state that the Capo has heard rumors that O'Hagorty's past indiscretions were about to resurface again. Vince Cibotti told Bruno that one of his lieutenants found out that Richie Rugnetta was going to confront the Monsignor and make him publicly admit to fathering a child with a cloistered nun. That Richie was the result of that "sinful union." Bruno added in bold print, **"An embarrassment for my Church and the Cardinal that I cannot allow."**

Bruno accepted the contract on the Monsignor on the condition he was given permission to "ice" Richie. No one gets whacked in South Philly without first getting permission from the Capo di tutti capi, the boss of the bosses. Not a drug dealer. Not a rat. No one without first "kissing the ring."

Bruno got his permission to eliminate the "little shit who knocked up my kid" and used his contacts in the PPD and the PFD to "take care of the Monsignor." Bruno went to his grave never knowing his own daughter was molested by the Monsignor. Or that Concetta and Richie Rugnetta were due to be married and that "Dad" was to give away the bride.

††††

With the help of Captain Devlin; Michelle Cunay, Editor-in-Chief of the Philadelphia Daily; and Katherine McBride, Philadelphia's second-term DA, young Terrell "Stitches" Soetoro received his scholarship to Roman Catholic High School at Broad and Vine Street. During all four years at Roman, Terrell was an honor student and won all Catholic status in baseball and cross country. Upon graduation, he received a full scholarship to Temple University. Terrell then attends the James E. Beasley School of Law. After graduation he hopes to work in the District Attorney's Office.

††††

When the smoke cleared on the 3rd District's corruption probe, Mickey was still standing tall, career untarnished. Not the outcome the Commissioner and Deputy Fannille were aiming for when they sent him there in the first place. In fact, once again Mickey, albeit unintentionally, outshined the PD's top cop and exposed his never-ending genius for being on the wrong side of a bad situation.

Mickey's predecessor, Captain Blackstone, was eventually convicted and fired. He's now serving seven to fifteen years, along with the remnants of his "3rd District posse," at a secure Federal facility in the Carolinas.

Mickey requested to remain in the 3rd District. The PC against the advice of Deputy Fannille approved Mickey's request. He felt duty-bound to get the 3rd District back on the road to what Lieutenant Linda MacGraft called "real police work." The PC also approved the "swap transfer" of two 3rd District officers to another patrol district. Supposedly, the officers feared blowback for their "stealthy allegiance" to Deputy Fannille. A similar request by a South Street sergeant was "temporarily denied" due to her recent status change, maternity leave. Mickey is fairly confident that the "3rd District Fannille Spy Syndicate" has for the time being been shelved.

††††

Mickey's decision to stay in the 3rd District came at a price. For six months, Deputy Antonio Fannille tried to pick up where the PC left off. His tactics became more covert, using other "associates" inside and out of the PPD to challenge Captain Devlin's authority and attacking his reputation.

Within the Department Fannille used his spy network to inform him on all of Devlin's endeavors, hoping to impede them before they gained support. Outside the PPD, Fannille used the owner of a famous deli to fabricate a rumor that Devlin was anti-Semitic. That tactic feel flat when the Mayor's communications director dispelled that farse immediately. The deli owner reluctantly called Devlin to apologies and offered to write a letter of "good character" if ever needed. Devlin accepted the apology and respectfully turned down the letter.

The first public skirmish to hit the local press was over "special beats" for an walk-up steak take-out property owned by a close friend of Fannille. That was quickly followed by the Deputy's mandate to establish a "special beat" in front of a South Philly bakery owned by the Deputy's family. The next clash cam over Devlin sending cops out to ticket all illegal parking in the middle of South Broad Street. People actually drove in from New Jersey and parked illegally all day. A practice permitted for years by Fannille when he was the Inspector on South Division. In that case Devlin actually received the support of two city council members and future mayor. Each of these "special arrangements" were turned down by Devlin and blasted by all the neighborhood papers. Devlin came out looking the bigger man in every case.

Cartoonists had a field day with images of Fannille ordering cops to stand guard at steak-shop takeout windows and bakeries as part of his "Pro-active Approach Initiative" for combating serious crime in South Philly. Under pressure from neighborhood groups, negative press and the Mayor called for a "Review of the Deputy's questionable crime-fighting initiatives," Fannille again had to back off thus ending his constant interference with Mickey's command.

But the biggest conflict came over Fannille's attempt to impede the election process in a South Philly-based labor union. Once Mickey got wind of what the Deputy was covertly attempting to do for another "associate," he again tried doing the right thing, chain of command be damned. He was hoping by going directly to the IAB Chief, he would also do the right thing. But that was not to be.

Michelle Cunay's Philadelphia Daily Paper called the so-called investigation by Internal Affairs into the Deputy's interference a complete "Whitewash." So named because of Fannille's ability to have IAB paint him as a victim of anti-Italian bigotry and vindictive subordinates. Not surprising, Fannille was cleared of any "inappropriate or corrupt behavior." The Police Commissioner was more than happy to sign off quickly on what he announced as IAB's "comprehensive and impartial investigation into groundless allegations of a good man who's dedicated his life to public service."

The FOP was outraged by the skewed manner in which the Chief of IAB conducted himself during the "deeply flawed investigation." The President of the FOP made his position known at a press conference in front of Lodge 5 on Spring Garden Street.

"This whole Fannille thing is just another example of how the Commissioner has a double standard when it comes to the discipline process. There's one set of rules for street cops and another set of rules for bosses. Especially, bosses with offices in the West Wing. It just highlights once again IAB's inability to conduct an impartial investigation. One that is actually based on fact and not 'West Wing Shenanigans.'"

At the monthly FOP meeting Mickey received a standing ovation for "having the balls to go up against Fannille and his IAB goons."

The Deputy will soon have a larger controversy to contend with. The New Jersey State Police reopened their probe into Fannille's "dubious business ventures" with the Atlantic City Mob, most recently being his one-third partnership in a South Jersey cement company. However, the investigation will come to a screeching halt after one of the prime targets, AC's Deputy Mayor, was found nailed, crucified style, under Atlantic City's famous boardwalk. Initially, the ACPD outrageously classified the death a suicide. That absurd classification immediately broadened the State Police probe.

Not unnoticed by the local and national media was the endless support Deputy Fannille kept receiving from Cardinal Dominic Vuotto's replacement and the newly elected Philadelphia City Council President, Victoria Russo. In the end not even their influence could save him.

††††

The Mayor's "hold-order" on PPD promotions was finally lifted in May during police week, clearing the way for Mickey's August 7th promotion to Inspector. Mick's son was also promoted to Sergeant the same day. It was a grand day for the Devlin Clan.

Frustrated with his inability to finally "Get Devlin," Fannille decided to take one last shot at Mickey and call it a day. He used his remaining influence over the lame-duck commissioner to have the newly promoted Inspector Mickey Devlin sent back to the "Black Hole for Commanders," CIB. Inspector Devlin once again took it in stride and told family and friends that he looked forward to working with his old squad.

††††

Concetta Bruno had her baby. She named him Richard after his father. Her mother talked her into filing a suit against the Catholic Church for the rape she endured by Monsignor O'Hagorty when she was a student at Our Lady of Sorrows Elementary. At the urging of Mickey, Michelle Cunay investigated and was successful in locating Richie's birth mother. After being contacted and informed of the pending suit, Sister Bernadette, now thirty-eight, a Carmelite nun stationed in Italy, decided to leave the order and join Concetta's adjudication. She said she was doing it for her son Richard and her new grandson. Legal aid is being supplied by Kline, Leonard and Swartz, the firm where Angelo Lombardo had been a partner.

At Richie's funeral mass, Concetta Bruno, Terrell "Stitches" Soetoro and Bernadette Salerno, Richie's birth mother, all shared their thoughts about Richard Rugnetta to a packed Our Lady of Sorrows Church. Richie's adapted parents never returned to Philadelphia. His brothers, Salvatore and Rocco, did not attend Richie's funeral. Mickey arranged a police escort to the gravesite.

††††

Over the next decade and a half the parishioners of Our Lady of Sorrows and other will be forced to deal with Church's lax stewardship, hideous neglect and repugnant cover up of the molestation of countless innocent children. Many worshippers will leave the flock never to return.

Some of Our Lady of Sorrows' parishioners are uncertain if their Church will survive. They pray it will. But as they like to say, "It's in God's hands now."

††††

At the close of 1997 with crime at an all-time high and no "Super Stars" on the PPD bench to save the day, the Mayor felt forced to look outside the Philadelphia Police Department for new leadership. In March of the following year, he hired the second in command with the NYPD, Brian Delany. Commissioner Delany just happened to be a close personal friend of Chief Superintendent Kevin O'Clooney, a peer Mickey befriended on his '96 trip to Ireland. It was O'Clooney who was instrumental in helping Mickey bring a cop killer back to Philly. A feat that almost cost Mickey and the Chief their lives.

When Mickey got a call from the Mayor's office after work early one morning to set up a meeting between him and the new Commissioner, he knew it was his Irish brother in arms, Chief O'Clooney, who arranged it. After a short but to the point meeting with Commissioner Delany, Inspector Devlin was offered a position as "Special Assistant to the Commissioner." Mickey's first question for the new Top Cop was "Special assistant of what?"

The commissioner taken aback a bit smiled. "I heard you're a tough Mick...Inspector. That's good. So am I. We'll get along just fine. You'll be my utility man. You'll work on whatever...whatever I think needs those very special abilities...that gut thing...I keep hearing you have."

Mickey's new position would end up being "one hell of a ride." Neither the Commissioner nor most of the PPD were quite ready for the new "Special Assistant." Not by a long shot. Commissioner Delany will later write about Mickey Devlin being his "first find" in the Philly PD. They will remain friends even after the commissioner moves on to other pursuits and new challenges in other cities.

†††

Michelle Cunay postponed her original three-part article titled, *"IT TAKES A SNIPER,"* exposing the attempts by the PPD and others to corrupt the murder investigations of Richard Rugnetta and defrocked Monsignor O'Hagorty. Instead, she published the story of a hero within the ranks of the Philadelphia Police Department. Michelle chose to focus on Lieutenant Linda MacGraft's career being tragically cut short by a crazed and disgraced Mob-connected father.

Her front-page piece told of the Lieutenant's actions in a dark sub-basement on South 7th Street on the morning of February 5th when she saved lives with her bravery. Sadly, Linda joined the list of sixty-six officers "Killed in the Line of Duty." 1997, sixteen percent higher than the previous year, all but four were killed by firearms. The much applauded limited series put Michelle in line for another string of honors.

††††

Imperfect Contrition Major Character List

Bell, Bob – 4TH District Commanding officer

Blackstone, Delbert, - Corrupt 3RD District Captain

Brady, Gil – 5 Platoon Senior Officer

Brown, Nora – 3RD District Captain's Clerk

Bruno, Concetta – Richie's Fiancée

Bruno, "The Gimp" Francis – Concetta's Father

Capaccio, Grace – Deputy Fanelli's Ex-wife

Claus, Nick – 3RD District Turnkey

Clemens, Samuel Longhorn – Mickey Devlin's Alter Ego

Conti, Gino – Last Out Sergeant 3RD District

Davis, Cliff – Catholic School Maintenance

Deloria, Joann – EMT Medic 27

Demarco JR, Frank – Stakeout Officer

Devlin, Mickey - Captain 3RD District/Protagonist

Devlin, Pat – Mickey's Wife

DeStefano, James – Monsignor O'Hagorty's Doctor

Ebner, Alan – Michelle Cunay's Camera Man

Fannille, Antonio – Deputy Commissioner PPD

Gallo, "Worms" Carmine –Deputy Commissioner Fanelli's Aid

Guckin, Stu – 3RD District Police Officer

Johnson. Deshaun – South Division Detective/Negotiator

Ligambi, Nicolas – Philadelphia Fire Department EMT

Lombardo, Angelo Esquire – Mob Consigliere

MacGraft, Linda – One Platoon Lieutenant 3RD District

O'Drain, Don – Cellmate of Polina, "Little John" Johnny

O'Hagorty, Mario – Monsignor Catholic Church

Polina, "Little John" Johnny – Rectory Burglar

Rossi, Tony – Last Out Lieutenant 3RD District

Rugnetta, Richie – Hostage Taker

Rugnetta, Celeste – Richie's Stepmother

Rugnetta, Anthony – Richie's Stepfather

Rugnetta, Salvatore and Rocco – Richie's Stepbrothers

Russo, Victoria – Councilwoman

Ryan, Mike – Homicide Detective

Scott, Jesse – CO Crime Scene Unit

Sister Bernadette – Richie Rugnetta's Birth Mother

Soetoro, Samantha – Richie's Mother

Soetoro, "Stiches" Terrell – Close Friend of Richie Rugnetta

Steinberg, David – Philadelphia Chief Medical Examiner

Waters, Jimmy – Devlin's trusted 3RD District Aide

Vuotto, Dominic – Cardinal Philadelphia Archdioceses

Photo Gallery

Philadelphia Skyline

Ben Franklin Bridge

Washington Ave Egress

**2ND & Washington
Mummers Museum**

9TH & Washington
Italian Outdoor Market

12TH & Reed
Staging Area

Columbus Square Park
1200 Reed Scene Media Area

Our Lady of Sorrows School
Classroom 4

Our Lady of Sorrows Front Door

PFD Engine 10 at 12TH & Reed Sts.

3ᴿᴰ District & Our Lady of Sorrows School

3ᴿᴰ District @ 11ᵀᴴ & Wharton

3ᴿᴰ & 4ᵀᴴ District Property

3ᴿᴰ District Operations Room

3ᴿᴰ District Roll/Court Room

**Phila. Police Headquarters 8ᵀᴴ & Race Streets
Home of "The West Wing"**

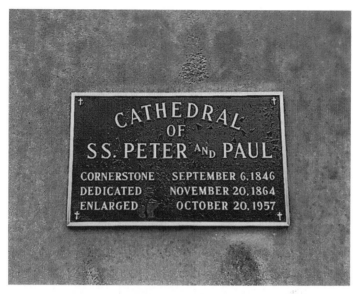

Saints Peter and Paul Commemorative Plaque
Logan Circle: Philadelphia PA

Cathedral of Saints Peter/Paul Confessionals

9TH Street Italian Market

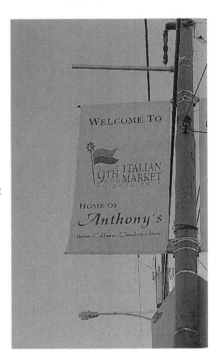

9TH & League St,
Rugnetta Residence

Rocky Plaque 9ᵀᴴ & Passyunk Ave.
Mr. Rugnetta "Rocky tappo" little.

Rugnetta Family Fruit & Vegetable Store

Italian Market 9TH & Washington Ave.

South Corridor Front South Street Bridge

2ND & South Street

Our Lady of Sorrows Rectory Burglary Scene

Our Lady of Sorrows Scene Day 2
School Locked Down

1150 Wharton School Crime Scene Day 2

St. Paul's "The Irish Church"
Lt. Linda MacGraft's Funeral Mass

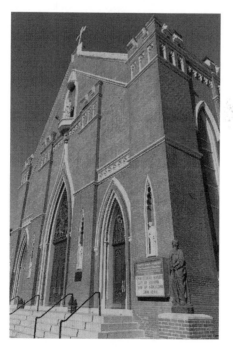

Saint Paul's Church 923 Christian St.

Rome, Cardinal Vuotto's retirement neighborhood

Venice: Officer Demarco's hideout ...temporarily